Barbara H. Solomon is a professor of English and Women's Studies at Iona College. Her major academic interests are twentieth-century American and world literature. The anthologies she has edited include: *The Awakening and Selected Stories of Kate Chopin*; *Other Voices, Other Vistas*; *Herland and Selected Stories of Charlotte Perkins Gilman*; and *The Haves and Have-Nots*. With Eileen Panetta, she has coedited *Once Upon a Childhood*; *Passages: 24 Modern Indian Stories*; and *Vampires, Zombies, Werewolves, and Ghosts: 25 Classic Stories of the Supernatural*.

Prof. W. Reginald Rampone Jr., is an associate professor of English who has taught at numerous colleges and universities. His research focuses on early modern English literature, especially Shakespeare's plays, and he has published *Sexuality in the Age of Shakespeare*. He is currently working on a book concerning Shakespeare's *Much Ado About Nothing* and a critical edition of Nicholas Goodman's *Hollands Leaguer*.

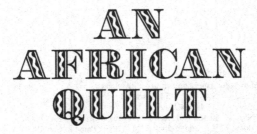

AN AFRICAN QUILT

24 Modern African Stories

Edited and with an Introduction by
Barbara H. Solomon
and W. Reginald Rampone Jr.

SIGNET CLASSICS

SIGNET CLASSICS
Published by New American Library, a division of
Penguin Group (USA) Inc., 375 Hudson Street,
New York, New York 10014, USA
Penguin Group (Canada), 90 Eglinton Avenue East, Suite 700, Toronto,
Ontario M4P 2Y3, Canada (a division of Pearson Penguin Canada Inc.)
Penguin Books Ltd., 80 Strand, London WC2R 0RL, England
Penguin Ireland, 25 St. Stephen's Green, Dublin 2,
Ireland (a division of Penguin Books Ltd.)
Penguin Group (Australia), 250 Camberwell Road, Camberwell, Victoria 3124,
Australia (a division of Pearson Australia Group Pty. Ltd.)
Penguin Books India Pvt. Ltd., 11 Community Centre, Panchsheel Park,
New Delhi - 110 017, India
Penguin Group (NZ), 67 Apollo Drive, Rosedale, Auckland 0632,
New Zealand (a division of Pearson New Zealand Ltd.)
Penguin Books (South Africa) (Pty.) Ltd., 24 Sturdee Avenue,
Rosebank, Johannesburg 2196, South Africa

Penguin Books Ltd., Registered Offices:
80 Strand, London WC2R 0RL, England

Published by Signet Classics, an imprint of New American Library,
a division of Penguin Group (USA) Inc.

First Signet Classics Printing, January 2013
10 9 8 7 6 5 4 3 2 1

In memory of Murray Paul Gruber, loving husband, father, and grandfather, caring uncle, philanthropist, and inspiration to all who pursue the American Dream.
—BHS

In memory of William Dave Wilkins, a concerned, generous and unfailingly kind man to all who knew him.
—WRR Jr.

ACKNOWLEDGMENTS

We wish to express our gratitude to Tracy Bernstein at New American Library for her enthusiastic support and endless patience. A great deal of expert assistance was provided by Edward L. Helmich of Ryan Library's Interlibrary Loan Program at Iona College.

Four people from the four corners of the world generously helped us to locate writers and copyright holders: Mary Jay, Kelly Norwood-Young, Irene Staunton, and Annari van der Merwe.

CONTENTS

INTRODUCTION

As this collection of stories vividly dramatizes, there are many Africas. There is the Africa of the brutal desert, of the snowcapped mountains, of dried-out wells and bubbling streams, of the bush and the jungle, of the veldt and the cities, and of the towns and tiny villages. Africa is a world filled with thousands of species of plants, birds, animals, and insects found on no other continent, including creatures of sizes, shapes, colors, numbers, and survival strategies that make the imagined species of science fiction seem feeble in comparison. There is tribal and village Africa as well as urban Africa; it is a continent of traditional ancestor worship, Protestants, Catholics, Muslims, and Jews. It is a world that has been divided into nations by outsiders for their own convenience. These outsiders, the European colonists, struggled for hundreds of years to mold those they viewed as diverse, intractable, and unruly inhabitants into a cheap workforce that would be docile and obedient, that would support their quest for riches from the diamond and gold mines, the farms and ranches, and the fecund jungle filled with wood and other precious resources. It is also a world where for many the land offers no source of wealth, where drought or delayed rainfall makes even subsistence farming and cattle raising a nightmare of powerlessness.

Africa is a land of the affluent few and the impoverished multitude, of conflicting allegiances that reach back through communal generations, a world splintered by an array of languages that reinforces a sense of separateness and defensiveness. Many Africans have two languages. If they were born in territory ruled by the British, they speak and study English. In the lands ruled by French or Belgian colonists, such as Ivory Coast or Senegal, they use French. If they live in Mozambique or Angola, they speak Portuguese. Long after the departure of the colonial rulers, many Africans find themselves needing to speak, write, or educate their children in the oppressors' language, because there are so many local languages within a single country that easy communication between different areas is impossible. Those who are not fluent in the European language are at an enormous economic and social disadvantage. They often feel scorned by politicians and by the successful, urban business class. Complicating the problems of the poor and impeding their upward mobility is the lack of free and available education, the education that is all-important and necessary for a good job. Sending a child to school involves tuition fees, room and board if there are no schools close by, the cost of uniforms and books. Often several family members must contribute to make one child's education possible.

It is not in the least surprising that the fiction of Africa often reflects the strife and suffering of a continent that was claimed by force. First, European colonists conquered the inhabitants by virtue of their more sophisticated weapons. Outnumbered by the natives, colonial administrators were pitiless in quelling any sign of rebellion in their territories. Murdering or jailing dissidents with impunity, they employed torture and public executions to demonstrate the power of the rulers and create a climate of fear. The message they sent to those they ruled was: "You have no rights." Then they sometimes went to war with other Europeans in order to gain additional land or to maintain the territory they had acquired, especially when the land was fertile or the natural resources were valuable. Unfortunately, the departure of the colonists and the arrival of national independence often did not bring an end to the rule of tyrants or improve the political and economic circumstances of millions of "citizens."

Threaded throughout this land of vast contrasts and seemingly intractable problems are the universal relationships between wives and husbands, parents and children, sisters and brothers, grandparents, aunts, uncles, and cousins, often made more difficult and intense by the transitions occasioned by the modern world. The rules and customs that have been entrenched and honored for generations are questioned or disregarded by some young people, especially those who have left their families and traditional homes and moved to the cities. In the urban environment, the desire for clothes and cars engulfs people who never had an opportunity to acquire such material goods at home. Living among strangers who know nothing about them, they're faced with competition to achieve status based on apparent wealth or good looks, rather than traditional skills such as hunting, fishing, raising cattle or cooking. Without a familial home for entertaining or the usual communal opportunities for making friends or meeting possible dates, the uprooted young people are often attracted to bars and clubs, as reflected in several of the stories here.

The Lives of Women

Stories such as Doreen Baingana's "First Kiss," Leila Aboulela's "The Museum," Chimamanda Ngozi Adichie's "A Private Experience," Ama Ata Aidoo's "Two Sisters," and Ngugi wa Thiong'o's "Minutes of Glory" explore the lives of women in very different circumstances. Baingana's "First Kiss" captures the poignant inner life of fourteen-year-old Ugandan Christine. The tyrant Idi Amin departed many years earlier, but the new rulers have merely presided over crumbling buildings and roads. Unexpectedly,

Christine is to be allowed to accompany her two older sisters to a party. She will borrow a pair of high heels, have her hair hot-combed, struggle into a tight pantsuit, and wear makeup. An avid reader of romantic novels depicting spirited heroines, she will now drink whiskey for the first time and dance with Nicholas, an attractive eighteen-year-old. From an affluent family, she belongs to a community that carefully differentiates itself from the poor village women who toil around them. She is expected to "Study hard, speak English well, get into one of the few good high schools, go to college." Adult life stretches out before her— different, challenging, and exciting.

In Aboulela's "The Museum," Shadia, a twenty-five-year-old graduate student from Sudan, is studying in Scotland for a master's degree in mathematics. She is practiced in pleasing others, has learned to be agreeable, to tell people what they want to hear. With Bryan, her Scots classmate, she realizes that she could stop playing this role and be herself rather than marry her fiancé, Fareed, a wealthy, materialistic sexist who dominates her. Bryan, who clearly loves her and wants to please her, does not really understand Shadia or her African roots. It is not his fault that he has the stereotypical images and distorted perspective with which he was raised, but Shadia is horrified by the way imperialism and exploitation are seen as part of the glorious past in Scotland.

In Adichie's "A Private Experience," two women take shelter in an abandoned shop after a bloody riot has broken out at the central marketplace. One woman, Chika, is an affluent medical student, sophisticated and well traveled. The other, unnamed, is a poor seller of onions, a mother of five children, a devout woman who prays during their time together. The divisions between the two are not only of wealth and education, but Chika is an Igbo Christian and her companion is a Hausa Muslim, members of the very groups engaged in a deadly battle in the streets around them. The bond that is formed as they help and comfort each other is powerful, but it can never be acknowledged or survive in the mad world outside the empty store.

The title characters of Aidoo's "Two Sisters" lead troubled lives for very different reasons. The problems of Mercy, the younger sister, stem from her materialistic and envious nature, while those of Connie, six years older, are rooted in the way her husband treats her. Mercy is a typist in a low-level job whose lover, a member of Parliament, has many wives and girlfriends. His wealth and power—certainly not the man himself—attract Mercy, who is eager to receive his gifts and to live in a government estate house. Connie, who is pregnant with her second child, must sleep with her face to the wall because her husband complains that seeing her stomach before falling asleep "always gave him nightmares." She suspects him of having affairs but he is dismissive of her questions. Although Connie worries about her sister's crass relationships with inappropriate men and her husband's infidelity, she is powerless to influence the behavior of either of the people she loves.

In "Minutes of Glory," by Ngugi wa Thiong'o, Wanjiru works as a barmaid/prostitute who is not generally popular with the male clients, typically wealthy, politically powerful, and arrogant, who frequent the bar. Just as Wanjiru is an outsider among the more popular prostitutes, her one regular client is an outsider who drives a big truck instead of a European luxury car. But she sees a bond in their parallel experiences to which he is oblivious.

Everyday Life

Several seemingly disparate stories are embedded in detailed descriptions of the characters' daily lives. While the crisis depicted in each is very different—sometimes a trivial event and sometimes a horrifying threat—in each case the problem is dramatized against a vivid pattern of days with characters who know very well (or soon learn) what to expect when they set out from home.

In "Another Day at the Office," Steve Chimombo dramatizes the routine workday of a government copy typist.

Dressed in the expected uniform of a low-level office worker, Chingaipe is very uncomfortable in his tight jacket, baggy pants, shirt and tie, and his badly fitting and well-worn shoes. He is well aware that he is twenty years older than the clerks who are his coworkers, that his typing skills have deteriorated somewhat with the passing of time, that he cannot compete successfully with the white female secretary who works for the highest official in the building. With his love for his wife and children, poverty, isolation at work, lack of status, and fear of the loss of his job, Chingaipe is a figure to inspire sympathy as he struggles to provide for his family and maintain his dignity.

In "Under New Pastoral Management," Tanure Ojaide provides a glimpse of the religious influence of a highly popular Pentecostal church. The Church of the New Dawn, headed by a charismatic pastor called Evangelist Peter, is housed in an imposing building characterized by impressive architecture, beautiful landscaping, and very comfortable furnishings. Each week the members of the church look forward eagerly to attending Sunday services. Dressed in their finery, they know that they will be energized by the songs and dances in which they regularly participate. Attending church is like going to a weekly festival. The prayers of the congregation, however, are not about cultivating virtue or receiving moral guidance or attaining salvation. Evangelist Peter promises, "Whatever you want God to do for you will come true in the Church of the New Dawn." Not surprisingly, among the devoted churchgoers are discontented workers who want to become rich, young women who want to find husbands, and wives whose husbands are womanizers or who are having difficulty in conceiving a child.

In "Who Will Stop the Dark?" by Charles Mungoshi, Zakeo is a thirteen-year-old who hates school. He does not do well in his studies but, more important, he is mercilessly bullied by the other boys. Zakeo would rather spend time with his grandfather, who is wise in the ways of hunting and fishing that were once at the center of village life. The old man spends two days with the boy, teaching him how to fish and trap mice, but deep down he knows that his daughter-in-law, whom he dislikes, is right about her son attending school; Zakeo's future depends upon his getting an education in subjects very different from the traditional skills the old man can teach him. If Zakeo continues to cut classes and escape to his loving grandfather, he will master the skills of the past but destroy his future.

In Chinua Achebe's "Civil Peace," Jonathan Iwegbu, an ex–coal miner, has survived a devastating civil war. Rather than dwell on his losses and the destruction all around him, he is overjoyed to find that the bicycle he had hidden during the war is in working order. Resuming normal life, he and his family are energetic and optimistic in pursuing work to support themselves. He uses the bicycle as a taxi to transport travelers to a paved road. His children pick mangoes and sell them for a few pennies while his wife fries breakfast akara balls to sell to the neighbors. Unfortunately, he lives in a postwar world where thugs and criminals can thrive because law and order have broken down. Rather than becoming despondent, he resigns himself to his situation and accepts the hardships that he experiences on a daily basis.

Interactions

A number of stories depict characters who either meet briefly or live alongside one another because of circumstances, but who are very different in background, education, values, perspectives, ambitions, and economic or social status. They are often of different races, of different religions, from different European nations, grew up in urban or rural environments, and have been transplanted to unfamiliar or uncongenial locations. Some are attempting to adapt to their new circumstances, some to dominate others, and often poverty and hard labor are the challenges they face. In some interactions, characters try to exploit or take advantage of another whom they perceive as weaker or lacking in power or status.

In Nadine Gordimer's "Inkalamu's Place," a first-person narrator who has not lived in Africa for many years revisits a grand house she had known as a child, when she accompanied her father to visit a pretentious Englishman who had sired children by his several native wives. He gloried in a privileged status he would never have achieved in England, and the narrator recalls him giving her candy while his own children stood watching, empty-handed, in the background. As she notes the ways in which the abandoned house is decaying and being destroyed by the elements, she is quite pleased to see the deterioration of this symbol of the old order.

Abdulrazak Gurnah's "Cages" depicts the life of an isolated, poor clerk in a grocery shop. Hamid's world has so contracted that he hardly ever leaves the shop and would have no destination if he did. The appearance one day of a new customer, an attractive young girl, fills him with longing. Hamid idealizes her as a girl who must be courted with songs and acts of courage, but with a few teasing remarks, she will dramatically disillusion this lonely and sad young man.

In Es'kia Mphahlele's "Mrs. Plum," which is set in a suburb of apartheid Johannesburg, a black woman recounts her experience working for an affluent white woman. The employer, Mrs. Plum, insists on using her servant's African name, Karabo, as well as having meals together. Mrs. Plum is a devoted activist, writing and campaigning on behalf of equal treatment and rights for black South Africans. She is glad that Karabo attends the Black Crow, a club where domestics meet on their Thursday afternoons off. She has no idea that the women there have a black teacher who tells them there can be no friendship between a servant and her master. On the other hand, when the police arrive at Mrs. Plum's house to conduct an invasive search of her servants' rooms, she turns the garden hose on them and is arrested. Given a choice by the court of paying a small fine or going to prison for fourteen days, she chooses the prison term. On the surface, it appears that no one could do more on behalf of the oppressed black people of South Africa, but Karabo will learn how wide the chasm is that divides blacks from whites and servants from those who employ them.

In Grace Ogot's "The Middle Door," the first-person narrator, Mrs. Muga, is an affluent writer, married to a Nairobi doctor. She has two unexpected encounters with strangers during the long train trip she is taking. The first is with a village woman who is traveling with a live rooster as well as a bunch of bananas and a sack of maize flour. Mrs. Muga repeatedly thinks about the amount of money she has paid to travel in her first-class sleeping compartment and she is determined to rid herself of the interloper. The presence of two policemen in an adjoining compartment at first provides the narrator with a sense of security. But they have concluded that she is an expensive prostitute available to men on the train. Trying to force their way into her compartment in the middle of the night, they display their contempt for women and their conviction that as police officers they can do anything they please with impunity.

In E. C. Osondu's "Voice of America," the interaction occurs between two people who never meet: a young man in his Nigerian village and an American high school student living on a farm in Iowa. Onwordi becomes the pen pal of Laura Williams, and her letter becomes a spark igniting the imagination of every boy in this group of friends. Perhaps, they conjecture, she will be willing to send Onwordi some money; perhaps he could become her boyfriend, even marry her and offer to move to America to be with her. Laura's few letters inspire glorious dreams and hopes for a romantic and luxurious future.

In Zoë Wicomb's "N2," a couple with a tense relationship, Mary and Harold, are traveling home on the N2 highway, a little nervous about being on the road late at night, having seen three black men dressed only in loincloths running across it earlier in the day. When their car, a silver Mercedes-Benz, has a flat tire, Harold is frustrated and angry at his inability to unscrew the bolts of the wheel to replace the tire with the spare. Themba, a tall, broad-shouldered black man, appears from a strip of bush along the road. Mary is so frightened by his appearance on the lonely highway that she aims a gun she carries in her purse at Themba. But his only intention is to help them, and Harold is embarrassed that this young man is able to do what he lacked the strength to accomplish. All in all, this is not the friendly encounter between equals that it might have been between people of the same race, but one of new and uneasy relationships.

Couples

Two vastly different stories depict married couples: "Earth Love" by Bessie Head, and "The Suit" by Can Themba. Head's story is somewhat unusual in that it does not dramatize any conflict or problem to be resolved, as most fiction does. In "Earth Love," the husband returns home to his wife and children after two months away in the bush. He has been successfully collecting animal skins that can be made into a blanket and sold. His gesture of feeding a nearby kitten reveals his kindly nature. The contentment of this couple is nicely contrasted with the behavior of others as his wife tells him the news of the village. Neighbors have become drunk, brutally beaten one another, had adulterous affairs, or been fired from their jobs for disgraceful behavior, but this pair, quiet, thoughtful, and well-suited, have made a good home for themselves and their children.

Themba's "The Suit" begins with a loving husband, Philemon, taking great pains not to disturb his sleeping wife, Tilly, as the day begins. He will prepare and serve a breakfast on a tray to her in bed. This contented man is shocked to be told that his wife has had a lover for three months, a man who arrives every morning after Philemon has left for work. When he returns home after hearing this news, he catches Tilly in bed with her lover. A bitter Philemon does not humiliate his wife in public, does not send her away, does not seem to vary from the contented routine he once enjoyed. Tilly mistakenly thinks that her husband will come to forgive or ignore her adultery, but this is not the case; instead, her furious and disillusioned husband will punish her endlessly for her transgression.

Political Turmoil, Violence, and Injustice

A considerable number of African stories and novels depict the historical and contemporary oppression and institutional brutality of much of the continent. Tribal hostilities that once led to warfare waged with spears or machetes now lead to civil wars with modern weapons. Many who once dreamed of the glory of freedom from European rule now face the bitter experience of deprivation, injustice, and cruelty at the hands of their own people.

In "Eighteen-Ninety-Nine," Olive Schreiner chronicles the life of an unnamed Boer woman whose first memory is that of a Zulu attack on a group of Boer settlers, including her parents, traveling in the Northern Transvaal to escape British rule. She and her cousin, the only survivors of that massacre, are adopted by a Boer family that settles close to the Witwatersrand. A strong and clever woman, she leads the life of a hardworking farm wife, a life marked by daily toil and isolation but also by the satisfaction of raising her sons, husbanding their stock, and bringing in successful crops of maize, pumpkins, sweet cane, and melons. Her hopes for the future are all focused on her grandson, Jan, who demonstrates his fine character and intelligence as a young boy. While there are many stained-glass windows in the churches of Scotland and England that are memorials to the brave British who lost their lives in the conflict with the Boers, this story serves as a moving memorial to those who fell on the Boer side.

Ironically, the violent events in Alex La Guma's "The Lemon Orchard" occur in a field that is touched by silvery moonlight and perfumed by the scent of the rows of lemon trees. In stark contrast to the setting, a group of at least five white men is marching their black prisoner, with bound wrists, to a spot where they plan to whip him severely—to teach him his place. Their victim's offense: being "cheeky." That is, he has had the temerity to bring two white men before a magistrate, seeking damages because they had beaten him. Referring to him as a "hotnot," they demand that their captive display his submission by responding with the words "Yes, baas."

In "Lomba," Helon Habila dramatizes a year in the life of a prisoner, a political detainee awaiting his trial that will probably never take place. A journalist, Lomba is accused of organizing antigovernment demonstrations, even though he was only covering the protest as a reporter. He describes the prison's physical conditions, the rats, mosquitoes, lice, beatings by guards, and the punishment by days in solitary confinement. Even more devastating is the psychological toll: the loneliness, the hopelessness, the loss of one's identity and sense of humanity. "Lomba" captures the plight of those who live in a land in which the powerful—often the legal military leaders—can do as they wish and the accused can be made to disappear behind prison walls.

The diverse stories in this collection reflect the lives of characters struggling to survive grinding poverty, tyrannical governments, cultural upheavals, and disintegrating relationships. Despite all of the very particular details of distant locations, readers can recognize and identify with the universal human condition that emerges at the heart of African fiction. Sadly, some of the authors whose stories appear in this collection have paid a heavy price for their commitment to the accurate depiction of life in Africa as they know it. In some instances, they have been physically attacked, made the victims of intimidation, or forced to flee their own countries to live in exile abroad. The work that they have created endures as a testament to the courage of the artists who attempted to bring insight, order, and meaning to a world that is often violent or chaotic.

AN
AFRICAN
QUILT

LEILA ABOULELA

Leila Aboulela was born in 1964 to an Egyptian mother and a Sudanese father. She grew up in Sudan, studying at the Khartoum American School and a Catholic missionary high school. Graduated from the University of Khartoum in 1985 with a degree in statistics, she earned MSc and MPhil degrees at the London School of Economics. Aboulela was awarded the first Caine Prize for African Writing in 2000 for the story "The Museum" and published the story collection *Coloured Lights* in 2001. She is the author of three novels: *Minaret* (2005), *The Translator* (a *New York Times* Notable Book in 2006), and *Lyrics Alley* (fiction winner of the Scottish Book Awards in 2011). All of these novels were longlisted for the Orange Prize. Aboulela, who has lived in Abu Dhabi and Aberdeen, currently lives in Qatar.

The Museum
(1997)

At first Shadia was afraid to ask him for his notes. The earring made her afraid; the straight long hair that he tied up with a rubber band. She had never seen a man with an earring and such long hair. But then she had never known such cold, so much rain. His silver earring was the strangeness of the West, another culture shock. She stared at it during classes, her eyes straying from the white scribbles on the board. Most times she could hardly understand anything. Only the notation was familiar. But how did it all fit together? How did *this* formula lead to *this*? Her ignorance and the impending exams were horrors she wanted to escape. His long hair was a dull colour between

1

yellow and brown. It reminded her of a doll she had when she was young. She had spent hours combing that doll's hair, stroking it. She had longed for such straight hair. When she went to Paradise she would have hair like that. When she ran it would fly behind her; if she bent her head down it would fall over her like silk and sweep the flowers on the grass. She watched his ponytail move as he wrote and then looked up at the board. She pictured her doll, vivid suddenly, after years, and felt sick that she was daydreaming in class, not learning a thing.

The first days of term, when the classes started for the M.Sc. in Statistics, she was like someone tossed around by monstrous waves — battered, as she lost her way to the different lecture rooms, fumbled with the photocopying machine, could not find anything in the library. She could scarcely hear or eat or see. Her eyes bulged with fright, watered from the cold. The course required a certain background, a background she didn't have. So she floundered, she and the other African students, the two Turkish girls, and the men from Brunei. Asafa, the short, round-faced Ethiopian, said, in his grave voice — as this collection from the Third World whispered their anxieties in grim Scottish corridors, the girls in nervous giggles — "Last year, last year a Nigerian on this very same course committed suicide. *Cut his wrists.*"

Us and them, she thought. The ones who would do well, the ones who would crawl and sweat and barely pass. Two predetermined groups. Asafa, generous and wise (he was the oldest), leaned over and whispered to Shadia: "The Spanish girl is good. Very good." His eyes bulged redder than Shadia's. He cushioned his fears every night in the university pub; she only cried. Their countries were next-door neighbours but he had never been to Sudan, and Shadia had never been to Ethiopia. "But we meet in Aberdeen!" she had shrieked when this information was exchanged, giggling furiously. Collective fear had its euphoria.

"That boy Bryan," said Asafa, "is excellent."

"The one with the earring?"

Asafa laughed and touched his own unadorned ear.

"The earring doesn't mean anything. He'll get the Distinction. He was an undergraduate here; got First Class Honours. That gives him an advantage. He knows all the lecturers, he knows the system."

So the idea occurred to her of asking Bryan for the notes of his graduate year. If she strengthened her background in stochastic processes and time series, she would be better able to cope with the new material they were bombarded with every day. She watched him to judge if he was approachable. Next to the courteous Malaysian students, he was devoid of manners. He mumbled and slouched and did not speak with respect to the lecturers. He spoke to them as if they were his equals. And he did silly things. When he wanted to throw a piece of paper in the bin, he squashed it into a ball and aimed it at the bin. If he missed, he muttered under his breath. She thought that he was immature. But he was the only one who was sailing through the course.

The glossy handbook for overseas students had explained about the "famous British reserve" and hinted that they should be grateful, things were worse further south, less "hospitable." In the cafeteria, drinking coffee with Asafa and the others, the picture of "hospitable Scotland" was something different. Badr, the Malaysian, blinked and whispered, "Yesterday our windows got smashed; my wife today is afraid to go out."

"Thieves?" asked Shadia, her eyes wider than anyone else's.

"Racists," said the Turkish girl, her lipstick chic, the word tripping out like silver, like ice.

Wisdom from Asafa, muted, before the collective silence: "These people think they own the world . . ." and around them the aura of the dead Nigerian student. They were ashamed of that brother they had never seen. He had weakened, caved in. In the cafeteria, Bryan never sat with them. They never sat with him. He sat alone, sometimes reading the local paper. When Shadia walked in front of him he didn't smile. "These people are strange . . . One day they greet you, the next day they don't . . ."

On Friday afternoon, as everyone was ready to leave the room after Linear Models, she gathered her courage and spoke to Bryan. He had spots on his chin and forehead, was taller than her, restless, as if he was in a hurry to go somewhere else. He put his calculator back in its case, his pen in his pocket. She asked him for his notes, and his blue eyes behind his glasses took on the blankest look she had ever seen in her life. What was all the surprise for? Did he think she was an insect? Was he surprised that she could speak?

A mumble for a reply, words strung together. So taken aback, he was. He pushed his chair back under the table with his foot.

"Pardon?"

He slowed down, separated each word. "Ah'll have them for ye on Monday."

"Thank you." She spoke English better than he did! How pathetic. The whole of him was pathetic. He wore the same shirt every blessed day. Grey and white stripe.

On the weekends, Shadia never went out of the halls and, unless someone telephoned long-distance from home, she spoke to no one. There was time to remember Thursday nights in Khartoum: a wedding to go to with Fareed, driving in his red Mercedes. Or the club with her sisters. Sitting by the pool drinking lemonade with ice, the waiters all dressed in white. Sometimes people swam at night, dived in the water—dark like the sky above. Here, in this country's weekend of Saturday and Sunday, Shadia washed her clothes and her hair. Her hair depressed her. The damp weather made it frizz up after she straightened it with hot tongs. So she had given up and now wore it in a bun all the time, tightly pulled back away from her face, the curls held down by pins and Vaseline Tonic. She didn't like this style, her corrugated hair, and in the mirror her eyes looked too large. The mirror in the public bathroom, at the end of the corridor to her room, had printed on it: "This is the face of someone with HIV." She had written about this mirror to her sister, something foreign and sensational like hail, and cars driving on the left. But she hadn't written that the mirror made her feel as if she had left her looks behind in Khartoum.

On the weekends, she made a list of the money she had spent: the sterling enough to keep a family alive back home. Yet she might fail her exams after all that expense, go back home empty-handed without a degree. Guilt was cold like the fog of this city. It came from everywhere. One day she forgot to pray in the morning. She reached the bus stop and then realized that she hadn't prayed. That morning folded out like the nightmare she sometimes had, of discovering that she had gone out into the street without any clothes.

In the evening, when she was staring at multidimensional scaling, the telephone in the hall rang. She ran to answer it. Fareed's cheerful greeting: "Here, Shadia, Mama and the girls want to speak to you." His mother's endearments: "They say it's so cold where you are . . ."

Shadia was engaged to Fareed. Fareed was a package that came with the 7UP franchise, the paper factory, the big house he was building, his sisters and widowed mother. Shadia was going to marry them all. She was going to be happy and make her mother happy. Her mother deserved happiness after the misfortunes of her life. A husband who left her for another woman. Six girls to bring up. People felt sorry for her mother. Six girls to educate and marry off. But your Lord is generous: each of the girls, it was often said, was lovelier than the other. They were clever too: dentist, pharmacist, architect, and all with the best of manners.

"We are just back from looking at the house." Fareed's turn again to talk. "It's coming along fine, they're putting the tiles down . . ."

"That's good, that's good," her voice strange from not talking to anyone all day.

"The bathroom suites. If I get them all the same colour for us and the girls and Mama, I could get them on a discount. Blue, the girls are in favour of blue," his voice echoed from one continent to another. Miles and miles.

"Blue is nice. Yes, better get them all the same colour."

He was building a block of flats, not a house. The ground-floor flat for his mother and the girls until they married, the first floor for him and Shadia. When Shadia had first got engaged to Fareed, he was the son of a rich man. A man with the franchise for 7UP and the paper factory which had a monopoly in ladies' sanitary towels. Fareed's sisters never had to buy sanitary towels; their house was abundant with boxes of *Pinky,* fresh from the production line. But Fareed's father died of an unexpected heart attack soon after the engagement party (five hundred guests at the Hilton). Now Shadia was going to marry the rich man himself. "You are a lucky, lucky girl," her mother had said, and Shadia had rubbed soap in her eyes so that Fareed would think she was weeping about his father's death.

There was no time to talk about her course on the telephone, no space for her anxieties. Fareed was not interested in her studies. He had said, "I am very broad-minded to allow you to study abroad. Other men would not have put up with this . . ." It was her mother who was keen for her to study, to get a postgraduate degree from Britain and then have a career after she got married. "This way," her mother had said, "you will have your in-laws' respect. They have money but you will have a degree. Don't end up like me. I left my education to marry your father and now . . ." Many conversations ended with her mother bitter; with her mother saying, "No one suffers like I suffer," and making Shadia droop. At night her mother sobbed in her sleep, noises that woke Shadia and her sisters.

No, on the long-distance line, there was no space for her worries. Talk about the Scottish weather. Picture Fareed, generously perspiring, his stomach straining the buttons of his shirt. Often she had nagged him to lose weight, without success. His mother's food was too good; his sisters were both overweight. On the long-distance line, listen to the Khartoum gossip as if listening to a radio play.

On Monday, without saying anything, Bryan slid two folders across the table towards her as if he did not want to come near her, did not want to talk to her. She wanted to say, "I won't take them till you hand them to me politely." But smarting, she said, "Thank you very much." *She* had manners. *She* was well brought up.

Back in her room, at her desk, the clearest handwriting she had ever seen. Sparse on the pages, clean. Clear and rounded like a child's, the tidiest notes. She cried over them, wept for no reason. She cried until she wetted one of the pages, smudged the ink, blurred one of the formulas. She dabbed at it with a tissue but the paper flaked and became transparent. Should she apologize about the stain, say that she was drinking water, say that it was rain? Or should she just keep quiet, hope he wouldn't notice? She chided herself for all that concern. *He* wasn't concerned about wearing the same shirt every day. She was giving him too much attention thinking about him. He was just an immature and closed-in sort of character. He probably came from a small town, his parents were probably poor, low-class. In Khartoum, she never mixed with people like that. Her mother liked her to be friends with people who were higher up. How else were she and her sisters going to marry well? She must study the notes and stop crying over this boy's handwriting. His handwriting had nothing to do with her, nothing to do with her at all.

Understanding after not understanding is fog lifting, pictures swinging into focus, missing pieces slotting into place. It is fragments gelling, a sound vivid whole, a basis to build on. His notes were the knowledge she needed, the gap filled. She struggled through them, not skimming them with the carelessness of incomprehension, but taking them in, making them a part of her, until in the depth of concentration, in the late hours of the nights, she lost awareness of time and place, and at last, when she slept she became epsilon and gamma, and she became a variable, making her way through discrete space from state "i" to state "j."

It felt natural to talk to him. As if now that she had spent hours and days with his handwriting, she knew him in some way. She forgot the offence she had taken when he had slid his folders across the table to her, all the times he didn't say hello.

In the computer room, at the end of the Statistical Packages class, she went to him and said: "Thanks for the notes. They are really good. I think I might not fail, after all. I might have a chance to pass." Her eyes were dry from all the nights she had stayed up. She was tired and grateful.

He nodded and they spoke a little about the Poisson distribution, queuing theory. Everything was clear in his mind; his brain was a clear pane of glass where all the concepts were written out boldly and neatly. Today, he seemed more at ease talking to her, though he still shifted about from foot to foot, avoiding her eyes.

He said, "Do ye want to go for a coffee?"

She looked up at him. He was tall and she was not used to speaking to people with blue eyes. Then she made a mistake. Perhaps because she had been up late last night, she made that mistake. Perhaps there were other reasons for that mistake. The mistake of shifting from one level to another.

She said, "I don't like your earring."

The expression in his eyes, a focusing, no longer shifting away. He lifted his hand to his ear and tugged the earring off. His earlobe without the silver looked red and scarred.

She giggled because she was afraid, because he wasn't smiling, wasn't saying anything. She covered her mouth with her hand, then wiped her forehead and eyes. A mistake had been made and it was too late to go back. She plunged ahead, careless now, reckless. "I don't like your long hair."

He turned and walked away.

The next morning, Multivariate Analysis, and she came in late, dishevelled from running and the rain. The professor, whose name she wasn't sure of (there were three who were Mc-something), smiled, unperturbed. All the lecturers were relaxed and urbane, in tweed jackets and polished shoes. Sometimes she wondered how the incoherent Bryan, if he did pursue an academic career, was going to transform himself into a professor like that. But it was none of her business.

Like most of the other students, she sat in the same seat in every class. Bryan sat a row ahead which was why she could always look at his hair. But he had cut it, there was no ponytail today! Just his neck and the collar of the grey and white striped shirt.

Notes to take down. *In discriminant analysis, a linear combination of variables serves as the basis for assigning cases to groups.*

She was made up of layers. Somewhere inside, deep inside, under the crust of vanity, in the untampered-with essence, she would glow and be in awe, and be humble and think, this is just for me, he cut his hair for me. But there were other layers, bolder, more to the surface. Giggling. Wanting to catch hold of a friend. Guess what? You wouldn't *believe* what this idiot did!

Find a weighted average of variables . . . The weights are estimated so that they result in the best separation between the groups.

After the class he came over and said very seriously, without a smile, "Ah've cut my hair."

A part of her hollered with laughter, sang: "You stupid boy, you stupid boy, I can see that, can't I?"

She said, "It looks nice." She said the wrong thing and her face felt hot and she made herself look away so that she would not know his reaction. It was true though, he did look nice; he looked decent now.

She should have said to Bryan, when they first held their coffee mugs in their hands and were searching for an empty table, "Let's sit with Asafa and the others." Mistakes follow mistakes. Across the cafeteria, the Turkish girl saw them together and raised her perfect eyebrows. Badr met Shadia's eyes and quickly looked away. Shadia looked at Bryan and he was different, different without the earring and the ponytail, transformed in some way. If he would put lemon juice on his spots . . . but it was none of her business. Maybe the boys who smashed Badr's windows looked like Bryan, but with fiercer eyes, no glasses. She must push him away from her. She must make him dislike her.

He asked her where she came from and when she replied, he said, "Where's that?"

"Africa," with sarcasm. "Do you know where *that* is?"

His nose and cheeks under the rims of his glasses went red. Good, she thought, good. He will leave me now in peace.

He said, "Ah know Sudan is in Africa, I meant where exactly in Africa."

"Northeast, south of Egypt. Where are *you* from?"

"Peterhead. It's north of here. By the sea."

It was hard to believe that there was anything north of Aberdeen. It seemed to her that they were on the northernmost corner of the world. She knew better now than to imagine suntanning and sandy beaches for his "by the sea." More likely dismal skies, pale, bad-tempered people shivering on the rocky shore.

"Your father works in Peterhead?"

"Aye, he does."

She had grown up listening to the proper English of the BBC World Service only to come to Britain and find people saying "yes" like it was said back home in Arabic: "aye."

"What does he do, your father?"

He looked surprised, his blue eyes surprised. "Ma dad's a joiner."

Fareed hired people like that to work on the house. Ordered them about.

"And your mother?" she asked.

He paused a little, stirred sugar in his coffee with a plastic spoon. "She's a lollipop lady."

Shadia smirked into her coffee, took a sip.

"My father," she said proudly, "is a doctor, a specialist." Her father was a gynaecologist. The woman who was now his wife had been one of his patients. Before that, Shadia's friends had teased her about her father's job, crude jokes that made her laugh. It was all so sordid now.

"And my mother," she blew the truth up out of proportion, "comes from a very big family. A ruling family. If British hadn't colonized us, my mother would have been a princess now."

"Ye walk like a princess," he said.

What a gullible, silly boy! She wiped her forehead with her hand and said, "You mean I am conceited and proud?"

"No, Ah didnae mean that, no . . ." The packet of sugar he was tearing open tipped from his hand, its contents scattered over the table. "Ah shit . . . sorry . . ." He tried to scoop up the sugar and knocked against his coffee mug, spilling a little on the table.

She took out a tissue from her bag, reached over and mopped up the stain. It was easy to pick up all the bits of sugar with the damp tissue.

"Thanks," he mumbled and they were silent. The cafeteria was busy: full of the humming, buzzing sound of people talking to each other, trays and dishes. In Khartoum, she avoided being alone with Fareed. She preferred it when they were with others: their families, their many mutual friends. If they were ever alone, she imagined that her mother or her sister was with them, could hear them, and she spoke to Fareed with that audience in mind.

Bryan was speaking to her, saying something about rowing on the River Dee. He went rowing on the weekends, he belonged to a rowing club.

To make herself pleasing to people was a skill Shadia was trained in. It was not difficult to please people. Agree with them, never dominate the conversation, be economical with the truth. Now, here was someone to whom all these rules needn't apply.

She said to him, "The Nile is superior to the Dee. I saw your Dee, it is nothing, it is like a stream. There are two Niles, the Blue and the White, named after their colours. They come from the south, from two different places. They travel for miles over countries with different names, never knowing they will meet. I think they get tired of running alone, it is such a long way to the sea. They want to reach the sea so that they can rest, stop running. There is a bridge in Khartoum, and under this bridge the two Niles meet. If you stand on the bridge and look down you can see the two waters mixing together."

"Do ye get homesick?" he asked. She felt tired now, all this talk of the river running to rest in the sea. She had never talked like this before. Luxury words, and this question he asked.

"Things I should miss I don't miss. Instead I miss things I didn't think I would miss. The *azan,* the Muslim call to prayer from the mosque. I don't know if you know about it. I miss that. At dawn it used to wake me up. I would hear 'prayer is better than sleep' and just go back to sleep. I never got up to pray." She looked down at her hands on the table. There was no relief in confessions, only his smile, young, and something like wonder in his eyes.

"We did Islam in school," he said. "Ah went on a trip to Mecca." He opened out his palms on the table.

"What!"

"In a book."

"Oh."

The coffee was finished. They should go now. She should go to the library before the next lecture and photocopy previous exam papers. Asafa, full of helpful advice, had shown her where to find them.

"What is your religion?" she asked.

"Dunno, nothing I suppose."

"That's terrible! That's really terrible!" Her voice was too loud, concerned.

His face went red again and he tapped his spoon against the empty mug.

Waive all politeness, make him dislike her. Badr had said, even before his windows got smashed, that here in the West they hate Islam. Standing up to go, she said flippantly, "Why don't you become a Muslim then?"

He shrugged. "Ah wouldnae mind travelling to Mecca, I was keen on that book."

Her eyes filled with tears. They blurred his face when he

stood up. In the West they hate Islam and he . . . She said, "Thanks for the coffee," and walked away, but he followed her.

"Shadiya, Shadiya," he pronounced her name wrongly, three syllables instead of two, "there's this museum about Africa. I've never been before. If you'd care to go, tomorrow . . ."

No sleep for the guilty, no rest, she should have said no, I can't go, no I have too much catching up to do. No sleep for the guilty, the memories come from another continent. Her father's new wife, happier than her mother, fewer worries. When Shadia visits she offers fruit in a glass bowl, icy oranges and guavas, soothing in the heat. Shadia's father hadn't wanted a divorce, hadn't wanted to leave them; he wanted two wives, not a divorce. But her mother had too much pride, she came from fading money, a family with a "name." Of the new wife her mother says, bitch, whore, the dregs of the earth, a nobody.

Tomorrow she need not show up at the museum, even though she said that she would. She should have told Bryan she was engaged to be married, mentioned it casually. What did he expect from her? Europeans had different rules, reduced, abrupt customs. If Fareed knew about this . . . her secret thoughts like snakes . . . Perhaps she was like her father, a traitor. Her mother said that her father was devious. Sometimes Shadia was devious. With Fareed in the car, she would deliberately say, "I need to stop at the grocer, we need things at home." At the grocer he would pay for all her shopping and she would say, "No, you shouldn't do that, no, you are too generous, you are embarrassing me." With the money she saved, she would buy a blouse for her mother, nail varnish for her mother, a magazine, imported apples.

It was strange to leave her desk, lock her room and go out on a Saturday. In the hall the telephone rang. It was Fareed. If he knew where she was going now . . . Guilt was like a hard-boiled egg stuck in her chest. A large cold egg.

"Shadia, I want you to buy some of the fixtures for the bathrooms. Taps and towel hangers. I'm going to send you a list of what I want exactly and the money . . ."

"I can't, I can't."

"What do you mean you can't? If you go into any large department store . . ."

"I can't, I wouldn't know where to put these things, how to send them."

There was a rustle on the line and she could hear someone whispering, Fareed distracted a little. He would be at work this time in the day, glass bottles filling up with clear effervescent, the words 7UP written in English and Arabic, white against the dark green.

"You can get good things, things that aren't available here. Gold would be good. It would match . . ."

Gold. Gold toilet seats!

"People are going to burn in hell for eating out of gold dishes, you want to sit on gold!"

He laughed. He was used to getting his own way, not easily threatened. "Are you joking with me?"

"No."

In a quieter voice, "This call is costing . . ."

She knew, she knew. He shouldn't have let her go away. She was not coping with the whole thing, she was not handling the stress. Like the Nigerian student.

"Shadia, gold-coloured, not gold. It's smart."

"Allah is going to punish us for this, it's not right . . ."

"Since when have you become so religious!"

Bryan was waiting for her on the steps of the museum, familiar-looking against the strange grey of the city streets where cars had their headlamps on in the middle of the afternoon. He wore a different shirt, a navy-blue jacket. He said, not looking at her, "Ah was beginning to think you wouldnae turn up."

There was no entry fee to the museum, no attendant handing out tickets. Bryan and Shadia walked on soft carpets; thick blue carpets that made Shadia want to take off her shoes. The first thing they saw was a Scottish man from Victorian times. He sat on a chair surrounded by possessions from Africa: overflowing trunks, an ancient map strewn on the floor of the glass cabinet. All the light in the room came from this and other glass cabinets and gleamed on the waxed floors. Shadia turned away; there was an ugliness in the lifelike wispiness of his hair, his determined expression, the way he sat. A hero who had gone away and come back, laden, ready to report.

Bryan began to conscientiously study every display cabinet, to read the posters on the wall. She followed him around and thought that he was studious, careful; that was why he did so well in his degree. She watched the intent expression on his face as he looked at everything. For her the posters were an effort to read, the information difficult to take in. It had been so long since she had read anything outside the requirements of the course. But she persevered, saying the words to herself, moving her lips . . . *"During the 18th and 19th centuries, northeast Scotland made a disproportionate impact on the world at large by contributing so many skilled and committed individuals. In serving an empire they gave and received, changed others and were themselves changed and often returned home with tangible reminders of their experiences."*

The tangible reminders were there to see, preserved in spite of the years. Her eyes skimmed over the disconnected objects out of place and time. Iron and copper, little statues. Nothing was of her, nothing belonged to her life at home, what she missed. Here was Europe's vision, the clichés about Africa: cold and old.

She had not expected the dim light and the hushed silence. Apart from Shadia and Bryan, there was only a man with a briefcase, a lady who took down notes, unless there were others out of sight on the second floor. Something electrical, the heating or the lights, gave out a humming sound like that of an air conditioner. It made Shadia feel as if they were in an aeroplane without windows, detached from the world outside.

"He looks like you, don't you think?" she said to Bryan. They stood in front of a portrait of a soldier who died in the first year of the twentieth century. It was the colour of his eyes and his hair. But Bryan did not answer her, did not agree with her. He was preoccupied with reading the caption. When she looked at the portrait again, she saw that she was mistaken. That strength in the eyes, the purpose, was something Bryan didn't have. They had strong faith in those days long ago.

Biographies of explorers who were educated in Edinburgh; they knew what to take to Africa: doctors, courage, Christianity, commerce, civilization. They knew what they wanted to bring back: cotton—watered by the Blue Nile, the Zambezi River. She walked after Bryan, felt his concentration, his interest in what was before him and thought, "In a photograph we would not look nice together."

She touched the glass of a cabinet showing papyrus rolls, copper pots. She pressed her forehead and nose against the cool glass. If she could enter the cabinet, she would not make a good exhibit. She wasn't right, she was too modern, too full of mathematics.

Only the carpet, its petroleum blue, pleased her. She had come to this museum expecting sunlight and photographs of the Nile, something to relieve her homesickness: a comfort, a message. But the messages were not for her, not for anyone like her. A letter from West Africa, 1762, an employee to his employer in Scotland. An employee trading European goods for African curiosities. *It was difficult to make the natives understand my meaning, even by an interpreter, it being a thing so seldom asked of them, but they have all undertaken to bring something and laughed heartily at me and said, I was a good man to love their country so much . . .*

Love my country so much. She should not be here, there was nothing for her here. She wanted to see minarets, boats fragile on the Nile, people. People like her father. The times she had sat in the waiting room of his clinic, among pregnant women, a pain in her heart because she was going to see him in a few minutes. His room, the air conditioner and the smell of his pipe, his white coat. When she hugged him, he smelled of Listerine mouthwash. He could never remember how old she was, what she was studying; six daughters, how could he keep track. In his confusion, there was freedom for her, games to play, a lot of teasing. She visited his clinic in secret, telling lies to her mother. She loved him more than she loved her mother. Her mother who did everything for her, tidied her room, sewed her clothes from *Burda* magazine. Shadia was twenty-five and her mother washed everything for her by hand, even her pants and bras.

"I know why they went away," said Bryan. "I understand why they travelled." At last he was talking. She had not seen him intense before. He spoke in a low voice. "They had to get away, to leave here . . ."

"To escape from the horrible weather . . ." She was making fun of him. She wanted to put him down. The imperialists who had humiliated her history were heroes in his eyes.

He looked at her. "To escape . . ." he repeated.

"They went to benefit themselves," she said, "people go away because they benefit in some way."

"I want to get away," he said.

She remembered when he had opened his palms on the table and said, "I went on a trip to Mecca." There had been pride in his voice.

"I should have gone somewhere else for the course," he went on. "A new place, somewhere down south."

He was on a plateau, not like her. She was fighting and struggling for a piece of paper that would say she was awarded an M.Sc. from a British university. For him, the course was a continuation.

"Come and see," he said, and he held her arm. No one had touched her before, not since she had hugged her mother goodbye. Months now in this country and no one had touched her.

She pulled her arm away. She walked away, quickly up the stairs. Metal steps rattled under her feet. She ran up the stairs to the next floor. Guns, a row of guns aiming at her. They had been waiting to blow her away. Scottish arms of centuries ago, gunfire in service of the empire.

Silver muzzles, a dirty grey now. They must have shone prettily once, under a sun far away. If they blew her away now, where would she fly and fall? A window that looked out at the hostile sky. She shivered in spite of the wool she was wearing, layers of clothes. Hell is not only blazing fire, a part of it is freezing cold, torturous ice and snow. In Scotland's winter you have a glimpse of this unseen world, feel the breath of it in your bones.

There was a bench and she sat down. There was no one here on this floor. She was alone with sketches of jungle animals, words on the wall. A diplomat away from home, in Ethiopia in 1903: Asafa's country long before Asafa was born. *It is difficult to imagine anything more satisfactory or better worth taking part in than a lion drive. We rode back to camp feeling very well indeed. Archie was quite right when he said that this was the first time since we have started that we have really been in Africa—the real Africa of jungle inhabited only by game, and plains where herds of antelope meet your eye in every direction.*

"Shadiya, don't cry." He still pronounced her name wrongly because she had not told him how to say it properly.

He sat next to her on the bench, the blur of his navy jacket blocking the guns, the wall-length pattern of antelope herds. She should explain that she cried easily, there was no need for the alarm on his face. His awkward voice: "Why are ye crying?"

He didn't know, he didn't understand. He was all wrong, not a substitute . . .

"They are telling lies in this museum," she said. "Don't believe them. It's all wrong. It's not jungles and antelopes, it's people. We have things like computers and cars. We have 7UP in Africa, and some people, a few people, have bathrooms with golden taps . . . I shouldn't be here with you. You shouldn't talk to me . . ."

He said, "Museums change, I can change . . ."

He didn't know it was a steep path she had no strength for. He didn't understand. Many things, years and landscapes, gulfs. If she had been strong she would have explained, and not tired of explaining. She would have patiently taught him another language, letters curved like the epsilon and gamma he knew from mathematics. She would have shown him that words could be read from right to left. If she had not been small in the museum, if she had been really strong, she would have made his trip to Mecca real, not only in a book.

Chinua Achebe

Chinua Achebe was born in 1930 in Ogidi, Nigeria, to an Igbo-speaking Christian family and learned English at the age of eight. He was educated at Government College, Umuahia, and the University College of Ibadan, where he was among the first graduates to earn a bachelor's degree. He was employed at the Nigerian Broadcasting Corporation from 1954 until 1966, where he created and directed the Voice of Nigeria. Later he became a senior research fellow at the Institute of African Studies at Nsukka, and then a professor of literature at the University of Nigeria. He has also taught at UCLA, the University of Connecticut, the University of Massachusetts–Amherst, and other Nigerian universities; he taught for many years at Bard College, and he is currently teaching at Brown University. He is a prolific author, writing in a multiplicity of genres, including poetry, essays, short stories, and novels. He is best known for his first novel, *Things Fall Apart* (1958), widely considered one of the most significant novels of the twentieth century and translated into more than forty-five languages. Among his many other notable works are *No Longer at Ease* (1960), *A Man of His People* (1966), *Anthills on the Savannah* (1988), *The Voter* (1994), and *Home and Exile* (2000).

Civil Peace
(1972)

Jonathan Iwegbu counted himself extraordinarily lucky. "Happy survival!" meant so much more to him than just a current fashion of greeting old friends in the first hazy days of peace. It went deep to his heart. He had come out of the war with five inestimable blessings—his head, his wife Maria's head and the heads of three out of their four children. As a bonus he also had his old bicycle—a miracle too but naturally not to be compared to the safety of five human heads.

The bicycle had a little history of its own. One day at the height of the war it was commandeered "for urgent military action." Hard as its loss would have been to him he would still have let it go without a thought had he not had some doubts about the genuineness of the officer. It wasn't his disreputable rags, nor the toes peeping out of one blue and one brown canvas shoe, nor yet the two stars of his rank done obviously in a hurry in biro, that troubled Jonathan; many good and heroic soldiers looked the same or worse. It was rather a certain lack of grip and firmness in his manner. So Jonathan, suspecting he might be amenable to influence, rummaged in his raffia bag and produced the two pounds with which he had been going to buy firewood which his wife, Maria, retailed to camp officials for extra stock-fish and cornmeal, and got his bicycle back. That night he buried it in the little clearing in the bush where the dead of the camp, including his own youngest son, were buried. When he dug it up again a year later after the surrender all it needed was a little palm-oil greasing. "Nothing puzzles God," he said in wonder.

He put it to immediate use as a taxi and accumulated a small pile of Biafran money ferrying camp officials and their families across the four-mile stretch to the nearest tarred road. His standard charge per trip was six pounds and those who had the money were only glad to be rid of

some of it in this way. At the end of a fortnight he had made
a small fortune of one hundred and fifteen pounds.

Then he made the journey to Enugu and found another
miracle waiting for him. It was unbelievable. He rubbed his
eyes and looked again and it was still standing there before
him. But, needless to say, even that monumental blessing
must be accounted also totally inferior to the five heads in
the family. This newest miracle was his little house in Ogui
Overside. Indeed nothing puzzles God! Only two houses
away a huge concrete edifice some wealthy contractor had
put up just before the war was a mountain of rubble. And
here was Jonathan's little zinc house of no regrets built with
mud blocks quite intact! Of course the doors and windows
were missing and five sheets off the roof. But what was
that? And anyhow he had returned to Enugu early enough
to pick up bits of old zinc and wood and soggy sheets of
cardboard lying around the neighbourhood before thousands more came out of their forest holes looking for the
same things. He got a destitute carpenter with one old hammer, a blunt plane and a few bent and rusty nails in his tool
bag to turn this assortment of wood, paper and metal into
door and window shutters for five Nigerian shillings or fifty
Biafran pounds. He paid the pounds, and moved in with his
overjoyed family carrying five heads on their shoulders.

His children picked mangoes near the military cemetery
and sold them to soldiers' wives for a few pennies—real pennies this time—and his wife started making breakfast akara
balls for neighbours in a hurry to start life again. With his
family earnings he took his bicycle to the villages around and
bought fresh palm-wine which he mixed generously in his
rooms with the water which had recently started running
again in the public tap down the road, and opened up a bar
for soldiers and other lucky people with good money.

At first he went daily, then every other day and finally
once a week, to the offices of the Coal Corporation where
he used to be a miner, to find out what was what. The only
thing he did find out in the end was that that little house of
his was even a greater blessing than he had thought. Some

of his fellow ex-miners who had nowhere to return at the end of the day's waiting just slept outside the doors of the offices and cooked what meal they could scrounge together in Bournvita tins. As the weeks lengthened and still nobody could say what was what Jonathan discontinued his weekly visits altogether and faced his palm-wine bar.

But nothing puzzles God. Came the day of the windfall when after five days of endless scuffles in queues and counter-queues in the sun outside the Treasury he had twenty pounds counted into his palms as ex-gratia award for the rebel money he had turned in. It was like Christmas for him and for many others like him when the payments began. They called it (since few could manage its proper official name) *egg-rasher*.

As soon as the pound notes were placed in his palm Jonathan simply closed it tight over them and buried fist and money inside his trouser pocket. He had to be extra careful because he had seen a man a couple of days earlier collapse into near-madness in an instant before that oceanic crowd because no sooner had he got his twenty pounds than some heartless ruffian picked it off him. Though it was not right that a man in such an extremity of agony should be blamed yet many in the queues that day were able to remark quietly at the victim's carelessness, especially after he pulled out the innards of his pocket and revealed a hole in it big enough to pass a thief's head. But of course he had insisted that the money had been in the other pocket, pulling it out too to show its comparative wholeness. So one had to be careful.

Jonathan soon transferred the money to his left hand and pocket so as to leave his right free for shaking hands should the need arise, though by fixing his gaze at such an elevation as to miss all approaching human faces he made sure that the need did not arise, until he got home.

He was normally a heavy sleeper but that night he heard all the neighbourhood noises die down one after another. Even the night watchman who knocked the hour on some metal somewhere in the distance had fallen silent after knocking one o'clock. That must have been the last thought in Jonathan's mind before he was finally carried away himself. He couldn't have been gone for long, though, when he was violently awakened again.

"Who is knocking?" whispered his wife lying beside him on the floor.

"I don't know," he whispered back breathlessly.

The second time the knocking came it was so loud and imperious that the rickety old door could have fallen down.

"Who is knocking?" he asked then, his voice parched and trembling.

"Na tief-man and him people," came the cool reply. "Make you hopen de door." This was followed by the heaviest knocking of all.

Maria was the first to raise the alarm; then he followed and all their children.

"Police-o! Thieves-o! Neighbours-o! Police-o! We are lost! We are dead! Neighbours, are you asleep? Wake up! Police-o!"

This went on for a long time and then stopped suddenly. Perhaps they had scared the thief away. There was total silence. But only for a short while.

"You done finish?" asked the voice outside. "Make we help you small. Oya, everybody!"

"Police-o! Tief-man-so! Neighbours-o! we done loss-o! Police-o! . . ."

There were at least five other voices besides the leader's.

Jonathan and his family were now completely paralysed by terror. Maria and the children sobbed inaudibly like lost souls. Jonathan groaned continuously.

The silence that followed the thieves' alarm vibrated horribly. Jonathan all but begged their leader to speak again and be done with it.

"My frien," said he at long last, "we don try our best for call dem but I tink say dem all done sleep-o . . . So wetin we go do now? Sometaim you wan call soja? Or you wan make we call dem for you? Soja better pass police. No be so?"

"Na so!" replied his men. Jonathan thought he heard

even more voices now than before and groaned heavily. His legs were sagging under him and his throat felt like sandpaper.

"My frien, why you no de talk again? I de ask you say you wan make we call soja?"

"No."

"Awrighto. Now make we talk business. We no be bad tief. We no like for make trouble. Trouble done finish. War done finish and all the katakata wey de for inside. No Civil War again. This time na Civil Peace. No be so?"

"Na so!" answered the horrible chorus.

"What do you want from me? I am a poor man. Everything I had went with this war. Why do you come to me? You know people who have money. We . . ."

"Awright! We know say you no get plenty money. But we sef no get even anini. So derefore make you open dis window and give us one hundred pound and we go commot. Orderwise we de come for inside now to show you guitar-boy like dis . . ."

A volley of automatic fire rang through the sky. Maria and the children began to weep aloud again.

"Ah, missisi de cry again. No need for dat. We done talk say we na good tief. We just take our small money and go nwayorly. No molest. Abi we de molest?"

"At all!" sang the chorus.

"My friends," began Jonathan hoarsely. "I hear what you say and I thank you. If I had one hundred pounds . . ."

"Lookia my frien, no be play we come play for your house. If we make mistake and step for inside you no go like am-o. So derefore . . ."

"To God who made me: if you come inside and find one hundred pounds, take it and shoot me and shoot my wife and children. I swear to God. The only money I have in this life is this twenty-pounds *egg-rasher* they gave me today . . ."

"OK. Time de go. Make you open dis window and bring the twenty pound. We go manage am like dat."

There were now loud murmurs of dissent among the

chorus: "Na lie de man de lie; e get plenty money . . . Make we go inside and search properly well . . . Wetin be twenty pound? . . ."

"Shurrup!" rang the leader's voice like a lone shot in the sky and silenced the murmuring at once. "Are you dere? Bring the money quick!"

"I am coming," said Jonathan, fumbling in the darkness with the key of the small wooden box he kept by his side on the mat.

At the first sign of light as neighbours and others assembled to commiserate with him he was already strapping his five-gallon demijohn to his bicycle carrier and his wife, sweating in the open fire, was turning over akara balls in a wide clay bowl of boiling oil. In the corner his eldest son was rinsing out dregs of yesterday's palm-wine from old beer bottles.

"I count it as nothing," he told his sympathizers, his eyes on the rope he was tying. "What is *egg-rasher*? Did I depend on it last week? Or is it greater than other things that went with the war? I say, let *egg-rasher* perish in the flames! Let it go where everything else has gone. Nothing puzzles God."

CHIMAMANDA NGOZI ADICHIE

Adichie was born in 1977 in Enugu, Nigeria, the fifth of six children of a professor of statistics and the first female registrar of the University of Nigeria. After attending the University of Nigeria, where she was the editor of *The Compass,* a magazine for the university's Catholic medical students, she decided to come to America. She graduated summa cum laude from Eastern Connecticut State University and then took a master's degree in creative writing from Johns Hopkins University and a master's degree in African Studies from Yale University. Her first novel, *Purple Hibiscus* (2004), won the Orange Prize for Fiction and the Commonwealth Prize for Best First Book. Her second book, *Half of a Yellow Sun,* was published in 2008 and was followed by *The Thing Around Your Neck,* a collection of short stories, published in 2009.

A Private Experience
(2009)

Chika climbs in through the store window first and then holds the shutter as the woman climbs in after her. The store looks as if it was deserted long before the riots started; the empty rows of wooden shelves are covered in yellow dust, as are the metal containers stacked in a corner. The store is small, smaller than Chika's walk-in closet back home. The woman climbs in and the window shutters squeak as Chika lets go of them. Chika's hands are trembling, her calves burning after the unsteady run from the market in her high-heeled sandals. She wants to thank the woman, for stopping her as she dashed past, for saying "No run that way!" and for leading her, instead, to this empty store where they could hide. But before she can say thank you, the woman says, reaching out to touch her bare neck, "My necklace lost when I'm running."

"I dropped everything," Chika says. "I was buying oranges and I dropped the oranges and my handbag." She does not add that the handbag was a Burberry, an original one that her mother had bought on a recent trip to London.

The woman sighs and Chika imagines that she is thinking of her necklace, probably plastic beads threaded on a piece of string. Even without the woman's strong Hausa accent, Chika can tell she is a Northerner, from the narrowness of her face, the unfamiliar rise of her cheekbones; and that she is Muslim, because of the scarf. It hangs around the woman's neck now, but it was probably wound loosely round her face before, covering her ears. A long, flimsy pink and black scarf, with the garish prettiness of cheap things. Chika wonders if the woman is looking at her as well, if the woman can tell, from her light complexion and the silver finger rosary her mother insists she wear, that she is Igbo and Christian. Later, Chika will learn that, as she and the woman are speaking, Hausa Muslims are hacking down Igbo Christians with machetes, clubbing them with stones. But now she says, "Thank you for calling me. Everything happened so fast and everybody ran and I was suddenly alone and I didn't know what I was doing. Thank you."

"This place safe," the woman says, in a voice that is so soft it sounds like a whisper. "Them not going to small-small shop, only big-big shop and market."

"Yes," Chika says. But she has no reason to agree or disagree, she knows nothing about riots: the closest she has come is the pro-democracy rally at the university a few weeks ago, where she had held a bright green branch and joined in chanting "The military must go! Abacha must go! Democracy now!" Besides, she would not even have participated in that rally if her sister Nnedi had not been one of the organizers who had gone from hostel to hostel to hand out fliers and talk to students about the importance of "having our voices heard."

Chika's hands are still trembling. Just half an hour ago, she was in the market with Nnedi. She was buying oranges and Nnedi had walked farther down to buy groundnuts and then there was shouting in English, in pidgin, in Hausa, in Igbo. "Riot! Trouble is coming, oh! They have killed a man!" Then people around her were running, pushing against one another, overturning wheelbarrows full of yams, leaving behind bruised vegetables they had just bargained hard for. Chika smelled the sweat and fear and she ran, too, across wide streets, into this narrow one, which she feared—felt—was dangerous, until she saw the woman.

She and the woman stand silently in the store for a while, looking out of the window they have just climbed through, its squeaky wooden shutters swinging in the air. The street is quiet at first, and then they hear the sound of running feet. They both move away from the window, instinctively, although Chika can still see a man and a woman walking past, the woman holding her wrapper up above her knees, a baby tied to her back. The man is speaking swiftly in Igbo and all Chika hears is "She may have run to Uncle's house."

"Close window," the woman says.

Chika shuts the windows and without the air from the street flowing in, the dust in the room is suddenly so thick she can see it, billowing above her. The room is stuffy and smells nothing like the streets outside, which smell like the kind of sky-colored smoke that wafts around during Christmas when people throw goat carcasses into fires to burn the hair off the skin. The streets where she ran blindly, not sure in which direction Nnedi had run, not sure if the man running beside her was a friend or an enemy, not sure if she should stop and pick up one of the bewildered-looking children separated from their mothers in the rush, not even sure who was who or who was killing whom.

Later she will see the hulks of burned cars, jagged holes in place of their windows and windshields, and she will

imagine the burning cars dotting the city like picnic bon-
fires, silent witnesses to so much. She will find out it had all
started at the motor park, when a man drove over a copy of
the Holy Koran that lay on the roadside, a man who happened to be Igbo and Christian. The men nearby, men who
sat around all day playing draughts, men who happened to
be Muslim, pulled him out of his pickup truck, cut his head
off with one flash of a machete, and carried it to the market,
asking others to join in; the infidel had desecrated the Holy
Book. Chika will imagine the man's head, his skin ashen in
death, and she will throw up and retch until her stomach is
sore. But now, she asks the woman, "Can you still smell the
smoke?"

"Yes," the woman says. She unties her green wrapper and
spreads it on the dusty floor. She has on only a blouse and a
shimmery black slip torn at the seams. "Come and sit."

Chika looks at the threadbare wrapper on the floor; it is
probably one of the two the woman owns. She looks down
at her own denim skirt and red T-shirt embossed with a
picture of the Statue of Liberty, both of which she bought
when she and Nnedi spent a few summer weeks with relatives in New York. "No, your wrapper will get dirty," she
says.

"Sit," the woman says. "We are waiting here long time."

"Do you know how long . . . ?"

"This night or tomorrow morning."

Chika raises her hand to her forehead, as though check-
ing for a malaria fever. The touch of her cool palm usually
calms her, but this time her palm is moist and sweaty. "I left
my sister buying groundnuts. I don't know where she is."

"She is going safe place."

"Nnedi."

"Eh?"

"My sister. Her name is Nnedi."

"Nnedi," the woman repeats, and her Hausa accent
sheaths the Igbo name in a feathery gentleness.

Later, Chika will comb the hospital mortuaries looking
for Nnedi; she will go to newspaper offices clutching the

photo of herself and Nnedi taken at a wedding just the week before, the one where she has a stupid half smile on her face because Nnedi pinched her just before the photo was taken, the two of them wearing matching off-the-shoulder Ankara gowns. She will tape copies of the photo on the walls of the market and the nearby stores. She will not find Nnedi. She will never find Nnedi. But now she says to the woman, "Nnedi and I came up here last week to visit our aunty. We are on vacation from school."

"Where you go school?" the woman asks.

"We are at the University of Lagos. I am reading medicine. Nnedi is in political science." Chika wonders if the woman even knows what going to university means. And she wonders, too, if she mentioned school only to feed herself the reality she needs now—that Nnedi is not lost in a riot, that Nnedi is safe somewhere, probably laughing in her easy, mouth-all-open way, probably making one of her political arguments. Like how the government of General Abacha was using its foreign policy to legitimize itself in the eyes of other African countries. Or how the huge popularity in blond hair attachments was a direct result of British colonialism.

"We have only spent a week here with our aunty, we have never even been to Kano before," Chika says, and she realizes that what she feels is this: she and her sister should not be affected by the riot. Riots like this were what she read about in newspapers. Riots like this were what happened to other people.

"Your aunty is in market?" the woman asks.

"No, she's at work. She is the director at the secretariat." Chika raises her hand to her forehead again. She lowers herself and sits, much closer to the woman than she ordinarily would have, so as to rest her body entirely on the wrapper. She smells something on the woman, something harsh like the bar soap their housegirl uses to wash the bed linen.

"Your aunty is going safe place."

"Yes," Chika says. The conversation seems surreal; she

feels as if she is watching herself. "I still can't believe this is happening, this riot."

The woman is staring straight ahead. Everything about her is long and slender, her legs stretched out in front of her, her fingers with henna-stained nails, her feet. "It is work of evil," she says finally.

Chika wonders if that is all the woman thinks of the riots, if that is all she sees them as—evil. She wishes Nnedi were here. She imagines the cocoa brown of Nnedi's eyes lighting up, her lips moving quickly, explaining that riots do not happen in a vacuum, that religion and ethnicity are often politicized because the ruler is safe if the hungry ruled are killing one another. Then Chika feels a prick of guilt for wondering if this woman's mind is large enough to grasp any of that.

"In school you are seeing sick people now?" the woman asks.

Chika averts her gaze quickly so that the woman will not see the surprise. "My clinicals? Yes, we started last year. We see patients at the Teaching Hospital." She does not add that she often feels attacks of uncertainty, that she slouches at the back of the group of six or seven students, avoiding the senior registrar's eyes, hoping she would not be asked to examine a patient and give her differential diagnosis.

"I am trader," the woman says. "I'm selling onions."

Chika listens for sarcasm or reproach in the tone, but there is none. The voice is as steady and as low, a woman simply telling what she does.

"I hope they will not destroy market stalls," Chika replies; she does not know what else to say.

"Every time when they are rioting, they break market," the woman says.

Chika wants to ask the woman how many riots she has witnessed but she does not. She has read about the others in the past: Hausa Muslim zealots attacking Igbo Christians, and sometimes Igbo Christians going on murderous missions of revenge. She does not want a conversation of naming names.

"My nipple is burning like pepper," the woman says.

"What?"

"My nipple is burning like pepper."

Before Chika can swallow the bubble of surprise in her throat and say anything, the woman pulls up her blouse and unhooks the front clasp of a worn black bra. She brings out the money, ten- and twenty-naira notes, folded inside her bra, before freeing her full breasts.

"Burning-burning like pepper," she says, cupping her breasts and leaning toward Chika, as though in an offering. Chika shifts. She remembers the pediatrics rotation only a week ago: the senior registrar, Dr. Olunloyo, wanted all the students to feel the stage 4 heart murmur of a little boy, who was watching them with curious eyes. The doctor asked her to go first and she became sweaty, her mind blank, no longer sure where the heart was. She had finally placed a shaky hand on the left side of the boy's nipple, and the *brrr-brrr-brrr* vibration of swishing blood going the wrong way, pulsing against her fingers, made her stutter and say "Sorry, sorry" to the boy, even though he was smiling at her.

The woman's nipples are nothing like that boy's. They are cracked, taut and dark brown, the areolas lighter-toned. Chika looks carefully at them, reaches out and feels them. "Do you have a baby?" she asks.

"Yes. One year."

"Your nipples are dry, but they don't look infected. After you feed the baby, you have to use some lotion. And while you are feeding, you have to make sure the nipple and also this other part, the areola, fit inside the baby's mouth."

The woman gives Chika a long look. "First time of this. I'm having five children."

"It was the same with my mother. Her nipples cracked when the sixth child came, and she didn't know what caused it, until a friend told her that she had to moisturize," Chika says. She hardly ever lies, but the few times she does, there is always a purpose behind the lie. She wonders what purpose this lie serves, this need to draw on a fictional past similar to the woman's; she and Nnedi are her mother's only children. Besides, her mother always had Dr. Igbokwe, with his British training and affectation, a phone call away.

"What is your mother rubbing on her nipple?" the woman asks.

"Cocoa butter. The cracks healed fast."

"Eh?" The woman watches Chika for a while, as if this disclosure has created a bond. "All right, I get it and use." She plays with her scarf for a moment and then says, "I am looking for my daughter. We go market together this morning. She is selling groundnut near bus stop, because there are many customers. Then riot begin and I am looking up and down market for her."

"The baby?" Chika asks, knowing how stupid she sounds even as she asks.

The woman shakes her head and there is a flash of impatience, even anger, in her eyes. "You have ear problem? You don't hear what I am saying?"

"Sorry," Chika says.

"Baby is at home! This one is first daughter. Halima." The woman starts to cry. She cries quietly, her shoulders heaving up and down, not the kind of loud sobbing that the women Chika knows do, the kind that screams *Hold me and comfort me because I cannot deal with this alone.* The woman's crying is private, as though she is carrying out a necessary ritual that involves no one else.

Later, when Chika will wish that she and Nnedi had not decided to take a taxi to the market just to see a little of the ancient city of Kano outside their aunt's neighborhood, she will wish also that the woman's daughter, Halima, had been sick or tired or lazy that morning, so that she would not have sold groundnuts that day.

The woman wipes her eyes with one end of her blouse. "Allah keep your sister and Halima in safe place," she says. And because Chika is not sure what Muslims say to show agreement—it cannot be "amen"—she simply nods.

*   *   *

The woman has discovered a rusted tap at a corner of the store, near the metal containers. Perhaps where the trader washed his or her hands, she says, telling Chika that the stores on this street were abandoned months ago, after the government declared them illegal structures to be demolished. The woman turns on the tap and they both watch—surprised—as water trickles out. Brownish, and so metallic Chika can smell it already. Still, it runs.

"I wash and pray," the woman says, her voice louder now, and she smiles for the first time to show even-sized teeth, the front ones stained brown. Her dimples sink into her cheeks, deep enough to swallow half a finger, and unusual in a face so lean. The woman clumsily washes her hands and face at the tap, then removes her scarf from her neck and places it down on the floor. Chika looks away. She knows the woman is on her knees, facing Mecca, but she does not look. It is like the woman's tears, a private experience, and she wishes that she could leave the store. Or that she, too, could pray, could believe in a god, see an omniscient presence in the stale air of the store. She cannot remember when her idea of God has not been cloudy, like the reflection from a steamy bathroom mirror, and she cannot remember ever trying to clean the mirror.

She touches the finger rosary that she still wears, sometimes on her pinky or her forefinger, to please her mother. Nnedi no longer wears hers, once saying with that throaty laugh, "Rosaries are really magical potions, and I don't need those, thank you."

Later, the family will offer Masses over and over for Nnedi to be found safe, though never for the repose of Nnedi's soul. And Chika will think about this woman, praying with her head to the dust floor, and she will change her mind about telling her mother that offering Masses is a waste of money, that it is just fund-raising for the church.

When the woman rises, Chika feels strangely energized. More than three hours have passed and she imagines that the riot is quieted, the rioters drifted away. She has to leave, she has to make her way home and make sure Nnedi and her aunty are fine.

"I must go," Chika says.

Again the look of impatience on the woman's face. "Outside is danger."

"I think they have gone. I can't even smell any more smoke."

The woman says nothing, seats herself back down on the wrapper. Chika watches her for a while, disappointed without knowing why. Maybe she wants a blessing from the woman, something. "How far away is your house?" she asks.

"Far. I'm taking two buses."

"Then I will come back with my aunty's driver and take you home," Chika says.

The woman looks away. Chika walks slowly to the window and opens it. She expects to hear the woman ask her to stop, to come back, not to be rash. But the woman says nothing and Chika feels the quiet eyes on her back as she climbs out of the window.

The streets are silent. The sun is falling, and in the evening dimness Chika looks around, unsure which way to go. She prays that a taxi will appear, by magic, by luck, by God's hand. Then she prays that Nnedi will be inside the taxi, asking her where the hell she has been, they have been so worried about her. Chika has not reached the end of the second street, toward the market, when she sees the body. She almost doesn't see it, walks so close to it that she feels its heat. The body must have been very recently burned. The smell is sickening, of roasted flesh, unlike that of any she has ever smelled.

Later, when Chika and her aunt go searching throughout Kano, a policeman in the front seat of her aunt's air-conditioned car, she will see other bodies, many burned, lying lengthwise along the sides of the street, as though someone carefully pushed them there, straightening them. She will look at only one of the corpses, naked, stiff, face-down, and it will strike her that she cannot tell if the partially burned man is Igbo or Hausa, Christian or Muslim, from looking at that charred flesh. She will listen to BBC radio and hear the accounts of the deaths and the riots—"religious with undertones of ethnic tension" the voice will say. And she will fling the radio to the wall and a fierce red rage will run through her at how it has all been packaged and sanitized and made to fit into so few words, all those bodies. But now, the heat from the burned body is so close to her, so present and warm that she turns and dashes back toward the store. She feels a sharp pain along her lower leg as she runs. She gets to the store and raps on the window, and she keeps rapping until the woman opens it.

Chika sits on the floor and looks closely, in the failing light, at the line of blood crawling down her leg. Her eyes swim restlessly in her head. It looks alien, the blood, as though someone had squirted tomato paste on her.

"Your leg. There is blood," the woman says, a little wearily. She wets one end of her scarf at the tap and cleans the cut on Chika's leg, then ties the wet scarf around it, knotting it at the calf.

"Thank you," Chika says.

"You want toilet?"

"Toilet? No."

"The containers there, we are using for toilet," the woman says. She takes one of the containers to the back of the store, and soon the smell fills Chika's nose, mixes with the smells of dust and metallic water, makes her feel lightheaded and queasy. She closes her eyes.

"Sorry, oh! My stomach is bad. Everything happening today," the woman says from behind her. Afterwards, the woman opens the window and places the container outside, then washes her hands at the tap. She comes back and she and Chika sit side by side in silence; after a while they hear raucous chanting in the distance, words Chika cannot make out. The store is almost completely dark when the woman stretches out on the floor, her upper body on the wrapper and the rest of her not.

Later, Chika will read in *The Guardian* that "the reactionary Hausa-speaking Muslims in the North have a history of violence against non-Muslims," and in the middle of her grief, she will stop to remember that she examined the nipples and experienced the gentleness of a woman who is Hausa and Muslim.

Chika hardly sleeps all night. The window is shut tight; the air is stuffy, and the dust, thick and gritty, crawls up her nose. She keeps seeing the blackened corpse floating in a halo by the window, pointing accusingly at her. Finally she hears the woman get up and open the window, letting in the dull blue of early dawn. The woman stands there for a while before climbing out. Chika can hear footsteps, people walking past. She hears the woman call out, voice raised in recognition, followed by rapid Hausa that Chika does not understand.

The woman climbs back into the store. "Danger is finished. It is Abu. He is selling provisions. He is going to see his store. Everywhere policeman with tear gas. Soldier-man is coming. I go now before soldier-man will begin to harass somebody."

Chika stands slowly and stretches; her joints ache. She will walk all the way back to her aunty's home in the gated estate, because there are no taxis on the street, there are only army jeeps and battered police station wagons. She will find her aunty, wandering from one room to the next with a glass of water in her hand, muttering in Igbo, over and over, "Why did I ask you and Nnedi to visit? Why did my chi deceive me like this?" And Chika will grasp her aunty's shoulders tightly and lead her to a sofa.

Now, Chika unties the scarf from her leg, shakes it as though to shake the bloodstains out, and hands it to the woman. "Thank you."

"Wash your leg well-well. Greet your sister, greet your people," the woman says, tightening her wrapper around her waist.

"Greet your people also. Greet your baby and Halima,"

Chika says. Later, as she walks home, she will pick up a stone stained the copper of dried blood and hold the ghoulish souvenir to her chest. And she will suspect right then, in a strange flash while clutching the stone, that she will never find Nnedi, that her sister is gone. But now, she turns to the woman and adds, "May I keep your scarf? The bleeding might start again."

The woman looks for a moment as if she does not understand; then she nods. There is perhaps the beginning of future grief on her face, but she smiles a slight, distracted smile before she hands the scarf back to Chika and turns to climb out of the window.

AMA ATA AIDOO

Ama Ata Aidoo was born in 1942, the daughter of a Fante chief. She received her college education at the University of Ghana in Legon, where she majored in English, and around this time wrote her first play, *The Dilemma of a Ghost*. When it appeared in 1965, she became the first published African playwright. She has been a lecturer at the University of Cape Coast and a research fellow at the Institute of African Studies at the University of Ghana, and, in addition to her academic career, served as Minister of Education in 1982–83. Aidoo has lived in America, Britain, Germany, and Zimbabwe. Most recently, she held the post of visiting professor in the Africana Studies Department at Brown University. In the course of her prolific career, she has published the short story collections *No Sweetness Here* (1970) and *The Girl Who Can and Other Stories* (1997); poetry collections such as *Someone Talking to Sometime* (1986), *Birds and Other Poems* (1987), and *An Angry Letter in January* (1992); and the novels *Our Sister Killjoy* (1977), *The Eagle and the Chicken* (1986), and *Changes: A Love Story* (1991). She won the 1987 Nelson Mandela Award for Poetry and the 1992 Commonwealth Writers' Prize for Africa.

Two Sisters

(1970)

s she shakes out the typewriter cover and covers the machine with it, the thought of the bus she has to hurry to catch goes through her like a pain. It is her luck, she thinks. Everything is just her luck. Why, if she had one of those graduates for a boyfriend, wouldn't he come and take her home every evening? And she knows that a girl does not herself have to be a graduate to get one of those boys. Certainly, Joe is dying to do exactly that—with his taxi. And he is as handsome as anything, and a good man, but you know . . . Besides, there are cars and there are cars. As for the possibility of the other actually coming to fetch her—oh well. She has to admit it will take some time before she can bring herself to make demands of that sort on *him*. She has also to admit that the temptation is extremely strong. Would it really be so dangerously indiscreet? Doesn't one government car look like another? The hugeness of it? Its shaded glass? The uniformed chauffeur? She can already see herself stepping out to greet the dead-with-envy glances of the other girls. To begin with, she will insist on a little discretion. The driver can drop her under the *neem* trees in the morning and pick her up from there in the evening . . . anyway, she will have to wait a little while for that and it is all her luck.

There are other ways, surely. One of these, for some reason, she has sworn to have nothing of. Her boss has a car and does not look bad. In fact, the man is all right. But she keeps telling herself that she does not fancy having some old and dried-out housewife walking into the office one afternoon to tear her hair out and make a row . . . Mm, so for the meantime it is going to continue to be the municipal bus with its grimy seats, its common passengers and impudent conductors . . . Jesus! She doesn't wish herself dead or anything as stupidly final as that. Oh no. She just wishes she could sleep deep and only wake up on the morning of her glory.

The new pair of black shoes are more realistic than their owner, though. As she walks down the corridor, they sing:

> *Count, Mercy, count your blessings*
> *Count, Mercy, count your blessings*
> *Count, count, count your blessings.*

They sing along the corridor, into the avenue, across the

road, and into the bus. And they resume their song along
the gravel path as she opens the front gate and crosses the
cemented courtyard to the door.

"Sissie!" she called.

"*Hei* Mercy." And the door opened to show the face of
Connie, big sister, six years or more older and now heavy
with her second child. Mercy collapsed into the nearest chair.

"Welcome home. How was the office today?"

"Sister, don't ask. Look at my hands. My fingers are dead
with typing. Oh God, I don't know what to do."

"Why, what is wrong?"

"You tell me what is right. Why should I be a typist?"

"What else would you be?"

"What a strange question. Is typing the only thing one
can do in this world? You are a teacher, are you not?"

"But . . . but . . ."

"But what? Or you want me to know that if I had done
better in the exams, I could have trained to be a teacher
too, eh, sister? Or even a proper secretary?"

"Mercy, what is the matter? What have I done? What
have I done? Why have you come home so angry?"

Mercy broke into tears.

"Oh I am sorry. I am sorry, Sissie. It's just that I am sick
of everything. The office, living with you and your husband.
I want a husband of my own, children. I want . . . I want . . ."

"But you are so beautiful."

"Thank you. But so are you."

"You are young and beautiful. As for marriage, it's you
who are postponing it. Look at all these people who are
running after you."

"Sissie, I don't like what you are doing. So stop it."

"Okay, okay, okay."

And there was a silence.

"Which of them could I marry? Joe is—mm, fine—but,
but I just don't like him."

"You mean . . ."

"Oh, Sissie!"

"Little sister, you and I can be truthful with one another."

"Oh yes."

"What I would like to say is that I am not that old or wise. But still I could advise you a little. Joe drives someone's car now. Well, you never know. Lots of taxi drivers come to own their taxis, sometimes fleets of cars."

"Of course. But it's a pity you are married already. Or I could be a go-between for you and Joe!"

And the two of them burst out laughing. It was when she rose to go to the bedroom that Connie noticed the new shoes.

"*Ei*, those are beautiful shoes. Are they new?"

From the other room, Mercy's voice came interrupted by the motions of her body as she undressed and then dressed again. However, the uncertainty in it was due to something entirely different.

"Oh, I forgot to tell you about them. In fact, I was going to show them to you. I think it was on Tuesday I bought them. Or was it Wednesday? When I came home from the office, you and James had taken Akosua out. And later I forgot all about them."

"I see. But they are very pretty. Were they expensive?"

"No, not really." This reply was too hurriedly said.

And she said only last week that she didn't have a penny on her. And I believed her because I know what they pay her is just not enough to last anyone through any month, even minus rent . . . I have been thinking she manages very well. But these shoes. And she is not the type who would borrow money just to buy a pair of shoes, when she could have gone on wearing her old pairs until things get better. Oh, I wish I knew what to do. I mean, I am not her mother. And I wonder how James will see these problems.

"Sissie, you look worried."

"Hmm, when don't I? With the baby due in a couple of months and the government's new ruling on salaries and all. On top of everything, I have reliable information that James is running after a new girl."

Mercy laughed. "Oh, Sissie. You always get reliable information on these things."

"But yes. And I don't know why."

"Sissie, men are like that."

"They are selfish."

"No, it's just that women allow them to behave the way they do instead of seizing some freedom themselves."

"But I am sure that even if we were free to carry on in the same way, I wouldn't make use of it."

"But why not?"

"Because I love James. I love James and I am not interested in any other man." Her voice was full of tears.

But Mercy was amused. "Oh God. Now listen to that. It's women like you who keep all of us down."

"Well, I am sorry but it's how the good God created me."

"Mm. I am sure that I can love several men at the same time."

"Mercy!"

They burst out laughing again. And yet they are sad. But laughter is always best.

Mercy complained of hunger and so they went to the kitchen to heat up some food and eat. The two sisters alone. It is no use waiting for James. And this evening a friend of Connie's has come to take out the baby girl, Akosua, and had threatened to keep her until her bedtime.

"Sissie, I am going to see a film." This from Mercy.

"Where?"

"The Globe."

"Are you going with Joe?"

"No."

"Are you going alone?"

"No."

Careful Connie.

"Whom are you going with?"

Careful Connie, please. Little sister's nostrils are widening dangerously. Look at the sudden creasing up of her mouth and between her brows. Connie, a sister is a good thing. Even a younger sister. Especially when you have no mother or father.

"Mercy, whom are you going out with?"

"Well, I had food in my mouth! And I had to swallow it down before I could answer you, no?"

"I am sorry." How softly said.

"And anyway, do I have to tell you everything?"

"Oh no. It's just that I didn't think it was a question I should not have asked."

There was more silence. Then Mercy sucked her teeth with irritation and Connie cleared her throat with fear.

"I am going out with Mensar-Arthur."

As Connie asked the next question, she wondered if the words were leaving her lips. "Mensar-Arthur?"

"Yes."

"Which one?"

"How many do you know?"

Her fingers were too numb to pick up the food. She put the plate down. Something jumped in her chest and she wondered what it was. Perhaps it was the baby.

"Do you mean that Member of Parliament?"

"Yes."

"But, Mercy . . ."

Little sister only sits and chews her food.

"But, Mercy . . ."

Chew, chew, chew.

"But, Mercy . . ."

"What?"

She startled Connie.

"He is so old."

Chew, chew, chew.

"Perhaps, I mean, perhaps that really doesn't matter, does it? Not very much anyway. But they say he has so many wives and girlfriends."

Please little sister. I am not trying to interfere in your private life. You said yourself a little while ago that you wanted a man of your own. That man belongs to so many women already . . .

That silence again. Then there was only Mercy's foot-steps as she went to put her plate in the kitchen sink, run-ning water as she washed her plate and her hands. She drank some water and coughed. Then, as tears streamed down her sister's averted face, there was the sound of her footsteps as she left the kitchen. At the end of it all, she banged a door. Connie only said something like, "O Lord, O Lord," and continued sitting in the kitchen. She had hardly eaten anything at all. Very soon Mercy went to have a bath. Then Connie heard her getting ready to leave the house. The shoes. Then she was gone. She needn't have carried on like that, eh? Because Connie had not meant to probe or bring on a quarrel. What use is there in this old world for a sister, if you can't have a chat with her? What's more, things like this never happen to people like Mercy. Their parents were good Presbyterians. They feared God. Mama had not managed to give them all the rules of life before she died. But Connie knows that running around with an old and depraved public man would have been considered an abomination by the parents.

A big car with a super-smooth engine purred into the drive. It actually purrs, this huge machine from the white man's land. Indeed, its well-mannered protest as the tires slid onto the gravel seemed like a lullaby compared to the loud thumping of the girl's stiletto shoes. When Mensar-Arthur saw Mercy, he stretched his arm and opened the door to the passenger seat. She sat down and the door closed with a civilized thud. The engine hummed into motion and the car sailed away.

After a distance of a mile or so from the house, the man started a conversation.

"And how is my darling today?"

"I am well," and only the words did not imply tragedy.

"You look solemn today, why?"

She remained silent and still.

"My dear, what is the matter?"

"Nothing."

"Oh . . ." He cleared his throat again. "Eh, and how were the shoes?"

"Very nice. In fact, I am wearing them now. They pinch a little but then all new shoes are like that."

"And the handbag?"

"I like it very much, too . . . My sister noticed them. I mean the shoes." The tragedy was announced.

"Did she ask you where you got them from?"

"No."

He cleared his throat again. "Where did we agree to go tonight?"

"The Globe, but I don't want to see a film."

"Is that so? Mm, I am glad because people always notice things."

"But they won't be too surprised."

"What are you saying, my dear?"

"Nothing."

"Okay, so what shall we do?"

"I don't know."

"Shall I drive to the Seaway?"

"Oh yes."

He drove to the Seaway. To a section of the beach they knew very well. She loves it here. This wide expanse of sand and the old sea. She has often wished she could do what she fancied: one thing she fancies. Which is to drive very near to the end of the sands until the tires of the car touched the water. Of course it is a very foolish idea, as he pointed out sharply to her the first time she thought aloud about it. It was in his occasional I-am-more-than-old-enough-to-be-your-father tone. There are always disadvantages. Things could be different. Like if one had a younger lover. Handsome, maybe not rich like this man here, but well off, sufficiently well off to be able to afford a sports car. A little something very much like those in the films driven by the white racing drivers. With tires that can do everything . . . and they would drive to exactly where the sea and the sand meet.

"We are here."

"Don't let's get out. Let's just sit inside and talk."

"Talk?"

"Yes."

"Okay. But what is it, my darling?"

"I have told my sister about you."

"Good God. Why?"

"But I had to. I couldn't keep it to myself any longer."

"Childish. It was not necessary at all. She is not your mother."

"No. But she is all I have. And she has been very good to me."

"Well, it was her duty."

"Then it is my duty to tell her about something like this. I may get into trouble."

"Don't be silly," he said. "I normally take good care of my girlfriends."

"I see," she said, and for the first time in the one month since she agreed to be this man's lover, the tears which suddenly rose into her eyes were not forced.

"And you promised you wouldn't tell her." It was Father's voice now.

"Don't be angry. After all, people talk so much, as you said a little while ago. She was bound to hear it one day."

"My darling, you are too wise. What did she say?"

"She was pained."

"Don't worry. Find out something she wants very much but cannot get in this country because of the import restrictions."

"I know for sure she wants an electric motor for her sewing machine."

"Is that all?"

"That's what I know of."

"Mm. I am going to London next week on some delegation, so if you bring me the details on the make of the machine, I shall get her the motor."

"Thank you."

"What else is worrying my Black Beauty?"

"Nothing."

"And by the way, let me know as soon as you want to leave your sister's place. I have got you one of the government estate houses."

"Oh . . . oh," she said, pleased, contented for the first time since this typically ghastly day had begun, at half past six in the morning.

Dear little child came back from the playground with her toe bruised. Shall we just blow cold air from our mouth on it or put on a salve? Nothing matters really. Just see that she does not feel unattended. And the old sea roars on. This is a calm sea, generally. Too calm in fact, this Gulf of Guinea. The natives sacrifice to him on Tuesdays and once a year celebrate him. They might save their chickens, their eggs, and their yams. And as for the feast once a year, he doesn't pay much attention to it either. They are always celebrating one thing or another and they surely don't need him for an excuse to celebrate one day more. He has seen things happen along these beaches. Different things. Contradictory things. Or just repetitions of old patterns. He never interferes in their affairs. Why should he? Except in places like Keta, where he eats houses away because they leave him no choice. Otherwise, he never allows them to see his passions. People are worms, and even the God who created them is immensely bored with their antics. Here is a fifty-year-old "big man" who thinks he is somebody. And a twenty-three-year-old child who chooses a silly way to conquer unconquerable problems. Well, what did one expect of human beings? And so, as those two settled on the back seat of the car to play with each other's bodies, he, the Gulf of Guinea, shut his eyes with boredom. It is right. He could sleep, no? He spread himself and moved farther ashore. But the car was parked at a very safe distance and the rising tides could not wet its tires.

James has come home late. But then he has been coming back late for the past few weeks. Connie is crying and he knows it as soon as he enters the bedroom. He hates tears, for, like so many men, he knows it is one of the most potent weapons in women's bitchy and inexhaustible arsenal. She speaks first.

"James."

"Oh, are you still awake?" He always tries to deal with these nightly funeral parlor doings by pretending not to know what they are about.

"I couldn't sleep."

"What is wrong?"

"Nothing."

So he moves quickly and sits beside her. "Connie, what is the matter? You have been crying again."

"You are very late again."

"Is that why you are crying? Or is there something else?"

"Yes."

"Yes to what?"

"James, where were you?"

"Connie, I have warned you about what I shall do if you don't stop examining me, as though I were your prisoner, every time I am a little late."

She sat up. "A little late! It is nearly two o'clock."

"Anyway, you won't believe me if I told you the truth, so why do you want me to waste my breath?"

"Oh well." She lies down again and turns her face to the wall. He stands up but does not walk away. He looks down at her. So she remembers every night: they have agreed, after many arguments, that she should sleep like this. During her first pregnancy, he kept saying after the third month or so that the sight of her tummy the last thing before he slept always gave him nightmares. Now he regrets all this. The bed creaks as he throws himself down by her.

"James."

"Yes."

"There is something much more serious."

"You have heard about my newest affair?"

"Yes, but that is not what I am referring to."

"Jesus, is it possible that there is anything more important than that?"

And as they laugh they know that something has happened. One of those things which, with luck, will keep them together for some time to come.

"He teases me on top of everything."

"What else can one do to you but tease when you are in this state?"

"James! How profane!"

"It is your dirty mind which gave my statement its shocking meaning."

"Okay! But what shall I do?"

"About what?"

"Mercy. Listen, she is having an affair with Mensar-Arthur."

"Wonderful."

She sits up and he sits up.

"James, we must do something about it. It is very serious."

"Is that why you were crying?"

"Of course."

"Why shouldn't she?"

"But it is wrong. And she is ruining herself."

"Since every other girl she knows has ruined herself prosperously, why shouldn't she? Just forget for once that you are a teacher. Or at least remember she is not your pupil."

"I don't like your answers."

"What would you like me to say? Every morning her friends who don't earn any more than she does wear new dresses, shoes, wigs, and what-have-you to work. What would you have her do?"

"The fact that other girls do it does not mean that Mercy should do it, too."

"You are being very silly. If I were Mercy, I am sure that's exactly what I would do. And you know I mean it, too."

James is cruel. He is terrible and mean. Connie breaks into fresh tears and James comforts her. There is one point he must drive home, though.

"In fact, encourage her. He may be able to intercede with the Ministry for you so that after the baby is born they will not transfer you from here for some time."

"James, you want me to use my sister!"

"She is using herself, remember."

"James, you are wicked."

"And maybe he would even agree to get us a new car from abroad. I shall pay for everything. That would be better than paying a fortune for that old thing I was thinking of buying. Think of that."

"You will ride in it alone."

"Well . . ."

That was a few months before the coup. Mensar-Arthur did go to London for a conference and bought something for all his wives and girlfriends, including Mercy. He even remembered the motor for Connie's machine. When Mercy took it to her she was quite confused. She had wanted this thing for a long time, and it would make everything so much easier, like the clothes for the new baby. And yet one side of her said that accepting it was a betrayal. Of what, she wasn't even sure. She and Mercy could never bring the whole business into the open and discuss it. And there was always James supporting Mercy, to Connie's bewilderment. She took the motor with thanks and sold even her right to dissent. In a short while, Mercy left the house to go and live in the estate house Mensar-Arthur had procured for her. Then, a couple of weeks later, the coup. Mercy left her new place before anyone could evict her. James never got his car. Connie's new baby was born. Of the three, the one who greeted the new order with undisguised relief was Connie. She is not really a demonstrative person but it was obvious from her eyes that she was happy. As far as she was concerned, the old order as symbolized by Mensar-Arthur was a threat to her sister and therefore to her own peace of mind. With it gone, things could return to normal. Mercy would move back to the house, perhaps start to date someone more—ordinary, let's say. Eventually, she would get married and then the nightmare of those past weeks would be forgotten. God being so good, he brought the coup early before the news of the affair could spread and brand her sister . . .

The arrival of the new baby has magically waved away the difficulties between James and Connie. He is that kind of man, and she that kind of woman. Mercy has not been seen for many days. Connie is beginning to get worried . . .

James heard the baby yelling—a familiar noise, by now—the moment he opened the front gate. He ran in, clutching to his chest the few things he had bought on his way home.

"We are in here."

"I certainly could hear you. If there is anything people of this country have, it is a big mouth."

"Don't I agree? But on the whole, we are well. He is eating normally and everything. You?"

"Nothing new. Same routine. More stories about the overthrown politicians."

"What do you mean, nothing new? Look at the excellent job the soldiers have done, cleaning up the country of all that dirt. I feel free already and I am dying to get out and enjoy it."

James laughed mirthlessly. "All I know is that Mensar-Arthur is in jail. No use. And I am not getting my car. Rough deal."

"I never took you seriously on that car business."

"Honestly, if this were in the ancient days, I could brand you a witch. You don't want me, your husband, to prosper?"

"Not out of my sister's ruin."

"Ruin, ruin, ruin! Christ! See, Connie, the funny thing is that I am sure you are the only person who thought it was a disaster to have a sister who was the girlfriend of a big man."

"Okay; now all is over, and don't let's quarrel."

"I bet the coup could have succeeded on your prayers alone."

And Connie wondered why he said that with so much bitterness. She wondered if . . .

"Has Mercy been here?"

"Not yet, later, maybe. Mm. I had hoped she would move back here and start all over again."

"I am not surprised she hasn't. In fact, if I were her, I wouldn't come back here either. Not to your nagging, no thank you, big sister."

And as the argument progressed, as always, each was forced into a more aggressive defensive stand.

"Well, just say what pleases you, I am very glad about the soldiers. Mercy is my only sister, brother; everything. I can't sit and see her life going wrong without feeling it. I am grateful to whatever forces there are which put a stop to that. What pains me now is that she should be so vague about where she is living at the moment. She makes mention of a girlfriend but I am not sure that I know her."

"If I were you, I would stop worrying because it seems Mercy can look after herself quite well."

"Hmm" was all she tried to say.

Who heard something like the sound of a car pulling into the drive? Ah, but the footsteps were unmistakably Mercy's. Are those shoes the old pair which were new a couple of months ago? Or are they the newest pair? And here she is herself, the pretty one. A gay Mercy.

"Hello, hello, my clan!" And she makes a lot of her nephew. "Dow-dah-dee-day! And how is my dear young man today? My lord, grow up fast and come to take care of Auntie Mercy."

Both Connie and James cannot take their eyes off her. Connie says, "He says to Auntie Mercy he is fine."

Still they watch her, horrified, fascinated, and wondering what it's all about. Because they both know it is about something.

"Listen, people, I brought a friend to meet you. A man."

"Where is he?" from James.

"Bring him in," from Connie.

"You know, Sissie, you are a new mother. I thought I'd come and ask you if it's all right."

"Of course," say James and Connie, and for some reason they are both very nervous.

"He is Captain Ashley."

"Which one?"

"How many do you know?"

James still thinks it is impossible. "Eh . . . do you mean the officer who has been appointed the . . . the . . ."

"Yes."

"Wasn't there a picture in *The Crystal* over the weekend of his daughter's wedding? And another one of him with his wife and children and grandchildren?"

"Yes."

"And he is heading a commission to investigate something or other?"

"Yes."

Connie just sits there with her mouth open that wide . . .

DOREEN BAINGANA

Doreen Baingana was born in Uganda, one of the nine children of a physician father and a mother who served as Permanent Secretary of the Public Service Commission. She earned a law degree at Makerere University in Uganda and an MFA in Creative Writing at the University of Maryland, where she was a writer-in-residence. Her stories have appeared in *Glimmer Train, African American Review, Calladoo,* and *The Guardian.* Her short story collection, *Tropical Fish: Tales from Entebbe,* won the 2006 Commonwealth Writers' Prize for Best First Book and an AWP Short Fiction Award. An active member of FEMRITE, a Ugandan women writers' association, she currently lives in Rockville, Maryland.

First Kiss
(2005)

Christine's romance was one day old. She was going to meet Nicholas again this afternoon. It was a hot empty Sunday in Entebbe, so bright you couldn't see. She didn't want anyone to know, but wondered how her sisters, Patti and Rosa, could not sense her excitement. The air itself felt different. Christine lay in bed late into the morning, plotting her escape. Her first date! With a boy! She was fourteen. Nicholas was older, eighteen maybe? Not Nick, or Nicky, but Nicholas. That was classy, she thought.

Having older sisters made Christine feel and talk older. She learned a lot that her school friends didn't know, like the words to more than four Jackson Five songs, and that the fashionable narrow trousers were called "pipes." Christine couldn't wait for adult things to happen. To wear a bra for a good reason, dance at parties, talk to boys nonchalantly, then giggle over them with her girlfriends. Move to Kampala instead of dying of boredom in Entebbe. But however much she copied her sisters, she still felt smaller, thinner, inadequate.

Anyway, what would she wear? How would she escape the house without anyone knowing? They would poke their noses into her business, ask her this and that. She had met him, Nicholas, the day before. He was as tall as a windmill. As foreign and familiar as one, too. A boy. No, a man. Help! Christine's world had been made up of women even before Taata died three years ago. He had been quiet and remote or drunk and to be avoided. Her sisters, mother, and aunts had converged protectively over and around her. In primary school it had been a scandal even to *talk* to boys; they were alien creatures.

Nicholas wasn't a stranger, though; she knew the whole Bajombora family. They had all gone to Lake Victoria Primary School—Lake Vic—once the best school in Entebbe. Back before Uganda's independence, in the early sixties, it had been for whites only. Some textbooks still had the stamp "The European School." But by 1973, with Idi Amin's regime in full force, there were about two *bazungu* left in the whole school.

Nicholas's youngest brother had been in her class. Even though the Bajomboras were always last in class, they were the best dressed in the whole school, with sharply ironed khaki shorts, shirts new and dazzling white, and black shoes so shiny you could see your face in them. Not that she got that close; they were boys! Rough and rude, or should have been. Their shoe heels were never worn down to one side like most of the others'; that was a sign of money. The dumb, handsome Bajombora boys, six of them. They were a deep, dark, smooth black and were all prizes. Although they belonged to Christine's ethnic group, the Banyankore, they were Catholics, which made them completely different, at least in her mother's Protestant opinion. To Maama, Catholics were misguided fools, though she never said this, of course, but clearly let it be known by turning down her mouth, raising her eyebrows, and hurrmphing heavily. Don't even bring up Muslims.

The day before, when Christine's sisters were dressing up to go to the Bajomboras' party, she had asked jokingly, "Can I come?" She was bored. She had spent the whole day in bed reading a Georgette Heyer romance. They were best read all the way through, at once, to keep up the excitement. To keep believing, hoping, fantasizing. Fantasy was so much better than real life. Christine became the plucky heroine waving her fan, singing, *"My ship sailed from China / with a cargo of tea . . . ,"* as she strolled through spring gardens or the drafty halls of Rossborough Castle. She inevitably fell in love with the hero, the tall, dark (African?) Lord Wimbledon, long before he won the heart of the rebellious witty heroine, Lady Thomasina. She imagined his shapely thighs in tight white knickerbockers, his ponytail long like a pirate's. No, not a pirate; he was an aristocrat. No one could resist him, not even Lady Thomasina, who had a mind of her own, but no fortune, alas. It was a fun read, but left Christine with a vague feeling of disgust, the same sick satisfaction she felt after eating too many sweet oily *kabs*.

Christine was on holiday, which was better than starving at school, but flat. She listened and watched her sisters talking on the phone, going out, working on their figures, doing sit-ups, drinking endless glasses of lemon juice that supposedly were slimming, walking with books on their heads to learn grace, wrapping their hips tight to stop them from growing too big. Rosa and Patti were seventeen and eighteen. They had purpose. Christine read romance novels and napped.

Rosa brushed away Christine's plea the way she usually did, as though her sister was a bothersome fly. "Don't be silly, the party is not for kids. Me, I won't have time to look after you."

Patti, as expected, took Christine's side. "*Bambi,* you want to come with us? Why not? But ask Maama first."

"Don't waste your time; she won't agree. *Bannange,* who last used the hot comb, and left their *bi-hairs* in it! Eeeh!"

Christine found Maama in the sitting room watching a TV play. *Ensi Bwetyo*—"Life's Like That"—had run forever. Maama was drinking her usual black tea. Christine's voice squeaked nervously. "The Pattis said I could go with them to the Bajombora party."

"Since when, at your age?" Maama talked to the children in Runyankore, but for some reason they answered her back in English. Probably because they would have been punished at school for speaking their own language.

"It's for all ages."

"Are you sure?" Maama's attention was on the TV show; she didn't want to miss a word. Patti came to Christine's rescue. "*Bambi,* let her come. She'll stay with me full-time."

Maama slowly turned her eyes away from the TV and swept her gaze over the two of them, down, up, and back down again, as if she was trying to figure out who they were. She shrugged her shoulders and turned back to the TV, torturing them with time. "Don't come complaining to me about her afterwards," she said. Maama never came right out and said yes. That would be too kind; she might get taken advantage of.

Patti quickly hot-combed Christine's hair in the kitchen while Rosa complained that *the baby* would make them late. The heat of the comb close to Christine's scalp caused delicious shivers of fear down her neck and back. Anticipation felt like a mild fever. She was going to a real party. *Katondest!* she said over and over again silently. Christine's feet were already Patti's size, so she borrowed her sister's pair of red high heels, with long straps that crisscrossed up the calves. She became Lady Thomasina preparing for a ball. She put on a corduroy pantsuit her aunt brought her a year ago from London. It was getting too small; it pressed into her crotch and squeezed into the crack of her bum, but what else could she wear? At least it was the latest, sort of. She almost twisted her back trying to see her behind in the mirror. Rosa laughed. "No one's going to notice *you,* silly!"

Patti came to Christine's defense. "*Wamma* you look good, grown-up."

Rosa jeered back, "*Kyoka,* Patti, you can lie!"

"How come the Senior Fours borrowed it for two socials last term? It's still in." Christine posed dramatically in front of the mirror, one hand on her nonexistent hips.

"Lie yourself, then! It's not the trousers that are the problem; it's your stick figure. Anyway, let's go!"

Christine and Patti were used to Rosa's taunts; they simply ignored her. Patti drew dark eyebrows over Christine's own and painted her lips deep crimson. Christine was startled by her reflection, and Rosa laughed hysterically. "Don't let Maama see you!"

"No one will know she's fourteen." Patti was proud of her artwork.

Forget her face; Christine's worry was falling off the high heels, since they were walking to the party. It had just turned dark when they set off. The air was bluish, mysterious, and the crickets shrilled urgently, but the girls did not hear them. Each of them dwelt on her own separate excitement. Rosa was going to see Sam, her boyfriend, again. She preferred being with him in public, showing off their love, rather than when they were alone, which time she spent fighting off his roaming hands. That wasn't romantic. As for Patti, she was saved, but didn't believe dancing was a sin. She danced for the Lord, she said, like David in the Psalms. Okay, David hadn't danced "squeeze" with women, but neither did Patti with boys. Nor did she drink. Patti was a little worried about Christine, however, who was more like Rosa, in Patti's opinion, or at least wanted to be, which could be worse.

Christine almost fell a number of times in the high red shoes. The tarmac road, which had not been repaired since the late sixties, before Amin took over, was more like a dry riverbed. Most of the tarmac was gone, leaving huge potholes to be skirted around. Luckily it hadn't rained recently, so there were no pools of muddy water, only empty craters and dusty flyaway soil and stones. Cars that circled off the

road to avoid the potholes had widened it, creating yawning mouths with no teeth, only gaping dirty-brown holes. It
was safer to walk down the middle to avoid the cars that
bumped and swerved along the roadside. It would have
been better with no tarmac at all. The girls walked with
heads bowed down out of habit, picking their way through
unthinkingly. They did not see the solemn indigo beauty of
the sky, now glowing with far-off dots of light.

When they got to the party, Christine hung close to Patti
shyly until she saw Betty, the Bajomboras' cousin, who
lived with them. She was two years older than Christine but
had repeated classes in primary school, and so had ended
up in P.7 with Christine. Betty already had full breasts by
then, when everyone else had nothing or only tiny protruding plums that stretched their school uniforms tight across
the chest. One year later, at fourteen, Betty got pregnant
and had an abortion. It was a major scandal. She was sent
to her village, Ibanda, for a year. She came back subdued,
fat, and very *shera,* you could tell her tribe right away. She
said *mwana* all the time, and walked as slowly and as heavily as a cow. Well, that was considered graceful among the
village Banyankore. Christine had seen Betty only twice
since that time, by accident, but was so glad to see her now,
especially since she didn't want to trail after Patti like a
five-year-old. Betty looked like a woman, but, thank goodness, she didn't brush her off.

Betty gave Christine whisky mixed with Mirinda to cut
the sour taste and hide the alcohol. Christine didn't say she
had never drunk whisky before. She was surprised by how
it burnt going down, not like pepper, but like glowing warm
fire. The two girls danced together; they could do that, they
were young enough. But then some strange boy called
Betty outside, pointing with his head, and off she went. Too
willingly, Christine thought. She was alone again. She was
supposed to be having fun with other people; that's what
parties were for. Luckily or unluckily, Patti saw Christine
and asked one of the Bajombora boys, Nicholas, to dance
with her. He looked drunk, and smiled at Christine like he

was doing her a favor. It was a Congolese song, and it seemed to last forever. The dance was simple, dull, and repetitive: one step left, then back, another right and back, left, right, with an accompanying jiggle of the hips. Nicholas danced in his own stiff way, frowning with concentration. It made her smile. He noticed and smiled back, then said, "You're a good dancer," leaning over her as if he was about to topple. He was tall, tall. The Leaning Tower of Nicholas. She smiled at her own joke and stumbled on his foot. "Enough," he laughed. "Let's have a drink."

"Not in front of my sisters."

"Outside, then."

They sat on a low branch of a huge old mango tree. It wasn't mango season, but the leaves were heavy and reassuring, a dark green umbrella for everyone, a rich auntie. Christine wondered where all the ants that crawled the craggy bark of every mango tree went to at night. Nicholas had put more whisky than Mirinda into Christine's drink. It burned her throat and brought tears to her eyes. She forced it down with a cough. Then it seemed like a bright light turned itself on in her head as they sat in the warm clear dark. The stars, which she usually didn't notice, twinkled in an exaggerated way through her tears. Christine stopped herself from showing him the sky; that would be silly, but she bet Lady Thomasina would have. What next? Nicholas lit a cigarette and inhaled deeply. He didn't say anything. But somehow, casually, his arm went over her shoulder. He put out his cigarette on the branch; then his face closed in and his lips were on hers. "My lipstick!" she thought, as he chewed away at her lips, then snaked his tongue into her mouth and ate some more. His smoky smell reminded her of her father. Soon, she couldn't breathe, didn't know how to, but just in time, he broke away. "Nice," he said, as she wiped her mouth with the back of her hand. She jumped off the branch. "Wait, don't go," he said.

"Patti will be looking for me."

"Okay, why not meet me tomorrow? Christine?"

She cleared her throat. The whisky, or something, was bubbling in her brain.

"Where?"

"How about at Lake Vic? The school, not the hotel. In front of the Assembly Hall, okay? Around two?"

"Okay."

So *that* was kissing. That was it? She couldn't decide if it was yucky or nice. She wiped her lips with the back of her hand. Would Lady Thomasina be this confused? Would Rosa? Christine had been kissed before Patti, she was sure. Her head felt foggy. Was it the whisky, Nicholas, or both? What if Maama smelt her breath? But *he* wanted to see her again. To kiss her some more!

So there was Christine the next morning daydreaming in bed, and panicking too. It was already eleven, but staying in bed was about the only way to be alone in the shared room. What would she wear? Should she put on lipstick again? Nicholas must have liked the red. Her lips' natural color was a pinkish brown, which just wouldn't do. And what if she looked completely different without her eyebrows drawn over? Should she wear her blue jean skirt, or the yellow lace dress? No, it was too frilly; she'd look like a baby. But she couldn't borrow clothes from Rosa or Patti without being asked a million questions. Imagine, *she* had a date, and with an older man! Well, okay, a boy, but still a date. Look at her fingernails, bitten short and ugly. Had he noticed them yesterday? She hoped not.

One could never tell what was going to happen. The future, the not-yet. It was like reading a book. But with a book, the delicious end was right there in your hands; all you had to do was read and not peek ahead, and you'd get to it. Of course, with romance novels you already knew that the Lord would get the Lady, or was it vice versa? How, was the question, the thrill. In real life, the future didn't exist. You could try and make it up as you went along, like how you put on makeup deliberately, but when other people were involved, there was no way you could tell what they would do. You couldn't control them. They might turn away, or prefer sad endings.

Luckily for Christine, Maama had gone to the neighbors; Mrs. Mukasa was sewing her a dress. Patti had been sent to line up for sugar. Rumor was that one store in Kitoro had some; the owner's son was in the army. Rosa had refused to go. She spent her afternoons "borrowing books," which they all knew meant seeing Sam. That day, Christine was supposed to clean the living room, which she did quickly. She ate leftover cassava and beans for lunch, enjoying the rarely still, empty house, then bathed and dressed up, slowly, deliberately. She chose the blue jean skirt; it was casual but looked good. She wore a red top to match Patti's red shoes, which she borrowed again for good luck. There. Christine went out through the back door to the boys' quarters, where Akiki, the housegirl, was resting. Christine called out through her closed door, "Akiki, the house is empty. I'm off to Betty's," and rushed away before Akiki could get up and see her all dressed up.

Christine slowed down once she got to the street. She was sweating already. Why did Nicholas choose the afternoon? It would have been cooler later on, and the evening light more romantic. Christine giggled and practiced a womanly sway. The high heels definitely made her more feminine, though unbalanced. She smoothed her jean skirt over her still small hips. Was it the heat or this escapade that was making her leak sweat like a broken tap? Under a jacaranda tree by the side of the road, she got a small mirror, Patti's, from her bag, rubbed on Patti's lipstick, then walked on.

Everything was asleep; the road was dead, even the flies were too lazy and drunk with heat to do more than flop around. The sun was Christine's relentless witness. She reached the huge roundabout in front of Lake Vic, but had to walk around it because the grass was overgrown. Back when she and her school friends passed by every day on their way to school, they would find groups of five or six women hired by the Entebbe Town Council cutting the grass with long thin slashers. The women were always busy because the grass grew back as fast as ever. Poor women;

during Amin's "economic war" they were paid next to nothing. It now looked like the council had long given up the fight with nature. The grass, ignoring the emergency situation, kept on growing.

Christine could almost see those early morning scenes: most of the slasher women had babies tied onto their backs, who slept peacefully even as the women swung up and down, up and down with labor. The women wore old, faded *busutis* and head scarves wrapped shabbily over their hair. They were barefoot or wore thin rubber *sapatu*. They didn't speak English, of course. Christine and her friends didn't greet them, even though they looked just like their aunties back in the village, whose close, sticky hugs smelt of sweat and kitchen-fire smoke. They were comforting and discomforting all at the same time. But here in town, the lesson these women gave was so clear no one even said it: Study hard, speak English well, get into one of the few good high schools, go to college. Onward and upward. You are not these women. Do not become them.

It was now half past one. Christine was rarely early for anything, but this time she was almost at the school. Past the roundabout was a giant tree that seemed to have retained its immensity even as the school buildings ahead shrank as she grew older. It was an olive tree, though she didn't know that when she was at Lake Vic. The fruit, *empafu,* were green, hard, and bitter, or black, a little softer, but just as bitter. Christine grew to like their chewy texture; it was like an interesting thought to be turned over and over. The fruit left her tongue and inner cheeks rough, as though her mouth had become someone else's. That was the taste and feel of walking home from school all those years ago. The sound of the past was of the small hard fruit falling. They would drop on her head, plop! or just miss her, startling her out of her daydreams of being first in class; of how she would show them, whoever they were, after whatever slight; dreams of visiting an aunt in Kampala; of going somewhere even farther away, England perhaps. America! As her mind roved, she climbed on the curb, carefully balancing, her arms stretched out wide like wings, one foot straight in front of the other. She was a ballerina, a flying airplane, then plop! The hard nut's sudden fall surprised her into tripping. On other days, when she walked home with her friends Carol and Karen, they would playfully push each other off the black and white curb. Christine could almost hear the laughter, the running, the joking shouts of abuse. All those days merged into one carefree moment in her mind.

Now, the curb's paint had faded to gray and its edges crumbled to dust. All the same, Christine stepped up onto it, stifling a giggle. In Patti's red high heels, she felt like a chicken clumsily trying to fly. Her laughter rang out in the silent hot afternoon, making her catch herself. Nicholas would think she was crazy!

Here was the Upper School Assembly, another faded apology of its former imposing blue and white state. It was now ten to two. Christine was early, oh no, a sign of desperation. Coming on time was bad enough. This was a date, not a school appointment. She wished she had asked Patti or Rosa for advice. No, not Patti, she didn't go out with boys; she would have stopped her from going, called up the Bajomboras or something! Rosa wouldn't be much help either; she would have laughed at her and kept bringing it up forever to embarrass her. So much for big sisters. Well, she had the time to cool down, wipe off the sweat, check her lipstick.

Christine sat in the shade on the cement ledge in front of the Assembly Hall. She doubted the toilets were open or clean. She wouldn't look at her watch again. The Assembly had long glass doors all along one side to keep it cool, and long windows on the other. Some of the panes were cracked or empty. She looked into the darkness of the hall. As her eyes adjusted to the dark, the forms inside took on recognizable shape. What a mess. The curtain on the stage was torn; a piano's dark bulk squatted awkwardly to one side on only two feet, its lid broken and askew. A few small chairs were scattered around the huge dusty floor, and on one of them was a pile of neglected, ragged-looking exercise books. It was hard to believe this was the same school that had performed so well once that even Amin's children had joined it for two terms when they lived in Entebbe State House. It was only three years since Christine had left P.7; how come she hadn't noticed this mess? This *we-have-given-up-why-bother* state. Things must have started falling apart years ago. She hadn't noticed it then, probably because she was here every day. The change was gradual and the result normal, like many other things about Amin's time, including the everyday fear in the air. She remembered how everyone had laughed in astonishment, then got used to it, when Amin by decree banned minis and wigs. He made Friday, the Muslim day of prayer, a day off and Saturday a workday. Everyone adjusted to the upside-down week, the upside-down life, including other unbelievable and ugly things she didn't want to think about. The bad smell became familiar.

In this very hall, Christine had been through five years of morning hymns, prayers, and announcements. She remembered the cheerful routine of singing "We Wish You Many Happy Returns of the Day" for different students every week. The word "returns" had puzzled her; it still did. The headmaster, fat round Mr. Mubozi, had led assembly since Christine's first year in the Upper School, when she was eight. He looked kind and jolly, like Father Christmas, but he wasn't, oh no! She remembered him shouting at a kid once, "Wipe that grin off your face!" Everyone looked around in astonishment for a green face. Christine had gone to his wife's nursery school. She was white. She too was fat and round, but kind, giving them homemade toffee every week. The nursery school was a room at her house, with children's colorful drawings up on every wall. Most of the other kids were Indian. The lasting impression of that year was of their heavy black hair and spicy smell, and how they jostled up to the front, not afraid to seek the teacher's attention, while Christine hung back, waiting, as she had been taught to do. But in one week that year, 1972, the Indian kids disappeared; Idi Amin sent them all away. Christine remembered busloads of frightened faces heading down Circular Road past Saint John's Church to the International Airport, and the piles of comics and all sorts of toys she, Rosa, Patti, and so many others got for almost nothing. Those Indians were rich! Where were all those kids now? Christine wondered.

It was now ten past two. *Okay, calm down,* Christine told herself. At least she was in the shade. Out in the sun, two yellow butterflies chased each other round and round. At the corner of the school building was a huge flower bed with three plants. Someone had planted only three of them. Strange, this neat flower bed next to the dilapidated hall. God, it was quiet. Well, private too, which was good. How come there was a cooling wind in the shade and none in the sun? she wondered distractedly. She should have brought a book. She remembered the dirty book she had seen peeking out of Rosa's suitcase, about a year ago. There was a naked woman on the cover, her body twisted in a weird position. Christine's face went hot as she peeked through the pages. How could Rosa read this? People didn't really do these things! But Maama and Taata must have, at least three times! Christine now giggled at the thought, then guiltily murmured, "Taata, rest in peace."

Goodness, two thirty. Should she leave? Christine heard a clamor of voices and froze. A group of rough-looking kids came running by, boys chasing girls, dark round heads bobbing, all of them screeching and yelling as they ran past, wove round the corner, and, just as suddenly, went out of sight. Silence rose up and took over again. What was she doing there? Christine decided to walk around the school once. Nicholas would have to wait. She would not think past that.

Christine peeked into the P.3 classroom. The chairs were so tiny. Innocent looking. This was where her class had done experiments with beans, to see what made plants grow. They tried to grow one plant without light, one without water, one without soil, and one that got everything. It was science in a bean shell. A guided experiment about life that you could control and be sure of the results. How simple. A few years later in P.7, as a prefect, Christine had stood sternly like a policeman in this very class, tapping the end of a stick on one of her palms slowly, threateningly, barking *silence!* at the smaller kids. It had been a serious game.

Here was the P.4 classroom, where one of the Bajombora boys, not Nicholas, had jumped through a window because of a fire. It wasn't a real fire; someone had shouted *Fire!* as a joke, and he got scared. He jumped and broke his leg and became a mini-hero, even though the whole incident was laughed at. Girls didn't talk to boys, oh no, but they gossiped about boys all the time. How stupid he was, they said, as they secretly admired him. Christine would never have dreamt she'd be here waiting for his big brother.

Christine came to the steps where she had fought with Karen and Carol, her two best friends. It was a game at first: the person in between the other two was the queen. They playfully pushed at one another to get into the center, but gradually the game turned from playful to rough to mean. Before long Christine, the smallest, was pushed to the ground crying, while the other two ran home separately. She was left there sniffling, wiping off the mud. The next day they pretended nothing had happened, but were shamefaced and awkward with one another. They didn't speak about it ever, but now they knew that friendship was envy, admiration, anger, and longing all mixed together. Three years later, Carol's parents retired and the family moved to their village in Toro. Karen went to a different high school. The flow of letters between them gradually dried up. Had all that emotion been for nothing after all? Time passed by and stole it away.

And now, now, time was moving too slowly. Christine circled back to the huge silent Assembly. No Nicholas. A part of her couldn't believe it. So he actually wasn't going to show up. Had he even planned to? Anyhow, had she really, really expected *him* to come and see *her*? That would have been the shock. She should leave. But she wanted to sit there and wait. Just sit there. Not go on. Tear out the end of this book.

Christine's feet in borrowed grown-up shoes hurt her. She undid the long red straps. She was tired of this place, the whole of Entebbe, in fact, filled with buildings that had been alive in the past, but now were small and irrelevant, ruins, almost. The three flowering plants, the only sign of new life around, now looked so stridently and annoyingly red and perky. She glanced over her shoulder, then went and pulled at the plants roughly. The stems were tougher than she was: taut, elastic. She tore at the tender petals. The flyaway pollen made her sneeze. She used her hand to wipe her nose and cleaned it off on her skirt, staining her nice tight jean skirt. That made her even angrier. Christine pulled harder at the green stems, leaning her body back. *Aaaah,* she felt the roots tearing, the dark brown earth moving, loosening, the plant breaking free. The release made her stumble back, almost fall, and she laughed through her tears, holding the limp, useless plant in her hands. Now there was soil all over her borrowed open-toed shoes and her feet. She threw the plant carcass back onto the soil, disgusted and feeling silly. Childish. Christine wiped her tears with the back of her hand and cleaned it on her blouse, smudging it red and brown with lipstick, tears, and dirt. What a mess. Nicholas should see her now. She had better go home; they would all be back, asking for her. Maybe there would still be some cookies left for tea.

Steven Bernard Miles Chimombo was born in 1945, in Zomba, Malawi. He received his BA from the University of Malawi and a teaching diploma in English as a second language from the University of Wales. He earned an MA and PhD in teaching at Columbia University in New York City. After studying at the University of Leeds in the UK, he returned to Malawi, where he edited the literary bulletin *Outlook-lookout*. Currently, Chimombo is Professor Emeritus of English at Chancellor College at the University of Malawi. He has published in a variety of genres: plays, poetry, novels, short stories, children's literature, and criticism. Among his books are the novels *The Basket Girl* (1990) and *The Wrath of Napolo* (2000), the plays *The Rainmaker* (1978) and *Sister! Sister!* (1995), the collections of stories *Tell Me a Story* (1992), *The Hyena Wears Darkness* (2006), and *Of Life, Love, and Death* (2009), and a work of literary criticism, *The Culture of Democracy: Language, Literature, and the Arts and Politics in Malawi, 1992–1994* (1996).

Another Day at the Office
(2009)

He joined the throng of people at the top of the small street leading from the marketplace. The main road marked the central artery of the main stream of people. They formed a vague column of marching feet kept in line by the fact that where the shops did not prevent them from leaving the main column, the ditches or the embankment did so further down.

A quarter to seven. Plenty of time. From the shop at the corner, the street leading from the marketplace to the office would only take fifteen minutes using Adam's mode of transport. The bells and the whirl of bicycle chains sounded a quicker form of locomotion which kept to the edges of the tarmac. This ensured that they were not directly in the path of the four-wheeled monsters that were the owners of that black road. But sometimes the cyclists violated this truth, only to be rudely reminded by the horn of an irate motorist and an oath that tore past at fifty miles per hour to leave the culprit shivering from its passage.

His faded, size seven brown shoes pinched a little after turning the corner. As traffic was heavier here on the main road, he was forced to keep to the pedestrian path. The dust formed a fine film over the polish his wife had applied that morning, as he was hurriedly washing his face and gargling his mouth to get on the road in time. The shoe repairer who worked opposite the vegetable stall in the marketplace had remarked in a friendly manner, "Why don't you let me keep this pair for patches on other customers' shoes? Another repair job on them and the makers won't recognize their handiwork."

He had muttered something to the effect that he did not see anything remarkable in the shoes. Just because he wanted another patch added to the areas where they pinched most did not warrant that he should turn into a charitable institution. Did he want him to go barefooted to the office? Still, the man had done a good job. It would be another two months of daily wear before the customary slight limp reappeared.

The familiar face he met at the top of the street leading from the marketplace had greeted him amiably enough. "How are you this morning, Chingaipe?"

All he got in reply was the most overused cliché in the Civil Service — "Fifty-fifty" — which could be understood to mean anything from "I'm broke" to "I've got the grandfather of all hangovers." After that, Chingaipe did not show any signs of interest in developing the theme. The familiar face continued on its way, silently falling in behind Chingaipe.

The street leading from the marketplace was flanked by the Indian shops. Old structures built in a random, absent-minded fashion. Garish colors and dusty spaces sprinkled with wild grass. But as soon as you turned the corner at the top, you met the shops that made a pretence at being modern: cemented car parks for the customers, wide shop windows boasting imported merchandise. Chingaipe did not glance at them. His vision always centered on a spot vaguely ten feet in front of him.

The sound of water forming the background to the hum of engines, whirl of bicycle chains, and voices informed him he had left the shops far behind and was nearing the bridge over the small river they called Mzimundilinde. This receded as he climbed the long hill, still in the column of other workers heading for duties.

It usually took only fifteen minutes to walk from the top of the street leading from the marketplace to the office. Chingaipe noted subconsciously that he must have used ten minutes already, for the column of which he formed a part was now noticeably thicker and faster-moving. The October sun was already making itself felt. He traced the course of a trickle of sweat from his armpit along his ribs down to where his vest, shirt, underwear constricted him round his waist on account of the leather belt he used to keep his trousers up. The trickle down his thighs was from a different source altogether.

Chingaipe had dressed with his usual care. In spite of the hurry in the morning, he had looked at himself in the mirror to see that the parting on top of his head followed the usual groove. The spiked bamboo comb he used for this purpose never failed him. He could perform this action in the dark if the need arose. The small knot on the cotton tie had been slightly to the left. He had pulled it right and shouted to his wife, Nambewe, in the kitchen, that he was off. Apparently, she had not heard him. The children, who were preparing to go to school, were making too much noise.

The road rose steeply after the river. Chingaipe felt the tie round his neck also constrict him, but he did not loosen the knot. The Higher Clerical Officer would give him a cold, disapproving stare if he noticed something faulty in the appearance of his clothes. Chingaipe's cheeks puffed a little and he breathed with some difficulty as he trundled up the steep incline. Only fifty yards to go.

He checked a little as he turned into the drive that led to the department he worked in. It was a huge, sprawling building that had belonged to some top government official in the pre-independence days. With the shortage of offices, the government had converted the residence into a block of offices, without changing the original design or the gardens surrounding it. The green corrugated iron roof was also the same. If you wanted to use the front door, you climbed the steps and came to a short passageway that led to what used to be the drawing room. It was now used by half-a-dozen young clerks, fresh from their School Certificate. Chingaipe's desk occupied one corner of this room.

The smaller path led to the back of the house—now office. You went through a bewildering maze of little rooms, including the bathroom and toilet, before you came to the same drawing room—now office—where Chingaipe had his desk.

Chingaipe took the smaller path to the back door. He always used the back door to his office, and every morning the Higher Clerical Officer's short but effective speech came to his mind: "Mr. Thomson has approached me about having a word with you lot in this room. Miss Prim, his secretary, has complained that, each time you clerks pass her desk by the front door in the next office, you stare at her. She doesn't like the way you look at her. Where are your manners, you people? Have you never seen a white lady before in your lives? Why do you have to gape at her each time you walk past her desk? Imagine all six, no, seven, of you marching past with eyes on her. What do you think she feels with fourteen eyes piercing her? You should be ashamed of yourselves. From now on, all junior clerks, typists, messengers, and telephone operators must use the back door to get to this room. That's not all. The toilet and bathroom on the other side of this room are closed to all junior staff. You're to use the toilets in the servants' quarters at the back of the house. I don't want to hear any more of this nonsense. Is that clear to everybody? I am going to write a memo to that effect right now. Copy to Mr. Thomson, one to Miss Prim, and a third to be pinned on that notice board to remind all of you."

Chingaipe opened the back door. It was seven o'clock. It seemed the only people around were the messengers and laborers. The rooms were so quiet. Even the girl who operated the switchboard had not yet made her appearance.

It was cooler inside. Chingaipe breathed a little easier. He passed the Executive Officer's office. The next one was the Higher Clerical Officer's. Both had originally been bedrooms. The drip, drip, drip was from the bathroom.

Chingaipe opened the door to the lounge—now office. It too was empty. He crossed the room to the far corner where his desk stood. He opened the window nearest to him and sat down with a sigh. He eased his feet a little out of the shoes to rest them. He dared not take them off all the way—the Higher Clerical Officer might walk in suddenly and find him in his holey socks.

He took the plastic cover off the typewriter, folded it carefully, pulled open the bottom right-hand drawer, laid it on the top of the papers there, and pushed the drawer shut. The keys stared blankly at him. He glanced at the two trays on the desk. The "IN" tray looked as full as it had been yesterday morning, the day before yesterday, last week, last month. It never seemed to be empty. The only empty one was the "OUT" tray.

Chingaipe put his hands on the desk, looked at his fingers for a brief moment, and pulled the top right-hand drawer open. He felt inside for what he wanted, and his hand came out with a razor blade. He proceeded to cut his nails slowly, piling the bits in the ashtray in front of him.

The other clerks found him sharpening a pencil, and to

their enquiries about his state of health he said, without turning (he faced the window with his back to the room), "Half-half."

He recognized the individuals behind each voice and his tone of voice reflected how he felt about each of them. The six "Half-half's" varied slightly in their lukewarm nature. He felt rather out of place in this room. They were all products of secondary school, compared to his old Standard Three, taken twenty years ago. They must have thought him a bit odd too. Him with his slight limp, tight jacket, and baggy trousers, banging away like a thing possessed at an equally battered typewriter amidst their loud talk and sometimes lewd jokes.

Chingaipe looked up and noticed that the laborers outside had started work. That meant that the Higher Clerical Officer was coming. He opened the top file from the "IN" tray, took out a rough draft, and laid it on top. He pulled open the top left-hand drawer and took out three blank sheets of typing paper. He shut it, pulled open the drawer beneath, and counted two sheets of carbon paper, which he put between the typing paper. He shut the drawer and inserted all the sheets into the machine. He set the typewriter margins and began to type:

> *"Dear Sir,*
> *With reference to your communication dated . . ."*

He could not type as fast as Miss Prim. There had been a time when he could have competed with her and not come off the worse. What did she type for Mr. Thomson which he didn't or couldn't anyway? Her with her superior secretarial airs. She was just a wisp of a woman really. Short, thin, almost angular. Long nose, thin lips. No bosom, no buttocks, no meat. Did she really think the young African clerks had any designs upon her? They might be fresh, but they knew there was no juice from that quarter. If it had been the telephone operator . . . Now she was altogether different. The type that they really would turn and look at.

Not that they had not, but they had come to grief. They were no match for her. That girl could be rude. He remembered the time he had been ready to go for the lunch break. She had preceded him into the passage with a friend. She had been speaking Yao so he could not understand, or so she had thought.

"At four o'clock, Chingaipe will knock off," she announced. "Hurry to his wife. Mrs. Chingaipe will stop pounding maize and hurry to the kitchen. She'll prepare food for the tired husband who is a copy typist in a big government office. Ha! Ha! Ha!"

The girl had not realized how close to the truth she had been. Chingaipe paused in his typing. Neither had she realized how it had cut him to the core to be dissected and classified as she had done. True, his wife prepared food for him as soon as he reached home after work. Only because he did not go for lunch like the Executive Officer, like Miss Prim, like Mr. Thomson, like the telephone operator and her numerous well-paid boyfriends. The other junior staff had formed the Lunch Break Union and had their meals of *mgaiwa* and dried fish prepared for them by one of the laborers in the servants' quarters at the back of the house. The rest contented themselves with boiled or raw cassava and bananas down by the Post Office.

He did not go to lunch. He could not start now. He had trained his stomach not to expect such a luxury. Instead, he drank a glass of water at noon and then went in the usual direction to a definite spot under a tree in the extensive gardens. There he loosened his tie, took off his jacket and shoes, and with obvious relief lay down to sleep, ignoring the inevitable rumblings of his stomach.

The beginning of the afternoon session always found him back at his desk banging away furiously. He could go on like that the whole afternoon, the noises of the keys interrupted at intervals by the loud guffaws of laughter from the secondary school kids.

There were six of them, four boys and two girls. Chingaipe knew intuitively who was going out with whom from

the occasional snatches of dialogue he caught while changing carbons or rummaging in his drawers or puzzling over
the handwriting of the Higher Clerical Officer. In one of
them, he had heard the kid called Mavuto talking to the
older girl.

"Of course, there are different types of hair," he had remarked loudly.

"Mine is called love hair," she had replied, unabashed.

"I'm not talking about your wig, baby."

They would have gone on and on like that if one of the
others had not noticed how rigidly Chingaipe had sat and
so told the two to shut up. Chingaipe had continued to
grope about the bottom right-hand drawer, embarrassed.
He did not know where the world was going to. In his
day . . . In his day . . . He found what he was looking for.

True, he did not go to lunch and his wife prepared a meal
for him as soon as he reached home after work. Nambewe.
Up at half past five to heat the water for her husband. Up
at half past five to prepare porridge for their children to eat
before going to school. One of them was now at secondary
school. Chingaipe hoped he would not turn into a brash,
unmannered kid like Mavuto, in an office like this. He was
trying to teach *his* children the meaning of work, determi-
nation, perseverance. Nambewe. Up at half past five to get
her husband and children ready for the day. Nambewe,
washing dirty pots and plates. Cleaning. Pounding grain for
flour. Nambewe in her missionary blue *chirundu* and
nyakura, a load of firewood on her head down the mountain slopes. Nambewe, smiling tenderly at him before they
went off to sleep at night. Nambewe . . .

Chingaipe brought the puncher near the typewriter. He
stood up with a sheaf of papers and inserted them in the
space ready to punch holes in them. He tensed the muscles
of his right hand and pressed down. Crunch. There was only
one hole in the papers. The other half of the puncher had
broken under the force, and fell on the floor with a loud
clink.

The office was very still as Chingaipe groped about the

floor for the broken piece. He looked from it back to the puncher. He pulled the sheaf of papers and laid them flat on the table. He sat down again and stared at the single hole.

Nambewe. Up at half past five to . . .

Chingaipe stood up again. He picked up the puncher and the broken piece and went past the now busy young clerks ostentatiously poring over their files. He opened the door to the passage and knocked on the door marked "Higher Clerical Officer" in large letters. He entered on hearing the growl, "Come in."

He stood in front of the huge desk littered with trays, files, notebooks, ledger cards, and looked at the man behind. The Higher Officer was in his late forties. He had sparse hair—a fact which he attempted to hide by having his hair cut very short each time he went to the barber's. But one cannot hide a fast receding hairline. The cheap spectacles he wore glinted dully as he looked up slowly.

"Yes?"

"The puncher is broken, sir," Chingaipe said slowly.

"The puncher is broken, sir," mimicked the Higher Clerical Officer. "You mean 'I broke the puncher,' don't you?"

"Yes, sir."

"You junior clerks, copy typists, and messengers," he spat out, "you can't be trusted to do even a simple job without a catastrophe happening. What will happen to this department if equipment is broken every day?"

"I was only trying to punch holes in a few letters I had typed, sir," Chingaipe explained.

"And you decided to break the puncher in the process?" the Higher Clerical Officer enquired. "You will have to see Mr. Thomson about this. We cannot allow this sort of thing to happen every day. I'm tired of all you junior clerks' tricks and inefficiency on the job. I swear some of you will get the sack before month end."

Chingaipe stood quite still as the Higher Clerical Officer's face swam in front of him. Nambewe. Up at half past five to . . .

"You must report this personally to Mr. Thomson immediately," the Higher Clerical Officer announced. "I cannot deal with this case myself."

"Yes, sir."

Chingaipe walked mechanically out of the room and down the passage, the puncher heavy in his hand. He went on, knocked, and entered Mr. Thomson's office.

"Good afternoon, Chingaipe."

"Good afternoon, sir," Chingaipe stammered. "The Higher Clerical Officer told me to see you, sir. I was trying to punch holes . . ."

"And the puncher broke?"

"Yes, sir."

"Gosh!" Mr. Thomson exclaimed. "You must be strong, Chingaipe."

Chingaipe was silent.

"Tell the Higher Clerical Officer to make out a local purchase order for a dozen punchers."

"Yes, sir."

Four o'clock. Time to go home. Chingaipe opened the bottom right-hand drawer. He took out the dust cover, locked the typewriter, and covered it. He stood up to go. The "IN" tray was empty. So was the building as he left. He said a tired goodbye to the night watchman.

"Tidzaonananso mawa, achimwene."

NADINE GORDIMER

Nadine Gordimer was born in 1923 in a small town outside of Johannesburg, South Africa. Her mother was British and her father was a Jewish emigré from Lithuania. She was educated at private schools and the University of Witwatersrand, and was a longtime activist against apartheid. She published her first short story at the age of fifteen and was introduced to the wider reading public in 1951 with a story published in *The New Yorker*. Her narratives are rife with the politics and tension of life in South Africa. Several of her books were banned, leading to international protest. Since the end of apartheid, Gordimer has continued her active opposition to South Africa's censorship of radio, television, and print media. Among her many novels are *Occasion for Loving* (1963), *A Guest of Honor* (1970), *The Conservationist* (1974), *Burger's Daughter* (1979), *July's People* (1981), *A Sport of Nature* (1987), *The House Gun* (1998), and *No Time Like the Present* (2012). She is the recipient of numerous awards, including the 1991 Nobel Prize for literature.

Inkalamu's Place
(1965)

Inkalamu Williamson's house is sinking and I don't suppose it will last out the next few rainy seasons. The red lilies still bloom as if there were somebody there. The house was one of the wonders of our childhood and when I went back to the territory last month for the independence celebrations I thought that on my way to the

bauxite mines I'd turn off the main road to look for it. Like
our farm, it was miles from anywhere when I was a child,
but now it's only an hour or two away from the new capital.
I was a member of a United Nations demographic commission (chosen to accompany them, I suppose, because of my
old connection with the territory) and I left the big hotel in
the capital after breakfast. The Peking delegation, who
never spoke to any of us and never went out singly, came
down with me in the lift. You could stare at them minutely,
each in turn; neither they nor you were embarrassed. I
walked through the cocktail terrace where the tiny flags of
the nations stood on the tables from last night's reception,
and drove myself out along the all-weather road where you
can safely do eighty and drive straight on, no doubt, until
you come out at the top of the continent—I only think of
these things this way now; when I grew up here, this road
didn't go anywhere else but home.

I had expected that a lot of the forest would have been
cut down, but once outside the municipal boundary of the
capital, it was just the same as always. There were no animals and few people. How secretly Africa is populated;
when I got out of the car to drink coffee from my flask, I
wanted to shout: Anybody there? The earth was neatly
spaded back from the margins of the tar. I walked a few
steps into the sunny forest, and my shoes exploded twigs
and dry leaves like a plunderer. You must not start watching the big, egg-timer bodied ants: whole afternoons used
to go, like that.

The new tarred road cuts off some of the bends of the
old one, and when I got near the river I began to think I'd
overshot the turnoff to Inkalamu's place. But no. There it
was, the long avenue of jacarandas plunging into the hilly
valley, made unfamiliar because of a clearing beside the
main road and a cottage and little store that never used to
be there. A store built of concrete blocks, with iron bars on
the windows, and a veranda: the kind of thing that the Africans, who used to have to do their buying from Indians and
white people, are beginning to go in for in the territory,

now. The big mango tree was still there—a homemade sign was nailed to it: KWACHA BEER ALL BRANDS CIGARETTES. There were hens, and someone whose bicycle seemed to have collapsed on its side in the heat. I said to him, "Can I go up to the house?"

He came over holding his head to one shoulder, squinting against the flies.

"Is it all right?"

He shook his head.

"Does somebody live in the house, the big house?"

"Is nobody."

"I can go up and look?"

"You can go."

Most of the gravel was gone off the drive. There was just a hump in the middle that scraped along the underside of the low American car. The jacarandas were enormous; it was not their blooming time. It was said that Inkalamu Williamson had made this mile-and-a-half-long avenue to his house after the style of the carriage-way in his family estate in England; but it was more likely that, in the elevation of their social status that used to go on in people's minds when they came out to the colonies, his memory of that road to the great house was the village boy's game of imagining himself the owner as he trudged up on an errand. Inkalamu's style was that of the poor boy who has found himself the situation in which he can play at being the lordly eccentric, far from aristocrats who wouldn't so much as know he existed, and the jeers of his own kind.

I saw this now; I saw everything, now, as it had always been, and not as it had seemed to us in the time when we were children. As I came in sight of the shrubbery in front of the house, I saw that the red amaryllis, because they were indigenous anyway, continued to bloom without care or cultivation. Everything else was blurred with overgrowth. And there was the house itself: sagging under its own weight, the thatch over the dormer windows sliding towards the long grass it came from. I felt no nostalgia, only recognition.

It was a red mud house, as all our houses were then, in the early thirties, but Inkalamu had rather grandly defied the limitations of mud by building it three storeys tall, a sandcastle reproduction of a large, calendar-picture English country house, with steep thatch curving and a wide chimney at either end, and a flight of steps up to a portico. Everyone had said it would fall down on his head; it had lasted thirty years. His mango and orange trees crowded in upon it from the sides of the valley. There was the profound silence of a deserted man-made place—the silence of absence.

I tried to walk a little way into the mango grove, but year after year the crop must have been left to fall and rot, and between the rows of old trees hundreds of spindly saplings had grown up from seed, making a dark wood. I hadn't thought of going into the house, but walked around it to look for the view down the valley to the mountains that was on the other side; the rains had washed a moat at the foot of the eroded walls and I had to steady myself by holding on to the rusty elbows of plumbing that stuck out. The house was intimately close to me, like a body. The lopsided wooden windows on the ground floor with their tin panes, the windows of the second floor with their panes of wire mesh, hung half-open like the mouths of old people asleep. I found I could not get all the way round because the bush on the valley side had grown right to the walls, and instead I tried to pull myself up and look inside. Both the mud and wattle gave way under my feet, the earth mixture crumbling and the supporting structure—branches of trees neither straightened nor dressed—that it had plastered, collapsing, hollowed by ants. The house had not fallen on Inkalamu and his black children (as the settlers had predicted) but I felt I might pull it down upon myself. Wasps hovered at my mouth and eyes, as if they, too, wanted to look inside: me. Inkalamu's house, that could have housed at least ten people, was not enough for them.

At the front again, I went up the steps where we used to sit scratching noughts and crosses while my father was in the house. Not that our families had been friends; only the children, which didn't count—my father and mother were white, my father a member of the Legislative Assembly, and Inkalamu's wives were native women. Sometimes my father would pay a call on Inkalamu, in the way of business (Inkalamu, as well as being a trader and hunter—the Africans had given him the name Inkalamu, "the lion"—was a big landowner, once) but my mother never accompanied him. When my brothers and I came by ourselves, Inkalamu's children never took us to the house; it didn't seem to be *their* home in the way that our small farmhouse was our home, and perhaps their father didn't know that we came occasionally, on our own, to play, any more than our mother and father knew we secretly went there. But when we were with my father—there was a special attraction about going to that house openly, with him—we were always called in, after business was concluded, by Inkalamu Williamson, their white father, with his long yellow curly hair on to his shoulders, like Jesus, and his sun-red chest and belly folded one upon the other and visible through his unbuttoned shirt. He gave us sweets while those of his own children who had slipped inside stood in the background. We did not feel awkward, eating in front of them, for they were all shades of brown and yellow-brown, quite different from Inkalamu and my father and us.

Someone had tied the two handles of the double front door with a piece of dirty rag to prevent it from swinging open, but I looped the rag off with a stick, and it was easy to push the door and go in. The place was not quite empty. A carpenter's bench with a vise stood in the hall, some shelves had been wrenched from the wall and stood on the floor, through the archway into the sitting room I saw a chair and papers. At first I thought someone might still be living there. It was dim inside and smelled of earth, as always. But when my eyes got accustomed to the dark I saw that the parts of the vise were welded together in rust and a frayed strip was all that was left on the rexine upholstery of the chair. Bat and mouse droppings carpeted the floor.

Piles of books looked as if they had been dumped temporarily during a spring cleaning; when I opened one the
pages were webbed together by mould and the fine gran-
ules of red earth brought by the ants.

*The Tale of a Tub. Mr. Perrin and Mr. Traill. Twenty Thou-
sand Leagues Under the Sea.* Little old Everymans, mixed
up with the numbers of *The Farmer's Weekly* and *Titbits.*
This room with its crooked alcoves moulded out of mud
and painted pink and green, and its pillars worm-tracked
with mauve and blue by someone who had never seen marble to suggest marble to people who did not know what it
was—it had never looked habitable. Inkalamu's rolltop
desk, stuffed like a pigeon loft with accounts ready to take
off in any draught, used to stand on one of the uneven-
boarded landings that took up more space than the dingy
coop of rooms. Here in the sitting room he would perform
formalities like the distribution of sweets to us children. I
don't think anyone had ever actually sat between the pot-
ted ferns and read before a real fire in that fireplace. The
whole house, inside, had been curiously uninhabitable; it
looked almost the real thing, but within it was not the Englishman's castle but a naive artifact, an African mud-and-
wattle dream—like the VC10 made of mealie stalks that a
small African boy was hawking round the airport when I
arrived the previous week.

A grille of light gleamed through the board over my
head. When Inkalamu went upstairs to fetch something, his
big boots would send red sand down those spaces between
the boards. He was always dressed in character, with leather
leggings, and the cloudy-faced old watch on his huge round
wrist held by a strap made of snakeskin. I went back into
the hall and had a look at the stairs. They seemed all right,
except for a few missing steps. The banisters made of the
handrails of an old tram-car were still there, and as I
climbed, flakes of the aluminium paint that had once covered them stuck to my palms. I had forgotten how ugly the
house was upstairs, but I suppose I hadn't been up very often; it was never clear whether Inkalamu's children actually

lived in the house with him or slept down at the kraal with their mothers. I think his favourite daughters lived with him sometimes—anyway, they wore shoes, and used to have ribbons for their hair, rather pretty hair, reddish-dun and curly as bubbles; I hadn't understood when I was about six and my brothers rolled on the floor giggling when I remarked that I wished I had hair like the Williamson girls. But I soon grew old enough to understand, and I used to recount the story and giggle, too.

The upstairs rooms were murmurous with wasps and the little windows were high as those of a prison cell. How good that it was all being taken apart by insects, washed away by the rain, disappearing into the earth, carried away and digested, fragmented to compost. I was glad that Inkalamu's children were free of it, that none of them was left here in this house of that "character" of the territory, the old Africa hand whose pioneering spirit had kept their mothers down in the compound and allowed the children into the house like pets. I was glad that the school where they weren't admitted when *we* were going to school was open to their children, and our settlers' club that they could never have joined was closed, and that if I met them now they would understand as I did that when I was the child who stood and ate sweets under their eyes, both they and I were what our fathers, theirs and mine, had made of us . . . And here I was in Inkalamu Williamson's famous bathroom, the mark of his civilization, and the marvel of the district because those very pipes sticking out of the outside walls that I had clung to represented a feat of plumbing. The lavatory pan had been taken away but the little tank with its tail of chain was still on the wall, bearing green tears of verdigris. No one had bothered to throw his medicines away. He must have had a year or two of decline before he died, there must have been an end to the swaggering and the toughness and the hunting trips and the strength of ten men: medicines had been dispensed from afar, they bore the mouldering labels of pharmacists in towns thousands of miles away—Mr. Williamson, the mixture, the pills, three

times a day; when necessary; for pain. I was glad that the
Williamsons were rid of their white father, and could live.
Suddenly, I beat on one of the swollen windows with my fist
and it flung open.

The sight there, the silence of it, smoking heat, was a
hand laid to quiet me. Right up to the house the bush had
come, the thorn trees furry with yellow blossom, the over-
lapping umbrellas of rose, plum and green *msasa*, the shoul-
dering mahogany with castanet pods, and far up on either
side, withdrawn, moon-mountainous, the granite peaks,
lichen-spattered as if the roc perched there and left its
droppings. The exaltation of emptiness was taken into my
lungs. I opened my mouth and received it. Good God, that
valley!

And yet I did not stand there long. I went down the broken stairs and out of the house, leaving the window hanging
like the page of an open book, adding my destruction to all
the others just as careless, that were bringing the house to
the ground; more rain would come in, more swifts and bats
to nest. But it is the ants who bring the grave to the house,
in the end. As I pushed the swollen front doors roughly
closed behind me I saw them, in their moving chain from
life to death, carrying in the grains of red earth that will
cover it.

They were black, with bodies the shapes of egg-timers. I
looked up from them, guilty at waste of time, when I felt
someone watching me. In the drive there was a young man
without shoes, his hands arranged as if he had an imaginary
hat in them. I said good morning in the language of the
country—it suddenly came to my mouth—and he asked me
for work. Standing on the steps before the Williamsons'
house, I laughed: "I don't live here. It's empty."

"I have been one years without a work," he said mouth-
ingly in English, perhaps as a demonstration of an additional qualification.

I said, "I'm sorry. I live very far from here."

"I am cooking and garden too," he said.

Then we did not know what to say to each other. I went

to the car and gave him two shillings out of my bag and he did what I hadn't seen since I was a child, and one of Inkalamu's servants used to take something from him—he went on his knees, clapped once, and made a bowl of his hands to receive the money.

I bumped and rocked down the drive from that house that I should never see again, whose instant in time was already forgotten, renamed, like the public buildings and streets of the territory—it didn't matter how they did it. I only hoped that the old man had left plenty of money for those children of his, Joyce, Bessie—what were the other ones' names?—to enjoy now that they were citizens of their mothers' country. At the junction with the main road the bicycle on its side and the man were still there, and a woman was standing on the veranda of the store with a little girl. I thought she might have something to do with the people who owned the land, now, and that I ought to make some sort of acknowledgement for having entered the property, so I greeted her through the car window, and she said, "Was the road very bad?"

"Thank you, no. Thank you very much."

"Usually people walks up when they come, now. I'm afraid to let them take the cars. And when it's been raining!"

She had come down to the car with the smile of someone for whom the historic ruin is simply a place to hang the washing. She was young, Portuguese, or perhaps Indian, with piled curls of dull hair and large black eyes, inflamed and watering. She wore tarnished gilt earrings and a peacock brooch, but her feet swished across the sand in felt slippers. The child had sore eyes, too; the flies were at her.

"Did you buy the place, then?" I said.

"It's my father's," she said. "He died about seven years ago."

"Joyce," I said. "It's Joyce!"

She laughed like a child made to stand up in class. "I'm Nonny, the baby. Joyce is the next one, the one before."

Nonny. I used to push her round on my bicycle, her little

legs hanging from the knee over the handlebars. I told her
who I was, ready to exchange family news. But of course
our families had never been friends. She had never been in
our house. So I said, "I couldn't go past without going to see
if Inkalamu Williamson's house was still there."

"Oh yes," she said. "Quite often people comes to look at
the house. But it's in a terrible mess."

"And the others? Joyce, and Bessie, and Roger—?"

They were in this town or that; she was not even sure
which, in the case of some of them.

"Well, that's good," I said. "It's different here now,
there's so much to do, in the territory." I told her I had been
at the independence celebrations; I was conscious, with a
stab of satisfaction at the past, that we could share now as
we had never been able to.

"That's nice," she said.

"—And you're still here. The only one of us still here! Is
it a long time since it was lived in?" The house was present,
out of sight, behind us.

"My mother and I was there till—how long now—five
years ago"—she was smiling and holding up her hand to
keep the light from hurting her eyes—"but what can a person do there, it's so far from the road. So I started this little
place." Her smile took me into the confidence of the empty
road, the hot morning, the single customer with his bicycle.
"Well, I must try. What can you do?"

I asked, "And the other farms, I remember the big tobacco farm on the other side of the river?"

"Oh that, that was gone long before he died. I don't know
what happened to the farms. We found out he didn't have
them any more, he must have sold them, I don't know . . . or
what. He left the brothers a tobacco farm—you know, the
two elder brothers, not from my mother, from the second
mother—but it came out the bank had it already. I don't
know. My father never talk to us about these business
things, you know."

"But you've got this farm." We were of the new generation, she and I. "You could sell it, I'm sure. Land values are

going to rise again. They're prospecting all over this area between the bauxite mines and the capital. Sell it, and—well, do—you could go where you like."

"It's just the house. From the house to the road. Just this little bit," she said, and laughed. "The rest was sold before he died. It's just the house, that he left to my mother. But you got to live, I mean."

I said warmly, "The same with my father! Our ranch was ten thousand acres. And there was more up at Lebishe. If he'd have hung on to Lebishe alone we'd have made a fortune when the platinum deposits were found."

But of course it was not quite the same. She said sympathetically, "Really!" to me with my university-modulated voice. We were smiling at each other, one on either side of the window of the big American car. The child, with bows in its hair, hung on to her hand; the flies bothered its small face.

"You couldn't make some sort of hotel, I suppose."

"It's in a mess," she said, assuming the tone of a flighty, apologetic housewife. "I built this little place here for us and we just left it. It's so much rubbish there still."

"Yes, and the books. All those books. The ants are eating them." I smiled at the little girl as people without children of their own do. Behind, there was the store, and the cottage like the backyard quarters provided for servants in white houses. "Doesn't anyone want the books?"

"We don't know what to do with them. We just left them. Such a lot of books my father collected up." After all, I knew her father's eccentricities.

"And the mission school at Balondi's been taken over and made into a pretty good place?" I seemed to remember that Joyce and one of the brothers had been there; probably all Inkalamu's children. It was no longer a school meant for black children, as it had been in our time. But she seemed to have only a polite general interest: "Yes, somebody said something the other day."

"You went to school there, didn't you, in the old days?"

She giggled at herself and moved the child's arm. "I never been away from here."

"Really? Never!"

"My father taught me a bit. You'll even see the school-books among that lot up there. Really."

"Well, I suppose the shop might become quite a nice thing," I said.

She said, "If I could get a licence for brandy, though. It's only beer, you see. If I could get a licence for brandy . . . I'm telling you, I'd get the men coming." She giggled.

"Well, if I'm to reach the mines by three, I'd better move," I said.

She kept smiling to please me; I began to think she didn't remember me at all; why should she, she had been no bigger than her little daughter when I used to take her on the handlebars of my bicycle. But she said, "I'll bring my mother. She's inside." She turned and the child turned with her and they went into the shade of the veranda and into the store. In a moment they came out with a thin black woman bent either by age or in greeting—I was not sure. She wore a head-cloth and a full long skirt of the minutely-patterned blue-and-white cotton that used to be in bales on the counter of every store, in my childhood. I got out of the car and shook hands with her. She clapped and made an obeisance, never looking at me. She was very thin with a narrow breast under a shrunken yellow blouse pulled to-gether by a flower with gaps like those of missing teeth in its coloured glass corolla. Before the three of them, I turned to the child rubbing at her eyes with hands tangled in the tendrils of her hair. "So you've a daughter of your own now, Nonny."

She giggled and swung her forward.

I said to the little girl, "What's hurting you, dear?— Something wrong with her eyes?"

"Yes. It's all red and sore. Now I've got it too, but not so bad."

"It's conjunctivitis," I said. "She's infected you. You must go to the doctor."

She smiled and said, "I don't know what it is. She had it two weeks now."

Then we shook hands and I thought: I mustn't touch my face until I can wash them.

"You're going to Kalondwe, to the mine." The engine was running. She stood with her arms across her breasts, the attitude of one who is left behind.

"Yes, I believe old Doctor Madley's back in the territory, he's at the W.H.O. centre there." Dr. Madley had been the only doctor in the district when we were all children.

"Oh yes," she said in her exaggeratedly interested, conversational manner. "He didn't know my father was dead, you know, he came to see him!"

"I'll tell him I've seen you, then."

"Yes, tell him." She made the little girl's limp fat hand wave goodbye, pulling it away from her eyes—"Naughty, naughty." I suddenly remembered—"What's your name now, by the way?"; the times were gone when nobody ever bothered to know the married names of women who weren't white. And I didn't want to refer to her as Inkalamu's daughter. Thank God she was free of him, and the place he and his kind had made for her. All that was dead, Inkalamu was dead.

She stood twiddling her earrings, bridling, smiling, her face not embarrassed but warmly bashful with open culpability. "Oh, just Miss Williamson. Tell him Nonny."

I turned carefully on to the tar. I didn't want to leave with my dust in their faces. As I gathered speed I saw in the mirror that she still had the child by the wrist, waving its hand to me.

ABDULRAZAK GURNAH

Gurnah was born on the island of Zanzibar, a part of Tanzania, in 1948. He emigrated in 1968 to Great Britain, where he earned a doctorate at the University of Kent in 1982. For a brief period from 1980 to 1982, he was a lecturer at Bayero University Kano in Nigeria, but he has spent most of his academic career at the University of Kent, where he is a lecturer. Among his many novels are *Memory of Departure* (1987), *Dottie* (1990), *Paradise* (1994), *Admiring Silence* (1996), *By the Sea* (2001), *Desertion* (2005), and *The Last Gift* (2011). His fiction often reflects the enduring effects of colonialism and slavery on the problems experienced by Africans today. Gurnah's biography, *My Mother Lived on a Farm in Africa*, was published in 2006.

Cages
(1992)

There were times when it felt to Hamid as if he had been in the shop always, and that his life would end there. He no longer felt discomfort, nor did he hear the secret mutterings at the dead hours of night which had once emptied his heart in dread. He knew now that they came from the seasonal swamp which divided the city from the townships, and which teemed with life. The shop was in a good position, at a major crossroads from the city's suburbs. He opened it at first light when the earliest workers were shuffling by, and did not shut it again until all but the last stragglers had trailed home. He liked to say that at his station he saw all of life pass him by. At peak hours he would be on his feet all the time, talking and bantering with the custom-ers, courting them and taking pleasure in the skill with which he handled himself and his merchandise. Later he would sink exhausted on the boxed seat which served as his till.

The girl appeared at the shop late one evening, just as he was thinking it was time to close. He had caught himself nodding twice, a dangerous trick in such desperate times. The second time he had woken up with a start, thinking a large hand was clutching his throat and lifting him off the ground. She was standing in front of him, waiting with a look of disgust in her face.

"Ghee," she said after waiting for a long, insolent min-ute. "One shilling." As she spoke she half-turned away, as if the sight of him was irritating. A piece of cloth was wrapped round her body and tucked in under the armpits. The soft cotton clung to her, marking the outline of her graceful shape. Her shoulders were bare and glistened in the gloom. He took the bowl from her and bent down to the tin of ghee. He was filled with longing and a sudden ache. When he gave the bowl back to her, she looked vaguely at him, her eyes distant and glazed with tiredness. He saw that she was young, with a small round face and slim neck. Without a word, she turned and went back into the darkness, taking a huge stride to leap over the concrete ditch which divided the kerb from the road. Hamid watched her retreating form and wanted to cry out a warning for her to take care. How did she know that there wasn't something there in the dark? Only a feeble croak came out as he choked the im-pulse to call to her. He waited, half-expecting to hear her cry out but only heard the retreating slap of her sandals as she moved further into the night.

She was an attractive girl, and for some reason as he stood thinking about her and watched the hole in the night into which she had disappeared, he began to feel disgust for himself. She had been right to look at him with disdain. His body and his mouth felt stale. There was little cause to wash more than once every other day. The journey from bed to shop took a minute or so, and he never went anywhere else.

What was there to wash for? His legs were misshapen from lack of proper exercise. He had spent the day in bondage, months and years had passed like that, a fool stuck in a pen all his life. He shut up the shop wearily, knowing that during the night he would indulge the squalor of his nature.

The following evening, the girl came to the shop again. Hamid was talking to one of his regular customers, a man much older than him called Mansur who lived nearby and on some evenings came to the shop to talk. He was half-blind with cataracts, and people teased him about his affliction, playing cruel tricks on him. Some of them said of Mansur that he was going blind because his eyes were full of shit. He could not keep away from boys. Hamid sometimes wondered if Mansur hung around the shop after something, after him. But perhaps it was just malice and gossip. Mansur stopped talking when the girl approached, then squinted hard as he tried to make her out in the poor light.

"Do you have shoe polish? Black?" she asked.

"Yes," Hamid said. His voice sounded congealed, so he cleared his throat and repeated Yes. The girl smiled.

"Welcome, my love. How are you today?" Mansur asked. His accent was so pronounced, thick with a rolling flourish, that Hamid wondered if it was intended as a joke. "What a beautiful smell you have, such perfume! A voice like *zuwarde* and a body like a gazelle. Tell me, *msichana,* what time are you free tonight? I need someone to massage my back."

The girl ignored him. With his back to them, Hamid heard Mansur continue to chat to the girl, singing wild praises to her while he tried to fix a time. In his confusion Hamid could not find a tin of polish. When he turned round with it at last, he thought she had been watching him all the time, and was amused that he had been so flustered. He smiled, but she frowned and then paid him. Mansur was talking beside her, cajoling and flattering, rattling the coins in his jacket pocket, but she turned and left without a word.

"Look at her, as if the sun itself wouldn't dare shine on

her. So proud! But the truth is she's easy meat," Mansur said, his body gently rocking with suppressed laughter. "I'll be having that one before long. How much do you think she'll take? They always do that, these women, all these airs and disgusted looks . . . but once you've got them into bed, and you've got inside them, then they know who's the master."

Hamid found himself laughing, keeping the peace among men. But he did not think she was a girl to be purchased. She was so certain and comfortable in every action that he could not believe her abject enough for Mansur's designs. Again and again his mind returned to the girl, and when he was alone he imagined himself intimate with her. At night after he had shut up the shop, he went to sit for a few minutes with the old man, Fajir, who owned the shop and lived in the back. He could no longer see to himself and very rarely asked to leave his bed. A woman who lived nearby came to see to him during the day, and took free groceries from the shop in return, but at night the ailing old man liked to have Hamid sit with him for a little while. The smell of the dying man perfumed the room while they talked. There was not usually much to say, a ritual of complaints about poor business and plaintive prayers for the return of health. Sometimes when his spirits were low, Fajir talked tearfully of death and the life which awaited him there. Then Hamid would take the old man to the toilet, make sure his chamber-pot was clean and empty, and leave him. Late into the night, Fajir would talk to himself, sometimes his voice rising softly to call out Hamid's name.

Hamid slept outside in the inner yard. During the rains he cleared a space in the tiny store and slept there. He spent his nights alone and never went out. It was well over a year since he had even left the shop, and before then he had only gone out with Fajir, before the old man was bedridden. Fajir had taken him to the mosque every Friday, and Hamid remembered the throngs of people and the cracked pavements steaming in the rain. On the way home they went to the market, and the old man named the luscious fruit and the brightly coloured vegetables for him, picking up some of them to make him smell or touch. Since his teens, when he first came to live in this town, Hamid had worked for the old man. Fajir gave him his board and he worked in the shop. At the end of every day, he spent his nights alone, and often thought of his father and his mother, and the town of his birth. Even though he was no longer a boy, the memories made him weep and he was degraded by the feelings that would not leave him be.

When the girl came to the shop again, to buy beans and sugar, Hamid was generous with the measures. She noticed and smiled at him. He beamed with pleasure, even though he knew that her smile was laced with derision. The next time she actually said something to him, only a greeting, but spoken pleasantly. Later she told him that her name was Rukiya and that she had recently moved into the area to live with relatives.

"Where's your home?" he asked.

"Mwembemaringo," she said, flinging an arm out to indicate that it was a long way away. "But you have to go on back-roads and over hills."

He could see from the blue cotton dress she wore during the day that she worked as a domestic. When he asked her where she worked, she snorted softly first, as if to say that the question was unimportant. Then she told him that until she could find something better, she was a maid at one of the new hotels in the city.

"The best one, the Equator," she said. "There's a swimming pool and carpets everywhere. Almost everyone staying there is a *mzungu,* a European. We have a few Indians too, but none of these people from the bush who make the sheets smell."

He took to standing at the doorway of his backyard bed-chamber after he had shut the shop at night. The streets were empty and silent at that hour, not the teeming, dangerous places of the day. He thought of Rukiya often, and sometimes spoke her name, but thinking of her only made him more conscious of his isolation and squalor. He remembered how she had looked to him the first time, moving away in the late evening shadow. He wanted to touch her . . . Years in darkened places had done this to him, he thought, so that now he looked out on the streets of the foreign town and imagined that the touch of an unknown girl would be his salvation.

One night he stepped out into the street and latched the door behind him. He walked slowly towards the nearest streetlamp, then to the one after that. To his surprise he did not feel frightened. He heard something move but he did not look. If he did not know where he was going, there was no need to fear since anything could happen. There was comfort in that.

He turned a corner into a street lined with shops, one or two of which were lit, then turned another corner to escape the lights. He had not seen anyone, neither a policeman nor a night watchman. On the edge of a square he sat for a few minutes on a wooden bench, wondering that everything should seem so familiar. In one corner was a clock tower, clicking softly in the silent night. Metal posts lined the sides of the square, impassive and correct. Buses were parked in rows at one end, and in the distance he could hear the sound of the sea.

He made for the sound, and discovered that he was not far from the waterfront. The smell of the water suddenly made him think of his father's home. That town too had been by the sea, and once he had played on the beaches and in the shallows like all the other children. He no longer thought of it as somewhere he belonged to, somewhere that was his home. The water lapped gently at the foot of the sea-wall, and he stopped to peer at it breaking into white froth against the concrete. Lights were still shining brightly on one of the jetties and there was a hum of mechanical activity. It did not seem possible that anyone could be working at that hour of the night.

There were lights on across the bay, single isolated dots that were strung across a backdrop of darkness. Who lived there? he wondered. A shiver of fear ran through him. He tried to picture people living in that dark corner of the city. His mind gave him images of strong men with cruel faces, who peered at him and laughed. He saw dimly lit clearings where shadows lurked in wait for the stranger, and where later, men and women crowded over the body. He heard the sound of their feet pounding in an old ritual, and heard their cries of triumph as the blood of their enemies flowed into the pressed earth. But it was not only for the physical threat they posed that he feared the people who lived in the dark across the bay. It was because they knew where they were, and he was in the middle of nowhere.

He turned back towards the shop, unable to resist, despite everything, a feeling that he had dared something. It became a habit that after he had shut up the shop at night and had seen to Fajir, he went for a stroll to the waterfront. Fajir did not like it and complained about being left alone, but Hamid ignored his grumbles. Now and then he saw people, but they hurried past without a glance. During the day, he kept an eye out for the girl who now so filled his hours. At night he imagined himself with her. As he strolled the silent streets, he tried to think she was there with him, talking and smiling, and sometimes putting the palm of her hand on his neck. When she came to the shop, he always put in something extra, and waited for her to smile. Often they spoke, a few words of greeting and friendship. When there were shortages he served her from the secret reserves he kept for special customers. Whenever he dared he complimented her on her appearance, and squirmed with longing and confusion when she rewarded him with radiant smiles. Hamid laughed to himself as he remembered Mansur's boast about the girl. She was no girl to be bought with a few shillings, but one to be sung to, to be won with display and courage. And neither Mansur, half-blind with shit as he was, nor Hamid, had the words or the voice for such a feat.

Late one evening, Rukiya came to the shop to buy sugar. She was still in her blue work-dress, which was stained under the arms with sweat. There were no other customers, and she did not seem in a hurry. She began to tease him gently, saying something about how hard he worked.

"You must be very rich after all the hours you spend in the shop. Have you got a hole in the yard where you hide your money? Everyone knows shopkeepers have secret hoards . . . Are you saving to return to your town?"

"I don't have anything," he protested. "Nothing here belongs to me."

She chuckled disbelievingly. "But you work too hard, anyway," she said. "You don't have enough fun." Then she smiled as he put in an additional scoopful of sugar.

"Thank you," she said, leaning forward to take the package from him. She stayed that way for a moment longer than necessary; then she moved back slowly. "You're always giving me things. I know you'll want something in return. When you do, you'll have to give me more than these little gifts."

Hamid did not reply, overwhelmed with shame. The girl laughed lightly and moved away. She glanced round once, grinning at him before she plunged into the darkness.

HELON HABILA

Born in Nigeria, Helon Habila studied literature at the University of Jos and worked as a teacher and journalist. In 2002, he emigrated to Great Britain, where he became the African Writing Fellow at the University of East Anglia. In 2005, he was chosen to become the first Chinua Achebe Fellow at Bard College. Currently, he is a faculty member at George Mason University in Fairfax, Virginia. He is a founding member of the African Writers' Trust, which helps to bring together African writers in the Disapora and those on the Continent to enhance the abilities and knowledge of these two groups. His novels include *Waiting for an Angel* (2004), *Measuring Time* (2007), and *Oil on Water* (2010). He is editor or co-editor of *New Writing 14* (2006), *Dreams, Miracles, and Jazz: An Anthology of New Africa Fiction* (2007), and *The Granta Book of the African Short Story* (2011). A segment of *Waiting for an Angel* was awarded the Caine Prize for African Fiction in 2001 and the completed novel was chosen for the Commonwealth Writers' Prize for a best first book in Africa in 2003.

Lomba
(2002)

In the middle of his second year in prison, Lomba got access to pencil and paper and he started a diary. It was not easy. He had to write in secret, mostly in the early mornings when the night warders, tired of peeping through the door bars, waited impatiently for the morning

102

shift. Most of the entries he simply headed with the days of the week; the exact dates, when he used them, were often incorrect. The first entry was in July 1997, a Friday.

Friday, July 1997

Today I begin a diary, to say all the things I want to say, to myself, because here in prison there is no one to listen. I express myself. It stops me from standing in the centre of this narrow cell and screaming at the top of my voice. It stops me from jumping up suddenly and bashing my head repeatedly against the wall. Prison chains not so much your hands and feet as it does your voice.

I express myself. I let my mind soar above these walls to bring back distant, exotic bricks with which I seek to build a more endurable cell within this cell. Prison. Misprison. Dis. Un. Prisoner. See? I write of my state in words of derision, aiming thereby to reduce the weight of these walls on my shoulders, to rediscover my nullified individuality. Here in prison loss of self is often expressed as anger. Anger is the baffled prisoner's attempt to re-crystallize his slowly dissolving self. The anger creeps up on you, like twilight edging out the day. It builds in you silently until one day it explodes in violence, surprising you. I saw it happen in my first month in prison. A prisoner, without provocation, had attacked an unwary warder at the toilets. The prisoner had come out of a bath-stall and there was the warder before him, monitoring the morning ablutions. Suddenly the prisoner leaped upon him, pulling him by the neck to the ground, grinding him into the black, slimy water that ran in the gutter from the toilets. He pummeled the surprised face repeatedly until other warders came and dragged him away. They beat him to a pulp before throwing him into solitary.

Sometimes the anger leaves you as suddenly as it appeared; then you enter a state of tranquil acceptance. You realize the absolute puerility of your anger: it was nothing but acid, cancer, eating away your bowels in the dark. You accept the inescapability of your fate; and with that, you learn the craft of cunning. You learn ways of surviving—surviving the mindless banality of the walls around you, the incessant harassment from the warders; you learn to hide money in your anus, to hold a cigarette inside your mouth without wetting it. And each day survived is a victory against the jailer, a blow struck for freedom.

My anger lasted a whole year. I remember the exact day it left me. It was a Saturday, the day after a failed escape attempt by two convicted murderers. The warders were more than usually brutal that day; the inmates were on tenterhooks, not knowing from where the next blow would come. We were lined up in rows in our cell, waiting for hours to be addressed by the prison superintendent. When he came his scowl was hard as rock, his eyes were red and singeing, like fire. He paced up and down before us, systematically flagellating us with his harsh, staccato sentences. We listened, our heads bowed, our hearts quaking.

When he left, an inmate, just back from a week in solitary, broke down and began to weep. His hands shook, as if with a life of their own. "What's going to happen next?" he wailed, going from person to person, looking into each face, not waiting for an answer. "We'll be punished. If I go back there I'll die. I can't. I can't." Now he was standing before me, a skinny mass of eczema inflammations, and ringworm, and snot. He couldn't be more than twenty, I thought; what did he do to end up in this dungeon? Then, without thinking, I reached out and patted his shoulder. I even smiled. With a confidence I did not feel I said kindly, "No one will take you back." He collapsed into my arms, soaking my shirt with snot and tears and saliva. "Everything will be all right," I repeated over and over. That was the day the anger left me.

In the over two months that he wrote before he was discovered and his diary seized, Lomba managed to put in quite a large number of entries. Most of them were poems, and letters to various persons from his by now hazy, pre-prison life—letters he can't have meant to send. There were also

long soliloquies and desultory interior monologues. The
poems were mostly love poems, fugitive lines from poets he
had read in school: Donne, Shakespeare, Graves, Eliot, etc.
Some were his original compositions rewritten from memory; but a lot were fresh creations—tortured sentimental
effusions to women he had known and admired, and perhaps loved. Of course they might have been imaginary beings, fabricated in the smithy of his prison-fevered mind.
One of the poems reads like a prayer to a much doubted,
but fervently hoped for God:

> Lord, I've had days black as pitch
> And nights crimson as blood,
>
> But they have passed over me, like water.
> Let this one also pass over me, lightly,
> Like a smooth rock rolling down the hill,
> Down my back, my skin, like soothing water.

That, he wrote, was the prayer on his lips the day the cell
door opened without warning and the superintendent,
flanked by two baton-carrying warders, entered.

Monday, September
I had waited for this; perversely anticipated it with each
day that passed, with each surreptitious sentence that I
wrote. I knew it was me he came for when he stood there,
looking bigger than life, bigger than the low, narrow cell.
The two dogs with him licked their chops and growled.
Their eyes roved hungrily over the petrified inmates caught
sitting, or standing, or crouching; laughing, frowning,
scratching—like figures in a movie still.
    "Lomba, step forward!" his voice rang out suddenly. In
the frozen silence it sounded like glass breaking on concrete, but harsher, without the tinkling. I was on my mattress on the floor, my back propped against the damp wall.
I stood up. I stepped forward.
    He turned the scowl on me. "So, Lomba. You are."

"Yes. I am Lomba," I said. My voice did not fail me. Then he nodded, almost imperceptibly, to the two warders. They bounded forward eagerly, like game hounds scenting a rabbit. One went to a tiny crevice low in the wall, almost hidden by my mattress. He threw aside the mattress and poked two fingers into the triangular crack. He came out with a thick roll of papers. He looked triumphant as he handed it to the superintendent. Their informer had been exact. The other hound reached unerringly into a tiny hole in the sagging, rain-patterned ceiling and brought out another tube of papers.

"Search. More!" the superintendent barked. He unrolled the tubes. He appeared surprised at the number of sheets in his hands. I was. I didn't know I had written so much. When they were through with the holes and crevices, the dogs turned their noses to my personal effects. They picked up my mattress and shook and sniffed and poked. They ripped off the tattered cloth on its back. There were no papers there. They took the pillow-cum-rucksack (a jeans trouser-leg cut off at mid-thigh and knotted at the ankle) and poured out the contents on to the floor. Two threadbare shirts, one pair of trousers, one plastic comb, one toothbrush, one half-used bar of soap, and a pencil. They swooped on the pencil before it had finished rolling on the floor, almost knocking heads in their haste.

"A pencil!" the superintendent said, shaking his head, exaggerating his amazement. The prisoners were standing in a tight, silent arc. He walked the length of the arc, displaying the papers and pencil, clucking his tongue. "Papers. And pencil. In prison. Can you believe that? In my prison!"

I was sandwiched between the two hounds, watching the drama in silence. I felt removed from it all. Now the superintendent finally turned to me. He bent a little at the waist, pushing his face into mine. I smelt his grating smell; I picked out the white roots beneath his carefully dyed moustache.

"I will ask. Once. Who gave you. Papers?" He spoke like that, in jerky, truncated sentences.

I shook my head. I did my best to meet his red-hot glare. "I don't know."

Some of the inmates gasped, shocked; they mistook my answer for reckless intrepidity. They thought I was foolishly trying to protect my source. But in a few other eyes I saw sympathy. They understood that I had really forgotten where the papers came from.

"Hmm," the superintendent growled. His eyes were on the papers in his hands; he kept folding and unfolding them. I was surprised he had not pounced on me yet. Maybe he was giving me a spell to reconsider my hopeless decision to protect whoever it was I was protecting. The papers. They might have blown in through the door bars on the sentinel wind that sometimes patrolled the prison yard in the evenings. Maybe a sympathetic warder, seeing my yearning for self-expression emblazoned neonlike on my face, had secretly thrust the roll of papers into my hands as he passed me in the yard. Maybe— and this seems more probable—I bought them from another inmate (anything can be bought here in prison, from marijuana to a gun). But I had forgotten. In prison, memory short-circuit is an ally to be cultivated at all costs.

"I repeat. My question. Who gave you the papers?" he thundered into my face, spraying me with spit.

I shook my head. "I have forgotten."

I did not see it, but he must have nodded to one of the hounds. All I felt was the crushing blow on the back of my neck. I pitched forward, stunned by pain and the unexpectedness of it. My face struck the door bars and I fell before the superintendent's boots. I saw blood where my face had touched the floor. I waited. I stared, mesmerized, at the reflection of my eyes in the high gloss of the boots' toecaps. One boot rose and landed on my neck, grinding my face into the floor.

"So. You won't. Talk. You think you are. Tough," he shouted. "You are. Wrong. Twenty years! That is how long I have been dealing with miserable bastards like you. Let this be an example to all of you. Don't. Think you can deceive me. We have our sources of information. You can't. This insect will be taken to solitary and he will be properly dealt with. Until. He is willing to. Talk."

I imagined his eyes rolling balefully round the tight, narrow cell, branding each of the sixty inmates separately. The
boot pressed down harder on my neck; I felt a tooth bend
at the root.

"Don't think because you are political. Detainees you
are untouchable. Wrong. You are all rats. Saboteurs. Anti-
government rats. That is all. Rats."

But the superintendent was too well versed in the ways
of torture to throw me into solitary that very day. I waited
two days before they came and blindfolded me and took
me away to the solitary section. In the night. Forty-eight
hours. In the first twenty-four hours I waited with my eyes
fixed on the door, bracing myself whenever it opened; but
it was only the cooks bringing the meal, or the number-
check warders come to count the inmates for the night, or
the slop-disposal team. In the second twenty-four hours I
bowed my head into my chest and refused to look up. I was
tired. I refused to eat or speak or move. I was rehearsing for
solitary.

They came, at around ten at night. The two hounds. Banging their batons on the door bars, shouting my name, cursing and kicking at anyone in their path. I hastened to my
feet before they reached me, my trouser-leg rucksack
clutched like a shield in my hands. The light of their torch
on my face was like a blow.

"Lomba!"

"Come here! Move!"

"Oya, out. Now!"

I moved, stepping high over the stirring bodies on the
floor. The light fell on my rucksack.

"What's that in your hand, eh? Where you think say you
dey carry am go? Bring am. Come here! Move!"

Outside. The cell door clanked shut behind us. All the compounds were in darkness. Only security lights from poles
shone at the sentry posts. In the distance, the prison wall
loomed huge and merciless, like a mountain. Broken bot-

tles. Barbed wire. Then they threw the blindfold over my head. My hands instinctively started to rise, but they were held and forced behind me and cuffed.

"Follow me."

One was before me, the other was behind, prodding me with his baton. I followed the footsteps, stumbling. At first it was easy to say where we were. There were eight compounds within the prison yard; ours was the only one reserved for political detainees. There were four other Awaiting Trial men's compounds surrounding ours. Of the three compounds for convicted criminals, one was for lifers and one, situated far away from the other compounds, was for condemned criminals. Now we had passed the central lawn where the warders conducted their morning parade. We turned left towards the convicted prisoners' compounds, then right towards . . . we turned right again, then straight . . . I followed the boots, now totally disoriented. I realized that the forced march had no purpose to it, or rather its purpose was not to reach anywhere immediately. It was part of the torture. I walked. On and on. I bumped into the front warder whenever he stopped abruptly.

"What? You no de see? Idiot!"

Sometimes I heard their voices exchanging pleasantries and amused chuckles with other warders. We marched for over thirty minutes; my slippered feet were chipped and bloody from hitting into stones. My arms locked behind me robbed me of balance and often I fell down; then I'd be prodded and kicked. At some places—near the light poles—I was able to see brief shimmers of light. At other places the darkness was thick as walls, and eerie. I recalled the shuffling, chain-clanging steps we heard late at nights through our cell window. Reluctant, sad steps. Hanging victims going to the hanging room; or their ghosts returning. We'd lie in the dark, stricken by immobility as the shuffling grew distant and finally faded away.

Now we were on concrete, like a corridor. The steps in front halted. I waited. I heard metal knock against metal, then the creaking of hinges. A hand took my wrist, cold metal touched me as the handcuffs were unlocked. My hands felt light with relief. I must have been standing right before the cell door because when a hand on my back pushed me forward I stumbled inside. I was still blind-folded, but I felt the consistency of the darkness change: it grew thicker, I had to wade through it to feel the walls. That was all: walls so close together that I felt like a man in a hole. I reached down and touched a bunk. I sat down. I heard the door close. I heard footsteps retreating. When I removed the blindfold the darkness remained the same, only now a little air touched my face. I closed my eyes. I don't know how long I remained like that, hunched forward on the bunk, my sore, throbbing feet on the floor, my el-bows on my knees, my eyes closed.

As if realizing how close I was to tears, the smells got up from their corners, shook the dust off their buttocks and lined up to make my acquaintance — to distract me from my sad thoughts. I shook their hands one by one. Loneliness Smell, Anger Smell, Waiting Smell, Masturbation Smell, Fear Smell. The most noticeable was Fear Smell; it filled the tiny room from floor to ceiling, edging out the others. I did not cry. I opened my lips and slowly, like a Buddhist chant-ing his mantra, I prayed:

> *Let this one also pass over me, lightly,*
> *Like a smooth rock rolling down the hill,*
> *Down my back, my skin, like soothing water.*

He was in solitary for three days. This is how he described the cell in his diary: The floor was about six feet by ten, and the ceiling was about seven feet from the floor. There were two pieces of furniture: the iron bunk with its tattered, lice-ridden mat, and the slop bucket in the corner.

His only contact with the outside was when his mess of beans, once daily at six p.m., was pushed into the cell through a tiny flap at the bottom of the wrought-iron door, and at precisely eight p.m. when the cell door was opened for him to take out the slop bucket and replace it with a

fresh one. He wrote that the only way he distinguished
night from day was by the movement of his bowels—in
hunger or in purgation.

Then on the third day, late in the evening, things began
to happen. Like Nichodemus, the superintendent came to
him, covertly, seeking knowledge.

Third Day, Solitary Cell

When I heard metal touch the lock on the door I sat
down from my blind pacing. I composed my countenance.
The door opened, bringing in unaccustomed rays of light. I
blinked. *"Oh, sweet light, may your face meeting mine bring
me good fortune."* When my eyes had adjusted to the light,
the superintendent was standing on the threshold—the cell
entrance was a tight, brightly lit frame around his looming
form. He advanced into the cell and stood in the centre,
before me in my disadvantaged position on the bunk. His
legs were planted apart, like an A. He looked like a cartoon
figure: his jodhpur-like uniform trousers emphasized the
skinniness of his calves, where they disappeared into the
glass-glossy boots. His stomach bulged and hung like a
belted sack. He cleared his voice. When I looked at his face
I saw his blubber lips twitching with the effort of an attempted smile. But he couldn't quite carry it off. He started
to speak, then stopped abruptly and began to pace the tiny
space before the bunk. When he returned to his original
position he stopped. Now I noticed the sheaf of papers in
his hands. He gestured in my face with it.

"These. Are the. Your papers." His English was more
disfigured than usual. He was soaking wet with the effort of
saying whatever it was he wanted to say. "I read. All. I read
your file again. Also. You are journalist. This is your second
year. Here. Awaiting trial. For organizing violence. Demonstration against. Anti-government demonstration against
the military legal government." He did not thunder as
usual.

"It is not true."

"Eh?" The surprise on his face was comical. "You deny?"

"I did not organize a demonstration. I went there as a reporter."

"Well . . ." He shrugged. "That is not my business. The truth. Will come out at your. Trial."

"But when will that be? I have been forgotten. I am not allowed a lawyer, or visitors. I have been awaiting trial for two years now . . ."

"Do you complain? Look. Twenty years I've worked in prisons all over this country. Nigeria. North. South. East. West. Twenty years. Don't be stupid. Sometimes it is better this way. Can you win a case against government? Wait. Hope."

Now he lowered his voice, like a conspirator. "Maybe there'll be another coup, eh? Maybe the leader will collapse and die. He is mortal, after all. Maybe a civilian government will come. Then. There will be amnesty for all political prisoners. Amnesty. Don't worry. Enjoy yourself."

I looked at him, planted before me like a tree, his hands clasped behind him, the papier-mâché smile on his lips. *Enjoy yourself.* I turned the phrase over and over in my mind. When I lay to sleep rats kept me awake, and mosquitoes, and lice, and hunger, and loneliness. The rats bit at my toes and scuttled around in the low ceiling, sometimes falling on to my face from the holes in the ceiling. *Enjoy yourself.*

"Your papers," he said, thrusting them at me once more. I was not sure if he was offering them to me. "I read them. All. Poems. Letters. Poems, no problem. The letters, illegal. I burned them. Prisoners sometimes smuggle out letters to the press to make us look foolish. Embarrass the government. But the poems are harmless. Love poems. And diaries. You wrote the poems for your girl, isn't it?"

He bent forward, and clapped a hand on my shoulder. I realized with wonder that the man, in his awkward, flat-footed way, was making overtures of friendship to me. My eyes fell on the boot that had stepped on my neck just five days ago. What did he want?

"Perhaps because I work in prison. I wear uniform. You think I don't know poetry, eh? Soyinka, Okigbo, Shakespeare."

It was apparent that he wanted to talk about poems, but he was finding it hard to begin.

"What do you want?" I asked.

He drew back to his full height. "I write poems too. Sometimes," he added quickly when the wonder grew and grew on my face. He dipped his hand into his jacket pocket and came out with a foolscap sheet of paper. He unfolded it and handed it to me. "Read."

It was a poem; handwritten. The title was written in capital letters: "MY LOVE FOR YOU."

Like a man in a dream, I ran my eyes over the bold squiggles. After the first stanza I saw that it was a thinly veiled imitation of one of my poems. I sensed his waiting. He was hardly breathing. I let him wait. Lord, I can't remember another time when I had felt so good. So powerful. I was Samuel Johnson and he was an aspiring poet waiting anxiously for my verdict, asking tremulously, "Sir, is it poetry, is it Pindar?"

I wanted to say, with as much sarcasm as I could put into my voice, "Sir, your poem is both original and interesting, but the part that is interesting is not original, and the part that is original is not interesting." But all I said was, "Not bad, you need to work on it some more."

The eagerness went out of his face and for a fleeting moment the scowl returned. "I promised my lady a poem. She is educated, you know. A teacher. You will write a poem for me. For my lady."

"You want me to write a poem for you?" I tried to mask the surprise, the confusion and, yes, the eagerness in my voice. He was offering me a chance to write.

"I am glad you understand. Her name is Janice. She has been to the university. She has class. Not like other girls. She teaches in my son's school. That is how we met."

Even jailers fall in love, I thought inanely.

"At first she didn't take me seriously. She thought I only wanted to use her and dump her. And. Also. We are of different religion. She is Christian, I am Muslim. But no problem. I love her. But she still doubted. I did not know what to do. Then I saw one of your poems . . . yes, this one." He handed me the poem. "It said everything I wanted to tell her."

It was one of my early poems, rewritten from memory.

" 'Three Words.' I gave it to her yesterday when I took her out."

"You gave her my poem?"

"Yes."

"You . . . you told her you wrote it?"

"Yes, yes, of course. I wrote it again in my own hand," he said, unabashed. He had been speaking in a rush; now he drew himself together and, as though to reassert his authority, began to pace the room, speaking in a subdued, measured tone. "I can make life easy for you here. I am the prison superintendent. There is nothing I cannot do, if I want. So write. The poem. For me."

There is nothing I cannot do. You can get me cigarettes, I am sure, and food. You can remove me from solitary. But can you stand me outside these walls, free under the stars? Can you connect the tips of my upraised arms to the stars so that the surge of liberty passes down my body to the soft downy grass beneath my feet?

I asked for paper and pencil. And a book to read.

He was removed from the solitary section that day. The pencil and paper came, the book too. But not the one he had asked for. He wanted Wole Soyinka's prison notes, *The Man Died*; but when it came it was *A Brief History of West Africa*. While writing the poems in the cell, Lomba would sometimes let his mind wander; he'd picture the superintendent and his lady out on a date, how he'd bring out the poem and unfold it and hand it to her and say boldly, "I wrote it for you. Myself."

They sit outside on the verandah at her suggestion. The light from the hanging, wind-swayed Chinese lanterns falls softly on them. The breeze blowing from the lagoon below smells fresh to her nostrils; she loves its dampness on her bare arms and face. She looks at him across the circular table, with its vase holding a single rose. He appears nervous. A thin film of sweat covers his forehead. He removes his cap and dabs at his forehead with a white handkerchief.

"Do you like it, a Chinese restaurant?" he asks, like a father anxious to please his favourite child. It is their first outing together. He pestered her until she gave in. Sometimes she is at a loss what to make of his attentions. She sighs. She turns her plump face to the deep, blue lagoon. A white boat with dark stripes on its sides speeds past; a figure is crouched inside, almost invisible. Her light, flower-patterned gown shivers in the light breeze. She watches him covertly. He handles his chopsticks awkwardly, but determinedly.

"Waiter!" he barks, his mouth full of fish, startling her. "Bring another bottle of wine."

"No. I am all right, really," she says firmly, putting down her chopsticks.

After the meal, which has been quite delicious, he lifts the tiny, wine-filled porcelain cup before him and says: "To you. And me."

She sips her drink, avoiding his eyes.

"I love you, Janice. Very much. I know you think I am not serious. That I only want to suck the juice and throw away the peel. No." He suddenly dips his hand into the pocket of his well-ironed white kaftan and brings out a yellow paper.

"Read and see." He pushes the paper across the table to her. "I wrote it. For you. A poem."

She opens the paper. It smells faintly of sandalwood. She looks at the title: "Three Words." She reaches past the vase and its single, white rose, past the wine bottle, the wine glasses, and covers his hairy hand with hers briefly. "Thank you."

She reads the poem, shifting in her seat towards the swaying light of the lantern:

Three words

When I hear the waterfall clarity of your laughter
When I see the twilight softness of your eyes

I feel like draping you all over myself, like a cloak,
To be warmed by your warmth.

Your flower-petal innocence, your perennial
Sapling resilience — your endless charms

All these set my mind on wild flights of fancy:
I add word unto word,
I compare adjectives and coin exotic phrases
But they all seem jaded, corny, unworthy
Of saying all I want to say to you.

So I take refuge in these simple words,
Trusting my tone, my hand in yours, when I
Whisper them, to add depth and new
Twists of meaning to them. Three words:
I love you.

With his third or fourth poem for the superintendent, Lomba began to send Janice cryptic messages. She seemed to possess an insatiable appetite for love poems. Every day a warder came to the cell, in the evening, with the same request from the superintendent: "The poem." When he finally ran out of original poems, Lomba began to plagiarize the masters from memory. Here are the opening lines of one:

Janice, your beauty is to me
Like those treasures of gold . . .

Another one starts:

I wonder, my heart, what you and I
Did till we loved . . .

But it was Lomba's bowdlerization of Sappho's "Ode" that brought the superintendent to the cell door:

> *A peer of goddesses she seems to me*
> *The lady who sits over against me*
> *Face to face,*
> *Listening to the sweet tones of my voice,*
> *And the loveliness of my laughing.*
> *It is this that sets my heart fluttering*
> *In my chest,*
> *For if I gaze on you but for a little while*
> *I am no longer master of my voice,*
> *And my tongue lies useless*
> *And a delicate flame runs over my skin*
> *No more do I see with my eyes;*
> *The sweat pours down me*
> *I am all seized with trembling*
> *And I grow paler than the grass*
> *My strength fails me*
> *And I seem little short of dying.*

He came to the cell door less than twenty minutes after the poem had reached him, waving the paper in the air, a real smile splitting his granite face.

"Lomba, come out!" he hollered through the iron bars. Lomba was lying on his wafer-thin mattress, on his back, trying to imagine figures out of the rain designs on the ceiling. The door officer hastily threw open the door.

The superintendent threw a friendly arm over Lomba's shoulders. He was unable to stand still. He walked Lomba up and down the grassy courtyard.

"This poem. Excellent. With this poem. After. I'll ask her for marriage." He was incoherent in his excitement. He raised the paper and read aloud the first line, straining his eyes in the dying light: "'A peer of goddesses she seems to me.' Yes. Excellent. She will be happy. Do you think I should ask her for. Marriage. Today?"

He stood before Lomba, bent forward expectantly, his legs planted in their characteristic A formation.

"Why not?" Lomba answered. A passing warder stared at the superintendent and the prisoner curiously. Twilight fell dully on the broken bottles studded in the concrete of the prison wall.

"Yes. Why not. Good." The superintendent walked up and down, his hands clasped behind him, his head bowed in thought. Finally, he stopped before Lomba and declared gravely: "Tonight. I'll ask her."

Lomba smiled at him, sadly. The superintendent saw the smile; he did not see the sadness.

"Good. You are happy. I am happy too. I'll send you a packet of cigarettes. Two packets. Today. Enjoy. Now go back inside."

He turned abruptly on his heels and marched away.

September

Janice came to see me two days after I wrote her the Sappho. I thought, she has discovered my secret messages, my scriptive Morse tucked innocently in the lines of the poems I've written her.

Two o'clock is compulsory siesta time. The opening of the cell door brought me awake. My limbs felt heavy and lifeless. I feared I might have an infection. The warder came directly to me.

"Oya, get up. The superintendent wan see you." His skin was coarse, coal black. He was fat and his speech came out in laboured gasps. "Oya, get up. Get up," he repeated impatiently.

I was in that lethargic, somnambulistic state condemned people surely fall into when, in total inanition and despair, they await their fate—without fear or hope, because nothing can be changed. No dew-wet finger of light would come poking into the parched gloom of the abyss they tenant. I did not want to write any more poems for the superintendent's lover. I did not want any more of his cigarettes. I was tired of being pointed at behind my back, of being whispered about by the other inmates as the superintendent's informer, his fetch-water. I wanted to recover my lost dignity. Now I realized that I really had no "self" to express; that self had flown away from me the day the chains touched my hands. What is left here is nothing but a mass of protruding bones, unkempt hair and tearful eyes; an asshole for shitting and farting, and a penis that in the mornings grows turgid in vain. This leftover self, this sea-bleached wreck panting on the iron-filing sands of the shores of this penal island is nothing but hot air, and hair, and ears cocked, hopeful . . .

So I said to the warder, "I don't want to see him today. Tell him I'm sick."

The fat face contorted. He raised his baton in Pavlovian response. "What!" But our eyes met. He was smart enough to decipher the bold "No Trespassing" sign written in mine. Smart enough to obey. He moved back, shrugging. "Na you go suffer!" he blustered, and left.

I was aware of the curious eyes staring at me. I closed mine. I willed my mind over the prison walls to other places. Free. I dreamt of standing under the stars, my hands raised, their tips touching the blinking, pulsating electricity of the stars. The rain would be falling. There'd be nothing else: just me and rain and stars and my feet on the wet, downy grass earthing the electricity of freedom.

He returned almost immediately. There was a smirk on his fat face as he handed me a note. I recognized the superintendent's clumsy scrawl. It was brief, a one-liner: *Janice is here. Come. Now.* Truncated, even in writing. I got up and pulled on my sweat-grimed shirt. I slipped my feet into my old, worn-out slippers. I followed the warder. We passed the parade ground, and the convicted men's compound. An iron gate, far to our right, locked permanently, led to the women's wing of the prison. We passed the old laundry, which now served as a barber's shop on Saturdays—the prison's sanitation day. A gun-carrying warder opened a tiny door in the huge gate that led into a foreyard where the prison officials had their offices. I had been here before, once, on my first day in prison. There were cars parked before the offices; cadets in their well-starched uniforms came and went, their young faces looking comically stern. Female secretaries with time on their hands stood in the corridors gossiping. The superintendent's office was not far from the gate; a flight of three concrete steps led up to a thick wooden door, which bore the single word: SUPERINTENDENT.

My guide knocked on it timidly before turning the handle.

"The superintendent wan see am," he informed the secretary. She barely looked up from her typewriter; she nodded. Her eyes were bored, uncurious.

"Enter," the warder said to me, pointing to a curtained doorway beside the secretary's table. I entered. A lady sat in one of the two visitor's armchairs. Back to the door, her elbows rested on the huge Formica-topped table before her. Janice. She was alone. When she turned, I noted that my mental image of her was almost accurate. She was plump. Her face was warm and homely. She came halfway out of her chair, turning it slightly so that it faced the other chair. There was a tentative smile on her face as she asked, "Mr. Lomba?"

I almost said no, surprised by the "Mr." I nodded.

She pointed at the empty chair. "Please sit down." She extended a soft, pudgy hand to me. I took it and marveled at its softness. She was a teacher; the hardness would be in the fingers: the tips of the thumb and middle finger, and the side of the index finger.

"Muftau—the superintendent—will be here soon. He just stepped out," she said. Her voice was clear, a little high-pitched. Her English was correct, each word carefully pronounced and projected. Like in a classroom. I was struck by how clean she looked, squeaky clean; her skin glowed like a child's after a bath. She had obviously taken a lot of trouble with her appearance: her blue evening dress looked almost new, but a slash of red lipstick extended to the left cheek after missing the curve of the lip. She crossed and

uncrossed her legs, tapping the left foot on the floor. She
was nervous. That was when I realized I had not said a word
since I entered.

"Welcome to the prison," I said, unable to think of anything else.

She nodded. "Thank you. I told Muftau I wanted to see
you. The poems, I just knew it wasn't him writing them. I
went along with it for a while, but later I told him."

She opened the tiny handbag in her lap and took out
some papers. The poems. She put them on the table and
unfolded them, smoothing out the creases, uncurling the
edges. "After the Sappho I decided I must see you. It was
my favourite poem in school, and I like your version of it."

"Thank you," I said. I liked her directness, her sense of
humour.

"So I told him—look, I know who the writer is, he is one
of the prisoners, isn't he? That surprised him. He couldn't
figure out how I knew. But I was glad he didn't deny it. I
told him that. And if we are getting married, there shouldn't
be secrets between us, should there?"

Ah, I thought, so my Sappho has worked the magic.
Aloud I said, "Congratulations."

She nodded. "Thanks. Muftau is a nice person, really, when
you get to know him. His son, Farouk, was in my class—he's
finished now—really, you should see them together. So touching. I know he has his awkward side, and that he was once
married—but I don't care. After all, I have a little past too.
Who doesn't?" She added the last quickly, as if scared she was
revealing too much to a stranger. Her left hand went up and
down as she spoke, like a hypnotist, like a conductor. After a
brief pause, she continued, "After all the pain he's been
through with his other wife, he deserves some happiness. She
was in the hospital a whole year before she died."

Muftau. The superintendent had a name, and a history,
maybe even a soul. I looked at his portrait hanging on the
wall. He looked young in it, serious-faced and smart, like
the cadet warders outside. I turned to her and said suddenly and sincerely, "I am glad you came. Thanks."

Her face broke into a wide, dimpled smile. She was actually pretty. A little past her prime, past her sell-by date, but still nice, still viable. "Oh, no. I am the one that should be glad. I love meeting poets. I love your poems. Really I do."

"Not all of them are mine."

"I know—but you give them a different feel, a different tone. And also, I discovered your S.O.S. I had to come . . ." She picked the poems off the table and handed them to me. There were thirteen of them. Seven were my originals, six were purloined. She had carefully underlined in red ink certain lines of them—the same line, actually, recurring.

There was a waiting-to-be-congratulated smile on her face as she awaited my comment.

"You noticed," I said.

"Of course I did. S.O.S. It wasn't apparent at first. I began to notice the repetition with the fifth poem. 'Save my soul, a prisoner.' "

"Save my soul, a prisoner" . . . The first time I put down the words, in the third poem, it had been non-deliberate, I was just making alliteration. Then I began to repeat it in the subsequent poems. But how could I tell her that the message wasn't really for her, or for anyone else? It was for myself, perhaps, written by me to my own soul, to every other soul, the collective soul of the universe.

I told her, the first time I wrote it an inmate had died. His name was Thomas. He wasn't sick. He just started vomiting after the afternoon meal, and before the warders came to take him to the clinic, he died. Just like that. He died. Watching his stiffening face, with the mouth open and the eyes staring, as the inmates took him out of the cell, an irrational fear had gripped me. I saw myself being taken out like that, my lifeless arms dangling, brushing the ground. The fear made me sit down, shaking uncontrollably amidst the flurry of movements and voices excited by the tragedy. I was scared. I felt certain I was going to end up like that. Have you ever felt like that, certain that you are going to die? No? I did. I was going to die. My body would end up in some anonymous mortuary, and later in an unmarked grave, and no one would know. No one would care. It happens every day here. I am a political detainee; if I die I am just one antagonist less. That was when I wrote the S.O.S. It was just a message in a bottle, thrown without much hope into the sea . . . I stopped speaking when my hands started to shake. I wanted to put them in my pocket to hide them from her. But she had seen it. She left her seat and came to me. She took both my hands in hers.

"You'll not die. You'll get out alive. One day it will be all over," she said. Her perfume, mixed with her female smell, rose into my nostrils: flowery, musky. I had forgotten the last time a woman had stood so close to me. Sometimes, in our cell, when the wind blows from the female prison, we'll catch distant sounds of female screams and shouts and even laughter. That is the closest we ever come to women. Only when the wind blows, at the right time, in the right direction. Her hands on mine, her smell, her presence, acted like fire on some huge, prehistoric glacier locked deep in my chest. And when her hand touched my head and the back of my neck, I wept.

When the superintendent returned, my sobbing face was buried in Janice's ample bosom. Her hands were on my head, patting, consoling, like a mother, all the while cooing softly, "One day it will finish."

I pulled away from her. She gave me her handkerchief.

"What is going on? Why is he crying?"

He was standing just within the door—his voice was curious, with a hint of jealousy. I wiped my eyes; I subdued my body's spasms. He advanced slowly into the room and went round to his seat. He remained standing, his hairy hands resting on the table.

"Why is he crying?" he repeated to Janice.

"Because he is a prisoner," Janice replied simply. She was still standing beside me, facing the superintendent.

"Well. So? Is he realizing that just now?"

"Don't be so unkind, Muftau."

I returned the handkerchief to her.

"Muftau, you must help him."

"Help. How?"

"You are the prison superintendent. There's a lot you can do."

"But I can't help him. He is a political detainee. He has not even been tried."

"And you know that he is never going to be tried. He will be kept here forever, forgotten." Her voice became sharp and indignant. The superintendent drew back his seat and sat down. His eyes were lowered. When he looked up, he said earnestly, "Janice. There's nothing anyone can do for him. I'll be implicating myself. Besides, his lot is far easier than that of the other inmates. I give him things. Cigarettes. Soap. Books. And I let him. Write."

"How can you be so unfeeling! Put yourself in his shoes—two years away from friends, from family, without the power to do anything you wish to do. Two years in *chains*! How can you talk of cigarettes and soap, as if that were substitute enough for all that he has lost?" She was like a teacher confronting an erring student. Her left hand tapped the table for emphasis as she spoke.

"Well." He looked cowed. His scowl alternated rapidly with a smile. He stared at his portrait on the wall behind her. He spoke in a rush. "Well. I could have done something. Two weeks ago. The Amnesty International. People came. You know, white men. They wanted names of. Political detainees held. Without trial. To pressure the government to release them."

"Well?"

"Well." He still avoided her stare. His eyes touched mine and hastily passed. He picked up a pen and twirled it between his fingers. The pen slipped out of his fingers and fell to the floor.

"I didn't. Couldn't. You know . . . I thought he was comfortable. And, he was writing the poems, for you . . ." His voice was almost pleading. Surprisingly, I felt no anger towards him. He was just Man. Man in his basic, rudimentary state, easily moved by powerful emotions like love, lust, anger, greed and fear, but totally dumb to the finer, acquired emotions like pity, mercy, humour and justice.

Janice slowly picked up her bag from the table. There was enormous dignity to her movements. She clasped the bag under her left arm. Her words were slow, almost sad. "I see now that I've made a mistake. You are not really the man I thought you were . . ."

"Janice." He stood up and started coming round to her, but a gesture stopped him.

"No. Let me finish. I want you to contact these people. Give them his name. If you can't do that, then forget you ever knew me."

Her hand brushed my arm as she passed me. He started after her, then stopped halfway across the room. We stared in silence at the curtained doorway, listening to the sound of her heels on the bare floor till it finally died away. He returned slowly to his seat and slumped into it. The wood creaked audibly in the quiet office.

"Go," he said, not looking at me.

The above is the last entry in Lomba's diary. There's no record of how far the superintendent went to help him regain his freedom, but as he told Janice, there was very little to be done for a political detainee—especially since, about a week after that meeting, a coup was attempted against the military leader, General Sani Abacha, by some officers close to him. There was an immediate crackdown on all pro-democracy activists, and the prisons all over the country swelled with political detainees. A lot of those already in detention were transferred randomly to other prisons around the country, for security reasons. Lomba was among them. He was transferred to Agodi Prison in Ibadan. From there he was moved to the far north, to a small desert town called Gashuwa. There is no record of him after that.

A lot of these political prisoners died in detention, although the prominent ones made the headlines—people like Moshood Abiola and General Yar Adua.

But somehow it is hard to imagine that Lomba died. A lot seems to point to the contrary. His diary, his economical expressions show a very sedulous character at work. A survivor. The years in prison must have taught him not to hope too much, not to despair too much—that for the prisoner, nothing kills as surely as too much hope or too much despair. He had learned to survive in tiny atoms, piecemeal, a day at a time. It is probable that in 1998, when the military dictator Abacha died, and his successor, General Abdulsalam Abubakar, dared to open the gates to democracy, and to liberty for the political detainees, Lomba was in the ranks of those released.

This might have been how it happened: Lomba was seated in a dingy cell in Gashuwa, his eyes closed, his mind soaring above the glass-studded prison walls, mingling with the stars and the rain in elemental union of freedom; then the door clanked open, and when he opened his eyes Liberty was standing over him, smiling kindly, extending an arm.

And Liberty said softly, "Come. It is time to go."

And they left, arm in arm.

BESSIE HEAD

Bessie Amelia (Emery) Head was born in Pietermaritz-burg, South Africa, in 1937 to a mother from a well-to-do white family and an African who cared for horses. Because of her illicit relationship and unwed pregnancy, her mother was sent to a mental hospital, and Bessie was raised by two adoptive families, one Afrikaner and one "colored," both of whom ultimately rejected her, leading her to be sent to a missionary orphanage at age thirteen. She became a journalist and taught elementary school and, after a divorce, took her son and emigrated to Botswana. She worked for the Bamangwato Development Farm, where she grew vegetables and made guava jam to sell. There she was inspired by the lives of the men and women in her village of Serowe and began to write fiction. Her three novels are *When Rain Clouds Gather* (1969), *Maru* (1971), and *A Question of Power* (1974), a very autobiographical story about a biracial woman struggling to maintain her sanity as she works to gain acceptance in an African village. She also wrote two other works, *Serowe: Village of the Rain Wind* and *Bewitched Crossroad: An African Saga*, which combine sociological and historical accounts with elements of folklore, and *The Collector of Treasures and Other Botswana Village Tales*, a collection of related short stories. She died in 1986.

Earth Love
(1993)

The sky was a brilliant red glow when he came home that evening. He could have arrived home at midday, except that to do so was unthinkable. The message must be sent on ahead, passing from mouth to mouth, scurrying along the winding African footpaths. He must then delay, dallying here and there so that on arrival home the wife would have swept the hut, shaken out the sleeping mats and prepared a special meal of good food.

For two months he had been out in the wild bush, collecting the skins of jackal. Now he would sit at home and leisurely piece together these skins into a sleeping blanket. Always in demand, a well-made sleeping blanket can fetch a good price. A jackal blanket with its thick pattern of silver and black hair is very beautiful.

For two months he had lived on wild meat of wild animals, wild berries and wild bush-watermelon.

For two months there had been only the stunning, numbing silence of the bush. Above, in the sky at evening, the brilliant flight of the red-and-white flamingo birds; on the ground, the ceaseless, heavy jogtrot of the foolish kudu; or the startled, delicate flight of buck; or the rustle, rustle of small, round, furry animals among the low thorn bushes.

"Man can never separate himself from earth and sky," he would often think with tender amazement. "Always they are there, flamingo birds and kudu. Wild, beautiful sunset flamingo birds and the foolish kudu.

"What does a man love best?" he thought. "In the bush I am only a breathing man with eyes and ears alert for the treacherous jackal. Soon, village life will close about me again. I shall drink beer and make the rounds of the village courts, and listen to the repetitious tragedies and comedies of our life. Everywhere there is some sadness. In the village life and in the silence of the bush. Man must continually exchange one sadness for another to make his life a livable thing."

He felt a cold rush of wind on his face. He looked up at the sky and quickened his homeward pace. There were huge streaks of rain shadows on the east and southwest horizons. It was raining there, far in the distance, and the strong south wind had rushed through it and become a cold, fresh rain-wind. The earth was so flat and broad and wide and endless that the canopy of sky overhead had to stretch with all its might to keep pace with the breadth of the earth. The sky was always brooding about this. It did not like to be outdone by the earth. At evening, it dressed itself up in a brilliant splash of red and yellow glow, leaving the earth a black, stark silhouette of thorn trees. Man had to leave off his intense preoccupation with the earth and raise his eyes to the sky. Then, it seemed, the eyes and soul of man became the wild, beautiful sunset flamingo bird flying free in the limitless space of the sky. The ache and pain and uncertainty of earth life was drowned in the peace and freedom of the sky.

"How strange," he thought. "One part of me is the flamingo bird. The other the foolish kudu. More often I am the foolish kudu, my feet jogging heavily along the ground. I can see neither left nor right nor behind, but only straight ahead. All things beat down on me and I dart off in one blind direction, and another. I am a slow earth man of little wit. I am the foolish kudu. How is it then that my eyes and soul drown in the flight of the wild flamingo bird? Can I be two things at once—the flamingo bird and the foolish kudu? Man cannot separate himself from earth and sky."

There was a rumble of thunder and a flash of lightning as he entered the village. The rain-wind rushed along the village pathways and swirled about the circular mud huts. The wife was happy to see him but subdued about expressing this happiness. The children came shouting about and he spoke to them with rough, abashed male tenderness. They took the jackal skins to store away in the spare hut and fled out of the yard to continue their interrupted game.

The wife brought the basin of water so that he could wash. "Tell me the news," he said, taking off his tattered, soiled shirt.

"There isn't much to tell," she said, sitting on the ground near him. Then all at once a lot of words poured out so that he could hardly sort out one story from the other.

"Manga's quiet wife has left him. He beat her severely, so that she had to run to the police camp in the middle of the night. He immediately took in another woman. Then it appears that he made a young girl pregnant and when this young girl called at the house, this other woman beat the young girl. Manga was roaring drunk and beat his other woman almost to death. Her cries were so terrible that the police had to be called. Manga is now in jail. Three teachers and a principal were dismissed for making schoolgirls pregnant. Do you know Sylvia? She works in the shop. The one of whom people say she has no food at home, but dresses like a shop window? People are indignant about her behaviour. It is known that she has slept with many men in the village, but now it seems that her husband took up with a quiet young teacher who is now in the place. It seems that the story was whispered to Sylvia by a snake in the green grass. While the teacher was at work, Sylvia went to her house and opened her belongings. In a suitcase were many letters from Sylvia's husband. Sylvia waited there and when the young teacher returned home, Sylvia removed her high-heeled shoe and beat her about the head. She almost beat another woman's child to death. No one can forget this terrible story. Sylvia's husband has fled away, as he does not want to face the trouble. I received a report from the cattle-post that one of the bulls has his eye damaged. The young one who was not yet castrated. He got into a fight with one of the old bulls who put a horn in his eye. I thought of going to the cattle-post to attend to the matter but then I received word that you were on the way home, so instead I sent instructions about how the eye should be treated."

She was silent a moment. The husband commented almost to himself, smiling with quiet amusement: "We are all foolish kudus."

"What is that?" the wife asked, puzzled. She had never

heard that expression before. The husband did not reply, and the woman went about her business. She accepted him as he was, a quiet, reserved man. He could never be driven into a quarrel, and all the things in life he looked at with an interested detachment.

The wife brought him a plate of boiled ground millet over which she had put a piece of soft braised meat, spinach and pumpkin. In another plate she had two steaming fresh young mealies. While he ate, the storm clouds gathered overhead and the thunder rumbled. A small black kitten hovered near. Its eyes were grey-green and it was soft and beautiful. He tore off a long shred of meat and put it down. The kitten ate with great delicacy; then it sat down at his feet, shot one straight black leg upwards and began cleaning its tail. Also at his feet the large, fat, brown earth ants were as busy as anything. A huge team scattered over the earth, cutting down blades of grass and carrying them back to the edge of the hole. Another team gathered these deposits of grass from the edge of the hole and all the time he could see their fat round abdomens disappearing into the earth's depths. He placed his foot over the hole for a few seconds and at once caused great confusion among this well-organised community. The team outside fell back, consulting among themselves, then dropped their blades of grass and ran panic-stricken hither and hither. When he raised his foot, four large soldier ants, with menacing, shiny claws waving about, slowly emerged from the hole. They surveyed the surroundings. There was nothing wrong, just maybe some foolish kudu had temporarily interfered. They consulted with the panic-stricken workers, threw about their weight a little, then walked majestically back and disappeared into the hole. The rhythm of work replaced itself, but this time with a speeded-up tempo. The rain was near.

The wife called the children home. They had eaten a while ago and now, with the first isolated drops of rain, they came tumbling and shouting and tussling into the yard, and scattered to their separate sleeping huts.

The man felt tired and content. When he entered their

sleeping hut, the bed of jackal blankets was neatly prepared. There was an oil lamp, made from a Milo tin, burning in one corner. There was the thunder and rain outside.
There was this hut, and his wife's quiet, warm female body
which was very satisfying.

ALEXANDER KANENGONI

Born in 1951, Alexander Kanengoni was trained as a teacher before he joined ZANLA, an African nationalist guerrilla force. Much of his fiction was inspired by the anticolonial struggle and Zimbabwean war for liberation. After Zimbabwe gained its independence in 1980, he attended the University of Zimbabwe and majored in English literature. He became a member of the Ministry of Education and Culture, where he worked as a project officer and was responsible for overseeing the education of ex-soldiers and refugees. From 1988 to 2002 he worked for the Zimbabwe Broadcasting Service, but then returned to his familial roots when he became a farmer. He recalled that his father had owned his own land and that he himself had grown up "living on and knowing the land." He thinks that the relationship between the people and the land has an almost spiritual quality about it. Kanengoni's works include *Vicious Circle* (1983), *When the Rainbird Cries* (1988), *Echoing Silences* (1997), a collection of short stories titled *Effortless Tears* (1993), and *Writing Still* (2003).

Effortless Tears
(1993)

We buried my cousin, George Pasi, one bleak windswept afternoon: one of those afternoons that seem fit for nothing but funerals. Almost everyone there knew that George had died of an AIDS-related illness but no one mentioned it. What showed was only the fear and uncertainty in people's eyes; beyond that, silence.

Even as we traveled from Harare on that hired bus that morning, every one of us feared that at last AIDS had caught up with us. In the beginning, it was a distant, blurred phenomenon which we only came across in the newspapers and on radio and television, something peculiar to homosexuals. Then we began hearing isolated stories of people dying of AIDS in far-flung districts. After that came the rumors of sealed wards at Harare and Parirenyatwa, and of other hospitals teeming with people suffering from AIDS. But the truth is that it still seemed rather remote and did not seem to have any direct bearing on most of us.

When AIDS finally reached Highfield and Zengeza, and started claiming lives in the streets where we lived, that triggered the alarm bells inside our heads. AIDS had finally knocked on our doors.

For two months, we had watched George waste away at Harare Hospital. In desperation, his father—just like the rest of us—skeptical of the healing properties of modern medicine, had turned to traditional healers. Somehow, we just could not watch him die. We made futile journeys to all corners of the country while George wasted away. He finally died on our way home from some traditional healer in Mutare.

All the way from Harare to Wedza, the atmosphere was limp. January's scorching sun in the naked sky and the suffocating air intensified into a sense of looming crisis that could not be expressed in words. The rains were already very late and the frequent sight of untilled fields, helplessly confronting an unfulfilling sky, created images of seasons that could no longer be understood. The crops that had been planted with the first and only rains of the season had emerged only to fight a relentless war with the sun. Most had wilted and died. The few plants that still survived were struggling in the stifling heat.

Now, as we stood forlornly round the grave, the choir sang an ominous song about death: we named the prophets yielded up to heaven while the refrain repeated: "Can you see your name? Where is your name?"

This eerie question rang again and again in our minds until it became part of one's soul, exposing it to the nakedness of the Mutekedza communal land: land that was overcrowded, old, and tired. Interminable rows of huts stretched into the horizon, along winding roads that only seemed to lead to other funerals.

Not far away, a tattered scarecrow from some forgotten season flapped a silent dirge beneath the burning sun.

Lean cattle, their bones sticking out, their ribs moving painfully under their taut skin, nibbled at something on the dry ground: what it was, no one could make out. And around the grave the atmosphere was subdued and silent. Even the once phenomenal Save River, only a stone's throw away to the east, lay silent. This gigantic river, reduced to puddles between heaps of sand, seemed to be brooding on its sad predicament. And behind the dying river, Wedza Mountain stared at us with resignation, as if it, too, had given up trying to understand some of the strange things that were happening.

The preacher told the parable of the Ten Virgins. He warned that when the Lord unexpectedly came and knocked on our door, like the clever five virgins, we should be found ready and waiting to receive Him.

Everyone nodded silently.

George's grandfather mourned the strange doings of this earth. He wished it was he who had been taken away. But then such were the weird ways of witches and wizards that they preferred to pluck the youngest and plumpest— although George had grown thinner than the cattle we could see around us. We listened helplessly as the old man talked and talked until at last he broke down and cried like a small child.

George's father talked of an invisible enemy that had sneaked into our midst and threatened the very core of our existence. He warned us that we should change our ways immediately or die.

He never mentioned the word "Aids," the acronym AIDS.

Alexander Kanengoni

George's wife was beyond all weeping. She talked of a need for moral strength during such critical times. She readily admitted that she did not know where such strength could come from: it could be from the people; it could be from those gone beyond; it could be from God. But wherever it was from, she needed it. As if acting upon some invisible signal, people began to cry. We were not weeping for the dead. We were weeping for the living. And behind us, while Wedza Mountain gazed at us dejectedly, the Save River was silently dying.

The coffin was slowly lowered into the grave and we filed past, throwing in clods of soil. In the casket lay George, reduced to skin and bone. (Most people had refused a last glimpse of him.) During his heyday we had called him Mr. Bigstuff because of his fast and flashy style—that was long ago.

As we trudged back to the village, away from the wretched burial area, most of us were trying to decide which memory of George to take back with us: Mr. Bigstuff or that thread, that bundle of skin and bones which had died on our way back from some traditional healer in Mutare.

Out there, around the fire, late that Monday evening, all discussion was imbued with a painful sense of futility, a menacing uncertainty, and an overwhelming feeling that we were going nowhere.

Drought.

"Compared to the ravaging drought of 1947, this is child's play," said George's grandfather. "At that time, people survived on grass like cattle," he concluded, looking skeptically up into the deep night sky.

No one helped him take the discussion further.

Politics.

The village chairman of the party attempted a spirited explanation of the advantages of the government's economic reform program: "It means a general availability of goods and services and it means higher prices for the people's agricultural produce," he went on, looking up at the dark, cloudless sky. Then, with an inexplicable renewal of optimism peculiar to politicians, he went on to talk of programs and projects until, somehow, he, too, was overcome by the general weariness and took refuge in the silence around the dying fire.

"Aren't these religious denominations that are daily sprouting up a sign that the end of the world is coming?" asked George's grandfather.

"No, it's just people out to make a quick buck, nothing else," said George's younger brother.

"Don't you know that the end of the world is foretold in the Scriptures," said the Methodist lay preacher with sharp urgency. He continued: "All these things"—he waved his arms in a large general movement—"are undoubtedly signs of the Second Coming." Everyone looked down and sighed.

And then, inevitably, AIDS came up. It was a topic that everyone had been making a conscious effort to avoid, but then, like everything else, its turn came. Everyone referred to it in indirect terms: that animal, that phantom, that creature, that beast. It was not out of any respect for George. It was out of fear and despair.

"Whatever this scourge is"—George's father chuckled—"it has claimed more lives than all my three years in the Imperial Army against Hitler." He chuckled again helplessly.

"It seems as if these endless funerals have taken the place of farming."

"They are lucky, the ones who are still getting decent burials," chipped in someone from out of the dark. "Very soon, there will be no one to bury anybody."

The last glowing ember in the collected heap of ashes grew dimmer and finally died away. George's grandfather asked for an ox-hide drum and began playing it slowly at first and then with gathering ferocity. Something in me snapped.

Then he began to sing. The song told of an unfortunate woman's repeated pregnancies which always ended in miscarriages. I felt trapped.

When at last the old man, my father, stood up and began to dance, stamping the dry earth with his worn-out car-tire sandals, I knew there was no escape. I edged George's grandfather away from the drum and began a futile prayer on that moonless night. The throbbing resonance of the drum rose above our voices as we all became part of one great nothingness. Suddenly I was crying for the first time since George's death. Tears ran from my eyes like rivers in a good season. During those years, most of us firmly believed that the mighty Save River would roll on forever, perhaps until the end of time.

But not now, not any longer.

FARIDA KARODIA

Farida Karodia was born in 1942 in the Eastern Cape province of South Africa. She taught in Johannesburg, Zambia, and Swaziland, but while she was teaching in Zambia in 1968, she learned that she had been exiled by the South African government and emigrated to Canada. In 1994, she was able to return to South Africa, and she currently divides her time between those two nations. In India, in 1993, she wrote and produced *Midnight Embers,* a half hour television drama that won awards at three international film festivals. Her novels include *Daughters of the Twilight* (1986) and *Boundaries* (2003). *Coming Home* (1988), *A Shattering of Silence* (1993), *Against an African Sky* (1997) and *Other Secrets* (2011) are collections of short stories.

Cardboard Mansions
(1988)

66 “Chotoo! Eh Chotoo!”
   “Ja, Dadi-Ma?” the boy cried from the far side of the yard.

"Don't ja Dadi-Ma me! Come here!" the old woman called from the stoep. Leaning over the low abutment wall, she craned to peer around the corner but her view was obstructed by a pile of rubbish. She stepped back, knocking over the chipped enamel pail which was normally kept beside her bed at night. The empty pail rolled out of reach, clattering against the wall.

She waited for the boy, pulling the end of the faded green cotton sari over her head. Her wide, flat heels hung over the back of the blue rubber thongs almost two sizes smaller than her feet.

Dadi-Ma looked much older than her seventy-three years. She was a tall, heavily built woman with slow, tired movements. Her dark brown eyes were set deep in a face scored and marked with age and hardship. The gap in the front of her mouth was relieved only by three stumps of rotted teeth, bloodily stained by betel-nut.

In her youth she had been much admired for her beauty, with her dark lustrous eyes like those of a young doe. But there was no one left to remember her as she'd been then. Sonny, the youngest of her sons, and her grandson, Chotoo, were the only surviving members of her family. Three of her sons and her husband, like so many of the men who had toiled in the sugarcane fields, had all died of tuberculosis.

And now the only ones left to her were her grandchild, Chotoo, and her friend Ratnadevi. Dadi-Ma in her old age was left to gaze upon the world with the patient endurance of the old water buffalo they had once owned in India.

The boy, Chotoo, took a long time coming. His grandmother waited, her broad, varicose-veined feet and legs planted astride. A rip in her sari revealed a discoloured slip, unadorned and frayed. Her dark eyes stared out from under thick brows, slowly gathering in impatience.

"Chotoo!" she called again and sat down on the step to wait.

The row of shanties was all connected. At one time they had served as a shed, but an enterprising landlord had used sheets of corrugated iron to divide the shed into stalls which he rented to the poor. All the dividing walls stopped at least twelve inches short of the ceiling.

On Saturday night when Frank Chetty beat his wife, Nirmala, her cries swirled over the heads of the other tenants. Some ignored them. Others were just grateful that they were not in Nirmala's shoes. Dadi-Ma's daughter-in-law, Neela, had once remarked to their neighbour, Urmila, that no matter what Sonny was guilty of, this was one thing that he had not yet stooped to.

"Just you wait and see," Urmila said. "It'll happen when Sonny loses his job."

But even when Sonny lost his job he never raised a hand to his wife. Chotoo, however, was not so lucky and in his short life had been slapped many times, often for no apparent reason. Despite this, Dadi-Ma's pride in her son remained undiminished. She could hold up her head and say that he had never lifted a hand to his wife or his mother.

It had come as a terrible blow to Dadi-Ma when Neela had died in childbirth three years ago, leaving Sonny with the boy, Chotoo. But Sonny was hardly ever around and everything had fallen on her shoulders. Somehow they managed. Even when Sonny lost his job they still managed. Dadi-Ma used many of the ideas she had picked up from Ratnadevi who had a real knack for making do.

But eventually Sonny had fallen in with a bad crowd and everything seemed to come apart. Now there was a new element in their struggle, one that caused Dadi-Ma a great deal of anxiety. As Sonny was jobless, there was not a penny coming in any more, yet all weekend long Sonny smoked dagga. Sometimes he drew the reefers through a broken bottleneck making himself so crazy that he'd end up running amok with a knife. At times like these Dadi-Ma and Chotoo had to hide from him until the effects of the dagga wore off.

Without means to pay the rent there was constant friction between himself and the landlord. Sonny, desperate and irritable, pleaded with the landlord until they reached a state of open hostility. The tenants were all drawn into this conflict, all except Dadi-Ma. She alone remained aloof and detached. Sitting on the concrete step in front of their room, she listened in silence to the two men arguing when the landlord came to collect the rent. Sonny's response was always wild and abusive. Although she was afraid that he would harm the landlord, she remained impassive.

The landlord, Mr. Naidoo, grew to resent the old woman.

He thought that her silence was a way of showing contempt for him. Who was she to judge him, a man of means and property? He often wondered as he drove off in his Mercedes why it was that she never said anything. What thoughts crossed her mind as she sat there, implacable as a stone Buddha? In the end he grew to hate the old woman.

Then one day the inevitable happened: Sonny got into a drunken brawl and stabbed someone. He was arrested, sentenced and thrown into jail. Mr. Naidoo saw his opportunity to evict the old woman, but he hesitated, fearing censure from the other tenants, some of whom had contributed to help Dadi-Ma with her rent. He knew, though, that this situation could not continue indefinitely. Those who had supported her were themselves experiencing difficulty. So he bided his time.

It happened that a few months later the old woman fell so far behind with her rent that the others could no longer assist her. Now at last Mr. Naidoo could exercise his rights; he gave Dadi-Ma her notice.

She was devastated. She had tried so hard to keep the roof over their heads. There was nothing for her to do now but pack their few possessions. They would have to move, but where to? she fretted. Dadi-Ma's concern was more for her grandson than for herself. She did not have many more years left, but what would happen to this boy who was only starting out in life?

"What took you so long, hey?" Dadi-Ma demanded, feigning severity when the boy finally joined her.

He shrugged, his hands thrust deep in his pockets, emulating the cockiness of the older boys who hung out in the alley. She tousled his hair and he sat down on the step beside her, pressing close to her side where he felt safe and secure.

For a time they sat like this in silence, the boy content with this closeness while his grandmother brooded about the past and the problems which were driving them into the unknown. Her mind moved slowly and ponderously, like an ox picking its way over the stones, lingering on the good times.

Lately her thoughts had started returning to those happy years—to Ratnadevi and Stanger. The two women had shared a friendship that went back a long way. They had arrived on the same boat from India to marry two indentured labourers on the sugarcane fields in Natal. They had lived in the same compound, as close as sisters, sharing in each other's joys and tragedies.

"Why you like the skollies?" the old woman asked the boy, adjusting the sari over her head. "They no good."

"Why you say that, Dadi-Ma?" he asked. His enormous brown eyes turned up to her questioningly.

He was so young, she thought, how could he understand that she wanted him to make something of his life? How could he understand that if he didn't try, this was all he had to look forward to?

"Because they bad. They smoke dagga. You best go to school so you can be something, hey?" she said in her broken English.

"We don't do nothing wrong, Dadi-Ma, we just sit out there bullshitting."

The old woman shook her head wearily.

"They say old man Naidoo going to throw us out. Where we going to go, Dadi-Ma?"

Dadi-Ma felt a deep attachment to her grandson. She had been drawn to him from the moment he was born. It had been Dadi-Ma who took care of him right from that first day, not his mother who was too tired and sickly to care. From Chotoo came the only warmth and caring that life still apportioned to her. All that the boy had known of love and tenderness came from her; not from his mother, whom he could not remember. It was a bond that neither had words for. The only expression Dadi-Ma ever gave her grandson of her feelings was a rare and awkward pat on his cheek, or the tousling of his hair with her arthritic fingers.

The boy, undernourished and small for his age, with eyes as large and expressive as hers had once been, was conscious of his grandmother's love. The others, like his parents, had deserted him. But not her. She was the fulcrum in his fragile existence.

"I was thinking, Chotoo, maybe you and me, we go to Stanger. It will be a good place for us. This place is no good," she muttered.

"Where is Stanger, Dadi-Ma?" he asked, his voice catching in breathless excitement.

"It's not so far away."

"How will we go . . . by car, by train?" he asked, in his shrill little voice.

She nodded, smiling down at him. "We go by train."

Dadi-Ma had saved some money for just such an emergency. The money, fifty rands, was what she had amassed in her long lifetime. Money that she had artfully secreted. Many times the money had gone for some other emergency but somehow she had always managed to replace it. Sometimes it had been slow to accumulate: money from the sale of a few pieces of gold jewellery brought with her from India, a few cents here and there from what she could scrimp out of the money Sonny had given her to buy food and clothes in the good old days when he still had a job.

These savings were all that stood between them and destitution now. The previous night she had removed the money from its hiding place beneath the linoleum under her bed, and in the dim light of the lamp she had counted it carefully, stacking the small coins in even piles, smoothing out the crumpled notes. Then she had returned it to the hiding place for safekeeping.

After a while Chotoo started fidgeting and wriggled out from under her arm.

"You don't tell nobody," Dadi-Ma warned him. "If old man Naidoo find out he make big trouble for us."

Chotoo nodded. Despite his age, he understood. "Can I go and play now, Dadi-Ma?"

"Ja, you go and play, but you remember what I tell you."

"I won't tell nobody, Dadi-Ma."

She nodded and he sauntered off to the side of the house

where the dagga smokers hung out. She watched him go, legs thin and scaly, the knobbly knees protruding just below his short trousers, his feet rough and thickened from going barefoot.

The tenement somehow always reminded Dadi-Ma of the quarters they had once occupied on the sugarcane plantation. There she and her husband had lived in a barracks with dozens of other workers, separated from the rest by paper-thin walls, or frayed curtains. In summer the windowless barracks were like ovens and then when the rains came it was like the monsoons in India, lasting for weeks and turning the compound into a quagmire.

Further north along the east coast was the town of Stanger where Ratnadevi had eventually moved after her husband died. His death had released Ratnadevi and her family from the contract which had bound them to the plantation. When Dadi-Ma's own husband had died and Sonny had run off to the city, Dadi-Ma had also moved to Stanger to live with Ratnadevi.

She remembered every detail so clearly. The wooden shack set back from the road amidst a clump of mango, banana and litchi trees. There had been an abundance of everything on that small piece of property; even the birds flocked to feed off the ripening fruit. It was indeed a wonderful sight and one that Dadi-Ma had cherished since that time.

She had never been happier than during those days with Ratnadevi in that old shack in Stanger. The two of them had managed by taking in laundry from the white people, most of whom were English-speaking. They also used to weave baskets which they sold in the local community, or peddled in the marketplace where Ratnadevi had a hawker's barrow.

The house was at the end of a gravel road. It was the last house on the street with a larger corner lot where parts of an old picket fence still stood. On windy nights they could hear the pickets clattering and rattling against each other. Each sound had its own particular significance and was like music to Dadi-Ma's ears. Some nights when it was very quiet she imagined she could hear the strains of a flute, the same poignant sounds made by Manu, the confectioner in her village in India, when he sat on the front step of his hut playing to the night.

From one of the big trees in the front yard hung a swing carved from an old tyre. There had been enough room for a large garden and the eggs produced by the hens were taken to the market each day. Dadi-Ma learnt a great deal about survival from the years she had spent there.

Then to interrupt this happiness, something unexpected had happened which irreversibly altered the tempo of her life. Sonny, who had married and moved to Port Elizabeth, sent for her. He was her son; her only son, how could she have refused him? Without the slightest hesitation, Dadi-Ma packed her few belongings and went to live with her son and Neela, her daughter-in-law. Neela, she found, was a frail and sickly girl who was unable to withstand the rigours of married life. Dadi-Ma took care of them all.

Several years went by and to Dadi-Ma's dismay her daughter-in-law, Neela, had still not produced a child. For reasons that Dadi-Ma did not understand the young girl could not carry a single pregnancy to its full term, miscarrying each after only four months.

It was a difficult life but Dadi-Ma never complained, even though she hated city life and constantly longed for Stanger and for Ratnadevi. The years passed and memories of those happy days began to dim. Eventually she stopped thinking about them. For fifteen years she lived with Sonny and his wife, taking care of them, and suffering constant abuse at the hands of Neela who grew resentful of her role in the house. Then one day, five years ago, Neela gave birth to Chotoo and it was as though Dadi-Ma had finally found fulfilment.

Now, ever since the landlord had given them notice, her thoughts returned again to that little house at the end of the road with the swing in the front yard. She could see the trees and hear the plank veranda and fence creaking in the wind.

Dadi-Ma remained on the step, dreaming. There was a stench of urine and human excrement in the air which came from a blocked sewer. They were accustomed to the stench which mingled with the rancid smell of old ghee and curry.

In a way Dadi-Ma was relieved that they were leaving. It was too difficult to raise a boy in this environment. He needed to run free, to breathe air unpolluted by smoke and odours of decay. Dadi-Ma's thoughts drifted back to the long low line of hills in the north, to mango and litchi trees laden with fruit. She remembered how she and Ratnadevi had sat out on the veranda, identifying the gaily coloured birds as they swooped down into the trees.

She and Ratnadevi had spent so much of their time in the backyard, doing the washing, kneading and scrubbing the heavy linen against the fluted surface of the washboard. In their spare time they sat beneath the tree, weaving baskets. Sometimes they chatted about their life in India, or life on the plantation; other times they worked in easy companionable silence.

Chotoo returned to his grandmother's side, wanting to know more about this place called Stanger. She was smiling to herself now as she thought of how she and Ratnadevi would once again sit out in the yard. She remembered the long washing line and the sputtering sizzle as Ratnadevi deftly spat against the iron. She remembered the smell of lye and freshly ironed laundry.

They could weave baskets again. As if following her thoughts her fingers, now stiff with age and arthritis, fell awkwardly into the familiar movements of weaving. The boy, seeing this, pressed closer to her side. She looked down upon him sombrely and drew his head against her chest. She began to talk to him of the life she had once known. The boy listened and with her words felt a new sense of adventure.

That night Dadi-Ma bundled together their few possessions. Her plan was to leave under cover of darkness since she did not have the money to pay the landlord the rent that was owing.

They caught the train for Durban early the next morning. For Chotoo the adventure had begun. Through most of the journey he was awake, his nose flattened against the window. In the second-class coach they shared their compartment with two other women, who chatted amiably with his grandmother while he remained at her side.

When they arrived in Durban, he grabbed a handful of his grandmother's sari, and hung on while she carried the bundle of belongings on her head. In the street outside the station they got into the bus for Stanger.

It was a long drive and they passed fields of sugarcane. Dadi-Ma pointed out many things to him, drawing his attention to this or to that. He stood against the seat, his nose once again pressed to the window, lurching against her as the bus bumped and swayed. They stopped often to offload passengers on the road and it was afternoon before they arrived at their destination.

Dadi-Ma became excited as they approached the town. She asked the woman across the aisle about the bus stop. The woman told her that the bus went all the way to the market. Dadi-Ma was pleased. She knew her way from there.

They entered the town and Dadi-Ma looked around for familiar landmarks, but things had changed. The market was no longer where she had remembered it to be. It had been moved to a new location. Dadi-Ma was puzzled. She spoke to the woman again, asking where the old market was, but the woman shrugged, saying she didn't know. She did not live here, only visited occasionally.

"Ask the woman over there," she said.

Dadi-Ma got up from her seat and Chotoo followed her, clutching the end of her sari. In her anxiety she was impatient with him. "Stay there," she snapped.

Chotoo's eyes grew large and mournful and she was sorry that she had spoken sharply. She touched his cheek and explained that she would be back in a moment, that she was merely going to speak to the woman over there, near the front of the bus. She told him to remain in the seat so that no one could take it.

Chotoo understood and hung back.

Dadi-Ma spoke to this other woman for several minutes. Chotoo watched her and sensed her unease.

"What is it, Dadi-Ma?" he asked when she returned.

"We will have to walk a long distance," she told him.

"Why?" he asked.

"So many questions!" she exclaimed. Then she said, "The marketplace where the bus stops is no longer where I thought it would be, they have moved it."

The boy did not say anything; he sensed in her a new anxiety that bewildered him.

When they got off the bus at the marketplace, the woman Dadi-Ma had talked to in the front of the bus asked why they wanted to get to that particular street.

"It is where my friend Ratnadevi lives," she said.

"Your friend lives there?" the woman asked, surprised.

"Yes, she has a small house with big trees."

The woman fell silent. Then she shrugged her shoulders. Perhaps this friend was a servant in one of the big houses out there, she concluded.

Dadi-Ma smiled and thanked the woman.

The woman repeated her instructions, telling them to go to the end of the wide road and then to turn to the left and continue on for five more streets to where there was a big store. At that point they were to turn right and walk for several blocks until they reached the area of big houses and mansions. There they were to turn right again to the street Dadi-Ma was enquiring about. "But there is no small house there like the one you have described," the woman said.

"From there I will know my way," Dadi-Ma assured her. She thanked the woman, hoisted the bundle on to her head, and waited for Chotoo to get a good grip on her sari. Then she left. Her feet in the old champals flip-flopped as she walked away. The other woman watched them going.

Dadi-Ma and Chotoo walked a long way that day, stopping often to rest. Chotoo was tired and dragged on her sari and she had to urge him on with quiet words of encouragement. She talked about the trees and the birds, nurturing the anticipation which lightened his step. At the end of the road, they stopped. She took down the bundle from her head and carefully unwrapped it. Packed amongst their belongings was a bottle of water. She handed it to Chotoo who took a long drink; then after taking a sip herself, she screwed the cap back on and returned the bundle to her head.

They turned left and continued on. She recognized some of the landmarks, her heart lurching excitedly as she pointed these out to the boy. Then they turned right and suddenly nothing seemed familiar any more.

Nevertheless they pressed on, following the woman's directions. They walked all the way to the end of the street in silence. On both sides of the street were large houses surrounded by walls and fences. The open field she remembered was no longer there. Her legs automatically propelled her forward. The pain that had racked her limbs through the past few days now gave way to fear which turned her legs to jelly.

They had made the last right turn and supposedly this was the street where she had once lived. Her dark eyes looked out upon an area that was unrecognizable. Slowly and wearily they made their way to the end of the street, but Ratnadevi's house was no longer there; neither were the trees and the groves of bamboo. She took the bundle from her head. The boy raised his eyes to look at her. In her face he saw the bewilderment.

Dadi-Ma was tired now, her legs could no longer hold her weight and she sat down on the kerb, drawing the boy down beside her.

"What's wrong, Dadi-Ma? Where is Ratnadevi's house?"

Dadi-Ma's fingers moved, weaving an invisible basket.

"Dadi-Ma?" he said in a small voice.

"Hush, Chotoo. Don't worry. We'll rest a bit and then we'll find Ratnadevi's house."

Chotoo drew close to his grandmother, resting his head on her lap for he was tired and sleepy.

The woman must have made a mistake, she thought. Ratnadevi's house was probably at the end of some other street and she would find it. A small house with a plank veranda and many trees with birds. Chotoo would be able to climb trees and pick fruit to his heart's content and sometimes he'd help them to pick bamboo for baskets.

A servant who had seen them sitting there came out of one of the houses. "Why are you sitting here?" she asked.

Dadi-Ma described the house she was searching for.

"Yes, I remember that one," the woman said. "The house was torn down a long time ago."

"What happened to the people who once lived here?" Dadi-Ma asked.

The woman shrugged and shook her head.

Dadi-Ma sat back; the pain that had nagged her all day, numbing her arms, suddenly swelled in her chest. The woman noticed the way Dadi-Ma's colour had changed.

"Are you all right, Auntie?" she asked.

Dadi-Ma compressed her lips and nodded. She did not want to alarm Chotoo. Did not want him to be afraid. She struggled to get up, the woman helping her to her feet.

But Chotoo saw the expression on his grandmother's face and for the first time in his life he felt insecure and uncertain about the future; felt a dreadful apprehension of being wrenched from the only human being he had ever loved.

"Dadi-Ma, Dadi-Ma," he sobbed.

"It's all right, Chotoo, it's all right."

But he knew that it wasn't all right, that it would never be all right again.

ALEX LA GUMA

Alex La Guma was born in District Six of Cape Town, South Africa, in 1925. His father was an important official in the Industrial and Commercial Workers' Union and the South African Communist Party. La Guma graduated from a technical school in 1945, and was fired from his job at the Metal Box Company after he had organized the workers to strike. He became involved with the Young Communist League in 1947 and the next year joined the South African Communist Party. It was not until 1957 that he published his first short story, "Nocturne." In 1966, he left South Africa and spent the remainder of his life in exile. Among his works are *A Walk in the Night and Other Stories* (1962), *The Stone-Country* (1967), *In the Fog of the Seasons' End* (1972), *A Soviet Journey* (1978), and *Time of the Butcherbird* (1979). In 1969 La Guma was awarded the Lotus Prize for his contributions to literature. He died in 1985.

The Lemon Orchard
(1967)

The men came down between two long, regular rows of trees. The winter had not passed completely and there was a chill in the air; and the moon was hidden behind long, high parallels of cloud which hung like suspended streamers of dirty cotton-wool in the sky. All of the men but one wore thick clothes against the coolness of the night. The night and earth was cold and damp, and the shoes of the men sank into the soil and left exact, ridged footprints, but they could not be seen in the dark.

One of the men walked ahead holding a small cycle lantern that worked from a battery, leading the way down the avenue of trees while the others came behind in the dark. The night close around was quiet now that the crickets had stopped their small noises, but far out others that did not feel the presence of the men continued the monotonous creek-creek-creek. Somewhere, even further, a dog started barking in short high yaps, and then stopped abruptly. The men were walking through an orchard of lemons and the sharp, bittersweet citrus smell hung gently on the night air.

"Do not go so fast," the man who brought up the rear of the party called to the man with the lantern. "It's as dark as a kaffir's soul here at the back."

He called softly, as if the darkness demanded silence. He was a big man and wore khaki trousers and laced-up riding boots, and an old shooting jacket with leather patches on the right breast and the elbows.

The shotgun was loaded. In the dark this man's face was invisible except for a blur of shadowed hollows and lighter crags. Although he walked in the rear he was the leader of the party. The lantern-bearer slowed down for the rest to catch up with him.

"It's cold, too, Oom," another man said.

"Cold?" the man with the shotgun asked, speaking with sarcasm. "Are you colder than this verdomte hotnot, here?" And he gestured in the dark with the muzzle of the gun at the man who stumbled along in their midst and who was the only one not warmly dressed.

This man wore trousers and a raincoat which they had allowed him to pull on over his pyjamas when they had taken him from his lodgings, and he shivered now with chill, clenching his teeth to prevent them from chattering. He had not been given time to tie his shoes and the metal-covered ends of the laces clicked as he moved.

"Are you cold, hotnot?" the man with the light jeered.

The colored man did not reply. He was afraid, but his

fear was mixed with a stubbornness which forbade him to answer them.

"He is not cold," the fifth man in the party said. "He is shivering with fear. Is it not so, hotnot?"

The colored man said nothing, but stared ahead of himself into the half-light made by the small lantern. He could see the silhouette of the man who carried the light, but he did not want to look at the two who flanked him, the one who had complained of the cold, and the one who had spoken of his fear. They each carried a sjambok and every now and then one of them slapped a corduroyed leg with his.

"He is dumb, also," the one who had spoken last chuckled.

"No, Andries. Wait a minute," the leader who carried the shotgun said, and they all stopped between the row of trees. The man with the lantern turned and put the light on the rest of the party.

"What is it?" he asked.

"Wag'n oomblikkie. Wait a moment," the leader said, speaking with forced casualness. "He is not dumb. He is a slim hotnot; one of those educated bushmen. Listen, hotnot," he addressed the colored man, speaking angrily now. "When a baas speaks to you, you answer him. Do you hear?" The colored man's wrists were tied behind him with a riem and the leader brought the muzzle of the shotgun down, pressing it hard into the small of the man's back above where the wrists met. "Do you hear, hotnot? Answer me or I will shoot a hole through your spine."

The bound man felt the hard round metal of the gun muzzle through the loose raincoat and clenched his teeth. He was cold and tried to prevent himself from shivering in case it should be mistaken for cowardice. He heard the small metallic noise as the man with the gun thumbed back the hammer of the shotgun. In spite of the cold, little drops of sweat began to form on his upper lip under the overnight stubble.

"For God's sake, don't shoot him," the man with the light said, laughing a little nervously. "We don't want to be involved in any murder."

"What are you saying, man?" the leader asked. Now with the beam of the battery-lamp on his face the shadows in it were washed away to reveal the mass of tiny wrinkled and deep creases which covered the red-clay complexion of his face like the myriad lines which indicate rivers, streams, roads and railways on a map. They wound around the ridges of his chin and climbed the sharp range of his nose and the peaks of his chin and cheekbones, and his eyes were hard and blue like two frozen lakes.

"This is mos a slim hotnot," he said again. "A teacher in a school for which we pay. He lives off our sweat, and he had the audacity to be cheeky and uncivilized towards a minister of our church and no hotnot will be cheeky to a white man while I live."

"Ja, man," the lantern-bearer agreed. "But we are going to deal with him. There is no necessity to shoot him. We don't want that kind of trouble."

"I will shoot whatever hotnot or kaffir I desire, and see me get into trouble over it. I demand respect from these donders. Let them answer when they're spoken to."

He jabbed the muzzle suddenly into the colored man's back so that he stumbled, struggling to keep his balance. "Do you hear, jong? Did I not speak to you?" The man who had jeered about the prisoner's fear stepped up then, and hit him in the face, striking him on a cheekbone with the clenched fist which still held the sjambok. He was angry over the delay and wanted the man to submit so that they could proceed. "Listen, you hotnot bastard," he said loudly. "Why don't you answer?"

The man stumbled, caught himself and stood in the rambling shadow of one of the lemon trees. The lantern-light swung on him and he looked away from the center of the beam. He was afraid the leader would shoot him in anger and he had no wish to die. He straightened up and looked away from them.

"Well?" demanded the man who had struck him.

"Yes, baas," the bound man said, speaking with a mixture of dignity and contempt which was missed by those who surrounded him.

"Yes there," the man with the light said. "You could save yourself trouble. Next time you will remember. Now let us get on." The lantern swung forward again and he walked ahead. The leader shoved their prisoner on with the muzzle of the shotgun, and he stumbled after the bobbing lantern with the other men on each side of him.

"The amazing thing about it is that this bliksem should have taken the principal, and the meester of the church before the magistrate and demand payment for the hiding they gave him for being cheeky to them," the leader said to all in general. "This verdomte hotnot. I have never heard of such a thing in all my born days."

"Well, we will give him a better hiding," the man Andries said. "This time we will teach him a lesson, Oom. He won't demand damages from anybody when we're done with him."

"And afterwards he won't be seen around here again. He will pack his things and go and live in the city where they're not so particular about the dignity of the volk. Do you hear, hotnot?" This time they were not concerned about receiving a reply but the leader went on, saying, "We don't want any educated hottentots in our town."

"Neither black Englishmen," added one of the others.

The dog started barking again at the farmhouse which was invisible on the dark hillside at the other end of the little valley. "It's that Jagter," the man with the lantern said. "I wonder what bothers him. He is a good watchdog. I offered Meneer Marais five pounds for that dog, but he won't sell. I would like to have a dog like that. I would take great care of such a dog."

The blackness of the night crouched over the orchard and the leaves rustled with a harsh whispering that was inconsistent with the pleasant scent of the lemons. The chill in the air had increased, and far-off the creek-creek-creek of the crickets blended into solid strips of high-pitched sound. Then the moon came from behind the banks of cloud and its white light touched the leaves with wet silver, and the perfume of lemons seemed to grow stronger, as if the juice was being crushed from them.

They walked a little way further in the moonlight and the man with the lantern said, "This is as good a place as any, Oom."

They had come into a wide gap in the orchard, a small amphitheater surrounded by fragrant growth, and they all stopped within it. The moonlight clung for a while to the leaves and the angled branches, so that along their tips and edges the moisture gleamed with the quivering shine of scattered quicksilver.

DORIS LESSING

Doris May Lessing was born on October 22, 1919, in Iran (then called Persia) to a British army captain and his wife. Lessing was schooled at Dominican Convent High School, but left at the age of fifteen to work as a maid. Encouraged by her employer, who gave her books about politics and sociology, she began writing. After two marriages and divorces, she moved to London, where she launched her writing career. Lessing is the author of many celebrated novels including *The Grass Is Singing* (1950), *The Golden Notebook* (1962), *The Summer Before Dark* (1973), *The Fifth Child* (1985), *The Sweetest Dream* (2001), *The Cleft* (2007), and *Alfred and Emily* (2008), as well as numerous short story collections. She is justly celebrated for her humanitarian concern regarding the plight of Africans living under oppressive regimes. In 2007 Lessing was awarded the Nobel Prize; she was the oldest recipient of the literature prize and the third oldest Nobel Laureate in any category.

The Second Hut[*]
(1951)

Before that season and his wife's illness, he had thought things could get no worse: until then, poverty had meant not to deviate further than the snapping point from what he had been brought up to think of as a normal life.

Being a farmer (he had come to it late in life, in his forties) was the first test he had faced as an individual. Before he had always been supported, invisibly perhaps, but none the less strongly, by what his family expected of him. He had been a regular soldier, not an unsuccessful one, but his success had been at the cost of a continual straining against his own inclinations; and he did not know himself what his inclinations were. Something stubbornly unconforming kept him apart from his fellow officers. It was an inward difference: he did not think of himself as a soldier. Even in his appearance, square, close-bitten, disciplined, there had been a hint of softness, or of strain, showing itself in his smile, which was too quick, like the smile of a deaf person afraid of showing incomprehension, and in the anxious look of his eyes. After he left the army he quickly slackened into an almost slovenly carelessness of dress and carriage. Now, in his farm clothes there was nothing left to suggest the soldier. With a loose, stained felt hat on the back of his head, khaki shorts a little too long and too wide, sleeves flapping over spare brown arms, his wispy moustache hiding a strained, set mouth, Major Carruthers looked what he was, a gentleman farmer going to seed.

The house had that brave, worn appearance of those struggling to keep up appearances. It was a four-roomed shack, its red roof dulling to streaky brown. It was the sort of house an apprentice farmer builds as a temporary shelter till he can afford better. Inside, good but battered furniture stood over worn places in the rugs; the piano was out of tune and the notes stuck; the silver tea things from the big narrow house in England where his brother (a lawyer) now lived were used as ornaments, and inside were bits of paper, accounts, rubber rings, old corks.

The room where his wife lay, in a greenish sun-lanced gloom, was a place of seedy misery. The doctor said it was her heart; and Major Carruthers knew this was true: she had broken down through heartbreak over the conditions they lived in. She did not want to get better. The harsh light from outside was shut out with dark blinds, and she turned her face to the wall and lay there, hour after hour, inert and uncomplaining, in a stoicism of defeat nothing could penetrate. Even the children hardly moved her. It was as if she had said to herself: "If I cannot have what I wanted for them, then I wash my hands of life."

Sometimes Major Carruthers thought of her as she had been, and was filled with uneasy wonder and with guilt. That pleasant conventional pretty English girl had been bred to make a perfect wife for the professional soldier she had imagined him to be, but chance had wrenched her on to this isolated African farm, into a life which she submitted herself to, as if it had nothing to do with her. For the first few years she had faced the struggle humorously, courageously: it was a sprightly attitude towards life, almost flirtatious, as a woman flirts lightly with a man who means nothing to her. As the house grew shabby, and the furniture, and her clothes could not be replaced; when she looked into the mirror and saw her drying, untidy hair and roughening face, she would give a quick high laugh and say, "Dear me, the things one comes to!" She was facing this poverty as she would have faced, in England, poverty of a narrowing, but socially accepted kind. What she could not face was a different kind of fear; and Major Carruthers understood that too well, for it was now his own fear.

The two children were pale, fine-drawn creatures, almost transparent-looking in their thin nervous fairness, with the defensive and wary manners of the young who have been brought up to expect a better way of life than they enjoy. Their anxious solicitude wore on Major Carruthers' already over-sensitised nerves. Children had no right to feel the aching pity which showed on their faces whenever they looked at him. They were too polite, too careful, too scrupulous. When they went into their mother's room she grieved sorrowfully over them, and they submitted patiently to her emotion. All those weeks of the school holidays after she was taken ill, they moved about the farm like two strained and anxious ghosts, and whenever he saw them his sense of guilt throbbed like a wound. He was glad they were going back to school soon, for then—so he thought—it would be easier to manage. It was an intolerable strain, running the farm and coming back to the neglected house and the problems of food and clothing, and a sick wife who would not get better until he could offer her hope.

But when they had gone back, he found that after all, things were not much easier. He slept little, for his wife needed attention in the night; and he became afraid for his own health, worrying over what he ate and wore. He learnt to treat himself as if his health was not what he was, what made him, but something apart, a commodity like efficiency, which could be estimated in terms of money at the end of a season. His health stood between them and complete ruin; and soon there were medicine bottles beside his bed as well as beside his wife's.

One day, while he was carefully measuring out tonics for himself in the bedroom, he glanced up and saw his wife's small reddened eyes staring incredulously but ironically at him over the bedclothes. "What are you doing?" she asked.

"I need a tonic," he explained awkwardly, afraid to worry her by explanations.

She laughed, for the first time in weeks; then the slack tears began welling under the lids, and she turned to the wall again.

He understood that some vision of himself had been destroyed, finally, for her. Now she was left with an ageing, rather fussy gentleman, carefully measuring medicine after meals. But he did not blame her; he never had blamed her; not even though he knew her illness was a failure of will. He patted her cheek uncomfortably, and said: "It wouldn't do for me to get run down, would it?" Then he adjusted the curtains over the windows to shut out a streak of dancing light that threatened to fall over her face, set a glass nearer to her hand, and went out to arrange for her tray of slops to be carried in.

Then he took, in one swift, painful movement, as if he

were leaping over an obstacle, the decision he had known for weeks he must take sooner or later. With a straightening of his shoulders, an echo from his soldier past, he took on the strain of an extra burden: he must get an assistant, whether he liked it or not.

So much did he shrink from any self-exposure, that he did not even consider advertising. He sent a note by native bearer to his neighbour, a few miles off, asking that it should be spread abroad that he was wanting help. He knew he would not have to wait long. It was 1931, in the middle of a slump, and there was unemployment, which was a rare thing for this new, sparsely-populated country.

He wrote the following to his two sons at boarding-school:

> I expect you will be surprised to hear I'm getting another man on the place. Things are getting a bit too much, and as I plan to plant a bigger acreage of maize this year, I thought it would need two of us. Your mother is better this week, on the whole, so I think things are looking up. She is looking forward to your next holidays, and asks me to say she will write soon. Between you and me, I don't think she's up to writing at the moment. It will soon be getting cold, I think, so if you need any clothes, let me know, and I'll see what I can do . . .

A week later, he sat on the little verandah, towards evening, smoking, when he saw a man coming through the trees on a bicycle. He watched him closely, already trying to form an estimate of his character by the tests he had used all his life: the width between the eyes, the shape of the skull, the way the legs were set on to the body. Although he had been taken in a dozen times, his belief in these methods never wavered. He was an easy prey for any trickster, lending money he never saw again, taken in by professional adventurers who (it seemed to him, measuring others by his own decency and the quick warmth he felt towards people) were the essence of gentlemen. He used to say that being a gentleman was a question of instinct: one could not mistake a gentleman.

As the visitor stepped off his bicycle and wheeled it to the verandah, Major Carruthers saw he was young, thirty perhaps, sturdily built, with enormous strength in the thick arms and shoulders. His skin was burnt a healthy orange-brown colour. His close hair, smooth as the fur of an animal, reflected no light. His obtuse, generous features were set in a round face, and the eyes were pale grey, nearly colourless.

Major Carruthers instinctively dropped his standards of value as he looked, for this man was an Afrikaner, and thus came into an outside category. It was not that he disliked him for it, although his father had been killed in the Boer War, but he had never had anything to do with the Afrikaans people before, and his knowledge of them was hearsay, from Englishmen who had the old prejudice. But he liked the look of the man: he liked the honest and straightforward face.

As for Van Heerden, he immediately recognised his traditional enemy, and his inherited dislike was strong. For a moment he appeared obstinate and wary. But they needed each other too badly to nurse old hatreds, and Van Heerden sat down when he was asked, though awkwardly, suppressing reluctance, and began drawing patterns in the dust with a piece of straw he had held between his lips.

Major Carruthers did not need to wonder about the man's circumstances: his quick acceptance of what were poor terms spoke of a long search for work.

He said scrupulously: "I know the salary is low and the living quarters are bad, even for a single man. I've had a patch of bad luck, and I can't afford more. I'll quite understand if you refuse."

"What are the living quarters?" asked Van Heerden. His was the rough voice of the uneducated Afrikaner: because he was uncertain where the accent should fall in each sentence, his speech had a wavering, halting sound, though his look and manner were direct enough.

Major Carruthers pointed ahead of them. Before the house the bush sloped gently down to the fields. "At the foot of the hill there's a hut I've been using as a storehouse. It's quite well-built. You can put up a place for a kitchen."

Van Heerden rose. "Can I see it?"

They set off. It was not far away. The thatched hut stood in uncleared bush. Grass grew to the walls and reached up to meet the slanting thatch. Trees mingled their branches overhead. It was round, built of poles and mud and with a stamped dung floor. Inside there was a stale musty smell because of the ants and beetles that had been at the sacks of grain. The one window was boarded over, and it was quite dark. In the confusing shafts of light from the door, a thick sheet of felted spider web showed itself, like a curtain halving the interior, as full of small flies and insects as a butcherbird's cache. The spider crouched, vast and glittering, shaking gently, glaring at them with small red eyes, from the centre of the web. Van Heerden did what Major Carruthers would have died rather than do: he tore the web across with his bare hands, crushed the spider between his fingers, and brushed them lightly against the walls to free them from the clinging silky strands and the sticky mush of insect-body.

"It will do fine," he announced.

He would not accept the invitation to a meal, thus making it clear this was merely a business arrangement. But he asked, politely (hating that he had to beg a favour), for a month's salary in advance. Then he set off on his bicycle to the store, ten miles off, to buy what he needed for his living.

Major Carruthers went back to his sick wife with a burdened feeling, caused by his being responsible for another human being having to suffer such conditions. He could not have the man in the house: the idea came into his head and was quickly dismissed. They had nothing in common, they would make each other uncomfortable—that was how he put it to himself. Besides, there wasn't really any room. Underneath, Major Carruthers knew that if his new assistant had been an Englishman, with the same upbringing, he would have found a corner in his house and a welcome as a friend. Major Carruthers threw off these thoughts: he had enough to worry him without taking on another man's problems.

A person who had always hated the business of organisation, which meant dividing responsibility with others, he found it hard to arrange with Van Heerden how the work was to be done. But as the Dutchman was good with cattle, Major Carruthers handed over all the stock on the farm to his care, thus relieving his mind of its most nagging care, for he was useless with beasts, and knew it. So they began, each knowing exactly where they stood. Van Heerden would make laconic reports at the end of each week, in the manner of an expert foreman reporting to a boss ignorant of technicalities—and Major Carruthers accepted this attitude, for he liked to respect people, and it was easy to respect Van Heerden's inspired instinct for animals.

For a few weeks Major Carruthers was almost happy. The fear of having to apply for another loan to his brother—worse, asking for the passage money to England and a job, thus justifying his family's belief in him as a failure—was pushed away; for while taking on a manager did not in itself improve things, it was an action, a decision, and there was nothing that he found more dismaying than decisions. The thought of his family in England, and particularly his elder brother, pricked him into slow burning passions of resentment. His brother's letters galled him so that he had grown to hate mail-days. They were crisp, affectionate letters, without condescension, but about money, bank-drafts, and insurance policies. Major Carruthers did not see life like that. He had not written to his brother for over a year. His wife, when she was well, wrote once a week, in the spirit of one propitiating fate.

Even she seemed cheered by the manager's coming; she sensed her husband's irrational lightness of spirit during that short time. She stirred herself to ask about the farm; and he began to see that her interest in living would revive quickly if her sort of life came within reach again.

But some two months after Van Heerden's coming, Major Carruthers was walking along the farm road towards his lands, when he was astonished to see, disappearing into the bushes, a small flaxen-haired boy. He called, but the child froze as an animal freezes, flattening himself against the foliage. At last, since he could get no reply, Major Carruthers approached the child, who dissolved backwards through the trees, and followed him up the path to the hut. He was very angry, for he knew what he would see.

He had not been to the hut since he handed it over to Van Heerden. Now there was a clearing, and amongst the stumps of trees and the flattened grass were half a dozen children, each as towheaded as the first, with that bleached sapless look common to white children in the tropics who have been subjected to too much sun.

A lean-to had been built against the hut. It was merely a roof of beaten petrol tins, patched together like cloth with wire and nails and supported on two unpeeled sticks. There, holding a cooking pot over an open fire that was dangerously close to the thatch, stood a vast slatternly woman. She reminded him of a sow among her litter, as she lifted her head, the children crowding about her, and stared at him suspiciously from pale and white-lashed eyes.

"Where is your husband?" he demanded.

She did not answer. Her suspicion deepened into a glare of hate: clearly she knew no English.

Striding furiously to the door of the hut, he saw that it was crowded with two enormous native-style beds: strips of hide stretched over wooden poles embedded in the mud of the floor. What was left of the space was heaped with the stained and broken belongings of the family. Major Carruthers strode off in search of Van Heerden. His anger was now mingled with the shamed discomfort of trying to imagine what it must be to live in such squalor.

Fear rose high in him. For a few moments he inhabited the landscape of his dreams, a grey country full of sucking menace, where he suffered what he would not allow himself to think of while awake: the grim poverty that could overtake him if his luck did not turn, and if he refused to submit to his brother and return to England.

Walking through the fields, where the maize was now waving over his head, pale gold with a froth of white, the sharp dead leaves scything crisply against the wind, he could see nothing but that black foetid hut and the pathetic futureless children. That was the lowest he could bring his own children to! He felt moorless, helpless, afraid: his sweat ran cold on him. And he did not hesitate in his mind; driven by fear and anger, he told himself to be hard; he was searching in his mind for the words with which he would dismiss the Dutchman who had brought his worst nightmares to life, on his own farm, in glaring daylight, where they were inescapable.

He found him with a screaming rearing young ox that was being broken to the plough, handling it with his sure understanding of animals. At a cautious distance stood the natives who were assisting; but Van Heerden, fearless and purposeful, was fighting the beast at close range. He saw Major Carruthers, let go the plunging horn he held, and the ox shot away backwards, roaring with anger, into the crowd of natives, who gathered loosely about it with sticks and stones to prevent it running away altogether.

Van Heerden stood still, wiping the sweat off his face, still grinning with the satisfaction of the fight, waiting for his employer to speak.

"Van Heerden," said Major Carruthers, without preliminaries, "why didn't you tell me you had a family?"

As he spoke the Dutchman's face changed, first flushing into guilt, then setting hard and stubborn. "Because I've been out of work for a year, and I knew you would not take me if I told you."

The two men faced each other, Major Carruthers tall, flyaway, shambling, bent with responsibility; Van Heerden stiff and defiant. The natives remained about the ox, to prevent its escape—for them this was a brief intermission in the real work of the farm—and their shouts mingled with the incessant bellowing. It was a hot day; Van Heerden wiped the sweat from his eyes with the back of his hand.

"You can't keep a wife and all those children here — how many children?"

"Nine."

Major Carruthers thought of his own two, and his perpetual dull ache of worry over them; and his heart became grieved for Van Heerden. Two children, with all the trouble over everything they ate and wore and thought, and what would become of them, were too great a burden; how did this man, with nine, manage to look so young?

"How old are you?" he asked abruptly, in a different tone.

"Thirty-four," said Van Heerden, suspiciously, unable to understand the direction Major Carruthers followed.

The only marks on his face were sun-creases; it was impossible to think of him as the father of nine children and the husband of that terrible broken-down woman. As Major Carruthers gazed at him, he became conscious of the strained lines on his own face, and tried to loosen himself, because he took so badly what this man bore so well.

"You can't keep a wife and children in such conditions."

"We were living in a tent in the bush on mealie meal and what I shot for nine months, and that was through the wet season," said Van Heerden drily.

Major Carruthers knew he was beaten. "You've put me in a false position, Van Heerden," he said angrily. "You know I can't afford to give you more money. I don't know where I'm going to find my own children's school fees, as it is. I told you the position when you came. I can't afford to keep a man with such a family."

"Nobody can afford to have me either," said Van Heerden sullenly.

"How can I have you living on my place in such a fashion? Nine children! They should be at school. Didn't you know there is a law to make them go to school! Hasn't anybody been to see you about them?"

"They haven't got me yet. They won't get me unless someone tells them."

Against this challenge, which was also an unwilling appeal, Major Carruthers remained silent, until he said brusquely: "Remember, I'm not responsible." And he walked off, with all the appearance of anger.

Van Heerden looked after him, his face puzzled. He did not know whether or not he had been dismissed. After a few moments he moistened his dry lips with his tongue, wiped his hand again over his eyes, and turned back to the ox. Looking over his shoulder from the edge of the field, Major Carruthers could see his wiry, stocky figure leaping and bending about the ox whose bellowing made the whole farm ring with anger.

Major Carruthers decided, once and for all, to put the family out of his mind. But they haunted him; he even dreamed of them; and he could not determine whether it was his own or the Dutchman's children who filled his sleep with fear.

It was a very busy time of the year. Harassed, like all his fellow-farmers, by labour difficulties, apportioning out the farm tasks was a daily problem. All day his mind churned slowly over the necessities: this fencing was urgent, that field must be reaped at once. Yet, in spite of this, he decided it was his plain duty to build a second hut beside the first. It would do no more than take the edge off the discomfort of that miserable family, but he knew he could not rest until it was built.

Just as he had made up his mind and was wondering how the thing could be managed, the boss-boy came to him, saying that unless the Dutchman went, he and his friends would leave the farm.

"Why?" asked Major Carruthers, knowing what the answer would be. Van Heerden was a hard worker, and the cattle were improving week by week under his care, but he could not handle natives. He shouted at them, lost his temper, treated them like dogs. There was continual friction.

"Dutchmen are no good," said the boss-boy simply, voicing the hatred of the black man for that section of the white people he considers his most brutal oppressors.

Now, Major Carruthers was proud that at a time when

most farmers were forced to buy labour from the contractors, he was able to attract sufficient voluntary labour to run his farm. He was a good employer, proud of his reputation for fair dealing. Many of his natives had been with him for years, taking a few months off occasionally for a rest in their kraals, but always returning to him. His neighbours were complaining of the sullen attitude of their labourers: so far Major Carruthers had kept this side of that form of passive resistance which could ruin a farmer. It was walking on a knife-edge, but his simple human relationship with his workers was his greatest asset as a farmer, and he knew it.

He stood and thought, while his boss-boy, who had been on this farm twelve years, waited for a reply. A great deal was at stake. For a moment Major Carruthers thought of dismissing the Dutchman; he realized he could not bring himself to do it: what would happen to all those children? He decided on a course which was repugnant to him. He was going to appeal to his employee's pity.

"I have always treated you square?" he asked. "I've always helped you when you were in trouble?"

The boss-boy immediately and warmly assented.

"You know that my wife is ill, and that I'm having a lot of trouble just now? I don't want the Dutchman to go, just now when the work is so heavy. I'll speak to him, and if there is any more trouble with the men, then come to me and I'll deal with it myself."

It was a glittering blue day, with a chill edge on the air, that stirred Major Carruthers' thin blood as he stood, looking in appeal into the sullen face of the native. All at once, feeling the fresh air wash along his cheeks, watching the leaves shake with a ripple of gold on the trees down the slope, he felt superior to his difficulties, and able to face anything. "Come," he said, with his rare, diffident smile. "After all these years, when we have been working together for so long, surely you can do this for me. It won't be for very long."

He watched the man's face soften in response to his own; and wondered at the unconscious use of the last phrase, for there was no reason, on the face of things, why the situation should not continue as it was for a very long time.

They began laughing together and separated cheerfully, the African shaking his head ruefully over the magnitude of the sacrifice asked of him, thus making the incident into a joke; and he dived off into the bush to explain the position to his fellow-workers.

Repressing a strong desire to go after him, to spend the lovely fresh day walking for pleasure, Major Carruthers went into his wife's bedroom, inexplicably confident and walking like a young man.

She lay as always, face to the wall, her protruding shoulders visible beneath the cheap pink bed-jacket he had bought for her illness. She seemed neither better nor worse. But as she turned her head, his buoyancy infected her a little; perhaps, too, she was conscious of the exhilarating day outside her gloomy curtains.

What kind of a miraculous release was she waiting for? he wondered, as he delicately adjusted her sheets and pillows and laid his hand gently on her head. Over the bony cage of the skull, the skin was papery and blueish. What was she thinking? He had a vision of her brain as a small frightened animal pulsating under his fingers.

With her eyes still closed, she asked in her querulous thin voice: "Why don't you write to George?"

Involuntarily his fingers contracted on her hair, causing her to start and to open her reproachful, red-rimmed eyes. He waited for her usual appeal: the children, my health, our future. But she sighed and remained silent, still loyal to the man she had imagined she was marrying; and he could feel her thinking: *the lunatic stiff pride of men.*

Understanding that for her it was merely a question of waiting for his defeat, as her deliverance, he withdrew his hand, in dislike of her, saying: "Things are not as bad as that yet." The cheerfulness of his voice was genuine, holding still the courage and hope instilled into him by the bright day outside.

"Why, what has happened?" she asked swiftly, her voice suddenly strong, looking at him in hope.

"Nothing," he said; and the depression settled down over him again. Indeed, nothing had happened; and his confidence was a trick of the nerves. Soberly he left the bedroom, thinking: I must get that well built; and when that is done, I must do the drains, and then . . . He was thinking, too, that all these things must wait for the second hut.

Oddly, the comparatively small problem of that hut occupied his mind during the next few days. A slow and careful man, he set milestones for himself and overtook them one by one.

Since Christmas the labourers had been working a seven-day week, in order to keep ahead in the race against the weeds. They resented it, of course, but that was the custom. Now that the maize was grown, they expected work to slack off; they expected their Sundays to be restored to them. To ask even half a dozen of them to sacrifice their weekly holiday for the sake of the hated Dutchman might precipitate a crisis. Major Carruthers took his time, stalking his opportunity like a hunter, until one evening he was talking with his boss-boy as man to man, about farm problems; but when he broached the subject of a hut, Major Carruthers saw that it would be as he feared: the man at once turned stiff and unhelpful. Suddenly impatient, he said: "It must be done next Sunday. Six men could finish it in a day, if they worked hard."

The black man's glance became veiled and hostile. Responding to the authority in the voice he replied simply: "Yes, baas." He was accepting the order from above, and refusing responsibility: his cooperation was switched off; he had become a machine for transmitting orders. Nothing exasperated Major Carruthers more than when this happened. He said sternly: "I'm not having any nonsense. If that hut isn't built, there'll be trouble."

"Yes, baas," said the boss-boy again. He walked away, stopped some natives who were coming off the fields with their hoes over their shoulders, and transmitted the order in a neutral voice. Major Carruthers saw them glance at him in fierce antagonism; then they turned away their heads, and walked off, in a group, towards their compound.

It would be all right, he thought, in disproportionate relief. It would be difficult to say exactly what it was he feared, for the question of the hut had loomed so huge in his mind that he was beginning to feel an almost superstitious foreboding. Driven downwards through failure after failure, fate was becoming real to him as a cold malignant force; the careful balancing of unfriendly probabilities that underlay all his planning had developed in him an acute sensitivity to the future; and he had learned to respect his dreams and omens. Now he wondered at the strength of his desire to see that hut built, and whatever danger it represented behind him.

He went to the clearing to find Van Heerden and tell him what had been planned. He found him sitting on a candle-box in the doorway of the hut, playing good-humouredly with his children, as if they had been puppies, tumbling them over, snapping his fingers in their faces, and laughing outright with boyish exuberance when one little boy squared up his fists at him in a moment of temper against this casual, almost contemptuous treatment of them. Major Carruthers heard that boyish laugh with amazement; he looked blankly at the young Dutchman, and then from him to his wife, who was standing, as usual, over a petrol tin that balanced on the small fire. A smell of meat and pumpkin filled the clearing. The woman seemed to Major Carruthers less a human being than the expression of an elemental, irrepressible force: he saw her, in her vast sagging fleshiness, with her slow stupid face, her instinctive responses to her children, whether for affection or temper, as the symbol of fecundity, a strong, irresistible heave of matter. She frightened him. He turned his eyes from her and explained to Van Heerden that a second hut would be built here, beside the existing one.

Van Heerden was pleased. He softened into quick confiding friendship. He looked doubtfully behind him at the small hut that sheltered eleven human beings, and said that it was really not easy to live in such a small space with so many children. He glanced at the children, cuffing them affectionately as he spoke, smiling like a boy. He was proud of his family, of his own capacity for making children: Major Carruthers could see that. Almost, he smiled; then he glanced through the doorway at the grey squalor of the interior and hurried off, resolutely preventing himself from dwelling on the repulsive facts that such close-packed living implied.

The next Saturday evening he and Van Heerden paced the clearing with tape measure and spirit level, determining the area of the new hut. It was to be a large one. Already the sheaves of thatching grass had been stacked ready for next day, shining brassily in the evening sun; and the thorn poles for the walls lay about the clearing, stripped of bark, the smooth inner wood showing white as kernels.

Major Carruthers was waiting for the natives to come up from the compound for the building before daybreak that Sunday. He was there even before the family woke, afraid that without his presence something might go wrong. He feared the Dutchman's temper because of the labourers' sulky mood.

He leaned against a tree, watching the bush come awake, while the sky flooded slowly with light, and the birds sang about him. The hut was, for a long time, silent and dark. A sack hung crookedly over the door, and he could glimpse huddled shapes within. It seemed to him horrible, a stinking kennel shrinking ashamedly to the ground away from the wide hall of fresh blue sky. Then a child came out, and another; soon they were spilling out of the doorway, in their little rags of dresses, or hitching khaki pants up over the bony jut of a hip. They smiled shyly at him, offering him friendship. Then came the woman, moving sideways to ease herself through the narrow doorframe—she was so huge it was almost a fit. She lumbered slowly, thick and stupid with sleep, over to the cold fire, raising her arms in a yawn, so that wisps of dull yellow hair fell over her shoulders and her dark slack dress lifted in creases under her neck. Then she saw Major Carruthers and smiled at him. For the first time he saw her as a human being and not as something fatally ugly. There was something shy, yet frank, in that smile; so that he could imagine the strong, laughing adolescent girl, with the frank, inviting, healthy sensuality of the young Dutchwoman—so she had been when she married Van Heerden. She stooped painfully to stir up the ashes, and soon the fire spurted up under the leaning patch of tin roof. For a while Van Heerden did not appear; neither did the natives who were supposed to be here a long while since; Major Carruthers continued to lean against a tree, smiling at the children, who nevertheless kept their distance from him, unable to play naturally because of his presence there, smiling at Mrs. Van Heerden who was throwing handfuls of mealie meal into a petrol tin of boiling water, to make native-style porridge.

It was just on eight o'clock, after two hours of impatient waiting, that the labourers filed up the bushy incline, with the axes and picks over their shoulders, avoiding his eyes. He pressed down his anger: after all it was Sunday, and they had had no day off for weeks; he could not blame them.

They began by digging the circular trench that would hold the wall poles. As their picks rang out on the pebbly ground, Van Heerden came out of the hut, pushing aside the dangling sack with one hand and pulling up his trousers with the other, yawning broadly, then smiling at Major Carruthers apologetically. "I've had my sleep out," he said; he seemed to think his employer might be angry.

Major Carruthers stood close over the workers, wanting it to be understood by them and by Van Heerden that he was responsible. He was too conscious of their resentment, and knew that they would scamp the work if possible. If the hut was to be completed as planned, he would need all his tact and good humour. He stood there patiently all morning, watching the thin sparks flash up as the picks swung into the flinty earth. Van Heerden lingered nearby, unwilling to be thus publicly superseded in the responsibility for his own dwelling in the eyes of the natives.

When they flung their picks and went to fetch the poles, they did so with a side glance at Major Carruthers, challenging him to say the trench was not deep enough. He called them back, laughingly, saying: "Are you digging for a dog-kennel then, and not a hut for a man?" One smiled unwillingly in response; the others sulked. Perfunctorily they deepened the trench to the very minimum that Major Carruthers was likely to pass. By noon, the poles were leaning drunkenly in place, and the natives were stripping the binding from beneath the bark of nearby trees. Long fleshy strips of fibre, rose-coloured and apricot and yellow, lay tangled over the grass, and the wounded trees showed startling red gashes around the clearing. Swiftly the poles were laced together with this natural rope, so that when the frame was complete it showed up against green trees and sky like a slender gleaming white cage, interwoven lightly with rosy-yellow. Two natives climbed on top to bind the roof poles into their conical shape, while the others stamped a slushy mound of sand and earth to form plaster for the walls. Soon they stopped—the rest could wait until after the midday break.

Worn out by the strain of keeping the balance between the fiery Dutchman and the resentful workers, Major Carruthers went off home to eat. He had one and a half hour's break. He finished his meal in ten minutes, longing to be able to sleep for once till he woke naturally. His wife was dozing, so he lay down on the other bed and at once dropped off to sleep himself. When he woke it was long after the time he had set himself. It was after three. He rose in a panic and strode to the clearing, in the grip of one of his premonitions.

There stood the Dutchman, in a flaring temper, shouting at the natives who lounged in front of him, laughing openly. They had only just returned to work. As Major Carruthers approached, he saw Van Heerden using his open palms in a series of quick swinging slaps against their faces, knocking them sideways against each other: it was as if he were cuffing his own children in a fit of anger. Major Carruthers broke into a run, erupting into the group before anything else could happen. Van Heerden fell back on seeing him. He was beef-red with fury. The natives were bunched together, on the point of throwing down their tools and walking off the job.

"Get back to work," snapped Major Carruthers to the men: and to Van Heerden: "I'm dealing with this." His eyes were an appeal to recognise the need for tact, but Van Heerden stood squarely there in front of him, on planted legs, breathing heavily. "But Major Carruthers . . ." he began, implying that as a white man, with his employer not there, it was right that he should take the command. "Do as I say," said Major Carruthers. Van Heerden, with a deadly look at his opponents, swung on his heel and marched off into the hut. The slapping swing of the grain-bag was as if a door had been slammed. Major Carruthers turned to the natives. "Get on," he ordered briefly, in a calm decisive voice. There was a moment of uncertainty. Then they picked up their tools and went to work.

Some laced the framework of the roof; others slapped the mud on to the walls. This business of plastering was usually a festival, with laughter and raillery, for there were gaps between the poles, and a handful of mud could fly through a space into the face of a man standing behind: the thing could become a game, like children playing snowballs. Today there was no pretence at good humour. When the sun went down the men picked up their tools and filed off into the bush without a glance at Major Carruthers. The work had not prospered. The grass was laid untidily over the roof-frame, still uncut and reaching to the ground in long swatches. The first layer of mud had been unevenly flung on. It would be a shabby building.

"His own fault," thought Major Carruthers, sending his slow, tired blue glance to the hut where the Dutchman was still cherishing the seeds of wounded pride. Next day, when Major Carruthers was in another part of the farm, the Dutchman got his own back in a fine flaming scene with the ploughboys: they came to complain to the boss-boy, but not to Major Carruthers. This made him uneasy. All that week he waited for fresh complaints about the Dutchman's behaviour. So much was he keyed up, waiting for the scene between himself and a grudging boss-boy, that when nothing happened his apprehensions deepened into a deep foreboding.

The building was finished the following Sunday. The floors were stamped hard with new dung, the thatch trimmed, and the walls grained smooth. Another two weeks must elapse before the family could move in, for the place smelled of damp. They were weeks of worry for Major Carruthers. It was unnatural for the Africans to remain passive and sullen under the Dutchman's handling of them, and especially when they knew he was on their side. There was something he did not like in the way they would not meet his eyes and in the over-polite attitude of the boss-boy.

The beautiful clear weather that he usually loved so much, May weather, sharpened by cold, and crisp under deep clear skies, pungent with gusts of wind from the dying leaves and grasses of the veld, was spoilt for him this year: something was going to happen.

When the family eventually moved in, Major Carruthers became discouraged because the building of the hut had represented such trouble and worry, while now things seemed hardly better than before: what was the use of two small round huts for a family of eleven? But Van Heerden was very pleased, and expressed his gratitude in a way that moved Major Carruthers deeply: unable to show feeling himself, he was grateful when others did, so relieving him of the burden of his shyness. There was a ceremonial atmosphere on the evening when one of the great sagging beds was wrenched out of the floor of the first hut and its legs plastered down newly into the second hut.

That very same night he was awakened towards dawn by voices calling to him from outside his window. He started up, knowing that whatever he had dreaded was here, glad that the tension was over. Outside the back door stood his boss-boy, holding a hurricane lamp which momentarily blinded Major Carruthers.

"The hut is on fire."

Blinking his eyes, he turned to look. Away in the darkness flames were lapping over the trees, outlining branches so that as a gust of wind lifted them patterns of black leaves showed clear and fine against the flowing red light of the fire. The veld was illuminated with a fitful plunging glare. The two men ran off into the bush down the rough road, towards the blaze.

The clearing was lit up, as bright as morning, when they arrived. On the roof of the first hut squatted Van Heerden, lifting tins of water from a line of natives below, working from the water-butt, soaking the thatch to prevent it catching the flames from the second hut that was only a few yards off. That was a roaring pillar of fire. Its frail skeleton was still erect, but twisting and writhing incandescently within its envelope of flame, and it collapsed slowly as he came up, subsiding in a crash of sparks.

"The children," gasped Major Carruthers to Mrs. Van Heerden, who was watching the blaze fatalistically from where she sat on a scattered bundle of bedding, the tears soaking down her face, her arms tight round a swathed child.

As she spoke she opened the cloths to display the smallest infant. A swathe of burning grass from the roof had fallen across its head and shoulders. He sickened as he looked, for there was nothing but raw charred flesh. But it was alive: the limbs still twitched a little.

"I'll get the car and we'll take it in to the doctor."

He ran out of the clearing and fetched the car. As he tore down the slope back again he saw he was still in his pyjamas, and when he gained the clearing for the second time, Van Heerden was climbing down the roof, which dripped water as if there had been a storm. He bent over the burnt child.

"Too late," he said.

"But it's still alive."

Van Heerden almost shrugged; he appeared dazed. He continually turned his head to survey the glowing heap that had so recently sheltered his children. He licked his lips with a quick unconscious movement, because of their burning dryness. His face was grimed with smoke and inflamed from the great heat, so that his young eyes showed startlingly clear against the black skin.

"Get into the car," said Major Carruthers to the woman. She automatically moved towards the car, without looking at her husband, who said: "But it's too late, man."

Major Carruthers knew the child would die, but his protest against the waste and futility of the burning expressed itself in this way: that everything must be done to save this life, even against hope. He started the car and slid off down the hill. Before they had gone half a mile he felt his shoulder plucked from behind, and, turning, saw the child was now dead. He reversed the car into the dark bush off the road, and drove back to the clearing. Now the woman had begun wailing, a soft monotonous, almost automatic sound that kept him tight in his seat, waiting for the next cry.

The fire was now a dark heap, fanning softly to a glowing red as the wind passed over it. The children were standing in a half-circle, gazing fascinated at it. Van Heerden stood near them, laying his hands gently, restlessly, on their heads and shoulders, reassuring himself of their existence there, in the flesh and living, beside him.

Mrs. Van Heerden got clumsily out of the car, still wailing, and disappeared into the hut, clutching the bundled dead child.

Feeling out of place among that bereaved family, Major Carruthers went up to his house, where he drank cup after cup of tea, holding himself tight and controlled, conscious of over-strained nerves.

Then he stooped into his wife's room, which seemed small and dark and airless. The cave of a sick animal, he thought, in disgust; then, ashamed of himself, he returned out of doors, where the sky was filling with light. He sent a message for the boss-boy, and waited for him in a condition of tensed anger.

When the man came Major Carruthers asked immediately: "Why did that hut burn?"

The boss-boy looked at him straight and said: "How should I know?" Then, after a pause, with guileful innocence: "It was the fault of the kitchen, too close to the thatch."

Major Carruthers glared at him, trying to wear down the straight gaze with his own accusing eyes.

"That hut must be rebuilt at once. It must be rebuilt today."

The boss-boy seemed to say that it was a matter of indifference to him whether it was rebuilt or not. "I'll go and tell the others," he said, moving off.

"Stop," barked Major Carruthers. Then he paused, frightened, not so much at his rage, but his humiliation and guilt. He had foreseen it! He had foreseen it all! And yet, that thatch could so easily have caught alight from the small incautious fire that sent up sparks all day so close to it.

Almost, he burst out in wild reproaches. Then he pulled himself together and said: "Get away from me." What was the use? He knew perfectly well that one of the Africans whom Van Heerden had kicked or slapped or shouted at had fired that hut; no one could ever prove it.

He stood quite still, watching his boss-boy move off, tugging at the long wisps of his moustache in frustrated anger.

And what would happen now?

He ordered breakfast, drank a cup of tea, and spoilt a piece of toast. Then he glanced in again at his wife, who would sleep for a couple of hours yet.

Again tugging fretfully at his moustache, Major Carruthers set off for the clearing.

Everything was just as it had been, though the pile of black débris looked low and shabby now that morning had come and heightened the wild colour of sky and bush. The children were playing nearby, their hands and faces black, their rags of clothing black—everything seemed patched and smudged with black, and on one side the trees hung withered and grimy and the soil was hot underfoot.

Van Heerden leaned against the framework of the first hut. He looked subdued and tired, but otherwise normal. He greeted Major Carruthers, and did not move.

"How is your wife?" asked Major Carruthers. He could hear a moaning sound from inside the hut.

"She's doing well."

Major Carruthers imagined her weeping over the dead child, and said: "I'll take your baby into town for you and arrange for the funeral."

Van Heerden said: "I've buried her already." He jerked his thumb at the bush behind them.

"Didn't you register its birth?"

Van Heerden shook his head. His gaze challenged Major Carruthers as if to say: Who's to know if no one tells them? Major Carruthers could not speak: he was held in silence by the thought of that charred little body, huddled into a packing-case or wrapped in a piece of cloth, thrust into the ground, at the mercy of wild animals or of white ants.

"Well, one comes and another goes," said Van Heerden at last, slowly, reaching out for philosophy as a comfort, while his eyes filled with rough tears.

Major Carruthers stared: he could not understand. At last the meaning of the words came into him, and he heard the moaning from the hut with a new understanding.

The idea had never entered his head; it had been a complete failure of the imagination. If nine children, why not ten? Why not fifteen, for that matter, or twenty? Of course there would be more children.

"It was the shock," said Van Heerden. "It should be next month."

Major Carruthers leaned back against the wall of the hut and took out a cigarette clumsily. He felt weak. He felt as if Van Heerden had struck him, smiling. This was an absurd and unjust feeling, but for a moment he hated Van Heerden for standing there and saying: this grey country of poverty that you fear so much will take on a different look when you actually enter it. You will cease to exist; there is no energy left, when one is wrestling naked, with life, for your kind of fine feelings and scruples and regrets.

"We hope it will be a boy," volunteered Van Heerden, with a tentative friendliness, as if he thought it might be considered a familiarity to offer his private notions to Major Carruthers. "We have five boys and four girls—three girls," he corrected himself, his face contracting.

Major Carruthers asked stiffly: "Will she be all right?"

"I do it," said Van Heerden. "The last was born in the middle of the night, when it was raining. That was when we were in the tent. It's nothing to her," he added, with pride. He was listening, as he spoke, to the slow moaning from inside. "I'd better be getting in to her," he said, knocking out his pipe against the mud of the walls. Nodding to Major Carruthers, he lifted the sack and disappeared.

After a while Major Carruthers gathered himself together and forced himself to walk erect across the clearing under the curious gaze of the children. His mind was fixed and numb, but he walked as if moving to a destination. When he reached the house, he at once pulled paper and pen towards him and wrote, and each slow difficult word was a nail in the coffin of his pride as a man.

Some minutes later he went in to his wife. She was awake, turned on her side, watching the door for the relief of his coming. "I've written for a job at Home," he said simply, laying his hand on her thin dry wrist, and feeling the slow pulse beat up suddenly against his palm.

He watched curiously as her face crumpled and the tears of thankfulness and release ran slowly down her cheeks and soaked the pillow.

Es'kia Mphahlele

Ezekial Mphahlele (he later Africanized his first name) was born in 1919 in Marabastad, Pretoria, South Africa, and received his BA and MA in English literature from the University of South Africa. He was teaching high school when his first book of short stories, *Man Must Live,* was published in 1947. When he was barred from teaching for his anti-apartheid activities, he worked in clerical positions in order to provide for his family. Eventually he was able to obtain a position as a political reporter, sub-editor, and fiction editor for the magazine *Drum.* In 1957, he went to Nigeria to teach and then to Kenya as the director of the Chemchemi Cultural Centre. After stints in Zambia and France, he earned a doctorate from the University of Denver and thereafter taught at the University of Pennsylvania. Finally, in 1977, he returned to South Africa and took a position at the University of Witwatersrand, where he was the first black professor. Mphahlele is the author of a wide range of nonfiction and fiction, including *The African Image* (1962), *Voices in the Whirlwind and Other Essays* (1972), "ES'KIA" (2002) and "ES'KIA Continued" (2004), and the novels *The Wanderers* (1969), *Chirundu* (1970), and *Father Come Home* (1984). He also wrote two acclaimed memoirs, *Down Second Avenue* (1959) and *Afrika My Music* (1984), and numerous short stories. He died in 2008.

Mrs. Plum
(1967)

I

My madam's name was Mrs. Plum. She loved dogs and Africans and said that everyone must follow the law even if it hurt. These were three big things in Madam's life.

I came to work for Mrs. Plum in Greenside, not very far from the center of Johannesburg, after leaving two white families. The first white people I worked for as a cook and laundry woman were a man and his wife in Parktown North. They drank too much and always forgot to pay me. After five months I said to myself No. I am going to leave these drunks. So that was it. That day I was as angry as a red-hot iron when it meets water. The second house I cooked and washed for had five children who were badly brought up. This was in Belgravia. Many times they called me You Black Girl and I kept quiet. Because their mother heard them and said nothing. Also I was only new from Phokeng my home, far away near Rustenburg. I wanted to learn and know the white people before I knew how far to go with the others I would work for afterwards. The thing that drove me mad and made me pack and go was a man who came to visit them often. They said he was cousin or something like that. He came to the kitchen many times and tried to make me laugh. He patted me on the buttocks. I told the master. The man did it again and I asked the madam that very day to give me my money and let me go.

These were the first nine months after I had left Phokeng to work in Johannesburg. There were many of us girls and young women from Phokeng, from Zeerust, from Shuping, from Kosten, and many other places who came to work in the cities. So the suburbs were full of blackness. Most of us had already passed Standard Six and so we learned more English where we worked. None of us likes to

work for white farmers, because we know too much about
them on the farms near our homes. They do not pay well
and they are cruel people.

At Easter time so many of us went home for a long
weekend to see our people and to eat chicken and sour
milk and *morogo*—wild spinach. We also took home sugar
and condensed milk and tea and coffee and sweets and cus-
tard powder and tinned foods.

It was a home-girl of mine, Chimane, who called me to
take a job in Mrs. Plum's house, just next door to where she
worked. This is the third year now. I have been quite happy
with Mrs. Plum and her daughter Kate. By this I mean that
my place as a servant in Greenside is not as bad as that of
many others. Chimane too does not complain much. We are
paid six pounds a month with free food and free servant's
room. No one can ever say that they are well paid, so we go
on complaining somehow. Whenever we meet on Thursday
afternoons, which is time off for all of us black women in the
suburbs, we talk and talk and talk: about our people at home
and their letters; about their illnesses; about bad crops; about
a sister who wanted a school uniform and books and school
fees; about some of our madams and masters who are good,
or stingy with money or food, or stupid or full of nonsense,
or who kill themselves and each other, or who are dirty—
and so many things I cannot count them all.

Thursday afternoons we go to town to look at the shops,
to attend a woman's club, to see our boyfriends, to go to
bioscope some of us. We turn up smart, to show others the
clothes we bought from the black men who sell soft goods
to servants in the suburbs. We take a number of things and
they come round every month for a bit of money until we
finish paying. Then we dress the way of many white madams and girls. I think we look really smart. Sometimes we
catch the eyes of a white woman looking at us and we laugh
and laugh until we nearly drop on the ground because we
feel good inside ourselves.

II

What did the girl next door call you? Mrs. Plum asked me the first day I came to her. Jane, I replied. Was there not an African name? I said yes, Karabo. All right, Madam said. We'll call you Karabo, she said. She spoke as if she knew a name is a big thing. I knew so many whites who did not care what they called black people as long as it was all right for their tongue. This pleased me, I mean Mrs. Plum's use of *Karabo;* because the only time I heard the name was when I was home or when my friends spoke to me. Then she showed me what to do: meals, mealtimes, washing, and where all the things were that I was going to use.

My daughter will be here in the evening, Madam said. She is at school. When the daughter came, she added, she would tell me some of the things she wanted me to do for her every day.

Chimane, my friend next door, had told me about the daughter Kate, how wild she seemed to be, and about Mr. Plum who had killed himself with a gun in a house down the street. They had left the house and come to this one.

Madam is a tall woman. Not slender, not fat. She moves slowly, and speaks slowly. Her face looks very wise, her forehead seems to tell me she has a strong liver: she is not afraid of anything. Her eyes are always swollen at the lower eyelids like a white person who has not slept for many many nights or like a large frog. Perhaps it is because she smokes too much, like wet wood that will not know whether to go up in flames or stop burning. She looks me straight in the eyes when she talks to me, and I know she does this with other people too. At first this made me fear her; now I am used to her. She is not a lazy woman, and she does many things outside, in the city and in the suburbs.

This was the first thing her daughter Kate told me when she came and we met. Don't mind Mother, Kate told me. She said, She is sometimes mad with people for very small things. She will soon be all right and speak nicely to you again.

Kate, I like her very much, and she likes me too. She tells me many things a white woman does not tell a black servant. I mean things about what she likes and does not like, what her mother does or does not do, all these. At first I was unhappy and wanted to stop her, but now I do not mind.

Kate looks very much like her mother in the face. I think her shoulders will be just as round and strong-looking. She moves faster than Madam. I asked her why she was still at school when she was so big. She laughed. Then she tried to tell me that the school where she was was for big people, who had finished with lower school. She was learning big things about cooking and food. She can explain better, me I cannot. She came home on weekends.

Since I came to work for Mrs. Plum Kate has been teaching me plenty of cooking. I first learned from her and Madam the word *recipes*. When Kate was at the big school, Madam taught me how to read cookery books. I went on very slowly at first, slower than an ox-wagon. Now I know more. When Kate came home, she found I had read the recipe she left me. So we just cooked straightaway. Kate thinks I am fit to cook in a hotel. Madam thinks so too. Never never! I thought. Cooking in a hotel is like feeding oxen. No one can say thank you to you. After a few months I could cook the Sunday lunch and later I could cook specials for Madam's or Kate's guests.

Madam did not only teach me cooking. She taught me how to look after guests. She praised me when I did very very well; not like the white people I had worked for before. I do not know what runs crooked in the heads of other people. Madam also had classes in the evenings for servants to teach them how to read and write. She and two other women in Greenside taught in a church hall.

As I say, Kate tells me plenty of things about Madam. She says to me she says, My mother goes to meetings many times. I ask her I say, What for? She says to me she says, For your people. I ask her I say, My people are in Phokeng far away. They have got mouths, I say. Why does she want to say something for them? Does she know what my

mother and what my father want to say? They can speak
when they want to. Kate raises her shoulders and drops
them and says, How can I tell you, Karabo? I don't say
your people—your family only. I mean all the black people
in this country. I say Oh! What do the black people want to
say? Again she raises her shoulders and drops them, taking
a deep breath.

I ask her I say, With whom is she in the meeting?

She says, With other people who think like her.

I ask her I say, Do you say there are people in the world
who think the same things?

She nods her head.

I ask, What things?

So that a few of your people should one day be among
those who rule this country, get more money for what they
do for the white man, and—what did Kate say again? Yes,
that Madam and those who think like her also wanted my
people who have been to school to choose those who must
speak for them in the—I think she said it looks like a *Kgotla*
at home who rule the villages.

I say to Kate I say, Oh I see now. I say, Tell me, Kate, why
is Madam always writing on the machine, all the time every
day nearly?

She replies she says, Oh my mother is writing books.

I ask, You mean a book like those?—pointing at the
books on the shelves.

Yes, Kate says.

And she told me how Madam wrote books and other
things for newspapers and she wrote for the newspapers
and magazines to say things for the black people who
should be treated well, be paid more money, for the black
people who can read and write many things to choose those
who want to speak for them.

Kate also told me she said, My mother and other women
who think like her put on black belts over their shoulders
when they are sad and they want to show the white government they do not like the things being done by whites to
blacks. My mother and the others go and stand where the

people in government are going to enter or go out of a building.

I ask her I say, Does the government and the white people listen and stop their sins? She says No. But my mother is in another group of white people.

I ask, Do the people of the government give the women tea and cakes? Kate says, Karabo! How stupid; oh!

I say to her I say, Among my people if someone comes and stands in front of my house I tell him to come in and I give him food. You white people are wonderful. But they keep standing there and the government people do not give them anything.

She replies, You mean strange. How many times have I taught you not to say *wonderful* when you mean *strange*! Well, Kate says with a short heart and looking cross and she shouts, Well, they do not stand there the whole day to ask for tea and cakes, stupid. Oh dear!

Always when Madam finished to read her newspapers she gave them to me to read to help me speak and write better English. When I had read she asked me to tell her some of the things in it. In this way, I did better and better and my mind was opening and opening and I was learning and learning many things about the black people inside and outside the towns which I did not know in the least. When I found words that were too difficult or I did not understand some of the things I asked Madam. She always told me You see this, you see that, eh? with a heart that can carry on a long way. Yes, Madam writes many letters to the papers. She is always sore about the way the white police beat up black people; about the way black people who work for whites are made to sit at the Zoo Lake with their hearts hanging, because the white people say our people are making noise on Sunday afternoon when they want to rest in their houses and gardens; about many ugly things that happen when some white people meet black man on the pavement or street. So Madam writes to the papers to let others know, to ask the government to be kind to us.

In the first year Mrs. Plum wanted me to eat at table

with her. It was very hard, one because I was not used to
eating at table with a fork and knife, two because I heard of
no other kitchen worker who was handled like this. I was
afraid. Afraid of everybody, of Madam's guests if they
found me doing this. Madam said I must not be silly. I must
show that African servants can also eat at table. Number
three, I could not eat some of the things I loved very much:
mealie-meal porridge with sour milk or *morogo*, stamped
mealies mixed with butter beans, sour porridge for breakfast and other things. Also, except for morning porridge,
our food is nice when you eat with the hand. So nice that it
does not stop in the mouth or the throat to greet anyone
before it passes smoothly down.

We often had lunch together with Chimane next door
and our garden boy—Ha! I must remember never to say
boy again when I talk about a man. This makes me think of
a day during the first few weeks in Mrs. Plum's house. I was
talking about Dick her garden man and I said "garden boy."
And she says to me she says, Stop talking about a "boy,"
Karabo. Now listen here, she says, You Africans must learn
to speak properly about each other. And she says White
people won't talk kindly about you if you look down upon
each other.

I say to her I say Madam, I learned the word from the
white people I worked for, and all the kitchen maids say
"boy."

She replies she says to me, Those are white people who
know nothing, just low-class whites. I say to her I say I
thought white people know everything.

She said, You'll learn, my girl, and you must start in this
house, hear? She left me there thinking, my mind mixed up.

I learned. I grew up.

III

If any woman or girl does not know the Black Crow Club
in Bree Street, she does not know anything. I think nearly
everything takes place inside and outside that house. It is

just where the dirty part of the City begins, with factories and the market. After the market is the place where Indians and Coloured people live. It is also at the Black Crow that the buses turn round and back to the black townships. Noise, noise, noise all the time. There are woman who sell hot sweet potatoes and fruit and monkey nuts and boiled eggs in the winter, boiled mealies and the other things in the summer, all these on the pavements. The streets are always full of potato and fruit skins and monkey nut shells. There is always a strong smell of roast pork. I think it is because of Piel's cold storage down Bree Street.

Madam said she knew the black people who work in the Black Crow. She was happy that I was spending my afternoon on Thursday in such a club. You will learn sewing, knitting, she said, and other things that you like. Do you like to dance? I told her I said, Yes, I want to learn. She paid the two shillings fee for me each month.

We waited on the first floor, we the ones who were learning sewing; waiting for the teacher. We talked and laughed about madams and masters, and their children and their dogs and birds and whispered about our boyfriends.

Sies! My Madam you do not know—*mojuta oa'nete*—a real miser . . .

Jo—jo—jo! you should see our new dog. A big thing like this. People! Big in a foolish way . . .

What! Me, I take a master's bitch by the leg, me, and throw it away so that it keeps howling, *tjwe—tjwe! ngo—wu ngo—wu!* I don't play about with them, me . . .

Shame, poor thing! God sees you, true . . . !

They wanted me to take their dog out for a walk every afternoon and I told them I said It is not my work in other houses the garden man does it. I just said to myself I said they can go to the chickens. Let them bite their elbow before I take out a dog, I am not so mad yet . . .

Hei! It is not like the child of my white people who keeps a big white rat and you know what? He puts it on his bed when he goes to school. And let the blankets just begin to smell of urine and all the nonsense and they tell me to wash them. *Hei,* people . . . !

Did you hear about Rebone, people? Her Madam put her out, because her master was always tapping her buttocks with his fingers. And yesterday the madam saw the master press Rebone against himself . . .

Jo—jo—jo! people . . . !

Dirty white man!

No, not dirty. The madam smells too old for him.

Hei! Go and wash your mouth with soap, this girl's mouth is dirty . . .

Jo, Rebone, daughter-of-the-people! We must help her to find a job before she thinks of going back home.

The teacher came. A woman with strong legs, a strong face, and kind eyes. She had short hair and dressed in a simple but lovely floral frock. She stood well on her legs and hips. She had a black mark between the two top front teeth. She smiled as if we were her children. Our group began with games, and then Lilian Ngoyi took us for sewing. After this she gave a brief talk to all of us from the different classes.

I can never forget the things this woman said and how she put them to us. She told us that the time had passed for black girls and women in the suburbs to be satisfied with working, sending money to our people and going to see them once a year. We were to learn, she said, that the world would never be safe for black people until they were in the government with the power to make laws. The power should be given by the Africans who were more than the whites.

We asked her questions and she answered them with wisdom. I shall put some of them down in my own words as I remember them.

Shall we take the place of the white people in the government?

Some yes. But we shall be more than they as we are more in the country. But also the people of all colours will

come together and there are good white men we can choose
and there are Africans some white people will choose to be
in the government.

There are good madams and masters and bad ones.
Should we take the good ones for friends?

A master and a servant can never be friends. Never, so
put that out of your head, will you! You are not even sure if
the ones you say are good are not like that because they
cannot breathe or live without the work of your hands. As
long as you need their money, face them with respect. But
you must know that many sad things are happening in our
country and you, all of you, must always be learning, adding
to what you already know, and obey us when we ask you to
help us.

At other times Lilian Ngoyi told us she said, Remember
your poor people at home and the way in which the whites
are moving them from place to place like sheep and cattle.
And at other times again she told us she said, Remember
that a hand cannot wash itself, it needs another to do it.

I always thought of Madam when Lilian Ngoyi spoke. I
asked myself, What would she say if she knew that I was
listening to such words. Words like: A white man is looked
after by his black nanny and his mother when he is a baby.
When he grows up the white government looks after him,
sends him to school, makes it impossible for him to suffer
from the great hunger, keeps a job ready and open for him
as soon as he wants to leave school. Now Lilian Ngoyi
asked she said, How many white people can be born in a
white hospital, grow up in white streets, be clothed in lovely
cotton, lie on white cushions; how many whites can live all
their lives in a fenced place away from people of other colours and then, as men and women learn quickly the correct
ways of thinking, learn quickly to ask questions in their
minds, big questions that will throw over all the nice things
of a white man's life? How many? Very very few! For those
whites who have not begun to ask, it is too late. For those
who have begun and are joining us with both feet in our
house, we can only say Welcome!

I was learning. I was growing up. Every time I thought of Madam, she became more and more like a dark forest which one fears to enter, and which one will never know. But there were several times when I thought, This woman is easy to understand, she is like all other white women.

What else are they teaching you at the Black Crow, Karabo?

I tell her I say, nothing, Madam. I ask her I say Why does Madam ask?

You are changing.

What does Madam mean?

Well, you are changing.

But we are always changing Madam.

And she left me standing in the kitchen. This was a few days after I had told her that I did not want to read more than one white paper a day. The only magazines I wanted to read, I said to her, were those from overseas, if she had them. I told her that white papers had pictures of white people most of the time. They talked mostly about white people and their gardens, dogs, weddings and parties. I asked her if she could buy me a Sunday paper that spoke about my people. Madam bought it for me. I did not think she would do it.

There were mornings when, after hanging the white people's washing on the line, Chimane and I stole a little time to stand at the fence and talk. We always stood where we could be hidden by our rooms.

Hei, Karabo, you know what? That was Chimane.

No—what? Before you start, tell me, has Timi come back to you?

Ach, I do not care. He is still angry. But boys are fools they always come back dragging themselves on their empty bellies. *Hei* you know what?

Yes?

The Thursday past I saw Moruti K.K. I laughed until I dropped on the ground. He is standing in front of the Black Crow. I believe his big stomach was crying from hunger. Now he has a small dog in his armpit, and is standing before

a woman selling boiled eggs and—*hei,* home-girl!—tripe
and intestines are boiling in a pot—oh—the smell! you
could fill a hungry belly with it, the way it was good. I think
Moruti K.K. is waiting for the woman to buy a boiled egg. I
do not know what the woman was still doing. I am standing
nearby. The dog keeps wriggling and pushing out its nose,
looking at the boiling tripe. Moruti keeps patting it with his
free hand, not so? Again the dog wants to spill out of Moruti's hand and it gives a few sounds through the nose. *Hei*
man, home-girl! One two three the dog spills out to catch
some of the good meat! It misses falling into the hot gravy
in which the tripe is swimming I do not know how. Moruti
K.K. tries to chase it. It has tumbled on to the woman's eggs
and potatoes and all are in the dust. She stands up and goes
after K.K. She is shouting to him to pay, not so? Where am
I at that time? I am nearly dead with laughter the tears are
coming down so far.

I was myself holding tight on the fence so as not to fall
through laughing. I held my stomach to keep back a pain in
the side.

I ask her I say, Did Moruti K.K. come back to pay for the
wasted food?

Yes, he paid.

The dog?

He caught it. That is a good African dog. A dog must
look for its own food when it is not time for meals. Not
these stupid spoiled angels the whites keep giving tea and
biscuits.

Hmm.

Dick our garden man joined us, as he often did. When
the story was repeated to him the man nearly rolled on the
ground laughing.

He asks who is Reverend K.K.?

I say he is the owner of the Black Crow.

Oh!

We reminded each other, Chimane and I, of the round
minister. He would come into the club, look at us with a
smooth smile on his smooth round face. He would look at

each one of us, with that smile on all the time, as if he had forgotten that it was there. Perhaps he had, because as he looked at us, almost stripping us naked with his watery shining eyes—funny—he could have been a farmer looking at his ripe corn, thinking many things.

K.K. often spoke without shame about what he called ripe girls—*matjitjana*—with good firm breasts. He said such girls were pure without any nonsense in their heads and bodies. Everybody talked a great deal about him and what they thought he must be doing in his office whenever he called in so-and-so.

The Reverend K.K. did not belong to any church. He baptised, married, and buried people for a fee, who had no church to do such things for them. They said he had been driven out of the Presbyterian Church. He had formed his own, but it did not go far. Then he later came and opened the Black Crow. He knew just how far to go with Lilian Ngoyi. She said although she used his club to teach us things that would help us in life, she could not go on if he was doing any wicked things with the girls in his office. Moruti K.K. feared her, and kept his place.

IV

When I began to tell my story I thought I was going to tell you mostly about Mrs. Plum's two dogs. But I have been talking about people. I think Dick is right when he says What is a dog! And there are so many dogs cats and parrots in Greenside and other places that Mrs. Plum's dogs do not look special. But there was something special in the dog business in Madam's house. The way in which she loved them, maybe.

Monty is a tiny animal with long hair and small black eyes and a face nearly like that of an old woman. The other, Malan, is a bit bigger, with brown and white colours. It has small hair and looks naked by the side of the friend. They sleep in two separate baskets which stay in Madam's bedroom. They are to be washed often and brushed and sprayed and they sleep on pink linen. Monty has a pink ribbon which stays on his neck most of the time. They both carry a cover on their backs. They make me fed up when I see them in their baskets, looking fat, and as if they knew all that was going on everywhere.

It was Dick's work to look after Monty and Malan, to feed them, and to do everything for them. He did this together with garden work and cleaning of the house. He came at the beginning of this year. He just came, as if from nowhere, and Madam gave him the job as she had chased away two before him, she told me. In both those cases, she said that they could not look after Monty and Malan.

Dick had a long heart, even although he told me and Chimane that European dogs were stupid, spoiled. He said One day those white people will put earrings and toe rings and bangles on their dogs. That would be the day he would leave Mrs. Plum. For, he said, he was sure that she would want him to polish the rings and bangles with Brasso.

Although he had a long heart, Madam was still not sure of him. She often went to the dogs after a meal or after a cleaning and said to them Did Dick give you food, sweethearts? Or, Did Dick wash you sweethearts? Let me see. And I could see that Dick was blowing up like a balloon with anger. These things called white people! he said to me. Talking to dogs!

I say to him I say, People talk to oxen at home do I not say so?

Yes, he says, but at home do you not know that a man speaks to an ox because he wants to make it pull the plow or the wagon or to stop or to stand still for a person to inspan it. No one simply goes to an ox looking at him with eyes far apart and speaks to it. Let me ask you, do you ever see a person where we come from take a cow and press it to his stomach or his cheek? Tell me!

And I say to Dick I say, We were talking about an ox, not a cow.

He laughed with his broad mouth until tears came out of his eyes. At a certain point I laughed aloud too.

One day when you have time, Dick says to me, he says,
you should look into Madam's bedroom when she has put
a notice outside her door.

Dick, what are you saying? I ask.

I do not talk, me. I know deep inside me.

Dick was about our age, I and Chimane. So we always
said *moshiman'o* when we spoke about his tricks. Because
he was not too big to be a boy to us. He also said to us *Hei,
lona banyana kelona*—Hey, you girls, you! His large mouth
always seemed to be making ready to laugh. I think Madam
did not like this. Many times she would say What is there to
make you laugh here? Or in the garden she would say This
is a flower and when it wants water that is not funny! Or
again, If you did more work and stopped trying to water my
plants with your smile you would be more useful. Even
when Dick did not mean to smile. What Madam did not get
tired of saying was, If I left you to look after my dogs without anyone to look after you at the same time you would
drown the poor things.

Dick smiled at Mrs. Plum. Dick hurt Mrs. Plum's dogs?
Then cows can fly. He was really—really afraid of white
people, Dick. I think he tried very hard not to feel afraid.
For he was always showing me and Chimane in private how
Mrs. Plum walked, and spoke. He took two bowls and
pressed them to his chest, speaking softly to them as
Madam speaks to Monty and Malan. Or he sat at Madam's
table and acted the way she sits when writing. Now and
again he looked back over his shoulder, pulled his face long
like a horse's making as if he were looking over his glasses
while telling me something to do. Then he would sit on one
of the armchairs, cross his legs and act the way Madam
drank her tea; he held the cup he was thinking about between his thumb and the pointing finger, only letting their
nails meet. And he laughed after every act. He did these
things, of course, when Madam was not home. And where
was I at such times? Almost flat on my stomach, laughing.

But oh how Dick trembled when Mrs. Plum scolded
him! He did his housecleaning very well. Whatever mistake

he made, it was mostly with the dogs: their linen, their food. One white man came into the house one afternoon to tell Madam that Dick had been very careless when taking the dogs out for a walk. His own dog was waiting on Madam's stoop. He repeated that he had been driving down our street; and Dick had let loose Monty and Malan to cross the street. The white man made plenty of noise about this and I think wanted to let Madam know how useful he had been. He kept on saying Just one inch, *just* one inch. It was lucky I put on my brakes quick enough. . . . But your boy kept on smiling—Why? Strange. My boy would only do it twice and only twice and then . . . ! His pass. The man moved his hand like one writing, to mean that he would sign his servant's pass for him to go and never come back. When he left, the white man said Come on, Rusty, the boy is waiting to clean you. Dogs with names, men without, I thought.

Madam climbed on top of Dick for this, as we say.

Once one of the dogs, I don't know which—Malan or Monty—took my stocking—brand-new, you hear—and tore it with its teeth and paws. When I told Madam about it, my anger as high as my throat, she gave me money to buy another pair. It happened again. This time she said she was not going to give me money because I must also keep my stockings where the two gentlemen would not reach them. Mrs. Plum did not want us ever to say *Voetsek* when we wanted the dogs to go away. Me I said this when they came sniffing at my legs or fingers. I hate it.

In my third year in Mrs. Plum's house, many things happened, most of them all bad for her. There was trouble with Kate; Chimane had big trouble; my heart was twisted by two loves; and Monty and Malan became real dogs for a few days.

Madam had a number of suppers and parties. She invited Africans to some of them. Kate told me the reasons for some of the parties. Like her mother's books when finished, a visitor from across the seas and so on. I did not like the black people who came here to drink and eat. They spoke such difficult English like people who were full of all the books in the world. They looked at me as if I were right down there whom they thought little of—me a black person like them.

One day I heard Kate speak to her mother. She says I don't know why you ask so many Africans to the house. A few will do at a time. She said something about the government which I could not hear well. Madam replies she says to her You know some of them do not meet white people often, so far away in their dark houses. And she says to Kate that they do not come because they want her as a friend but they just want a drink for nothing.

I simply felt that I could not be the servant of white people and of blacks at the same time. At my home or in my room I could serve them without a feeling of shame. And now, if they were only coming to drink!

But one of the black men and his sister always came to the kitchen to talk to me. I must have looked unfriendly the first time, for Kate talked to me about it afterwards as she was in the kitchen when they came. I know that at that time I was not easy at all. I was ashamed and I felt that a white person's house was not the place for me to look happy in front of other black people while the white man looked on.

Another time it was easier. The man was alone. I shall never forget that night, as long as I live. He spoke kind words and I felt my heart grow big inside me. It caused it to tremble. There were several other visits. I knew that I loved him. I could never know what he really thought of me, I mean as a woman and he as a man. But I loved him, and I still think of him with a sore heart. Slowly I came to know the pain of it. Because he was a doctor and so full of knowledge and English I could not reach him. So I knew he could not stoop down to see me as someone who wanted him to love me.

Kate turned very wild. Mrs. Plum was very much worried. Suddenly it looked as if she were a new person, with new ways and new everything. I do not know what was wrong or right. She began to play the big gramophone aloud, as if the music were for the whole of Greenside. The music was wild and she twisted her waist all the time, with her mouth half-open. She did the same things in her room. She left the big school and every Saturday night now she went out. When I looked at her face, there was something deep and wild there on it, and when I thought she looked young she looked old, and when I thought she looked old she was young. We were both twenty-two years of age. I think that I could see the reason why her mother was so worried, why she was suffering.

Worse was to come.

They were now openly screaming at each other. They began in the sitting room and went upstairs together, speaking fast hot biting words, some of which I did not grasp. One day Madam comes to me and says You know Kate loves an African, you know the doctor who comes to supper here often. She says he loves her too and they will leave the country and marry outside. Tell me, Karabo, what do your people think of this kind of thing between a white woman and a black man? It *cannot* be right is it?

I reply and I say to her We have never seen it happen before where I come from.

That's right, Karabo, it is just madness.

Madam left. She looked like a hunted person.

These white women, I say to myself I say these white women, why do not they love their own men and leave us to love ours!

From that minute I knew that I would never want to speak to Kate. She appeared to me as a thief, as a fox that falls upon a flock of sheep at night. I hated her. To make it worse, he would never be allowed to come to the house again.

Whenever she was home there was silence between us. I no longer wanted to know anything about what she was doing, where or how.

I lay awake for hours on my bed. Lying like that, I seemed to feel parts of my body beat and throb inside me, the way I have seen big machines doing, pounding and pounding and pushing and pulling and pouring some water into one hole which came out at another end. I stretched myself so many times so as to feel tired and sleepy.

When I did sleep, my dreams were full of painful things.

One evening I made up my mind, after putting it off many times. I told my boyfriend that I did not want him any longer. He looked hurt, and that hurt me too. He left.

The thought of the African doctor was still with me and it pained me to know that I should never see him again; unless I met him in the street on a Thursday afternoon. But he had a car. Even if I did meet him by luck, how could I make him see that I loved him? Ach, I do not believe he would even stop to think what kind of woman I am. Part of that winter was a time of longing and burning for me. I say part because there are always things to keep servants busy whose white people go to the sea for the winter.

To tell the truth, winter was the time for servants; not nannies, because they went with their madams so as to look after the children. Those like me stayed behind to look after the house and dogs. In winter so many families went away that the dogs remained the masters and madams. You could see them walk like white people in the streets. Silent but with plenty of power. And when you saw them you knew that they were full of more nonsense and fancies in the house.

There was so little work to do.

One week word was whispered round that a home-boy of ours was going to hold a party in his room on Saturday. I think we all took it for a joke. How could the man be so bold and stupid? The police were always driving about at night looking for black people; and if the whites next door heard the party noise—*oho!* But still, we were full of joy and wanted to go. As for Dick, he opened his big mouth and nearly fainted when he heard of it and that I was really going.

During the day on the big Saturday Kate came.

She seemed a little less wild. But I was not ready to talk to her. I was surprised to hear myself answer her when she said to me Mother says you do not like a marriage between a white girl and a black man, Karabo.

Then she was silent.

She says But I want to help him, Karabo.

I ask her I say You want to help him to do what?

To go higher and higher, to the top.

I knew I wanted to say so much that was boiling in my chest. I could not say it. I thought of Lilian Ngoyi at the Black Crow, what she said to us. But I was mixed up in my head and in my blood.

You still agree with my mother?

All I could say was I said to your mother I had never seen a black man and a white woman marrying, you hear me? What I think about it is my business.

I remembered that I wanted to iron my party dress and so I left her. My mind was full of the party again and I was glad because Kate and the doctor would not worry my peace that day. And the next day the sun would shine for all of us, Kate or no Kate, doctor or no doctor.

The house where our home-boy worked was hidden from the main road by a number of trees. But although we asked a number of questions and counted many fingers of bad luck until we had no more hands for fingers, we put on our best pay-while-you-wear dresses and suits and clothes bought from boys who had stolen them, and went to our home-boy's party. We whispered all the way while we climbed up to the house. Someone who knew told us that the white people next door were away for the winter. Oh, so that is the thing! we said.

We poured into the garden through the back and stood in front of his room laughing quietly. He came from the big house behind us, and were we not struck dumb when he told us to go into the white people's house! Was he mad? We walked in with slow footsteps that seemed to be sniffing at the floor, not sure of anything. Soon we were standing and sitting all over on the nice warm cushions and the heaters were on. Our home-boy turned the lights low. I counted fifteen people inside. We saw how we loved one another's evening dress. The boys were smart too.

Our home-boy's girlfriend Naomi was busy in the

kitchen preparing food. He took out glasses and cold drinks—fruit juice, tomato juice, ginger beers, and so many other kinds of soft drink. It was just too nice. The tarts, the biscuits, the snacks, the cakes, *woo*, that was a party, I tell you. I think I ate more ginger cake than I had ever done in my life. Naomi had baked some of the things. Our home-boy came to me and said I do not want the police to come here and have reason to arrest us, so I am not serving hot drinks, not even beer. There is no law that we cannot have parties, is there? So we can feel free. Our use of this house is the master's business. If I had asked him he would have thought me mad.

I say to him I say, You have a strong liver to do such a thing.

He laughed.

He played pennywhistle music on gramophone records—Miriam Makeba, Dorothy Masuka, and other African singers and players. We danced and the party became more and more noisy and more happy. *Hai,* those girls Miriam and Dorothy, they can sing, I tell you! We ate more and laughed more and told more stories. In the middle of the party, our home-boy called us to listen to what he was going to say. Then he told us how he and a friend of his in Orlando collected money to bet on a horse for the July Handicap in Durban. They did this each year but lost. Now they had won two hundred pounds. We all clapped hands and cheered. Two hundred pounds *woo!*

You should go and sit at home and just eat time, I say to him. He laughs and says You have no understanding not one little bit.

To all of us he says Now my brothers and sisters enjoy yourselves. At home I should slaughter a goat for us to feast and thank our ancestors. But this is town life and we must thank them with tea and cake and all those sweet things. I know some people think I must be so bold that I could be midwife to a lion that is giving birth, but enjoy yourselves and have no fear.

Madam came back looking strong and fresh.

The very week she arrived the police had begun again to search servants' rooms. They were looking for what they called loafers and men without passes who they said were living with friends in the suburbs against the law. Our dog's-meat boys became scarce because of the police. A boy who had a girlfriend in the kitchens, as we say, always told his friends that he was coming for dog's meat when he meant he was visiting his girl. This was because we gave our boy-friends part of the meat the white people bought for the dogs and us.

One night a white and a black policeman entered Mrs. Plum's yard. They said they had come to search. She says no, they cannot. They say Yes, they must do it. She answers No. They forced their way to the back, to Dick's room and mine. Mrs. Plum took the hose that was running in the front garden and quickly went round to the back. I cut across the floor to see what she was going to say to the men. They were talking to Dick, using dirty words. Mrs. Plum did not wait, she just pointed the hose at the two policemen. This seemed to surprise them. They turned round and she pointed it into their faces. Without their seeing me I went to the tap at the corner of the house and opened it more. I could see Dick, like me, was trying to keep down his laughter. They shouted and tried to wave the water away, but she kept the hose pointing at them, now moving it up and down. They turned and ran through the back gate, swearing the while.

That fixes them, Mrs. Plum said.

The next day the morning paper reported it.

They arrived in the afternoon—the two policemen—with another. They pointed out Mrs. Plum and she was led to the police station. They took her away to answer for stopping the police while they were doing their work.

She came back and said she had paid bail.

At the magistrate's court, Madam was told that she had done a bad thing. She would have to pay a fine or else go to prison for fourteen days. She said she would go to jail to show that she felt she was not in the wrong.

Kate came and tried to tell her that she was doing some-thing silly going to jail for a small thing like that. She tells Madam she says This is not even a thing to take to the high court. Pay the money. What is £5?

Madam went to jail.

She looked very sad when she came out. I thought of what Lilian Ngoyi often said to us: You must be ready to go to jail for the things you believe are true and for which you are taken by the police. What did Mrs. Plum really believe about me, Chimane, Dick, and all the other black people? I asked myself. I did not know. But from all those things she was writing for the papers and all those meetings she was going to where white people talked about black people and the way they are treated by the government, from what those white women with black bands over their shoulders were doing standing where a white government man was going to pass, I said to myself I said This woman, *hai*, I do not know she seems to think very much of us black people. But why was she so sad?

Kate came back home to stay after this. She still played the big gramophone loud-loud-loud and twisted her body at her waist until I thought it was going to break. Then I saw a young white man come often to see her. I watched them through the opening near the hinges of the door between the kitchen and the sitting room where they sat. I saw them kiss each other for a long time. I saw him lift up Kate's dress and her white-white legs begin to tremble, and—oh I am afraid to say more, my heart was beating hard. She called him Jim. I thought it was funny because white people in the shops call black men Jim.

Kate had begun to play with Jim when I met a boy who loved me and I loved. He was much stronger than the one I sent away and I loved him more, much more. The face of the doctor came to my mind often, but it did not hurt me so any more. I stopped looking at Kate and her Jim through openings. We spoke to each other, Kate and I, almost as freely as before but not quite. She and her mother were friends again.

Hallo, Karabo, I heard Chimane call me one morning as I was starching my apron. I answered. I went to the line to hang it. I saw she was standing at the fence, so I knew she had something to tell me. I went to her.

Hallo!

Hallo, Chimane!

O kae?

Ke teng. Wena?

At that moment a woman came out through the back door of the house where Chimane was working.

I have not seen that one before, I say, pointing with my head.

Chimane looked back. Oh, that one. *Hei,* daughter-of-the-people, *hei,* you have not seen miracles. You know this is Madam's mother-in-law as you see her there. Did I never tell you about her?

No, never.

White people, nonsense. You know what? That poor woman is here now for two days. She has to cook for herself and I cook for the family.

On the same stove?

Yes. She comes after me when I have finished.

She has her own food to cook?

Yes, Karabo. White people have no heart no sense.

What will eat them up if they share their food?

Ask me, just ask me. God! She clapped her hands to show that only God knew, and it was His business, not ours.

Chimane asks me she says, Have you heard from home?

I tell her I say, Oh daughter-of-the-people, more and more deaths. Something is finishing the people at home. My mother has written. She says they are all right, my father too and my sisters, except for the people who have died. Malebo, the one who lived alone in the house I showed you last year, a white house, he is gone. Then teacher Sedimo. He was very thin and looked sick all the time. He taught my sisters not me. His mother-in-law you remember I told you died last year—no, the year before. Mother says also there is a woman she does not think I remember because I last saw her when I was a small girl she passed away in Zeerust she was my mother's greatest friend when they were girls. She would have gone to her burial if it was not because she has swollen feet.

How are the feet?

She says they are still giving her trouble. I ask Chimane, How are your people at Nokaneng? They have not written?

She shook her head.

I could see from her eyes that her mind was on another thing and not her people at that moment.

Wait for me Chimane eh, forgive me, I have scones in the oven, eh! I will just take them out and come back, eh!

When I came back to her Chimane was wiping her eyes. They were wet.

Karabo, you know what?

E—e. I shook my head.

I am heavy with child.

Hau!

There was a moment of silence.

Who is it, Chimane?

Timi. He came back only to give me this.

But he loves you. What does he say have you told him?

I told him yesterday. We met in town.

I remembered I had not seen her at the Black Crow.

Are you sure, Chimane? You have missed a month?

She nodded her head.

Timi himself—he did not use the thing?

I only saw after he finished, that he had not.

Why? What does he say?

He tells me he says I should not worry I can be his wife.

Timi is a good boy, Chimane. How many of these boys with town ways who know too much will even say Yes it is my child?

Hai, Karabo, you are telling me other things now. Do you not see that I have not worked long enough for my people? If I marry now who will look after them when I am the only child?

Hm. I hear your words. It is true. I tried to think of something soothing to say.

Then I say You can talk it over with Timi. You can go home and when the child is born you look after it for three months and when you are married you come to town to work and can put your money together to help the old people while they are looking after the child.

What shall we be eating all the time I am at home? It is not like those days gone past when we had land and our mother could go to the fields until the child was ready to arrive.

The light goes out in my mind and I cannot think of the right answer. How many times have I feared the same thing! Luck and the mercy of the gods that is all I live by. That is all we live by—all of us.

Listen, Karabo. I must be going to make tea for Madam. It will soon strike half-past ten.

I went back to the house. As Madam was not in yet, I threw myself on the divan in the sitting room. Malan came sniffing at my legs. I put my foot under its fat belly and shoved it up and away from me so that it cried *tjunk—tjunk—tjunk* as it went out. I say to it I say Go and tell your brother what I have done to you and tell him to try it and see what I will do. Tell your grandmother when she comes home too.

When I lifted my eyes he was standing in the kitchen door, Dick. He says to me he says *Hau!* now you have also begun to speak to dogs!

I did not reply. I just looked at him, his mouth ever stretched out like the mouth of a bag, and I passed to my room.

I sat on my bed and looked at my face in the mirror. Since the morning I had been feeling as if a black cloud were hanging over me, pressing on my head and shoulders. I do not know how long I sat there. Then I smelled Madam. What was it? Where was she? After a few moments I knew what it was. My perfume and scent. I used the same cosmetics as Mrs. Plum's. I should have been used to it by now. But this morning—why did I smell Mrs. Plum like this? Then, without knowing why, I asked myself I said, Why have I been using the same cosmetics as Madam? I wanted to throw them all out. I stopped. And then I took all the things and threw them into the dustbin. I was going to buy other kinds on Thursday; finished!

I could not sit down. I went out and into the white people's house. I walked through and the smell of the house made me sick and seemed to fill up my throat. I went to the bathroom without knowing why. It was full of the smell of Madam. Dick was cleaning the bath. I stood at the door and looked at him cleaning the dirt out of the bath, dirt from Madam's body. *Sies!* I said aloud. To myself I said, Why cannot people wash the dirt of their own bodies out of the bath? Before Dick knew I was near I went out. Ach, I said again to myself, why should I think about it now when I have been doing their washing for so long and cleaned the bath many times when Dick was ill. I had held worse things from her body times without number . . .

I went out and stood midway between the house and my room, looking into the next yard. The three-legged grey cat next door came to the fence and our eyes met. I do not know how long we stood like that looking at each other. I was thinking, Why don't you go and look at your grandmother like that? when it turned away and mewed hopping on the three legs. Just like someone who feels pity for you.

In my room I looked into the mirror on the chest of drawers. I thought Is this Karabo this?

Thursday came, and the afternoon off. At the Black Crow I did not see Chimane. I wondered about her. In the evening I found a note under my door. It told me if Chimane was not back that evening I should know that she was at 660 3rd Avenue, Alexandra Township. I was not to tell the white people.

I asked Dick if he could not go to Alexandra with me after I had washed the dishes. At first he was unwilling. But I said to him I said, Chimane will not believe that you refused to come with me when she sees me alone. He agreed.

On the bus Dick told me much about his younger sister whom he was helping with money to stay at school until she finished; so that she could become a nurse and a midwife. He was very fond of her, as far as I could find out. He said he prayed always that he should not lose his job, as he had done many times before, after staying a few weeks only at each job; because of this he had to borrow monies from people to pay his sister's school fees, to buy her clothes and books. He spoke of her as if she were his sweetheart. She was clever at school, pretty (she was this in the photo Dick had shown me before). She was in Orlando Township. She looked after his old people, although she was only thirteen years of age. He said to me he said Today I still owe many people because I keep losing my job. You must try to stay with Mrs. Plum, I said.

I cannot say that I had all my mind on what Dick was telling me. I was thinking of Chimane: what could she be doing? Why that note?

We found her in bed. In that terrible township where night and day are full of knives and bicycle chains and guns and the barking of hungry dogs and of people in trouble. I held my heart in my hands. She was in pain and her face, even in the candlelight, was grey. She turned her eyes at me. A fat woman was sitting in a chair. One arm rested on the other and held her chin in its palm. She had hardly opened the door for us after we had shouted our names when she was on her bench again as if there were nothing else to do.

She snorted, as if to let us know that she was going to speak. She said There is your friend. There she is my own-own niece who comes from the womb of my own sister, my sister who was made to spit out my mother's breast to give way for me. Why does she go and do such an evil thing. *Ao!* you young girls of today you do not know children die so fast these days that you have to thank God for sowing a seed in your womb to grow into a child. If she had let the child be born I should have looked after it or my sister would have been so happy to hold a grandchild on her lap, but what does it help? She has allowed a worm to cut the roots, I don't know.

Then I saw that Chimane's aunt was crying. Not once did she mention her niece by her name, so sore her heart must have been. Chimane only moaned.

Her aunt continued to talk, as if she was never going to stop for breath, until her voice seemed to move behind me, not one of the things I was thinking: trying to remember signs, however small, that could tell me more about this moment in a dim little room in a cruel township without street lights, near Chimane. Then I remembered the three-legged cat, its grey-green eyes, its *miau*. What was this shadow that seemed to walk about us but was not coming right in front of us?

I thanked the gods when Chimane came to work at the end of the week. She still looked weak, but that shadow was no longer there. I wondered Chimane had never told me about her aunt before. Even now I did not ask her.

I told her I told her white people that she was ill and had been fetched to Nokaneng by a brother. They would never try to find out. They seldom did, these people. Give them any lie, and it will do. For they seldom believe you whatever you say. And how can a black person work for white people and be afraid to tell them lies. They are always asking the questions, you are always the one to give the answers.

Chimane told me all about it. She had gone to a woman who did these things. Her way was to hold a sharp needle, cover the point with the finger, and guide it into the womb. She then fumbled in the womb until she found the egg and then pierced it. She gave you something to ease the bleeding. But the pain, spirits of our forefathers!

Mrs. Plum and Kate were talking about dogs one evening at dinner. Every time I brought something to table I tried to catch their words. Kate seemed to find it funny, because she laughed aloud. There was a word I could not hear well which began with *sem*—: whatever it was, it was to be for dogs. This I understood by putting a few words together. Mrs. Plum said it was something that was common in the big cities of America, like New York. It was also something Mrs. Plum wanted and Kate laughed at the thought. Then later I was to hear that Monty and Malan could be sure of a nice burial.

Chimane's voice came up to me in my room the next morning, across the fence. When I come out she tells me she says, *Hei*, child-of-my-father, here is something to tickle your ears. You know what? What? I say. She says, These white people can do things that make the gods angry. More godless people I have not seen. The madam of our house says the people of Greenside want to buy ground where they can bury their dogs. I heard them talk about it in the sitting room when I was giving them coffee last night. *Hei*, people, let our forefathers come and save us!

Yes, I say, I also heard the madam of our house talk about it with her daughter. I just heard it in pieces. By my mother one day these dogs will sit at table and use knife and fork. These things are to be treated like people now, like children who are never going to grow up.

Chimane sighed and she says *Hela batho,* why do they not give me some of that money they will spend on the ground and on gravestones to buy stockings! I have nothing to put on, by my mother.

Over her shoulder I saw the cat with three legs. I pointed with my head. When Chimane looked back and saw it she said *Hm,* even *they* live like kings. The mother-in-law found it on a chair and the madam said the woman should not drive it away. And there was no other chair, so the woman went to her room.

Hela!

I was going to leave when I remembered what I wanted to tell Chimane. It was that five of us had collected £1 each to lend her so that she could pay the woman of Alexandra for having done that thing for her. When Chimane's time came to receive money we collected each month and which we took in turns, she would pay us back. We were ten women and each gave £2 at a time. So one waited ten months to receive £20. Chimane thanked us for helping her.

I went to wake up Mrs. Plum as she had asked me. She was sleeping late this morning. I was going to knock at the

door when I heard strange noises in the bedroom. What is
the matter with Mrs. Plum? I asked myself. Should I call
her, in case she is ill? No, the noises were not those of a sick
person. They were happy noises but like those a person
makes in a dream, the voice full of sleep. I bent a little to
peep through the keyhole. What is this? I kept asking myself. Mrs. Plum! Malan! What is she doing this one? Her
arm was round Malan's belly and pressing its back against
her stomach at the navel, Mrs. Plum's body in a nightdress
moving in jerks like someone in fits . . . her leg rising and
falling . . . Malan silent like a thing to be owned without any
choice it can make to belong to another.

The gods save me! I heard myself saying, the words
sounding like wind rushing out of my mouth. So this is what
Dick said I would find out for myself!

No one could say where it all started; who talked about
it first; whether the police wanted to make a reason for
taking people without passes and people living with servants and working in town or not working at all. But the
story rushed through Johannesburg that servants were
going to poison the white people's dogs. Because they
were too much work for us: that was the reason. We heard
that letters were sent to the newspapers by white people
asking the police to watch over the dogs to stop any
wicked things. Some said that we the servants were not
really bad, we were being made to think of doing these
things by evil people in town and in the locations. Others
said the police should watch out lest we poison madams
and masters because black people did not know right
from wrong when they were angry. We were still children
at heart, others said. Mrs. Plum said that she had also
written to the papers.

Then it was the police came down on the suburbs like
locusts on a cornfield. There were lines and lines of men
who were arrested hour by hour in the day. They liked this
very much, the police. Everybody they took, everybody
who was working was asked, Where's the poison eh? Where
did you hide it? Who told you to poison the dogs eh? If you

tell us we'll leave you to go free, you hear? and so many other things.

Dick kept saying It is wrong this thing they want to do to kill poor dogs. What have these things of God done to be killed for? Is it the dogs that make us carry passes? Is it dogs that make the laws that give us pain? People are just mad they do not know what they want, stupid! But when white policeman spoke to him, Dick trembled and lost his tongue and the things he thought. He just shook his head. A few moments after they had gone through his pockets he still held his arms stretched out, like the man of straw who frightens away birds in a field. Only when I hissed and gave him a sign did he drop his arms. He rushed to a corner of the garden to go on with his work.

Mrs. Plum had put Monty and Malan in the sitting room, next to her. She looked very much worried. She called me. She asked me she said Karabo, you think Dick is a boy we can trust? I did not know how to answer. I did not know whom she was talking about when she said *we*. Then I said I do not know, Madam. You know! she said. I looked at her. I said I do not know what Madam thinks. She said she did not think anything, that was why she asked. I nearly laughed because she was telling a lie this time and not I.

At another time I should have been angry if she lied to me, perhaps. She and I often told each other lies, as Kate and I also did. Like when she came back from jail, after that day when she turned a hosepipe on two policemen. She said life had been good in jail. And yet I could see she was ashamed to have been there. Not like our black people who are always being put in jail and only look at it as the white man's evil game. Lilian Ngoyi often told us this, and Mrs. Plum showed me how true those words are. I am sure that we have kept to each other by lying to each other.

There was something in Mrs. Plum's face as she was speaking which made me fear her and pity her at the same time. I had seen her when she had come from prison; I had seen her when she was shouting at Kate and the girl left the house; now there was this thing about dog poisoning. But never had I seen her face like this before. The eyes, the nostrils, the lips, the teeth seemed to be full of hate, tired, fixed on doing something bad; and yet there was something on that face that told me she wanted me on her side.

Dick is all right, Madam, I found myself saying. She took Malan and Monty in her arms and pressed them to herself, running her hands over their heads. They looked so safe, like a child in a mother's arm.

Mrs. Plum said All right you may go. She said Do not tell anybody what I have asked about Dick eh?

When I told Dick about it, he seemed worried.

It is nothing, I told him.

I had been thinking before that I did not stand with those who wanted to poison the dogs, Dick said. But the police have come out, I do not care what happens to the dumb things, now.

I asked him I said Would you poison them if you were told by someone to do it?

No. But I do not care, he replied.

The police came again and again. They were having a good holiday, everyone could see that. A day later Mrs. Plum told Dick to go because she would not need his work any more.

Dick was almost crying when he left. Is Madam so unsure of me? he asked. I never thought a white person could fear me! And he left.

Chimane shouted from the other yard. She said, *Hei ngoana'rona,* the boers are fire-hot eh!

Mrs. Plum said she would hire a man after the trouble was over.

A letter came from my parents in Phokeng. In it they told me my uncle had passed away. He was my mother's brother. The letter also told me of other deaths. They said I would not remember some, I was sure to know the others. There were also names of sick people.

I went to Mrs. Plum to ask her if I could go home. She asks she says When did he die? I answer I say It is three days, Madam. She says So that they have buried him? I reply Yes, Madam. Why do you want to go home then? Because my uncle loved me very much, Madam. But what are you going to do there? To take my tears and words of grief to his grave and to my old aunt, Madam. No you cannot go, Karabo. You are working for me you know? Yes, Madam. I, and not your people pay you. I must go, Madam, that is how we do it among my people, Madam. She paused. She walked into the kitchen and came out again. If you want to go, Karabo, you must lose the money for the days you will be away. Lose my pay, Madam? Yes, Karabo.

The next day I went to Mrs. Plum and told her I was leaving for Phokeng and was not coming back to her. Could she give me a letter to say that I worked for her. She did, with her lips shut tight. I could feel that something between us was burning like raw chillies. The letter simply said that I had worked for Mrs. Plum for three years. Nothing more. The memory of Dick being sent away was still an open sore in my heart.

The night before the day I left, Chimane came to see me in my room. She had her own story to tell me. Timi, her boyfriend, had left her—for good. Why? Because I killed his baby. Had he not agreed that you should do it? No. Did he show he was worried when you told him you were heavy? He was worried, like me as you saw me, Karabo. Now he says if I kill one I shall eat all his children up when we are married. You think he means what he says? Yes, Karabo. He says his parents would have been very happy to know that the woman he was going to marry can make his seed grow.

Chimane was crying, softly.

I tried to speak to her, to tell her that if Timi left her just like that, he had not wanted to marry her in the first place. But I could not, no, I could not. All I could say was Do not cry, my sister, do not cry. I gave her my handkerchief.

Kate came back the morning I was leaving, from somewhere very far I cannot remember where. Her mother took no notice of what Kate said asking her to keep me, and I was not interested either.

One hour later I was on the railway bus to Phokeng. During the early part of the journey I did not feel anything about the Greenside house I had worked in. I was not really myself, my thoughts dancing between Mrs. Plum, my uncle, my parents, and Phokeng, my home. I slept and woke up many times during the bus ride. Right through the ride I seemed to see, sometimes in sleep, sometimes between sleep and waking, a red car passing our bus, then running behind us. Each time I looked out it was not there.

Dreams came and passed. He tells me he says You have killed my seed I wanted my mother to know you are a woman in whom my seed can grow . . . Before you make the police take you to jail make sure that it is for something big you should go to jail for, otherwise you will come out with a heart and mind that will bleed inside you and poison you . . .

The bus stopped for a short while, which made me wake up.

The Black Crow, the club women . . . *Hei,* listen! I lie to the madam of our house and I say I had a telegram from my mother telling me she is very very sick. I show her a telegram my sister sent me as if Mother were writing. So I went home for a nice weekend . . .

The laughter of the women woke me up, just in time for me to stop a line of saliva coming out over my lower lip. The bus was making plenty of dust now as it was running over part of the road they were digging up. I was sure the red car was just behind us, but it was not there when I woke.

Any one of you here who wants to be baptised or has a relative without a church who needs to be can come and see me in the office . . . A round man with a fat tummy and sharp hungry eyes, a smile that goes a long, long way . . .

The bus was going uphill, heavily and noisily.

I kick a white man's dog, me, or throw it there if it has not been told the black people's law . . . This is Mister Monty and this is Mister Malan. Now get up, you lazy boys, and meet Mister Kate. Hold out your hands and say hallo to him . . . Karabo, bring two glasses there . . . Wait a bit—

What will you chew boys while Mister Kate and I have a drink? Nothing? Sure?

We were now going nicely on a straight tarred road and the trees rushed back. Mister Kate. What nonsense, I thought.

Look, Karabo, Madam's dogs are dead. What? Poison. I killed them. She drove me out of a job did she not? For nothing. Now I want her to feel she drove me out for something. I came back when you were in your room and took the things and poisoned them . . . And you know what? She has buried them in clean pink sheets in the garden. *Ao,* clean clean good sheets. I am going to dig them out and take one sheet do you want the other one? Yes, give me the other one I will send it to my mother . . . *Hei,* Karabo, see here they come. Monty and Malan. The bloody fools they do not want to stay in their hole. Go back you silly fools. Oh you do not want to move eh? Come here, now I am going to throw you in the big pool. No, Dick! No, Dick! no, no! Dick! They cannot speak do not kill things that cannot speak. Madam can speak for them she always does. No! Dick . . . !

I woke up with a jump after I had screamed Dick's name, almost hitting the window. My forehead was full of sweat. The red car also shot out of my sleep and was gone. I remembered a friend of ours who told us how she and the garden man had saved two white sheets in which their white master had buried their two dogs. They went to throw the dogs in a dam.

When I told my parents my story Father says to me he says, So long as you are in good health, my child, it is good. The worker dies, work does not. There is always work. I know when I was a boy a strong sound body and a good mind were the biggest things in life. Work was always there, and the lazy man could never say there was no work. But today people see work as something bigger than everything else, bigger than health, because of money.

I reply I say, Those days are gone, Papa. I must go back to the city after resting a little to look for work. I must look after you. Today people are too poor to be able to help you.

I knew when I left Greenside that I was going to return

to Johannesburg to work. Money was little, but life was full and it was better than sitting in Phokeng and watching the sun rise and set. So I told Chimane to keep her eyes and ears open for a job.

I had been at Phokeng for one week when a red car arrived. Somebody was sitting in front with the driver, a white woman. At once I knew it to be that of Mrs. Plum. The man sitting beside her was showing her the way, for he pointed towards our house in front of which I was sitting. My heart missed a few beats. Both came out of the car. The white woman said Thank you to the man after he had spoken a few words to me.

I did not know what to do and how to look at her as she spoke to me. So I looked at the piece of cloth I was sewing pictures on. There was a tired but soft smile on her face. Then I remembered that she might want to sit. I went inside to fetch a low bench for her. When I remembered it afterwards, the thought came to me that there are things I never think white people can want to do at our homes when they visit for the first time: like sitting, drinking water or entering the house. This is how I thought when the white priest came to see us. One year at Easter Kate drove me home as she was going to the north. In the same way I was at a loss what to do for a few minutes.

Then Mrs. Plum says, I have come to ask you to come back to me, Karabo. Would you like to?

I say I do not know, I must think about it first.

She says, Can you think about it today? I can sleep at the town hotel and come back tomorrow morning, and if you want to you can return with me.

I wanted her to say she was sorry to have sent me away, I did not know how to make her say it because I know white people find it too much for them to say Sorry to a black person. As she was not saying it, I thought of two things to make it hard for her to get me back and maybe even lose me in the end.

I say, You must ask my father first, I do not know, should I call him?

Mrs. Plum says, Yes.

I fetched both Father and Mother. They greeted her while I brought benches. Then I told them what she wanted.

Father asks Mother and Mother asks Father. Father asks me. I say if they agree, I will think about it and tell her the next day.

Father says, It goes by what you feel, my child.

I tell Mrs. Plum I say, if you want me to think about it I must know if you will want to put my wages up from £6 because it is too little.

She asks me, How much will you want?

Up by £4.

She looked down for a few moments.

And then I want two weeks at Easter and not just the weekend. I thought if she really wanted me she would want to pay for it. This would also show how sorry she was to lose me.

Mrs. Plum says, I can give you one week. You see you already have something like a rest when I am in Durban in the winter.

I tell her I say I shall think about it.

She left.

The next day she found me packed and ready to return with her. She was very much pleased and looked kinder than I had ever known her. And me, I felt sure of myself more than I had ever done.

Mrs. Plum says to me, You will not find Monty and Malan.

Oh?

Yes, they were stolen the day after you left. The police have not found them yet. I think they are dead myself.

I thought of Dick . . . my dream. Could he? And she . . . did this woman come to ask me to return because she had lost two animals she loved?

Mrs. Plum says to me she says, You know, I like your people, Karabo, the Africans.

And Dick and me? I wondered.

Charles Mungoshi

Mungoshi was born in 1947 near Chivhu, Rhodesia (now Zimbabwe), to a Shona-speaking family. An acclaimed writer in both English and Shona, he has worked as a bookstore clerk, an editor at the Literature Bureau, literary director at Zimbabwe Publishing House, and writer-in-residence at the University of Zimbabwe. Many of his stories illustrate the tension within families as their members wrestle with maintaining loyalty to traditional, rural values that are in conflict with their desire to be successful in modern cities and a Western European educational system. His work has both won government prizes and been banned; his most prominent novel, *Waiting for the Rain* (1972), is now required reading at many Zimbabwean schools. Mungoshi is also a poet, and the author of the memoirs *Stories from a Shona Childhood* (1989), *One Day Long Ago: More Stories from a Shona Childhood* (1991), and *Walking Still* (1997). Among his many awards are the Commonwealth Literature Prize for Africa and two Rhodesian PEN awards.

Who Will Stop the Dark?
(1980)

The boy began to believe what the other boys at school said about his mother. In secret he began to watch her—her face, words and actions. He would also watch his father's bare arched back as he toiled at his basket-weaving from day to day. His mother could go wherever she wanted to go. His father could not. Every morning he would drag his useless lower limbs out of the hut and sit under the *muonde* tree. He would not leave the tree till late in the evening when he would drag himself again back into the hut for his evening meal and bed. And always the boy felt a stab of pain when he looked at the front of his father's wet urine-stiffened trousers.

The boy knew that his mother had something to do with this condition of his father. The tight lines round her mouth and her long silences that would sometimes erupt into unexpected bursts of red violence said so. The story was that his father had fallen off the roof he had been thatching and broken his back. But the boy didn't believe it. It worried him. He couldn't imagine it. One day his father had just been like any other boy's father in their village, and the next day he wasn't. It made him wonder about his mother. He felt that it wasn't safe in their house. So he began to spend most of his time with the old man, his grandfather.

"I want you in the house," his mother said, when she could afford words, but the boy knew she was saying it all the time by the way she tightened her mouth and lowered her looking-away-from-people eyes.

The boy remembered that his grandfather had lived under the same roof with them for a long time. He couldn't remember how he had then come to live alone in his own hut half a mile from their place.

"He is so childish," he heard his mother say one day.

"He is old," his father said, without raising his head from his work.

"And how old do you think my mother is?" The lines round his mother's mouth drew tighter and tauter.

"Women do not grow as weak as men in their old age," his father persisted.

"Because it's the men who have to bear the children—so they grow weak from the strain!" His mother's eyes flashed once—so that the boy held his breath—and then she looked away, her mouth wrinkled tightly into an obscene little hole that reminded the boy of a cow's behind just after dropping its dung. He thought now his father would keep quiet, He was surprised to hear him say, "A man's back is the man. Once his back is broken—" Another flash of his mother's eye silenced him and the boy couldn't stand it. He stood up to go out.

"And where are you going?" his mother shouted after him.

"To see Grandfather."

"What do you want there with him?"

The boy turned back and stayed round the yard until his mother disappeared into the house. Then he quietly slid off for his grandfather's place through the bush. His father pretended not to see him go.

The old man had a way of looking at the boy: like someone looking into a mirror to see how badly his face had been burned.

"A, Zakeo," the old man said when the boy entered the yard. He was sitting against the wall of his hut, smoking his pipe quietly, looking into the distance. He hadn't even looked in Zakeo's direction.

"Did you see me this time?" Zakeo asked, laughing. He never stopped being surprised by the way his grandfather seemed to know everyone by their footfalls and would greet them by their names without even looking at them.

"I don't have to look to know it's you," the old man said.

"But today I have changed my feet to those of a bird," the boy teased him.

"No." The old man shook his head. "You are still the cat in my ears."

The boy laughed over that and although the old man smoked on without changing his expression, the boy knew that he was laughing too.

"Father said to ask you how you have spent the day," the boy said, knowing that the old man would know that it was a lie. The boy knew he would be forgiven this lie because the old man knew that the boy always wished his father would send him with such a message to his own father.

"You don't have to always protect him like that," the old man growled, almost to himself.

"*Sekuru?*" The boy didn't always understand most of the grown-up things the old man said.

"I said get on with the work. Nothing ever came out of a muscular mouth and snail-slime hands."

The boy disappeared into the hut while the old man sat on, smoking.

Zakeo loved doing the household chores for his grandfather: sweeping out the room and lighting the fire, collecting firewood from the bush and fetching water from the well and cooking. The old man would just look on, not saying anything much, just smoking his pipe. When he worked the boy didn't talk. Don't use your mouth and hands at the same time, the old man had told him once, and whenever he forgot the old man reminded him by not answering his questions. It was a different silence they practiced in the old man's house, the boy felt. Here, it was always as if his grandfather was about to tell him a secret. And when he left his parents' place he felt he must get back to the old man at the earliest opportunity to hear the secret.

"Have you ever gone hunting for rabbits, boy?" his grandfather asked him one day.

"No, *Sekuru*. Have you?"

The old man didn't answer. He looked away at the darkening landscape, puffing at his pipe.

"Did you like it?" the boy asked.

"Like it? We lived for nothing else, boy. We were born hunters, stayed hunters all our life and most of us died hunters."

"What happened to those who weren't hunters?"

"They became tillers of the land, and some, weavers of bamboo baskets."

"You mean Father?"

"I am talking of friends I used to know."

"But didn't you ever teach Father to hunt, *Sekuru*?" The boy's voice was strained, anxious, pained. The old man looked at him briefly and then quickly away.

"I taught him everything a man ought to know," he said distantly.

"Basket-weaving too?"

"That was his mother," the old man said and then silently went on, *his mother, your grandmother, my wife, taught your father basket-weaving. She also had been taught by a neighbor who later gave me the lumbago.*

"You like basket-weaving?" he asked the boy.

"I hate it!" The old man suddenly turned, surprised at the boy's vehemence. He took the pipe out of his mouth for a minute, looking intently at the boy, then he looked away, returning the pipe to his mouth.

"Do you think we could go hunting together, *Sekuru?*" the boy asked.

The old man laughed.

"Sekuru?" The boy was puzzled.

The old man looked at him.

"Please?"

The old man stroked the boy's head. "Talk of fishing," he said. "Or mouse-trapping. Ever trapped for mice?"

"No."

"Of course, you wouldn't have." He looked away. "You go to school these days."

"I don't like school!" Again, the old man was taken by surprise at the boy's violence. He looked at his grandson. The first son of his first son and only child. The boy's thirteen-year-old fists were clenched tightly and little tears danced in his eyes. *Could he believe in a little snotty-arse boy's voice? He looks earnest enough. But who doesn't, at the I-shall-never-die age of thirteen?* The old man looked away as if from the sight of the boy's death.

"I tell you I *hate* school!" the boy hissed.

"I hear you," the old man said quietly but didn't look at him. He was aware of the boy looking at him, begging him to believe him, clenching tighter his puny fists, his big ignorant eyes daring him to try him out on whatever milk-scented dream of heroics the boy might be losing sleep over at this difficult time of his life. The old man felt desolate.

"You don't believe me, do you, *Sekuru?*"

"Of course. I do!"

The boy suddenly uncoiled, ashamed and began to wring his hands, looking down at the ground.

That was unnecessarily harsh, the old man felt. So he stroked the boy's head again. *Thank you, ancestors, for our physical language that will serve our sons and daughters till we are dust.* He wished he could say something in words, something that the boy would clearly remember without it creating echoes in his head. He didn't want to give the boy an echo which he would later on mistake for the genuine thing.

"Is mouse-trapping very hard, *Sekuru*?" the boy asked, after some time.

"Nothing is ever easy, boy. But then, nothing is ever really hard for one who wants to learn."

"I would like to try it. Will you teach me?"

Physically, the old man didn't show anything, but he recoiled inwardly, the warmth in the center of him turned cold. *Boys' pranks, like the honey-bird luring you to a snake's nest. If only it were not this world, if only it were some other place where what we did today weren't our future, to be always there, held against us, to always see ourselves in . . .*

"And school?" he asked, as if he needed the boy to remind him again.

It was the boy's turn to look away, silent, unforgiving, betrayed.

As if stepping on newly-laid eggs, the old man learned a new language: not to touch the boy's head any more.

"There is your mother," he said, looking away, the better to make his grandson realize the seriousness of what he was talking about. From the corner of his eye he watched his grandson struggling with it, and saw her dismissed—not quite in the old way—but in a way that filled him with regrets for opportunities lost and a hopeless future.

"And if she doesn't mind?" the boy asked mischievously.

"You mean you will run away from school?" The old man restrained from stroking the boy's head.

"Maneto ran away from school and home two weeks ago. They don't know where he is right now."

Echoes, the old man repeated to himself. "But your mother is your mother," he said. *After all is said and done, basket-weaving never killed anyone. What kills is the rain and the hailstorms and the cold and the hunger when you are like this, when the echoes come.*

"I want to learn mouse-trapping, *Sekuru,*" the boy said. "At school they don't teach us that. It's always figures and numbers and I don't know what they mean and they all laugh at me."

The grandfather carefully pinched, with right forefinger and thumb, the ridge of flesh just above the bridge of his nose, closed his eyes and sighed. The boy looked at him eagerly, excited, and when he saw his grandfather settle back comfortably against the wall, he clapped his hands, rising up. The old man looked at him and was touched by the boy's excitement and not for the first time, he wondered at the mystery that is called life.

"Good night, *Sekuru,*" the boy said.

"Sleep well, Zakeo. Tell her that I delayed you if she asks where you have been." But the boy had already gone. The old man shook his head and prepared himself for another night of battle with those things that his own parents never told him exist.

They left the old man's hut well before sunrise the following day.

The boy had just come in and dumped his books in a corner of the room and they had left without any questions from the old man.

The grandfather trailed slowly behind the boy who ran ahead of him, talking and gesticulating excitedly. The old man just listened to him and laughed with him.

It was already uncomfortably warm at this hour before sunrise. It was October. The white cowtracks spread out straight and flat before them, through and under the new thick flaming *musasa* leaves, so still in the morning air.

Through patches in the dense foliage the sky was rusty-metal blue, October-opaque; the end of the long dry season, towards the *gukurahundi,* the very first heavy rains that would cleanse the air and clean the cowdung threshing floors of chaff, change and harden the crimson and bright-yellow leaves into hard green flat blades and bring back the stork, the millipede and the centipede, the fresh water crickets and the frogs, and the tiny yellow bird—*jesa*—that builds its nest on the river-reeds with the mouth of the nest facing down.

The air was harsh and still, and the old man thought, with renewed pleasure, of how he had almost forgotten the piercing whistle of that October-thirst bird, the *nonono,* and the shrill jarring ring of the cicada.

The cowtracks fell toward the river. They left the bush and came out into the open where the earth, bare and black from the *chirimo* fires, was crisscrossed with thousands of cattle-tracks which focused on the water-holes. The old man smelt wet river clay.

"It's hot," the boy said.

"It's October, *Gumiguru,* the tenth and hottest month of the year." The old man couldn't resist telling the boy a bit of what he must be going through.

The boy took off his school shirt and wound it round his waist.

"With a dog worth the name of dog—when dogs were still dogs—a rabbit goes nowhere in this kind of terrain," the old man said, seeing how naturally the boy responded to—blended in with—the surroundings.

"Is that why people burn the grass?"

"Aa, so you know that, too?"

"Maneto told me."

"Well, it's partly why we burn the grass but mainly we burn it so that new grass grows for our animals."

Finally, the river, burnt down now by the long rainless months to a thin trickle of blood, running in the shallow, sandy bottom of a vlei. But there were still some fairly deep water holes and ponds where fish could be found.

"These ponds are great for *muramba,*" the old man said.
"You need fairly clean flowing water for *magwaya*—the flat
short-spear-blade fish."

They dug for worms in the wet clay on the river banks.
The old man taught the boy how to break the soft earth
with a digging stick for the worms.

"Worms are much easier to find," the old man said.
"They stay longer on the hook. But a maggot takes a fish
faster." Here the old man broke off, suddenly assailed with
a very vivid smell of three-day-old cowdung, its soft cool
feel and the entangled wriggling yellow mass of maggots
packed in it.

"Locusts and hoppers are good too, but in bigger rivers,
like Munyati where the fish are so big they would take another fish for a meal. Here the fish are smaller and cleverer.
They don't like hoppers."

The old man looked into the coffee tin into which they
were putting the worms and said, "Should be enough for
me one day. There is always some other place we can get
some more when these are finished. No need to use more
than we should."

"But if they should get finished, *Sekuru*? Look, the tin
isn't full yet." Zakeo looked intently at his grandfather. He
wanted to fit in all the fishing that he would ever do before
his mother discovered that he was playing truant from
school. The old man looked at him. He understood. But he
knew the greed of thirteen-year-olds and the retribution of
the land and the soil when well-known laws were not
obeyed.

"There will always be something when we get where
these worms run out."

They walked downstream along the bank, their feet
kicking up clouds of black and white ash.

The sun came up harsh and red-eyed upstream. They
followed a tall straight shadow and a short stooped one
along the stream until they came to a dark pool where the
water, though opaque, wasn't really dirty.

"Here we are. I will get us some reeds for fishing rods

while you prepare the lines. The hooks are already on the lines."

The old man produced from a plastic bag a mess of tangled lines and metal blue-painted hooks.

"Here you are. Straighten these out."

He then proceeded to cut some tall reeds on the river bank with a pocket knife the boy had seen him poking tobacco out of his pipe with.

"Excellent rods, look." He bent one of the reeds till the boy thought it was going to break, and when he let go, the rod shot back like a whip!

"See?" the old man said.

The boy smiled and the old man couldn't resist slapping him on the back.

The boy then watched the old man fasten the lines to the rods.

"In my day," the old man said, "there were woman knots and men knots. A woman knot is the kind that comes apart when you tug the line. A knot worth the name of whoever makes it shouldn't fall apart. Let the rod break, the line snap, but a knot, a real man's knot, should stay there."

They fished from a rock by a pool.

"Why do you spit on the bait before you throw the line into the pool, *Sekuru*?"

The old man grinned. "For luck, boy, there is nothing you do that fate has no hand in. Having a good hook, a good line, a good rod, good bait or a good pool is no guarantee that you will have good fishing. So little is knowledge, boy. The rest is just mere luck."

Zakeo caught a very small fish by the belly.

"What's this?" he asked.

"A very good example of what I call luck! They aren't usually caught by the belly. You need several all-way facing hooks in very clear water even without bait—for you to catch them like that!"

The boy laughed brightly and the old man suddenly heard the splash of a kingfisher as it flew away, fish in beak, and this mixed with the smell of damp-rotting leaves and moisty river clay made the old man think: nothing is changed since our time. Then, a little later: except me. Self-consciously, with a sly look at the boy to make sure he wasn't seeing him, the old man straightened his shoulders.

The boy's grandfather hooked a frog and dashed it against a rock.

"What's that?" the boy asked.

"Know why I killed that—that—criminal?" he asked the boy.

"No, *Sekuru.*"

"Bad luck. Throw it back into the pool and it's going to report to the fish."

"But what is it?"

"Uncle Frog."

"A frog!" The boy was surprised.

"Shhh," the old man said. "Not a frog. Uncle Frog. You hear?"

"But why Uncle Frog, *Sekuru?*"

"Just the way it is, boy. Like the rain. It comes on its own."

Once again, the boy didn't understand the old man's grown-up talk. The old man saw it and said, "That kind of criminal is only good for dashing against the rock. You don't eat frogs, do you?"

The boy saw that the old man was joking with him. "No," he said.

"So why should we catch him on our hook when we don't eat him or need him?"

"I don't know, *Sekuru.*" The boy was clearly puzzled.

"He is the spy of the fish," the old man said in such a way that the boy sincerely believed him.

"But won't the fish notice his absence and wonder where he has gone to?"

"They won't miss him much. When they begin to do we will be gone. And when we come back here, they will have forgotten. Fish are just like people. They forget too easily."

It was grown-up talk again but the boy thought he would better not ask the man what he meant because he knew he wouldn't be answered.

They fished downriver till they came to where the Chambara met the Suka River.

"From here they go into Munyati," the old man said to himself, talking about his old hunting grounds; and to the boy, talking about the rivers.

"Where the big fish are," the boy said.

"You know that too?" the old man said, surprised.

"Maneto and his father spent days and days fishing the Munyati and they caught fish as big as men," the boy said seriously.

"Did Maneto tell you that?"

"Yes. And he said his father told him that *you, Sekuru,* were the only hunter who ever got to where the Munyati gets into the big water, the sea. Is that true?"

The old man pulled out his pipe and packed it. They were sitting on a rock. He took a long time packing and lighting the pipe.

"Is it true?" the boy asked.

"I was lost once," the old man said. "The Munyati goes into just another small water—but bigger than itself—and more powerful."

The boy would have liked to ask the man some more questions on this one but he felt that the old man wouldn't talk about it.

"You aren't angry, *Sekuru*?" the boy asked, looking up earnestly at his grandfather.

The old man looked at him, surprised again. *How do these milk-nosed ones know what we feel about all this?*

"Let's get back home," he said.

Something was bothering the old man, the boy realized, but what it was he couldn't say. All he wanted him to tell him was the stories he had heard from Maneto—whether they were true or not.

They had caught a few fish, enough for their supper, the boy knew, but the old man seemed angry. And that, the boy couldn't understand.

When they got back home the boy lit the fire, and with directions from the old man helped him to gut and salt the fish. After a very silent supper of sadza and salted fish the boy said he was going.

"Be sure to come back tomorrow," the old man said.

And the boy knew that whatever wrong he had done the old man, he would be told the following day.

Very early the following morning the boy's mother paid her father-in-law a visit. She stood in front of the closed door for a long time before she knocked. She had to collect herself.

"Who is there?" the old man answered from within the hut. He had heard the footsteps approaching but he did not leave his blankets to open up for her.

"I would like to talk to you," she said, swallowing hard to contain her anger.

"Ah, it's Zakeo's mother?"

"Yes."

"And what bad winds blow you this way this early, *muroora*?"

"I want to talk to you about my son."

"Your son?"

She caught her breath quickly. There was a short silence. The old man wouldn't open the door.

"I want to talk about Zakeo," she called.

"What about him?"

"Please leave him alone."

"You are telling me that?"

"He must go to school."

"And so?"

She was quiet for a minute; then she said, "Please."

"What have I done to him?"

"He won't eat, he won't listen to me, and he doesn't want to go to school."

"And he won't listen to his father?" the old man asked.

"He listens to *you.*"

"And you have come here this early to beat me up?"

She swallowed hard. "He is the only one I have. Don't let him destroy his future."

"He does what he wants."

"At his age? What does he know?"

"Quite a lot."

She was very angry, he could feel it through the closed door.

She said, "He will only listen to you. Please, help us."

Through the door the old man could feel her tears coming. He said, "He won't even listen to his father?"

"His father?" he heard her snort.

"Children belong to the man, *you* know that," the old man warned her.

And he heard her angry feet as she went away.

Zakeo came an hour after his mother had left the old man's place. His grandfather didn't say anything to him. He watched the boy throw his school bag in the usual corner of the hut; then after the usual greetings, he went out to bring in the firewood.

"Leave the fire alone," the old man said. "I am not cold."

"Sekuru?" The boy looked up, hurt.

"Today we go mouse-trapping in the fields."

"Are we going right now?"

"Yes."

"I'll make the fire if you like. We can go later."

"No. Now." The old man was quiet for some time, looking away from the boy.

"Are you all right, *Sekuru?*"

"Yes."

"We will go later when it's warm if you like."

The old man didn't answer him.

And as they came into the open fields with the last season's corn crop stubble, the boy felt that the old man wasn't quite well.

"We can do it some other day, *Sekuru.*"

His grandfather didn't answer.

They looked for the smooth mouse-tracks in the corn stubble and the dry grass. Zakeo carried the flat stones that the old man pointed out to him to the places where he wanted to set up the traps. He watched his grandfather setting the traps with the stone and two sticks. The sticks were about seven inches long each. One of them was the male and the other the female stick. The female was in the shape of a Y and the male straight.

The old man would place the female stick upright in the ground with the forked end facing up. The male would be placed in the fork parallel to the ground to hold up one end of the stone across the mousepath. The near end of the male would have a string attached to it and at the other end of the string would be the "trigger"—a matchstick-sized bit of straw that would hold the bait-stick against the male stick. The stone would be kept one end up by the delicate tension in the string and if a mouse took the bait the trigger would fly and the whole thing fall across the path onto the unfortunate victim.

The boy learned all this without words from the old man, simply by carefully watching him set about ten traps all over the field that morning. Once he tried to ask a question and he was given a curt, "Mouths are for women." Then he too set up six traps and around noon the old man said, "Now we will wait."

They went to the edge of the field where they sat under the shade of a *mutsamwi* tree. The old man carefully, tiredly, rested his back against the trunk of the tree, stretched himself out, sighed, and closing his eyes, took out his pipe and tobacco pouch and began to load. The boy sat beside him, looking on. He sensed a tension he had never felt in his grandfather. Suddenly it wasn't fun any more. He looked away at the distant hills in the west. Somewhere behind those hills the Munyati went on to the sea, or the other bigger river which the old man hadn't told him about.

"Tell me a story, *Sekuru,*" Zakeo said, unable to sit in his grandfather's silence.

"Stories are for the night," the old man said without opening his mouth or taking out the pipe. "The day is for watching and listening and learning."

Zakeo stood up and went a little way into the bush at the edge of the field. Tears stung his eyes but he would not let himself cry. He came back a little later and lay down beside the old man. He had hardly closed his eyes in sleep, just at that moment when the voices of sleep were beginning to talk, when he felt the old man shaking him up.

"The day is not for sleeping," the old man said quietly but firmly. He still wasn't looking at Zakeo. The boy rubbed the sleep out of his eyes and blinked.

"Is that what they teach you at school?"

"Sekuru?"

The old man groaned in a way that told Zakeo what he thought of school.

The boy felt ashamed that he had hurt his grandfather. "I am sorry."

The grandfather didn't answer or look at him. Some time later he said, "Why don't you go and play with the other boys of your own age?"

"Where?"

"At school. Anywhere. Teach them what you have learned."

The boy looked away for some time. He felt deserted, the old man didn't want him around any more. Things began to blur in his eyes. He bit his lip and kept his head stiffly turned away from his grandfather.

"You can teach them all I have taught you. Huh?"

"I don't think they would listen to me," the boy answered, still looking away, trying to control his voice.

"Why?"

"They never listen to me."

"Why?"

"They—they—just don't." He bit his lower lip harder but a big tear plopped down on his hand. He quickly wiped away the tear and then for a terrible second they wouldn't stop coming. He was ashamed in front of his grandfather. The old man, who had never seen any harm in boys crying, let him be.

When the boy had stopped crying he said, "Forget them."

"Who?"

"Your friends."

"They are not my friends. They are always laughing at me."

"What about?"

"O, all sorts of silly things."

"That doesn't tell me what sort of things."

"O, O, *lots of things!*" The boy's face was contorted in an effort to contain himself. Then he couldn't stop himself, "They are always at me saying your father is your mother's horse. Your mother rides hyenas at night. Your mother is a witch. Your mother killed so-and-so's child. Your mother digs up graves at night and you all eat human flesh which she hunts for you." He stopped. "O, lots of things I don't know!" The boy's whole body was tensed with violent hatred. The old man looked at him, amused.

"Do they really say that, now?"

"Yes and I know I could beat them all in a fight but the headmaster said we shouldn't fight and Father doesn't want me to fight either. But I know I can lick them all in a fight."

The old man looked at the boy intensely for some time, his pipe in his hand; then he looked away to the side and spat out brown spittle. He returned the pipe to his mouth and said, "Forget them. They don't know a thing." He then sighed and closed his eyes once more and settled a little deeper against the tree.

The boy looked at him for a long time and said, "I don't want to go to school, *Sekuru.*"

"Because of your friends?"

"They are not *my friends*!" He glared blackly at his grandfather, eyes flashing brilliantly and then, ashamed, confused, rose and walked a short distance away.

The old man looked at him from the corner of his eyes and saw him standing, looking away, body tensed, stiff and stubborn. He called out to him quietly, with gentleness, "Come back, Zakeo. Come and sit here by me."

Later on the boy woke up from a deep sleep and asked the old man whether it was time yet for the traps. He had come out of sleep with a sudden startled movement as if he were a little strange animal that had been scared by hunting dogs.

"That must have been a very bad dream," the old man said.

Zakeo rubbed the sleep out of his eyes and blinked. He stared at the old man, then the sun which was very low in the west, painting everything with that ripe mango hue that always made him feel sad. Tall dark shadows were creeping eastward. He had that strange feeling that he had overslept into the next day. In his dream his mother had been shouting at him that he was late for school. A rather chilly wind was blowing across the desolate fields.

"Sit down here beside me and relax," the old man said. "We will give the mice one more hour to return home from visiting their friends. Or to fool themselves that it's already night and begin hunting."

Zakeo sat beside his grandfather and then he felt very relaxed.

"You see?" the old man said. "Sleep does you good when you are tired or worried. But otherwise don't trust sleeping during the day. When you get to my age you will learn to sleep without sleeping."

"How is that?"

"Never mind. It just happens."

Suddenly, sitting in silence with the old man didn't bother him any more.

"You can watch the shadows or the setting sun or the movement of the leaves in the wind—or the sudden agitation in the grass that tells you some little animal is moving in there. The day is for watching and listening and learning."

He had got lost somewhere in his thoughts when the old man said, "Time for the traps."

That evening the old man taught him how to gut the mice, burn off the fur in a low-burning flame, boil them till they were cooked and then arrange them in a flat open pan close to the fire to dry them so that they retained as little moisture as possible which made them firm but solidly pleasant on eating.

After supper the old man told him a story in which the

hero seemed to be always falling into one misfortune after another, but always getting out through his own resourcefulness only to fall into a much bigger misfortune—on and on without the possibility of a happily ever after. It seemed as if the old man could go on and on inventing more and more terrible situations for his hero and improvising solutions as he went on till the boy thought he would never hear the end of the story.

"The story had no ending," the old man told him when he asked. He was feeling sleepy and he was afraid his mother would put a definite stop to his visits to the old man's place, even if it meant sending him out to some distant relative.

"Carry her these mice," the old man said when Zakeo said good night and stood up to go. "I don't think she will beat you tonight. She loves mice," he said with a little laugh.

But when he got home his mother threw the mice to the dog.

"What did I tell you?" she demanded of him, holding the oxhide strop.

Zakeo didn't answer. He was looking at his mother without blinking, ready to take the strop like Ndatofa, the hero in the old man's story. In the corner of his eye he saw his father working at his baskets, his eyes watering from the guttering smoking lamp he used to give him light. The crow's-feet round his eyes made him appear as if he were wincing from some invisible pain.

"Don't you answer when I am talking to you?" his mother said.

The boy kept quiet, sitting erect, looking at his mother. Then she made a sound which he couldn't understand, a sound which she always uttered from some unliving part of her when she was mad. She was blind with rage but the boy held in his screams right down there where he knew screams and sobs came from. He gritted his teeth and felt the scalding lashes cutting deep into his back, right down to where they met the screams, where they couldn't go any farther. And each time the strop cut into him and he didn't scream his mother seemed to get madder and madder. His father tried to intervene but he quickly returned to his basket-weaving when the strop cracked into *his* back twice in quick merciless succession. It was then that Zakeo almost let out a deafening howl. He closed his eyes so tightly that veins stood out in his face. He felt on fire.

"I could kill you—you—you!" He heard his mother scream and he waited, tensed, for the strop and then suddenly as if someone had told him, he knew it wasn't coming. He opened his eyes and saw that his mother had dropped the strop and was crying herself. She rushed at him and began to hug him.

"My Zakeo! My own son. What are you doing this to me for? Tell me. What wrong have I done to you, ha? O, I know! I know very well who is doing this to you. He never wanted your father to marry me!"

He let her hug him without moving but he didn't let her hugging and crying get as far as the strop lashes. *That* was his own place. He just stopped her hugs and tears before they got *there*. And when he had had enough, he removed her arms from round him and stood up. His mother looked at him, surprised, empty hands that should have contained his body becoming emptier with the expression on her face.

"Where are you going, Zakeo?" It was as if *he* had slapped her.

"Do you care?"

"Zakeo! I am *your* mother! Do you know that? No one here cares for you more than I do! Not *him*!" pointing at his father. "And *not* even him!"—indicating in the direction of his grandfather's hut.

"You don't know anything," Zakeo said, without understanding what he meant by that but using it because he had heard it used of his classmates by the old man.

"You don't know anything." He repeated it, becoming more and more convinced of its magical effect on his mother who gaped at him as if she was about to sneeze.

As he walked out he caught sight of his father who was working furiously at his baskets, his head almost touching his knees and his back bent double.

The old man was awake when Zakeo walked in.

"Put another log on the fire," the old man said.

Zakeo quietly did so. His back ached but the heat had gone. He felt a little relaxedly cool.

"You didn't cry today."

The boy didn't answer.

"But you will cry one day."

The boy stopped raking the coals and looked at the old man, confused.

"You will cry one day and you will think your mother was right."

"But—" The boy stopped, lost. The night had turned suddenly chilly, freaky weather for October. He had been too involved with something else to notice it when he walked the half mile between their place and the old man's. Now he felt it at his back and he shivered.

"Get into the blankets, you will catch a cold," the old man said.

Zakeo took off his shirt and left the shorts on. He got into the blankets beside the old man, on the side away from the fire.

"One day you will want to cry but you won't be able to," the old man said.

"Sekuru?"

"I said get into the blankets."

The boy lay down on his left side, facing the wall, away from the old man and drew up his knees with his hands between them. He knew he wouldn't be able to sleep on his back that night.

"Thirteen," the old man said, shaking his head.

"Sekuru?"

"Sleep now. I must have been dreaming."

Zakeo pulled the smoke-and-tobacco-smelling ancient blankets over his head.

"Who doesn't want to cry a good cry once in a while but there are just not enough tears to go round all of us?"

"Sekuru?"

"You still awake?"

"Yes."

"You want to go to school?"

"No."

"Go to sleep then."

"I can't."

"Why?"

"I just can't."

"Try. It's good for you. Think of fishing."

"Yes, *Sekuru.*"

"Or mouse-trapping."

"And hunting?"

"Yes. Think all you like of hunting."

"You will take me hunting some day, won't you, *Sekuru*?"

"Yes," the old man said and then after some time, "When the moon becomes your mother's necklace."

"You spoke, *Sekuru*?"

"I said yes."

"Thank you, *Sekuru.* Thank you very much."

"Thank you, *Sekuru,* thank you very much." The old man mimicked the boy, shook his head sadly—knowing that the following day the boy would be going to school. Soon, he too was fast asleep, dreaming of that mountain which he had never been able to climb since he was a boy.

GRACE OGOT

Grace Ogot was born in Kenya in 1930 and was educated at Ngiya and Butere Girls' High Schools. She
trained as a nurse in Uganda and England, but also
worked as a journalist and tutor before becoming one
of the first women in Parliament and the only woman to
serve as an assistant minister in the cabinet of President Daniel arap Moi. She was later a founding member
of the Writers Association of Kenya. She was a prolific
writer, who published several novels and two collections of short stories. Her first novel, *The Promised
Land* (1966), is the powerful story of a family's decision
to emigrate and its tragic consequences. She is well-
known for her compelling stories of the challenges that
women must overcome in a patriarchal society and often described village life. Among her many works are
The Graduate (1980), *The Strange Bride* (1989), and
The Island of Tears (1980). She died in 2010.

The Middle Door
(1976)

It was already 5:30 p.m., but my husband was nowhere
to be seen. In sheer panic I called a taxi.

"You can't catch that train," the taxi-driver said.

"Please try," I pleaded. "I just must catch it, please!"

"As you like, madam." The heavy slamming down of the
receiver, and his voice, indicated that it did not matter to
him either way. He would be paid whether I missed the
train or caught it.

My heart raced—apprehension about my husband's

safety, and the fear of missing the train made my eyes watery as Osanya and I rushed to the yard with the luggage to wait for the taxi. A thought came to me, "Cancel the journey—you cannot go on such a long journey without seeing your husband. How can you tell what has happened to him?" But before I could make up my mind the taxi zoomed in at breakneck speed, stopping just a few inches from my feet. The man flung both doors open. We jumped in without a word, my suitcase propped up beside me, and Osanya sitting with the driver in front.

We wriggled our way between the buses and the large cars, taking narrow chances at every roundabout. At the junction of Jamhuri Avenue and Uhuru Highway we only just missed two pedestrians who had expected the taxi to slow down. We swerved right, left, and then right again, to get out of the way of a Mercedes Benz which was coming at a high speed on the outer lane on the left-hand side. Its throaty hooter nearly blew us off the road. As they passed us, the driver, clad in starched uniform and a peaked hat, gave us a dirty and accusing look while a rotund figure in a black suit and wearing thick rimmed glasses sat in the middle of the back seat holding a strap. Dignity and power distorted what would have been, at first sight, a very handsome face. He eyed us much longer than his driver did, obviously feeling insulted that the rickety taxi did not move out of his way quickly enough.

I clung tight to the back seat. The driver swore under his breath, "Shenzi, we all pay for our licence." Osanya muttered something about *"Bwana mkubwa"* but I did not comment. We took another risk at the next roundabout opposite the railway station and stopped the car at the "Staff Only" white lines.

The large clock at the entrance to the station read a minute or so to six o'clock. I rushed through the gate without even showing my ticket. Osanya and the taxi man were running behind me.

My left foot was still on the pavement when the whistle went, announcing the departure of the train. How the taxi-

driver and Osanya got my luggage in my compartment, I do
not know. I just managed to get the right foot on the train
before it moved away. Perspiration ran down freely under
my arm and then rolled down along my side. I dashed to
the window in compartment D.

"Pesa, mama, pesa."

"Oh my God," I gasped. The ten shilling note for the
taxi-driver was still in my sweaty hand. The train was already moving, but the two men ran faster. I threw the ten
shilling note at them. They caught it in the air, to the laughter of all. Now they waved and I waved back genuinely—to
chase away the evil thought which nagged at me.

"All other passengers are seen off by their beloved ones,
while all you have is a taxi-driver and a gardener."

"Tell the Doctor to ring Kisumu, Osanya, eh—don't forget, or I will have nobody to meet me the other side."

He said something which I did not hear. The train had
gathered momentum and the gap between us widened. I
waved till we took a bend and were out of sight.

We entered a tunnel and there was complete temporary
darkness. I wondered now why I had decided to travel by
train after six years! Suddenly we came out into the open,
and the landscape facing Limuru was a magnificent sight.
Here and there ridges rose high revealing rich red soil between the shrubs only to taper down gradually into a valley
below. The rusty tin-roofed huts standing together marked
out a small family homestead on the ridges, leaving the
sloping land and the valley below for cultivation. Here and
there smoke curled skywards where women were preparing the evening meal. As it was harvesting season, the
aroma of the new maize on the cobs, being roasted by the
boys on the open fires, filled the air, and sent saliva jetting
out from our mouths.

Heavy footsteps at my door drew my attention from the
beautiful scenery. My eyes rested on a woman carrying a
huge *kikapu*. She was trying to push her way through my
compartment door. Behind her a porter whose khaki uniform carried the letters E.A.R. & H. also entered the room

carrying a big red cock and a three-foot bunch of unripe bananas. He dumped the bananas and the cock on the floor and, completely ignoring me, said to the woman, "I hope you will now feel comfortable."

The cock, with legs tied and wings left free, flapped dangerously towards me. I moved my legs in haste to protect my new pair of stockings. The woman pulled the cock away. She then rearranged the *kikapu* and the bunch of bananas in the small space between us, and made herself comfortable next to me. She broke the silence.

"*Misawa,*" she said.

"*Misawa,*" I replied coldly.

"Where are you going?" she asked.

"To Kisumu," I said half in a temper.

"Oh, we have the same destination," she said politely.

The train rocked away, and my stomach churned. Anger welled up in me. Could this be true? I pay sh 128 for a first-class compartment, only to land with that amount of luggage and a squawking cock on top of it. No, this could only be a big joke. I threw a side-glance at the newcomer. Her face was slightly turned towards the door, so that I could clearly see her without her knowing. She was perhaps younger than I. Her dark face was smooth and without any wrinkles or sordid makeup. Her dress with simple gathers, as was worn in the village, hung just below her knees. Her head-cloth was a bright multicolour print. She was fat, but was somewhat heavily built, revealing the comfortable life she led.

Many thoughts raced through my mind—"Tell her to move from here at once, this is a first class compartment. This is not your place, not your place, not with a cock anyway. Tell her I paid sh 128 to be alone."

But then I could not summon up enough courage. The words "independence," "equal rights for all" were written everywhere I looked. Did equality mean inconvenience? Did freedom give licence for chickens to travel first class? I got really annoyed, yet I could not pull myself together to throw this woman out of my room. Then a thought came to me which cooled me down a little. I got out my writing case and sorted out the papers which I wanted to work on—and piled them between the woman and myself. Now I turned to the woman whose eyes were fixed on the papers, out of curiosity.

"I was thinking that perhaps they could get you a different compartment," I told her.

"Why?" she asked politely. "There are two beds here."

Her well-mannered attitude annoyed me. I was in for a quarrel. I wanted an excuse to have a row, an excuse to tell her what was in my mind. I cleared my throat and then said, "I write books you see, that's why I travel by train. I have urgent work here which I must finish tonight, so I shall be keeping all the lights on. You will not be able to sleep." She hesitated, and I thought her temper was rising. But I was wrong. She eyed me from head to foot and then said:

"You write books for children, do you?"

"For everyone," I said, wondering if she could tell the difference between children's and adults' books.

"That is very important," she said in a matter-of-fact way.

I was furious with her. I was expecting her to be impressed and to say something like, "Oh you are so clever to be writing books." But instead, she continued in her indifferent style, "Children of today need good books to read, they are no longer listening to their parents."

At that point, a forced smile crept to my lips. The lady obviously had assumed that I was employed by the government to write books on delinquency. That, of course, was an important aspect of nation-building, and one did not have to be clever to be able to do it.

Now she eyed me closely and said, "Don't worry about me, madam. Lights don't worry me once I have slept. But even if they did, in public transport one has to dispense with the comforts of one's own house."

I looked at this woman unbelievingly. Our eyes met. Her eyes were soft and calm while mine were a flame of bewilderment. It was I who in the end had to look away. I could not stand the self-confidence of this simple village woman whose place with her crazy luggage was in the third class.

I took a piece of paper and started scribbling what I could not really follow. I could feel the woman's eyes on me. Eyes not full of hatred like mine, but eyes full of pity. She regarded me as a young woman who through luck or historical accident had managed to get education from the tax she paid. I had managed to marry some lucky man holding a big position in government where he sat on money and wielded undreamt-of power.

I felt her eyes accusing me. "Do you know who I am, you rich woman, eh? Where were you at the time when I and my kind nursed the wounded men during the struggle for independence? Where were you when we went without food and water? You, rich woman, when we carried the little food we could steal to feed our men, where were you? And what do you know about dying or sacrificing for a nation? Now you are proud because you are educated. You can write books. You have good clothes. Yes, you are very proud. But it is not my choice that I am the village woman, it is fate. It was just two weeks before our examination when the war broke out. The *Mzungu* seized our school and turned it into an army camp. That day we left the school and ran for our lives. The few girls they caught were tortured to death—we too were caught later. We were beaten and stripped naked before our families. We were tortured to reveal where our men were—but we would not give in. We looked at the soil our forefathers had fought for and weighed this against the reward the *Mzungu* would give us if we would betray our men, our own brothers and fathers. Ah, it was better and sweeter to die rather than hold hands with a *Mzungu*, a visitor who had now turned a ruler and a killer.

"For four years we knew nothing but hunger and death—and the smell of blood. Hope had gone. Schools and exams were soon forgotten, and sorrow quickly turned us into old women. The only thing we were longing for was the comfort and protection of a man which alone was capable of restoring the beauty of our womanhood which had been defiled by the white man. But men were rounded up daily and shot with big guns at night. We knew then that we would never know the worth of a man. The world was coming to an end."

I felt her anger was mounting and she was asking me threateningly, "Why, then, rich woman, can't I also enjoy the comforts of the freedom which the black man fought for, the fight which turned us into old women at a tender age? Eh? Tell me . . . I see your long pink nails, your powdered face and your prickly false hairpiece. You look much younger than you really are. You write books too, that is good. But now you leave me alone, you rich woman. Write your books till morning. I will sleep, I will not complain of the bright lights."

As I put my writing down and turned to admire the landscape, the woman's pitying eyes were still fixed on me. The sun was setting and the entire landscape was bathed in its delicate rays. At a sharp bend, the full length of the passenger train slid along the winding hills like a snake among rocks. My tricks had failed and short of creating a scene, the woman had no intention of moving.

At that point the gong went, very musically.

"What is that gong for?" my companion asked innocently.

"For food," I said curtly.

"I see," she said. Then silence.

The restaurant car was already full when I went for supper. Then I noticed the Ticket Examiner sitting at the snack bar on the left.

"Excuse me, sir," I said humbly.

"Yes, madam." He put down his knife and fork and got up.

"Sorry, sir, may I sit by you a minute while I wait for a table?"

"Sure, madam, and please sit down."

He pulled the chair out for me. I thanked him, then sat down.

"Eh . . . I thoroughly enjoyed your last book about a man with four wives. My favourite chapter is where the man orders his wives to work together, cook together, as one family, and they swear before him that the first one to break the rule must go. It is a great book. It is . . . we men love it."

He swallowed a mouthful of egg sandwich, and then faced me, half whispering like a person who is uncertain of his statement.

"Now your hand has been strengthened, my dear. The government has gone ahead and legalised polygamy. All women married to one man are to be equal in status. That combined with the sort of teamwork you advocate in your book—eh! For once, the men have a very fair deal! Just like it used to be during our grandmothers' days when polygamy was accepted as part of life, our heritage. In those days polygamy was a sign of dignity and wealth and the elder wife brought a girl of her own choice for her husband to marry. Eh!" He laughed loudly.

"In your next book, tell these educated, selfish and headstrong women who want to monopolise a man for themselves that a man is a dynamic being capable of caring for more than one wife."

"I am glad you enjoyed the book," I lied. I had no courage to tell him that I believed neither in polygamy nor in the misguided government law which recognised polygamy and demanded that the co-wives be treated as equals. I was not the author of the terrible anthropological book which had caused so much controversy in the country.

Anyway for the time being it did not pay to contradict the Ticket Examiner. His alleged interest in my books had broken the ice.

"Are you writing anything at the moment?" He pushed aside his empty cup.

"Oh yes," I said with a smile, "I'm always scribbling. This one is about urban life. I will send you a copy when it comes out."

"I would be delighted," he said after swallowing the last crust of bread.

I cleared my throat and then faced him.

"Sir, kindly do me a favour." A wicked smile played on my lips, for I never call anybody "sir," unless I am about to act devilishly.

"Most obliged," he said, wiping his mouth with a starched table napkin.

"I know I am asking too much, sir, but then the Bible says, 'Knock and it shall be opened unto you; ask and you shall receive.' I do write books and that is why I prefer travelling by train. Unfortunately tonight when I have very urgent work to finish, I am supposed to share a compartment with a lady who has a very noisy cock. Besides she has a large bunch of bananas and a big *kikapu* made of papyrus, and these, as you can imagine, don't leave me much room to work in. If it were possible, sir, I would greatly appreciate it if I could be moved to another compartment, so that I can concentrate."

"A lady with a cock and a bunch of bananas in a first class compartment? You can't be serious." He pulled out a small board from under his table on which he had the names of passengers. All compartments were fully booked. There were only three women in the first class coaches. That was me, a Mrs. Smith, and a Miss Larina Patel.

"I did not see Mrs. Smith with a cock or bananas, nor did Miss Patel carry these items!" He looked at me in utter disbelief.

"The lady is in my compartment right now as I speak to you. I don't really mind her staying if she can find another place for the cock and at least remove either the *kikapu* or the banana bunch. It is true that in an independent country we are all equal, and should learn to share facilities and amenities." I was trying to be sarcastic, but he was too shocked to notice it. His reaction to my report was quite violent.

"There cannot be a cock crowing in a first class compartment, independence or not. The East African Community has spent a fortune to make those places comfortable since the fare was doubled last September. I can't allow anybody to mess them up with chicken droppings simply because we are now independent.

"Look here, madam." He leaned forward. "In any country there are small people, middle people and big people. Community Ministers were not fools to create first class, second class and third class on these trains. This law is not peculiar to Kenya. It is practised in every country from the time of Jesus. Give honour to those who are in high positions. There must be a mistake somewhere. While you are having food, I will investigate this matter and deal with it accordingly."

"But please don't give the lady the impression that I am discriminating against her because of her class. This is not India where you have a class of untouchables. I would hate to feel that I am using my position to deny her the comfort she is entitled to."

"Don't waste your energy." The Ticket Examiner waved his hand in the air. "Leave it to me. You paid for a first class compartment. You must get your comfort." Then he left.

When I came back from supper, I could not believe my eyes. The woman, the cock, the banana bunch and the *kikapu* were no longer there. The compartment had been tidied and my bed made. Only traces of fine flour dotted the floor where the *kikapu* containing maize flour had rested. This is one thing my husband would not have accepted. A film of sadness blotted my eyes, making them moist. It was a pity to live with and love a man whose attitude to life was so different from one's own. Muga strongly believed in suffering with or without bitterness, while I avoided suffering of any sort.

I was working on chapter eleven of my next novel, *Thorns Among Flesh,* when I heard a squeaking noise. I quickly looked at the door—the bolt was in its place. My eyes moved slowly—and as they did, I saw the middle door which separated me from the next compartment starting to bulge inwards. For a moment I went stiff with fear. I had already changed into a thin transparent cotton nightdress because the evening was hot and oppressive. The bulge got bigger towards me, knocking down the suitcase which rested against the door. Instinctively, I jumped up from the lower seat where I was going to sleep, pushed the door with all my might, and then twiddled the bolt in its place. Was somebody trying to open the door from the other side? Now I stood with my back against the door, barefooted. My eyes darted around my compartment. The first thing that caught my eye was the notice — "ALARM SIGNAL: To stop the train pull the chain downwards." The chain glared at me, but my eyes moved away from it quickly. Then my eyes rested on the £200 fine or six months imprisonment or both, should you touch that chain without a grave reason. The other sign below the alarm signal was "It is dangerous to lean out of the window." That had nothing to do with me at night. The third sign was "IMPORTANT," written in red capital letters, followed with "BOLT FIRMLY the door of your compartment before you retire for the night." That was important. I had done that as soon as I came from supper. Still I checked on the main door again and made doubly sure that it was bolted — the middle door, too, was locked and then I made sure the window had been pulled to the very top.

Was somebody really trying to open the door from the other side? It could not be. There were two policemen next door. I had seen them there when I entered the train, heard them talking, saw them walking up and down the corridors. Then later on when I came from supper, they were sitting there with their door wide open. In fact I had felt quite happy and safe to have the police next door. I had not travelled by train for six years and had many hidden fears until I saw these policemen and my fears vanished. Now no drunk would wander along our corridor. Next to me on the other side was a couple with one son but there was no door between us.

I decided that I was imagining things. I had heard stories of cowards who, at night, would mistake trees for night-runners! Surely policemen would not open my door? My conclusion was that the apparent bulging of the door had been caused by the rocking of the train. But how could I be sure? I decided to go and inform the Ticket Examiner of my suspicion. But when I looked at my watch, it was past midnight. I had no idea where he slept, and, having thrown one passenger out of my compartment, I was scared of possible repercussions if my accusation of the policemen proved false. At best I would be dismissed as a persecution maniac or a person suffering from hysteria or hallucinations. At worst I could be charged with imputing improper motives in public servants engaged in their duty. I therefore decided to remove my bedding to the upper bed which was near the chain. That took me quite some time. After climbing onto the upper bed, I pushed the ladder away from it, and rested it instead against the door where it stood precariously. But it was better there.

Now I could not concentrate on anything. I decided to stay awake and watch that door. For a long time I watched while the train stopped at, and started from, several stations, but nothing happened beside the normal squeaking noises and rocking movement of a fast-moving train. It must have been my imagination, I concluded. I looked at my watch and it was 2:00 a.m. and my eyes could not stay open any more. I switched all the lights off and immediately fell asleep.

It was not a dream—in my sleep I could hear a squeaking noise coming from the same direction as before. I shook myself up and put on the lights above my head. But there was nothing unusual. The suspected door stood still with the bolt in its place and my suitcase against it. I must be crazy or sick, I blamed myself. A crazy woman. Everyone in the first class berth must have slept long ago while only one hysterical woman was still awake imagining things. I was being stupid.

I switched off the lights and slept, cursing myself for acting like a child. My mind was tired and the sleep was sweet. I heard squeaking noises for a long time—but because I was perhaps too tired, I did not bother any more, until the suitcase fell down with a big bang and the small wooden ladder standing against the door followed suit with a loud crash on the floor. I sat up instinctively and blasted on the main switch at the door. And there, wedged in the doorway in full uniform, all buttons down, were the two policemen, to whom I had entrusted my life. I felt sick, and numb. But the confusion left me quickly. These policemen no longer looked like friends. My eyes fixed on them, I moved upwards as I asked them in a trembling voice: "What do you two want, eh? . . . What do you want?" My thin nightdress left all the upper part of my chest bare. I had no sleeves except for a narrow strap that held the nightdress onto my body. The two men did not see me move towards the chain as their eyes were glued on the soft skin just above my breasts where the sun never reaches.

"We want you," one of the policemen answered, and his voice was cold, confident with an air of "there is nothing you can do about it, we get what we want."

"I don't understand you," I said.

"Alright, *Kisura* (Beautiful Face), maybe our English is not as good as yours. We don't write books as you do—we are saying, we both want you. You know, the way a man wants a woman. If you are not difficult, we are both experienced men just as you are. We will be quick, just the two of us."

I think it was their smile that sent me wild. "You are out of your mind," I shouted. "Completely out of your mind to think that I came here to be wanted by the police!" I spat on the clean floor just to emphasise the degree of contempt I had for them which I could not put into words. The spittle narrowly missed the black boots of the policeman on the right.

"Now, baby," the younger one said coldly. "There is no need to be rude, eh? I don't think you know us. You are new in your game, we are experienced in ours. Just give us what we want and you will come to no harm."

"You get out of here, or I will shout!"

"You can't shout," he said—and I saw his hand moving towards the unwieldy gun standing just by the doorway.

"You can't shout," he said. "You give it to other men—who give you money. We must have it too, with or without money. Look at your painted nails. Look at your hair and polished face. You are not married to one man, we know it. The type married to one man are the ones like the woman you chased away from your compartment. The simple housewife. Not you."

Now my heartbeat accelerated. Whichever way I looked, death stared me in the face.

"If you touch that gun," I swore, "I will pull the chain and stop the train." My eyes had turned red and my breathing was fast. All along then these men had assumed that I simply came to this train to look for men. What did they mean by saying that I didn't look like a simple housewife?

"You are acting stupid," the older policeman told me. "It would be all over by now if you behaved like a good girl. Nobody need ever know."

"Don't waste your time," I thundered. "I love my husband. He is the father of my three children."

They looked at one another and laughed. It was a kind of mocking laughter that was meant to remind me that as far as they were concerned, a woman was a woman.

"Alright," the younger policeman said, dropping his pants on the floor. "I am going to have it when you are dead. You don't think a policeman is as important as the men you lure to take you in their arms."

He grabbed the gun and sure enough dug his hands into the jacket pocket to pull out the bullets.

"If you take your hand out of your pocket I will shoot." In a split second I had pulled out a pistol from under the pillow and was pointing at the policeman with the gun.

"No jokes now, Mr. Policeman." My voice was coarse and sure. "I will kill both of you in cold blood. The gun is fully loaded."

My body was nothing but sweat. The strap on my right shoulder had fallen below my elbow revealing the rounded part of my right breast. But I did not care any more. Soon I would be dead and completely naked before these bastards.

"Take your hand off that chain," the older policeman ordered me.

"I will not," I answered rudely. "And unless that man lets go that gun, I am shooting both of you."

"So you harlots walk with pistols, eh? And automatic ones too?"

"I am not your wife," I said. "Only my husband tells me what to do."

Before I knew where I was, I saw a big white spittle flying towards me from the old policeman's mouth. The thick coughed-up sputum landed on my chest just above my breast. I felt the slimy stuff roll under my nightdress, over my breast and then on to my belly, but I did not move.

"You stupid whore," he said. "You will soon know who is stronger."

Then they retreated and slammed the door shut.

I mopped the sputum from my stomach with a towel. My hand remained on the gun till morning.

I dressed clumsily just before we got to Kisumu Station and flung my door open. My head was light and the near tragedy of the previous night still haunted me. Those men could have done anything to me!

Kisumu Station came into view and I got my luggage ready. As we entered the station, I saw my brother Jemka and his wife waiting for me. It was then that my tears ran freely. Jemka was four years older than I. He would know how to help me put my case to the stationmaster, and if possible to the police.

I jumped out immediately the train came to a halt.

But I had no chance to greet my people. Four policemen stood before me. One with several medals on his chest took his identity card out and showed it to me.

"Do you mind coming with us to the police station? We have a few things to ask you."

"What things?" I asked in surprise.

"You just come with us." I broke through their grip and fell into the arms of my brother. But they followed me there and said forcefully, "We have no time to waste."

As the police led me away, my brother Jemka and his wife, both speechless, followed me. I insisted that my brother must come with me in the Black Maria. At first the police refused but then, when I would not enter into the car, they allowed him to come. His wife followed us in their own car.

Unbelievingly, I found the two men who had terrorised me during the night already standing behind the counter at the police station. Their eyes were hostile when I was pushed into a corner away from my brother. It was clear that they were saying—"You know now who is stronger."

Without any formality, the fat senior superintendent looked at me critically and said: "I am told you are Mrs. Muga—wife of a Doctor practising in Nairobi?"

"Yes," I said.

"Mrs. Muga, could you please hand me the pistol you were seen with in the train?"

"Who saw me with a gun in the train?" I asked sulkily. And all of a sudden, I saw my sister-in-law leaning against the wall. She felt faint at the thought that I had a gun! "Let me put it this way, Mrs. Muga, and remember you are talking to the police, not a lawyer: have you got a gun in your possession?"

"Yes," I said without hesitation.

"Abura!" my brother shouted, almost in a fit. He opened his mouth to say more but then closed it again.

"Hand me the gun, will you."

The senior policeman got up from his chair. And, before I knew where I was, two men had jumped forward and handcuffed me. They were rough and my precious watch went flying on the cement floor, breaking into two pieces.

"Officer," I said, with tears in my eyes, "I paid a lot of money for that watch. I hope your men will put it together again." Instead of replying, he looked at me defiantly and asked: "Show me where the gun is."

"You can see the gun, Officer, but you cannot have it. I bought it for my brother's son. It is mine." Now I looked at the policeman defiantly—then I kicked the suitcase towards him.

"The gun is in that suitcase. You can have a look at it, if you like. But be careful! I have dirty pants in the suitcase."

Hate flamed in the officer's eyes as he flung the suitcase open. I heard the policeman who had spat on my breast whisper to the officer: "Be careful. The gun is loaded."

The officer forced the suitcase open. The gun was lying on top of my clothes. He looked at it suspiciously and then carefully picked it up.

First I fixed my eyes on the officer and then turned them to my molesters. I would have loved to have shouted at them that "Power and wisdom are two different things." Instead I said quietly: "You don't need my nephew's toy gun, Officer, do you?"

Instead of kicking me, the officer threw the toy gun back into the suitcase and kicked it shut.

I picked up my broken watch and my suitcase and walked out of the police station to narrate the incredible story to my stunned brother and sister-in-law.

Up to this day, my husband teases me to tears whenever there is a rowdy party at home.

"Eh," he will say. "Watch out for that devil—she held two policemen at gunpoint."

TANURE OJAIDE

Tanure Ojaide, born in 1948 in Nigeria, is a prolific writer of both poetry and fiction. Among his numerous honors are the Commonwealth Poetry Prize for the Africa Region in 1987, the BBC Arts and Africa Poetry Award in 1988, the All-Africa Okigbo Prize for Poetry in 1988 and 1997, and the Association of Nigerian Authors' Poetry Prize in 1988 and 1994. He is the author of novels such as *Sovereign Body* (2004), *The Activist* (2006), and *Matters of Moment* (2009), as well as more than a dozen poetry collections, including *Children of Ironko and Other Poems* (1973), *The Eagle's Vision* (1987), *The Blood of Peace* (1991), *When It No Longer Matters Where You Live* (1999), and *Waiting for the Hatching of a Cockerel* (2008).

Under New Pastoral Management
(2009)

In Effurun, the Pentecostal churches had mushroomed in the streets at a weekly regularity that amazed many residents. A banner, bell, or crusade would invite passersby to such new churches. Often presided over by a single pastor or a couple, each new church took the form of a private or family business. However, a majority of the new churches that made Effurun look like a Christian town despite the many public shrines to native gods did not grow beyond their first few months, before becoming stunted. But there were a few exceptions.

The Church of the New Dawn had established itself as the most popular of the many new Pentecostal churches in the town. Nobody made fun of it as a family business center, as they did of the very small ones. Its congregation was a mixture of Christians from other faiths such as the Roman Catholic, Baptist, and Anglican, as well as converts attracted by the charismatic evangelist's heartwarming sermons about here and now.

Those stricken by malaria too often, and who believed it was not caused by mosquito bites but some sinister power, came to Evangelist Peter for a permanent cure. So did those who believed they were working very hard and not becoming rich, but sinking deeper into hardship and penury; they came to the Church of the New Dawn for special prayers, for an upturn in their fortune. And many young women who could not find husbands, as well as married women whose husbands were philanderers, also came to the church for answers to their problems.

Men and women who dreamed of riches did not go to work on the days that Evangelist Peter wanted to say prayers about personal breakthroughs. Women who found it difficult to conceive came to break the curse on their wombs in the Church of the New Dawn. Such women left their men at home to attend regular all-night prayer vigils so that the evangelist could crush the demons making them sterile. Since most of the people suffered from diseases, hardship, and broken hearts, they came in droves for relief.

"It's always never too late to get a cure for your problems," Evangelist Peter would exhort his attentive congregation.

He often characterized his work as that of a spiritual doctor.

"You are currently besieged by dark forces of night, but you will certainly come into a new dawn!" he would tell his new converts.

"Alleluia!" they chorused.

"Whatever you want God to do for you will come true in the Church of the New Dawn," he said.

"Amen!" reverberated in the church.

There was so much enthusiasm for this church that wives disobeyed their husbands and left the churches they had married in for the Church of the New Dawn.

Evangelist Peter was in his late thirties and still single. He was rather chubby but very agile in movement. He was the only single pastor of the many Pentecostal churches around. He had in one sermon wondered out loud why men and women hurried to marry when Jesus died still a bachelor at thirty-three. His congregation believed he wanted to give his whole energy, time, and attention to God's work.

Evangelist Peter also cited the many mature women such as Martha and Mary Magdalene who did not marry, but assisted Jesus in his mission. Members of his congregation did not know how to interpret his many reflections on marriage, but felt he was biding his time to get a wife suitable for his pastoral mission. Better to be patient to catch the right woman than be impatient and be ruined by a jezebel, such people reasoned to explain the marital status of Evangelist Peter.

He was always dressed neatly in a white, blue, or black suit and appeared well groomed for every service, which was an opportunity for him to show how kind God had been to him. His choice of the type of suit to wear for service was informed by the spirit of the time. On happy days, thanksgiving services, and the annual harvest, he wore immaculate white. Dark blue was for ordinary times, while the black suit was for sober moments.

"God is so kind, God is so good; my God is fantastic," he asked his congregation to repeat.

And they did so with rebounding passion. They expected so much from God and they believed that, through Evangelist Peter's intervention, their hopes would be realized.

"My God is a trustworthy God," he sang.

There is nothing a good Christian wants that God will not give to the person; through prayers the human and the divine can dialogue, he told his church members.

On Sundays, as Evangelist Peter railed against witches,

wizards, and demons from the pulpit, loudspeakers, specially mounted on the church's rooftop, would blaze his message of defeating evil forces with special prayers. Every passerby heard his holy message. The neighborhood heard him.

"Jesus will make you vanquish all sorts of demons. No witch or wizard can penetrate one covered by the blood of Jesus. You in the arms of Jesus are the winner. Say 'I am a winner!'"

"I am a winner!" the congregation would chorus.

"Praise the Lord!"

"Alleluia!"

Those who felt vulnerable before suspected diabolic forces holding them down in life or threatened with poverty, accidents, sickness, or death flocked to the church for protection. Evangelist Peter was their shield against evil forces. His church would also ensure their salvation. These salvation-seekers had something to hold on to so as to be secure and safe from a myriad of perils. In Evangelist Peter's view, Jesus was a giant that his flock held to or just came to for protection. The presence of a giant or his proximity was great protection for the neighbors. Jesus was their family man or neighbor, he explained.

"If now you have no food to eat, Jesus will fill your plate with enough yams to last you all your life. Believe in the Son of God and He will work miracles for you!" he preached.

The frequent split and subsequent breakups in the Baptist and Anglican churches benefited the Church of the New Dawn. Every personality squabble in the other churches left a group drifting to Evangelist Peter's church rather than suffering the humiliation of their faction being defeated.

Also those Catholics who felt that their church was too rigid and took no cognizance of modern life found it convenient to become members of the Church of the New Dawn. Among such were divorcees who could not remarry in the Catholic Church but were allowed to have new partners in the Church of the New Dawn. Evangelist Peter was silent on polygamy.

"Only God the Father is the judge," he told his congregation on this issue.

That opened the way for a few polygamists in the church to pass the word to others outside who needed a church to worship in. Evangelist Peter welcomed everybody who wanted to know God into his church.

The rather tall and smooth-faced evangelist was happy. He glowed. He walked with a swagger, which, though it looked natural, came from confidence in his pastoral mission. His crowded church was the envy of other new churches that could barely draw fifty people into the rented or uncompleted buildings they used for Sunday worship or service at other times. Two nearby mushroom churches whose services used to be drowned by the loudspeakers of the Church of the New Dawn closed to join Evangelist Peter's congregation. He praised the Lord for His kind mercies.

Evangelist Peter practiced what his congregation called humility and modesty. He had a Mercedes Benz 280 and not a Toyota Land Cruiser or a Lincoln Navigator that other pastors of the few bigger churches around drove. Besides, he drove himself. He had rejected pleas by his congregation for him to have a driver.

"What do I need a driver for when I can drive myself?" he asked those who made such a suggestion to him.

"Maybe when I become older, I'll need a driver. Certainly not now," he told them.

He often took along one or two of his church members as he desired on trips that were described as "church mission." His congregation so revered him that whoever was chosen for a "church mission" felt blessed. Others yearned for such a blessing but discovered that Evangelist Peter tended to select the same woman or others for his trips to advance the faith.

The church building was imposing not only because of its size but also because of its sophisticated architecture. It was oval, rather like a dome in shape. Perched on the hilly part of town and surrounded by lush green vegetation it stood alone, dominating the landscape. From the low surroundings, the valley that was the main town, one could not look up north without being captured by the spectacle of the oval house of God. It was grand even from a distance. It was like the huge mansion of a rich man with refined tastes. And it held in its precincts a solemnity comparable to any cathedral that the evangelist had entered in Rome in one of his several pilgrimages there.

The church compound was floored with concrete and the roads were tiled. From the spacious parking lot to the church was laid a red carpet of shiny tiles. Different types of plants and flowers beautified the landscape. Eucalyptus, whispering pines, hibiscus, crotons, and exotic palms brought a certain natural harmony to the church compound.

The floor of the church itself was of terrazzo and glazed when cleaned, as was often done by a group of women volunteers led by Magdalene, wife of Elder James Ogbe. The seats were the most comfortable of any church around and had cushions; the evangelist's special chair was of imported Italian leather and burgundy in color—he was, as head of the flock, a special shepherd and his seat was comparable to a monarch's throne.

The eye-catching building had imitation fresco windows at the upper level and real frescoes at the bottom. The ceiling was a splendid work of art. The heavy cross hanging above the altar shone day and night, displaying the suffering Christ with blood splattered over his body. It was heartrending to look at this image for too long. Suffering such nerve-racking pain that He could have avoided as the Son of God was the ultimate sacrifice, Evangelist Peter told his congregation, mindful that in the society no son of the king would suffer for the sake of his father's subjects.

Five years earlier, Evangelist Peter, moved by missionary zeal after waking from a dream of one day becoming a saintly man, after years of debauchery, had gone to the United States to raise money to convert the many pagans that still frustrated God's work and needed to be converted into light, as he told his various white donors who lavishly contributed towards his church in Nigeria. He felt he needed the American connection since his country men and women respected what came from outside rather than what was homegrown. He had seen how American and European pastors drew mammoth crowds in their crusading missions all over the country.

"The devil is having a field day among my people. I need to bring God to rout Satan and his evil angels from their midst. Today my people live in darkness; they need God to see light. Your dollars will bring light and God to them," he had pleaded.

The pastor of the American host church he had visited saw a cause that needed to be pursued with vigor and so challenged his congregation to come out with a sufficient amount of dollars to make God proud of them. It was just after the Thanksgiving holiday and everybody was looking forward to the Christmas season.

"Instead of spending all your money in buying gifts in a few days, let your gift go to God," he said.

"Amen," the congregation chorused.

"This is the only opportunity we all have to contribute our little quota to the building of the house of light in dark Africa. Do you want to be counted out of this noble cause?" he asked.

"No!" was the thunderous response.

"Let your best gift this season be given to the needy people of Africa," he admonished them. "God will reward you a hundredfold for the saving of lives that your contribution will bring about in Africa. Let them in Africa see God and light!"

"Amen," the congregation chorused.

"Let the lost people of Africa be saved!" he shouted.

"Amen!"

And the American Christians gave what pleased the visiting pastor and his host church. Those who had inherited money from slave-owning parents saw an opportunity to be free from the moral burden that was always weighing heavily on their minds. Such donors gave out hefty sums. Those who gambled regularly and made it, but knew that Jesus had condemned gambling in the temple, saw the opportunity to relieve their minds of that age-old sin. Many whites who had felt guilty in their racist treatment of blacks throughout their lives wanted to redeem themselves by being supporters of the cause of Christianizing Africa. Different groups for their own reasons gave out so much money to free their minds from excoriating thoughts and deeds of the past.

It was enough money to build a fine church. Peter felt contented because his foreign mission was worth the pain of the physical exertion and personal humiliation at European airports where young men in uniform questioned him as if he were a drug smuggler or someone running from his country for residence in Europe or North America. His youth and boyish looks fitted the profile of drug traffickers and illegal immigrants that airport security worldwide screened thoroughly; that caused so much embarrassment to a man wearing a golden cross and a pastor's collar.

The American donors would not have been disappointed with what the African evangelist did with the money he had raised from them. The impressive church building spoke loudly and clearly for itself.

The pastor had from the inauguration of the church taken the name of Evangelist Peter. He had become the rock upon which the new church would stand and grow. The church would be the beacon of light in a dark landscape, he had envisaged.

Five years later the church was as solidly rooted in the community as if it had been there from the beginning of times. Even the older churches did not have as passionate and devoted a congregation as the Church of the New Dawn's. No service in any other church in town could boast of more numbers. No church event elsewhere in town was more crowded than anything done in the Church of the New Dawn. No congregation was more loyal and more generous than that of the Church of the New Dawn. Members of the church took literally the paying of tithes and did so without Evangelist Peter beating it into their ears as other pastors did, but without success. The Church of the New Dawn had become a model church in the area. All other Christians looked to the church on the green-clad hill with envy and admiration.

One Sunday morning, in the season of Lent, only two weeks to Easter, at 11 a.m. the congregation of the church came as usual to their place of worship for their weekly service which usually lasted from late morning to late afternoon. The church members looked to the service as to a great event in their lives and had dressed as for a popular festival. The Sunday service was a weekly festival that they waited for to fulfill a strong yearning that was at once social and spiritual and so compelling. Despite the five hours of service, they looked to the hours spent there as the time they had dedicated to God. The drumming, singing, and dancing brought spiritual energy that radiated into every pore of the body. They were too busy the rest of the week to think of God. The rest of the week they put into practice Evangelist Peter's recommendations about achieving wealth and fighting diabolical forces that stood in their way to success. During that period they sought the breakthroughs that their pastor told them to expect from God.

Evangelist Peter had always kept the main door of the church shut on Sundays until fifteen minutes before the service began. Members of the congregation who came early had to stay in a line and, as soon as the door opened, would rush in to occupy the front seats. They were usually in their fine clothes and jewelries, and would converse and shake hands. The men would shake hands with the women, and the women had the same opportunity to shake hands with men, which was not common practice outside the church premises. Sometimes Evangelist Peter would shake the hands of the first fifty people or so in the queue before they were let into the church. He would hug a few women who often took responsibilities for church activities. Magdalene Ogbe always came early and often received a hug from the evangelist; her husband would receive a handshake. Many members of the congregation believed Evangelist Peter was a modern-day prophet with his hands soft like a ripe banana.

This Sunday the usual humming of conversation could be heard. Many women showed off the latest fashions. New headties, new styles of blouses, and new fabrics bought from Lagos or imported from Marks & Spencer in London or from Dubai. They wore the different types of gold they craved for—Saudi, Italian, English, Dubai, or Indian. The men talked about where they had visited or the new contracts they had got from government agencies. This was a good part of Sunday, the showing-off time before the service began.

However, those coming late could see that the crowd had grown and there was no line to fall into. It was a large crowd but in groups of threes, fours, and fives—a forest full of clumps of trees.

This situation was because the early birds had found out that the church door was still shut even when it was already eleven o'clock. Was Evangelist Peter, always punctual to the minute, late this morning or why were people still outside? the latecomers wondered. He had never been late for service and they did not think that he was late that very Sunday morning. The evangelist had the mind of God and so could not forget time, more so the time for worship on Sunday. He would not want to keep his flock waiting to worship God. Something must be amiss, they thought, but could not guess from a distance. There had been no word that their pastor was sick or that he had traveled. Evangelist Peter was always well especially as he had boasted of being covered by the blood of Christ that repelled all physical and spiritual ailments from him.

The Sunday service attendants who had come first, and so were in front, saw what they thought was a prank. Who would intrude into the church premises at night to do this?

What they saw was not only one poster but many. Could this happen? they asked. Their church building had been sold to another pastor. On the hand-carved huge front door was posted the boldly written "Under New Pastoral Management." The same poster was pasted on different parts of the front wall of the church.

The new pastor, an imposing man like a tall boxer, and his wife, both dressed as if they belonged to royalty, introduced themselves as the new owners and pastors of the church, which they had bought from the former owner— Evangelist Peter.

"I am Pastor Emmanuel and my wife is Magdalene," the new pastor said.

They showed the signed agreement to those close enough to read the paper they flaunted before the crowd and asked the people to go in for worship.

"After all, the house remains the house of God. I am only God's messenger to bring you good news," Pastor Emmanuel said.

He was wearing a black suit as Evangelist Peter did on some Sundays. It was humid. He brought out a white handkerchief from one of his pockets and wiped sweat from his face. The sun was bright and one could feel the intense heat it had in store for the rest of the day.

There was division among the congregation as to whether to go in or leave.

"Let's go in for worship," one member of the congregation said; "you never can tell that this is God's working and we have to accept it—He definitely works in a mysterious way. If the Almighty deems it necessary to give us a new pastor, let's accept him. He may well be what we truly need."

Adam had never liked Evangelist Peter and had felt he favored the pretty women over other members of the congregation.

"A church is not property that you sell for profit and then disappear to buy a cheaper one somewhere else," Samuel argued.

Samuel was one of the few men that Evangelist Peter took out on church missions. He was in the church's Finance Committee that rarely met and only to approve Evangelist Peter's accounts, but still felt favored by being in the committee.

"We came to worship in Evangelist Peter's church; now we are asked to be in Pastor Emmanuel's church. It is only one God in the churches, really one church," Adam said.

"Why did you leave the Catholic Church for the Church of the New Dawn if it is all one church?" Samuel asked Adam.

"We have put in so much energy and tithes into this church and whether or not it is sold, it remains our church," a church member added.

"I can't imagine myself worshiping in another church," Adam told them.

"But the building alone is not the church. The pastor matters as well as the type of church," another church member said.

"Evangelist Peter and I are both men of God chosen to minister to you. Let's not argue before God's house. Don't be a doubting Thomas! Go in and you will be satisfied that God never fails in His mysterious ways," Pastor Emmanuel told the gathered crowd at the door of his newly acquired church.

He could not imagine the people leaving. The failure of his takeover of the much coveted Church of the New Dawn would be disastrous for him. He had invested so much money into this new church and wanted it to continue to prosper so that he could give praise to the Lord for His kindness. Eighteen million naira was a huge sum of money to pay for a building and its congregation, but without the congregation the investment would be ruined, he pondered. The building was designed as a church and could not be converted into a block of flats, Pastor Emmanuel reflected. He just had to succeed by all means, if he was to avoid a business disaster.

Pastor Emmanuel had acquired the art of persuasion

from a source that would remain a secret all his pastoral life. He believed that to fight the devil, he had to use all means necessary, including devilish techniques. That was how he justified to himself his going to a medicine man to make the charm of persuasion. The traditional healer had used a needle to poke his tongue to bleed and rubbed it with some medicine as he chanted an esoteric invocation. That, he assured the pastor, would make whoever listened to him accept what he said as truth and also carry out what he asked to be done. What was important in the end was his ability to convert more people to his church and exercise authority over their lives. With that Pastor Emmanuel felt he could enforce the paying of tithes without any hassle and preside over a prosperous church.

Pastor Emmanuel's wife, Magdalene, was very support-ive of her husband. She used to be called Grace but he made her change her name to Magdalene as soon as he became a pastor. That was a better Christian name than just Grace, he felt. Magdalene was the woman who had stood by Jesus even after his death. She had anointed Jesus. If Jesus had been an ordinary human, who wanted to marry, Pastor Emmanuel felt, the Son of God would have married no other woman but Magdalene.

Magdalene was a very charming woman whose dress, face, and smiles were as persuasive as the pastor's words. She was tall and had a well-proportioned shape. She walked with grace and whatever she wore gave her a unique charm. Pastor Emmanuel remembered what it had taken him to succeed among her many suitors. He had spent hundreds of thousands of naira in cash and kind to earn her attention and affection. He had planned ahead his successful life of a God's servant. Emmanuel and Mag-dalene formed a good partnership in the crusade against darkness and demons. Each found the other's company fortunate, as their partnership became strong with an ever-expanding beatitude.

At the end of a long debate, which each side thought it would win or lose, depending on their tenacity to their viewpoint, the congregation was swayed over to enter the church by the new pastor and his wife.

"Can't you give me the benefit of the doubt?" he asked, when he saw the opposing argument as gaining more support.

"My husband is a man of God that makes things to really happen. He knows how to pray, as a warrior knows how to fight his enemies," Magdalene interjected.

The congregation, feeling guilty for arguing so noisily with a man of God beside his newly acquired church, decided to give him the benefit of the doubt that he asked for and went in. Though the old order of entering the church was not respected, they sat in their usual seats.

Nothing in the church had changed. The altar section, like other parts of the church, remained in the way they used to be arranged. Only one thing was absent and none there noticed it: the rose or other flower that Magdalene Ogbe used to place at the altar before Evangelist Peter started service. But that beautification only took place when Peter was there.

It was as if it was a normal Sunday service but without Evangelist Peter, whose baritone voice always held them spellbound. He could sing and he could dance. His lilting voice would rise to a crescendo as the percussion instruments brought his dance steps to a staccato movement. He had been the lead singer and the rest of the congregation the chorus. Similarly, he had been the lead dancer and his congregation followed his graceful and agile steps. In their minds, they wondered if Pastor Emmanuel could match the evangelist's dexterity and talents in song and dance.

This first service at the Church of the New Dawn under new pastoral management proved to be a great success and more than pleased all present. There was something in Pastor Emmanuel's voice that made them feel he could be trusted. Though he was in his forties, he preached like a wise old man who knew life and could advise others. He had a different voice from the evangelist's, but his was like a river running leisurely towards the ocean, sure of where it was going and dissolving itself into the wide waters.

When it came to preaching, Pastor Emmanuel performed the sermon he had practiced meticulously at home for weeks. He knew the consequence of not doing his utmost best in his first sermon in the new church.

"Alleluia!"

"Praise the Lord!" echoed from the pews.

"I say Alleluia," he repeated in a stronger voice.

"Praise the Lord!" the church reverberated thunderously.

"Al-le-lu-ia!"

"Praise the Lord!"

He was now primed enough to start to perform his sermon.

As his sermon progressed, many people began nodding approval of his lessons. Some rose to shout "Amen!" to his prayers. And the whole church was on its feet to dance with Pastor Emmanuel and his wife. The congregation did not want the long service to end. It was as though they were suspended in a planet of pleasurable spirituality.

Pastor Emmanuel was an artist and knew how to weave functionality and beauty into his craft. He was an experienced performer who took the cues from his enthusiastic audience. He knew how to connect with his audience and did wonderfully with the new congregation.

Pastor Emmanuel and his wife felt his first day in his new church was a huge success. The three offerings accompanied by drumming and dancing fetched a staggering amount that made them smile. No wonder, they thought, Evangelist Peter struck a hard bargain with them. No pastor who made so much money every Sunday would sell his church unless he really had to, they now realized.

Once back home, some members of Pastor Emmanuel's congregation started to hear strange things about Evangelist Peter. They started to add so many things together. It started as a rumor, which gossip easily transmitted to every attentive ear. The absence of Elder James Ogbe's wife at church the past Sunday fueled the rumors and gossip. Some women had looked out for her when Pastor Emmanuel introduced his wife as Magdalene, the same name as Elder James' wife. The Magdalene they knew, Mrs. Ogbe, was not in church that day. Now they remembered that the ritual of the flower being placed on the altar was not performed. "Where was Magdalene today?" many started to ask. They imagined she had not heard about the change of ownership of the church and might still be on an assignment that Evangelist Peter had arranged before he sold the church.

"Did she get wind of the sale of the church and had stayed home in protest?" others started to ask.

It was common knowledge that Magdalene Ogbe had been a favorite of Evangelist Peter. At thirty-seven, she was much younger than her husband in his late fifties. She had had no child in their ten years of marriage and looked very much in her prime in beauty. She was the leader of the women's group and reported to the evangelist their discussions and resolutions. She had traveled many times with Evangelist Peter on church duties out of town, and to conventions out of state that lasted many days.

Evangelist Peter had complimented her service publicly in the church. He always embraced and hugged her on Sunday mornings before worship, when he came to her; he shook hands with most other women.

Magdalene, the name that the evangelist had given to her, stuck. She had been Agnes, which the evangelist said was not as Christian as Magdalene. Unknown to Elder James Ogbe, his wife and Evangelist Peter had been having a secret relationship and she had received numerous favors from the evangelist—always in the delegation traveling on behalf of the church. Rumors had started, but none wanted to imagine that the evangelist could do such an immoral thing as sleeping with his church member's wife.

Magdalene went often to see Evangelist Peter to pray for her at different times of the day. Church members noticed her frequenting the pastor's office and home but their minds did not wander beyond her not conceiving all the years of marriage. They pitied her and her husband—such a gentle and godly couple!

There were rumors too that Elder James Ogbe was either impotent or weak as a man, but again, nobody wanted to imagine such a beautiful woman married to a eunuch.

"How could that beautiful woman have married such a mature man without a taste of the thing first?" They asked many questions.

When such rumors first came, the bearers were seen as agents of Satan.

"Don't defame a man of God," one member of the church had said.

"The good ones will always be smeared by the rumor-mongers of this world," another had added.

"Those who perjure the evangelist will roast in hell," another swore.

Magdalene Ogbe had conceived. It was a miracle that only she and Evangelist Peter knew about. They did not expect it, but it happened. They accepted the crop whose seed they had been planting.

The two secret lovers went underground for a few days. Only Pastor Emmanuel and his Magdalene knew that Evangelist Peter and Magdalene Ogbe had migrated to the United States to start a new life. As part of the contract that included the sale of the Church of the New Dawn, Pastor Emmanuel had secretly married Evangelist Peter and Magdalene before they took off. That was after they confessed their sins to Pastor Emmanuel who forgave them. That also was part of the contract. Only his wife, the namesake of the new bride, was witness to the ceremony that took place in Pastor Emmanuel's house after midnight.

"We are entering a new dawn," Evangelist Peter quipped.

"God bless both of you!" the pastor pronounced.

"And God also bless you with the Church of the New Dawn that I hand over to you," Peter told the pastor and his wife, as he handed to them the keys of the church.

That night Evangelist Peter and Magdalene headed into darkness not to spend a conjugal night in bed but to travel fast to catch their plane taking off from Lagos later that

morning. Their minds were focused on where they were going and the new life as husband and wife they were going to
live in God's own country.

No member of the Church of the New Dawn, including
Elder James Ogbe, knew where they had emigrated that
night. Magdalene had told her husband that she was going
for a retreat in Lagos and would be away for a week. He did
not ask her any questions about her travels for religious
events, including this one for which she had filled a big
trunk with clothes, shoes, and jewelry.

To the congregation of the Church of the New Dawn,
Evangelist Peter and Magdalene might as well have died or
gone to heaven. Or hell, if members of the church knew
what had really transpired between them in the many years
they had been under the pastoral leadership of Evangelist
Peter! As for Magdalene, the women would say, "She was
looking for more than conception or a baby from God under cover of prayers—a new and virile man!"

IFEOMA OKOYE

Ifeoma Okoye earned a BA in English at the University of Nigeria, Nsukka, and an MSC in Teaching English for Specific Purposes at Aston University in Birmingham, England. She has authored numerous well-known children's books beginning with *The Village Boy* (1978), which won the Macmillan Children's Literature Prize. Among her other children's books are *The Adventures of Tulu the Monkey* (1980), *Only Bread for Eze* (1980), *No School for Eze* (1980), *Neka Goes to Market* (1995), *Ayo and His Pencil* (1995), and *Chika's House* (1995). Among her adult novels are *Behind the Clouds* (1983), *Men Without Ears* (1984), which won the Association of Nigerian Authors' Best Fiction of the Year Award, *Chimere* (1992), and *No Where to Hide* (2000). Many of her stories are collected in *The Trial and Other Stories* (2005). She was married to the late civil rights activist Mokwugo Okoye and has five children.

The Power of a Plate of Rice
(1999)

I walked hurriedly to Mr. Aziza's office, breathing heavily in steadily rising anger. The January sun was blazing in fury, taking undue advantage of the temporary withdrawal of the seasonal harmattan. As I arrived at the office which was at the end of the administration block, I remembered one of my mother's precepts: "Do nothing in anger. Wait till your anger melts like thick palm oil placed under the sun." Mother was a philosopher of sorts. Poor woman. She died before I could reward her for all the sacrifices she made on my behalf, forgoing many comforts just so that I could get some education, and for carrying the financial burden of the family during my father's protracted illness and even after his premature death. In deference to Mother, I stood by Mr. Aziza's door for a few seconds, trying to stifle my anger, but failing woefully. Only an angel or an idiot would remain calm in my situation.

At last I knocked at the mottled green door.

"Come in."

Mr. Aziza's authoritative voice hit me like a blow, startling me. I opened the door and walked in, my anger still smouldering . . .

Mr. Aziza, the principal of the secondary school where I was teaching, was seated behind a medium-sized desk made of cheap white wood and thickly coated with varnish. Books, files, letter trays and loose sheets of paper jostled for a place on the desk. He raised his coconut-shaped head, closed the file he was reading, removed his plastic-framed spectacles and peered at me.

"Yes, Mrs. Cheta Adu. What do you want?" His voice was on the defensive and the look on his ridged face was intimidating.

I took a deep breath. "The bursar has just told me, Sir, that you told him to withhold my salary."

We were paid irregularly. Although it was the end of January, the salary in question was for October of the previous year. Four months without any salary and yet we went to work regularly.

"Yes, I did, Mrs. Cheta Adu." Mr. Aziza's small, narrow eyes pierced me like a lethal weapon. As one teacher had put it, he paralysed his prey with his eyes before dealing a death blow to them.

"What have I done, Sir?" I asked, trying to load the word *Sir* with as much sarcasm as I could to indicate how I felt inside.

Mr. Aziza fingered his bulbous nose, a part of his body which had been the butt of many a teacher's joke. He was

known to love food more than anything else, and one female teacher had once said that most of what he ate went
into his nose.

"You were away from school without permission for
four days last week," Mr. Aziza finally declared.

My anger, which a few minutes ago had reduced to a
simmer, suddenly began to bubble like a pot of *ogbono*
soup when the fire under it is poked.

I said as calmly as I could, "In those four days, Sir, I almost lost my baby. I had already explained the circumstances to you. My baby became very ill suddenly. I had to
rush him to hospital. For those four days, Sir, he battled for
his life."

"And so?" Mr. Aziza intoned.

Someone knocked at the door and I turned to see the
Second Vice-Principal's bearded face appear as he opened
it. "I'll be back," a thin-lipped, hair-fringed mouth said and
disappeared. The appearance of the bearded face was like a
comic scene in a Shakespearean tragedy.

I turned to Mr. Aziza and, in answer to his question, I
reminded him that I had sent someone to tell him that my
baby was in hospital.

"After you've been away from school for days," Mr.
Aziza complained.

"Yes, Sir, but my baby was in real danger and I was too
upset to write. I had thought you would understand."

"And did you bother to find out whether your friend
gave your message to me or not?"

"She told me she delivered it a day after I sent her to
you. You were not in the office when she first called, and
then she forgot all about it till the next day. I've already
apologized for all the delay, Sir."

Mr. Aziza opened another file and began to flip through
it. "You will receive your salary at the end of February," he
said.

I gasped, "Do you mean I'll have to wait till the end of
February before I receive my salary?"

"Exactly."

"That would make it five whole months without a salary!"

"I'm not interested in your calculations."

Mr. Aziza was known for punishing his teachers by with-holding their salaries. But I had not known him to withhold any teacher's salary for more than two weeks at the most. He had always felt, and had said so in words and in action, that he was doing his teachers a favour by paying them even though the school belonged to, and was funded by, the state government.

"How am I going to feed my two sons, Sir?" I asked.

"That's your problem, not mine," Mr. Aziza replied.

I refused to think about this problem. January, as every low- and medium-salaried worker in my country knows from experience, was the longest month of the year. After the enormous compulsive and often senseless spending during Christmas and the New Year, a salaried worker was left with little money for the rest of January. And for those who had children in school, paying school fees and buying books and school uniforms for the new school year often became a nightmare. This year was worse for me because I and all the other teachers in the school were last paid in September of the year before.

"I am a widow, Sir," I pleaded with Mr. Aziza. "I am the sole breadwinner for my family. Times are hard. My children cannot survive till the end of February without my next salary."

Mr. Aziza said, "I don't want to know, Mrs. Cheta Adu. My decision is final."

He stood up, hitched his trousers up with his elbows, and walked to a window on his right and peered out of it. He was a small, wiry man, the type my mother often told me to beware of.

Helpless, I stood watching him, a man known for his in-flexibility. I knew from my colleagues' experiences that tak-ing my case to the State Schools Management Board would be futile as Mr. Aziza had ingratiated himself with the pow-erful and high-ranking officers of the Board. As the princi-pal of one of the elite schools in the state, he had helped them to get their children admitted into his school even when the spoilt ones amongst them did not pass the entrance examination. I also knew that taking Mr. Aziza to court was out of the question. Where would I get the money for a lawyer? Besides, civil cases had been known to last for months or even years because of unnecessary and often deliberate court adjournments.

Mr. Aziza walked back to his chair and sat down.

I looked hard at him and, without saying anything more, left his office. In a taxi taking me home, I thought about nothing else but Mr. Aziza. This was the second time I had found myself at his mercy. The first time was when, five years before, I was transferred to his school from a secondary school in Onitsha where I was teaching before my marriage. On reading the letter posting me to his school—I had delivered it to him personally—he had flung it at me and had declared, "I don't want any more female teachers in my school, especially married ones."

"What have we done?" I had wanted to know.

"You're a lazy lot," he had said. "You always find excuses to be away from school. Today it's this child of yours becoming ill who must be taken to hospital, and tomorrow it's the funeral of one relation or another."

When he officially refused to give me a place in his school, I resorted to a tactic I had used successfully before. I kept calling at his office every day, often without uttering a word, until I broke his resistance and made him accept me. This time, however, I had the feeling that he would not budge, no matter what I did.

When I arrived home after five in the evening, my mother-in-law was walking up and down in front of my flat with my two-year-old son, Rapulu, tied on her back, and four-year-old Dulue trailing behind her.

"You're late, Cheta," my mother-in-law said. "I was beginning to think you were not going to come home." She looked weary and worried.

"Sorry, Mama, I have some problems at school." I

walked to her after hugging Dulue, who had trotted to me. "And how is Rap?" I asked.

"He's ill."

I placed the back of my hand on my younger son's forehead. It was piping hot.

"You're not going to be ill again, Rapulu?" I said under my breath. Aloud I asked, "How long has he been running a temperature, Mama?"

"A short while after you left for school in the morning," my mother-in-law replied.

I helped her untie Rapulu from her back and took him in, Dulue trotting behind me. I stripped Rapulu of his clothes, put him on the settee, fetched a bowl of cold water and a towel and began to sponge him down. He yelled and kicked, but I ignored him. Dulue, with his thumb in his mouth, kept on mumbling that he was hungry, while my mother-in-law stood speechless, watching me.

Presently, I remembered that I should have given Rapulu some fever medicine. I ran into the only bedroom in the flat and dashed out with a small bottle. Taking Rapulu in my arms, I gave him a teaspoonful of the bittersweet medicine and began to sponge him again.

My mother-in-law soon dozed off. Poor woman, she must have had a trying day. She was a widow too and I had brought her to help me look after my children. Bless her, for what could I have done if she had refused my offer? Another reason why I brought her to live with me was to save costs. I used to send her money every month to supplement the meagre proceeds from her farms.

We had a late lunch of yam and raw palm oil. It was the last piece of yam in the house. I skipped supper because I wanted to make sure that the *garri* and *egusi* soup which I had left would last for two nights.

The night was a long one. First I lay awake for fear that Rapulu might become worse, but fortunately the fever did not persist. Then I reviewed all that I had gone through since I lost Afam, my husband, who was an only child, in a ghastly motor accident a little more than a year before. He was a brilliant banker. We were at the university together, he studying banking and I mathematics. As luck would have it, we were posted to the same state for our National Youth Service. We became engaged at the end of our service and married shortly after. He died a fortnight after our fifth wedding anniversary and, ever since, my life had become an endless journey into the land of hardship and frustration. I had, under great pressure, spent all our savings to give my husband what my people and his had called a befitting burial, and what I saw as a senseless waste of hard-earned money.

For the better part of the night, I worried over how I was going to pay the January rent, how I was going to feed my two sons and my mother-in-law, and what I was going to do if Rapulu became so ill that he had to be hospitalized again. I already owed two of my friends some money and could not see myself summoning up the courage to go to them again.

I borrowed money again and for two long weeks I managed to feed my family, sometimes going without meals myself. I became irritable, and students complained that I was being too hard on them. My good-natured mother-in-law became equally touchy and nagged me incessantly. My two sons threw tantrums, spending a great deal of time crying. Soon I had no money left and no one to lend me more. I had reached a point when I had to do something drastic or allow my sons to die of hunger.

On the 23rd of February, after school hours, I went to Mr. Aziza's office and once again pleaded with him to pay me.

"You're wasting your time, Mrs. Cheta Adu," he said. "I never change my mind. You will receive your salary on the twenty-eighth of February and not even one day earlier."

I left his office and waited for him in the outer room. At four o'clock he left his office. I followed him to his house, which was situated near the school main gate, and he turned and asked me why I was following him. I remained silent. He opened the door and walked in. Quietly, I followed him into his sitting room and sat down without any invitation to do so. The room was sparsely furnished. A black-and-white television stood on top of the shelf next to a small transistor radio. Near the bookshelf was a small dining table and a steel-back chair.

Mr. Aziza lived alone. His wife and six children lived at Onitsha about one hundred and twenty kilometres away.

Mr. Aziza turned and faced me. "Look, Mrs. Adu, you'll achieve nothing by following me like a dog. You may stay here forever, but you'll not make me change my mind." He disappeared through a door on the right.

Presently, his houseboy walked into the room and began to lay the table. The smell of *jollof* rice wafted around my nostrils, reactivating in me the hunger which had been suppressed by anger, depression, and desperation. The houseboy finished laying the table and left.

On impulse I left my chair, walked to the dining table and sat down on the chair beside it. Removing the lid on the plate, I stared at the appetizing mound of *jollof* rice. Then I grabbed the spoon beside the plate and began to eat. I ate quickly, and not only with relish, but also with vengeance and animosity.

I heard a door squeak and turned to see Mr. Aziza walk into the sitting room. His jaw dropped and his mouth remained open as he stared at me.

"What do you think you're doing, Mrs. Cheta Adu?" he bellowed, finding his tongue at last. Disbelief was writen all over his face.

I ignored the question and continued to help myself to the rice. I scooped a large piece of meat and some rice into my mouth, my cheeks bulging.

Mr. Aziza strode to the table, snatched the spoon from me with his right hand and with his left snatched the plate of rice away from me. It was almost empty by now. I rose from the chair and moved a little bit back from him, thinking he was going to hit me.

He faced me, his eyes deadly. "Get out of my house, I say, get out!"

"Not until I receive my salary," I said calmly. Desperation had given me a form of courage I had not experienced before. "I'll wait for supper."

Mr. Aziza barked at me, "Get out. Go to the bursar. Tell him I said he can pay you now."

I said calmly, "He'll not believe me. Why not give me a note for him?"

He scribbled a note, threw it at me and I grabbed it. Trying hard to suppress a smile, I said, "Thank you, Sir," and left the room, still chewing the rubbery meat in my mouth.

E. C. Osondu

E. C. Osondu was born in 1966 in Lagos, Nigeria, and worked in advertising before earning an MFA in Fiction at Syracuse University, where he was a fellow in the creative writing program. His short fiction has appeared in publications such as *Agni, Guernica, Vice, Fiction,* and *The Atlantic.* The story "Waiting" was awarded the prestigious Caine Prize for African Literature in 2009. In his collection of eighteen stories, *Voice of America,* published in 2010, Osondu dramatizes the plight of Nigerians desperate to leave the country as well as the disillusioning experiences they have upon arriving in America. He is currently a professor of English at Providence College in Rhode Island, where he teaches creative writing and a variety of other English courses.

Voice of America
(2007)

I

We were sitting in front of Ambo's provision store drinking the local gin *ogogoro* and Coke and listening to a program called *Music Time in Africa* on the Voice of America. We were mostly young men who were spending our long summer holidays in the village. Some of us whose parents were too poor to pay our school fees spent the period of the long vacation doing odd jobs in the village to enable us to save money to pay our school fees. Someone remarked on how clear the broadcast was, compared to our local radio broadcasts, which were filled with static. The presenter announced that there was a special request from an American girl whose name was Laura Williams for an African song and that she was also interested in pen pals from every part of Africa, especially Nigeria. Onwordi, who had been pensive all this while, rushed to Ambo the shopkeeper, collected a pen and began to take down her address. This immediately led to a scramble among us to get the address, too. We all took it down and folded the piece of paper and put it in our pockets and promised we were going to write as soon as we got home that night.

A debate soon ensued among us concerning the girl who wanted pen pals from Africa.

"Before our letter gets to her, she would have received thousands from the big boys who live in the city of Lagos and would throw our letters into the trash can," Dennis said.

"Yes, you may be right," remarked Sunday, "and besides even if she writes you, both of you may not have anything in common to share. But the boys who live in the city go to night clubs and know the lyrics of the latest songs by Michael Jackson and Dynasty. They are the ones who see the latest movies, not the dead Chinese kung-fu and Sonny Chiba films that Fantasia Cinema screens for us in the village once every month."

"But you can never tell with these Americans, she could be interested in being friends with a real village boy because she lives in the big city herself and is probably tired of city boys." Lucky, who said this, was the oldest among us and had spent three years repeating form four.

"I once met an American lady in Onitsha where I went to buy goods for my shop," Ambo the shopkeeper said. He hardly spoke to us, only listening and smiling and looking at the figures in his *Daily Reckoner* notebook.

We all turned to Ambo in surprise. We knew that he traveled to the famous Onitsha market, which was the biggest market in West Africa, to buy goods every week; we could hardly believe that he had met an American lady.

Again, Onitsha market was said to be so big that half of those who came there to buy and sell were not humans but spirits. It was said that a simple way of seeing the spirits when in the market was to bend down and look through your legs at the feet of people walking through. If you looked well and closely enough, you would notice that some of them had feet whose soles did not touch the ground when they walked. These were the spirits. If they got a good bargain from a trader he would discover that the money in his money box miraculously grew every day, but any trader who cheats them would find his money disappearing from his money box without any rational explanation.

"She was wearing an ordinary Ankara skirt and blouse made from local fabrics and had come to buy a leather purse and hat from the Hausa traders; she even exchanged a few words in Hausa with the traders. The way she said *ina kwu ana nkwu* was so sweet and melodious it was like listening to a canary singing."

"She was probably a volunteer schoolteacher in one of the girls' secondary schools around Onitsha and has lived here for so long she does not count as an American. We are talking of a real American girl living on American soil." Jekwu, who said this, was Ambo's adversary as a result of a dispute over an old debt and was permanently on the opposite side of any argument with Ambo.

"Well, what I was trying to say was that she may be interested in a village boy. Like the one I saw in Onitsha who was wearing a local dress and spoke Hausa, I am sure she will be interested in a village boy," Ambo said and buried his head in his *Daily Reckoner*.

Someone ordered another round of *ogogoro* and Coke and we all began to drink and became silent as we thought our own thoughts. The moon dipped and everywhere suddenly became dark. One by one we rose and left for our homes.

II

We were sitting in Ambo's shop one evening when Onwordi swaggered in holding a white envelope with a small
American stamp which had an eagle painted on it on its
side. He waved it in our faces and was smiling. He called for
drinks and we all rushed to him trying to snatch the envelope from his hands.

"She has replied," he said, looking very proud like a man
who had unexpectedly caught a big fish with a hook in the
small village river. The truth was that we had all forgotten
about the announcement on the radio program and I had
actually washed the shorts in whose back pocket I had put
the paper where I jotted down the address.

Onwordi began to read from the letter to us. The girl's
name was Laura Williams. She had recently moved with her
parents to a farm in Iowa from a much larger city. She had
one more year before finishing high school. She was going
to take a class on Africa, Its People and Culture in the fall
and was curious to know more about African culture. She
wanted to know whether Onwordi lived in the city or in a
village. She also wanted to know if he lived close to lots of
wild animals like giraffes, lions and chimpanzees. And what
kind of foods did he generally eat, were they spicy? and
how were they prepared? She also wanted to know if he
came from a large family. She ended the letter with the
phrase *"Yours Laura."*

"Oh my God," Lucky said, "this is a love letter. The
American lady is searching for an African husband."

"Eehen, why do you say that?" Onwordi said, clearly
very excited about such a prospect. Though he had read the
letter over a hundred times and was hoping for such a
stroke of good fortune, he had not seen any hint of such in
the letter.

"See the way she ended the letter, she was practically
telling you that she was yours from now on."

"I think that is the American way of ending letters,"
Dennis said. He was the most well read amongst us, having

read the entire oeuvre of James Hadley Chase and Nick Carter. He used big words and would occasionally refer to some girl in the village as a *doll* and some other as a *dead-beat floozy.*

"But that is not even the main issue; she can become your girlfriend in due course if you know how to play your game very well. You could tell her that you have a giraffe farm and that you ride on the back of a tiger to your farm," he continued.

"But she is soon going to ask for your photograph and you know we have no giraffes here and the last we heard of a lion was when one was said to have been sighted by a hunter well over ten years ago," Jekwu said. "You should ask her to send you a ten dollar bill, tell her you want to see what it looks like and when she sends it we can change it in the 'black market' at Onitsha for one thousand naira and use the money for *ogogoro.*" Jekwu took a drink and wiped his eyes, which were misting over from the drink.

"If you ask her for money, you are going to scare her away. White women are interested in love and romance. Write her a love letter professing your love for her and asking for her hand in marriage, tell her that you would love to come and join her in America and see what she has to say to that," Dennis said.

"Promise her you'll send her some records by Rex Jim Lawson if she can send you Dynasty's 'Do Me Right,' " Lucky added.

"A guy in my school once had a female pen pal from India, she would ask him to place her letters under his pillow when he slept. At night she would appear in his dreams and make love to him. He said he always woke up in the mornings exhausted and worn out after the marathon love-making sessions in the dreams. We do not know how it happened, but he later found out the girl had died years back."

We were all shocked into silence by Dennis's story. Ambo turned up the volume of the radio and we began to listen to the news in special English. The war in Palestine was progressing apace, Blacks in South Africa were still ri-

oting in Soweto and children were dying of hunger in Ethiopia and Eritrea.

Onwordi said nothing. He smiled at our comments,
holding the letter close to his chest like somehow hugging
a lover. He thanked us for our suggestions and was the first
to leave Ambo's shop that night.

III

Two weeks later, Onwordi walked into the shop again smiling and holding an envelope with an American flag stamp
close to his chest once more. We circled him and began to
ask him questions. She had written once again. She thanked
him for his mail. She was glad to know he lived in a village.
She was interested in knowing what life was like in a typical
African village. What kind of house did he live in, how did
he get his drinking water? What kind of school did he attend and how did he learn to write in English? She said she
would love to see his photograph, though she did not have
any of hers that she could share with him at the present
time. Postal regulations would not permit her to send
money by mail but she could take a picture of a ten dollar
bill and send it to him if all he really wanted was to see
what it looked like. She also said she was interested in
knowing about African Talking Drums, did they really
talk? She said she looked forward to hearing from him
again. We were silent as we listened to him and then we all
began to speak at once.

"I was right about her being interested in you; otherwise
why would she request for your picture without sending
you hers?"

"This shows that women all over the world are coy. She
was only being cunning. She really wants to know what you
look like before she gets involved with you."

"You should go and borrow a suit from the schoolteacher and go to Sim Paul's Photo Studio in the morning
when he is not yet drunk and let him take a nice shot of you
so you can send it to her."

"How about you borrow the schoolteacher's suit and Ambo's shirt and Dennis's black school tie and Lucky's silk flower patterned shirt and Sim Paul's shoes and tell the schoolteacher's wife to lend you her stretching comb to straighten your hair if you can't afford Wellastrech cream; then you'll be like the most handsome suitor in the folktale."

"Who is the most handsome suitor?" Onwordi asked. "I have never heard that folktale." Jekwu cleared his throat and took a sip from his *ogogoro* and Coke and began his story.

"Once in the land of Idu there lived a girl who was the prettiest girl in the entire kingdom. Her beauty shone like the sun and her teeth glittered like pearls whenever she smiled. All the young men in the kingdom asked for her hand in marriage but she turned them down. She turned down the men either because they were too tall or too short or too hairy or not hairy enough. She said since she was the most beautiful girl in the kingdom she could only marry the most handsome man. Her fame soon got to the land of the spirits and the most wicked spirit of them all, Tongo, heard about her and said he was going to marry her. Not only was Tongo the most wicked, he was also the most ugly, possessing only a cracked skull for a head. He was all bones and when he walked his bones rattled. Before setting out to ask for the hand of the maiden in marriage, Tongo went round the land of the spirits to borrow body parts. From the spirit with the straightest pair of legs, he borrowed a straight pair of legs and from the one with the best skin he borrowed a smooth and glowing skin. He went round borrowing body parts until he was transformed into the most handsome man there was. As soon as he walked into Idu on the market day and the maiden set eyes on him, she began following him around until he turned, smiled at her and asked for her hand in marriage. She took him to her parents and hurriedly packed her things, waved them goodbye and followed the handsome suitor.

"On their way to his home, which was across seven riv-

ers and seven hills, she was so busy admiring his handsome-
ness that she did not grow tired and was not bothered by
the fact that they were leaving all the human habitations
behind. It was only when they crossed into the land of the
spirits and he walked into the first house and came out
crooked because he had returned the straight legs to their
owner that she began to sense that something was wrong.
And so she continued to watch as he returned the skin, the
arms, the hair and the other borrowed body parts so that by
the time they got to his house, it was only his skull that was
left. She wept when she realized she had married an ugly
spirit but she knew it was too late to return to the land of
the living so she bided her time. When Tongo approached
her for lovemaking, she told him to go and borrow all the
body parts he had on when he married her. Because Tongo
loved her headstrong nature, he agreed. Each time they
made love he went round borrowing body parts and when
they had a child, the child was a very handsome child and
grew into the most handsome man."

We all laughed at the story and advised Onwordi to
work at transforming himself into the most handsome man.
Ambo advised him to dress in traditional African clothes,
that, from what he knew about white people, this was likely
to appeal to her more.

"So what are you going to do?" we asked Onwordi, but
he only smiled and held his letter tightly as he drank.

The next time *Music Time in Africa* was on the air, we
had our pens ready to take down the names of pen pals, but
the few that were announced were listeners from other
parts of Africa and we all felt disappointed.

We waited for Onwordi to walk in with a letter but he
did not for quite some time. We wondered what had happened. When he finally walked in after some days, he
looked dejected and would not say a word to any of us.

"Hope you have not upset her with your last mail?"
Lucky said. "You know white people are very sensitive and
you may have hurt her feelings without knowing it."

"This is why we told you to always let us see the letter

before you send it to her; when we put our heads together and craft a letter to her, she will pack her things and move into your house, leaking roof and all. As the elders say, 'When you piss on one spot, it is more likely to froth.' "

"But exactly what did you write to her that has made her silent?" Lucky asked. Onwordi was silent but he smiled liked a dumb man that had accidentally glimpsed a young woman's pointed breast and ordered more drinks. "Or have you started hiding her mail from us? Maybe the contents are too intimate for our eyes. Or now that you have become closer has she started kissing her letters with lipstick-painted lips and sealing the letters with kisses?" Ambo teased. But nothing we said would make Onwordi say a word.

Onwordi walked into Ambo's shop after a period of three weeks holding the envelope that we had become used to by now and looking morose. We all turned to him and began to speak at once.

"What happened, has she confessed that she has a husband or why are you looking so sad?"

"Has she fallen in love with another man? I hear white women fall out of love as quickly as they fall in love."

"If you have her telephone number I can take you to the Post and Telegrams Office in Onitsha if you have the money and help you make a call to her," Ambo suggested.

Onwordi opened the envelope and brought out a photograph. We all crowded around him to take a closer look. It was the picture of the American girl Laura Williams. It was a portrait that showed only her face. She had an open friendly face with brown hair and slightly chubby cheeks. She was smiling brightly in the photograph. Our damp fingers were already leaving a smudge on the face.

"She is beautiful and looks really friendly but why did she not send you a photograph where her legs are showing? That way you do not end up marrying a cripple."

Onwordi was not smiling.

"So what did she say in her letter or have the contents become too intimate for you to share with us?"

"She says that this was going to be her last letter to me. She says she's done with her paper and she did very well and illustrated her paper with some of the things I had told her about African culture. But she says her parents are moving back to the city, that the farm had not worked out as planned. She also said she has become interested in Japanese haiku and was in search of new friends from Japan."

"Is that why you are looking sad like a dog whose juicy morsel fell on the sand? You should thank God for saving you from a relationship where each time the lady clears her throat you have to jump. Sit down and drink with us, forget your sorrows and let the devil be ashamed," Jekwu said.

We all laughed but Onwordi did not laugh with us, he walked away in a slight daze. From that time onwards we never saw him at Ambo's shop again. Some people who went to check in on him said they found him lying on his bed with Laura Williams's letters and picture on his chest as he stared up into the tin roof.

OLIVE SCHREINER

Born in 1855 to a missionary couple at the Wesleyan Missionary Society station near Herschel, South Africa, Olive Schreiner grew up in a religious household, where she was taught discipline and self-control, but by the time she was a teenager, she had begun to renounce Christianity. She worked as a governess and in 1883 published her first and most successful novel, *The Story of an African Farm,* under a male pseudonym. Severe asthma and lack of money prevented her from pursuing her first choice of career, medicine, so she used writing to try to improve the lives of women and black South Africans. She was also a pacifist who campaigned against the events that led to the Boer War, writing *The South African Question by an English South African.* She lived in Europe during several periods of her life, returning to South Africa after World War I and dying in 1920.

Eighteen-Ninety-Nine
(1906)

"Thou fool, that which thou sowest is not quickened unless it die."

I

It was a warm night: the stars shone down through the thick soft air of the Northern Transvaal into the dark earth, where a little daub-and-wattle house of two rooms lay among the long, grassy slopes.

A light shone through the small window of the house,

though it was past midnight. Presently the upper half of the door opened and then the lower, and the tall figure of a woman stepped out into the darkness. She closed the door behind her and walked towards the back of the house where a large round hut stood; beside it lay a pile of stumps and branches quite visible when once the eyes grew accustomed to the darkness. The woman stooped and broke off twigs till she had her apron full, and then returned slowly, and went into the house.

The room to which she returned was a small, bare room, with brown earthen walls and a mud floor; a naked deal table stood in the centre, and a few dark wooden chairs, homemade, with seats of undressed leather, stood round the walls. In the corner opposite the door was an open fireplace, and on the earthen hearth stood an iron three-foot, on which stood a large black kettle, under which coals were smouldering, though the night was hot and close. Against the wall on the left side of the room hung a gun-rack with three guns upon it, and below it a large hunting-watch hung from two nails by its silver chain.

In the corner by the fireplace was a little table with a coffeepot upon it and a dish containing cups and saucers covered with water, and above it were a few shelves with crockery and a large Bible; but the dim light of the tallow candle which burnt on the table, with its wick of twisted rag, hardly made the corners visible. Beside the table sat a young woman, her head resting on her folded arms, the light of the tallow candle falling full on her head of pale flaxen hair, a little tumbled, and drawn behind into a large knot. The arms crossed on the table, from which the cotton sleeves had fallen back, were the full, rounded arms of one very young.

The older woman, who had just entered, walked to the fireplace, and kneeling down before it took from her apron the twigs and sticks she had gathered and heaped them under the kettle till a blaze sprang up which illumined the whole room. Then she rose up and sat down on a chair before the fire, but facing the table, with her hands crossed on her brown apron.

She was a woman of fifty, spare and broad-shouldered, with black hair, already slightly streaked with grey; from below high, arched eyebrows, and a high forehead, full dark eyes looked keenly, and a sharply cut aquiline nose gave strength to the face; but the mouth below was somewhat sensitive, and not over-full. She crossed and recrossed her knotted hands on her brown apron.

The woman at the table moaned and moved her head from side to side.

"What time is it?" she asked.

The older woman crossed the room to where the hunting-watch hung on the wall.

It showed a quarter-past one, she said, and went back to her seat before the fire, and sat watching the figure beside the table, the firelight bathing her strong upright form and sharp aquiline profile.

Nearly fifty years before, her parents had left the Cape Colony, and had set out on the long trek northward, and she, a young child, had been brought with them. She had no remembrance of the colonial home. Her first dim memories were of travelling in an ox-wagon; of dark nights when a fire was lighted in the open air, and people sat round it on the ground, and some faces seemed to stand out more than others in her memory which she thought must be those of her father and mother and of an old grandmother; she could remember lying awake in the back of the wagon while it was moving on, and the stars were shining down on her; and she had a vague memory of great wide plains with buck on them, which she thought must have been in the Free State. But the first thing which sprang out sharp and clear from the past was a day when she and another child, a little boy cousin of her own age, were playing among the bushes on the bank of a stream; she remembered how suddenly, as they looked through the bushes, they saw black men leap out, and mount the ox-wagon outspanned under the trees; she remembered how they shouted and dragged people along, and stabbed them; she remembered how the blood gushed, and how they, the two young children among the bushes, lay flat on their stomachs and did not move or breathe, with that strange self-preserving instinct found in the young of animals or men who grow up in the open.

She remembered how black smoke came out at the back of the wagon and then red tongues of flame through the top; and even that some of the branches of the tree under which the wagon stood caught fire. She remembered later, when the black men had gone, and it was dark, that they were very hungry, and crept out to where the wagon had stood, and that they looked about on the ground for any scraps of food they might pick up, and that when they could not find any they cried. She remembered nothing clearly after that till some men with large beards and large hats rode up on horseback: it might have been next day or the day after. She remembered how they jumped off their horses and took them up in their arms, and how they cried; but that they, the children, did not cry, they only asked for food. She remembered how one man took a bit of thick, cold roaster-cake out of his pocket, and gave it to her, and how nice it tasted. And she remembered that the men took them up before them on their horses, and that one man tied her close to him with a large red handkerchief.

In the years that came she learnt to know that that which she remembered so clearly was the great and terrible day when, at Weenen, and in the country round, hundreds of women and children and youths and old men fell before the Zulus, and the assegais of Dingaan's braves drank blood.

She learnt that on that day all of her house and name, from the grandmother to the baby in arms, fell, and that she only and the boy cousin, who had hidden with her among the bushes, were left of all her kin in that northern world. She learnt, too, that the man who tied her to him with the red handkerchief took them back to his wagon, and that he and his wife adopted them, and brought them up among their own children.

She remembered, though less clearly than the day of the fire, how a few years later they trekked away from Natal, and went through great mountain ranges, ranges in and near which lay those places the world was to know later as Laings Nek, and Amajuba, and Ingogo; Elandslaagte, Nicholson Nek, and Spion Kop. She remembered how at last after many wanderings they settled down near the Witwatersrand where game was plentiful and wild beasts were dangerous, but there were no natives, and they were far from the English rule.

There the two children grew up among the children of those who had adopted them, and were kindly treated by them as though they were their own; it yet was but natural that these two of the same name and blood should grow up with a peculiar tenderness for each other. And so it came to pass that when they were both eighteen years old they asked consent of the old people, who gave it gladly, that they should marry. For a time the young couple lived on in the house with the old, but after three years they gathered together all their few goods and in their wagon, with their guns and ammunition and a few sheep and cattle, they moved away northwards to found their own home.

For a time they travelled here and travelled there, but at last they settled on a spot where game was plentiful and the soil good, and there among the low undulating slopes, near the bank of a dry sloot, the young man built at last, with his own hands, a little house of two rooms.

On the long slope across the sloot before the house, he ploughed a piece of land and enclosed it, and he built kraals for his stock and so struck root in the land and wandered no more. Those were brave, glad, free days to the young couple. They lived largely on the game which the gun brought down, antelope and wildebeest that wandered even past the doors at night; and now and again a lion was killed: one no farther than the door of the round hut behind the house where the meat and the milk were stored, and two were killed at the kraals. Sometimes, too, traders came with their wagons and in exchange for skins and fine horns sold sugar and coffee and print and tan-cord, and such things as the little household had need of. The lands yielded richly to them, in maize, and pumpkins, and sweet-cane, and melons; and they had nothing to wish for. Then in time three little sons were born to them, who grew as strong and vigorous in the free life of the open veld as the young lions in the long grass and scrub near the river four miles away. Those were joyous, free years for the man and woman, in which disease, and carking care, and anxiety played no part.

Then came a day when their eldest son was ten years old, and the father went out a-hunting with his Kaffir servants: in the evening they brought him home with a wound eight inches long in his side where a lioness had torn him; they brought back her skin also, as he had shot her at last in the hand-to-throat struggle. He lingered for three days and then died. His wife buried him on the low slope to the left of the house; she and her Kaffir servants alone made the grave and put him in it, for there were no white men near. Then she and her sons lived on there; a new root driven deep into the soil and binding them to it through the grave on the hillside. She hung her husband's large hunting-watch up on the wall, and put three of his guns over it on the rack, and the gun he had in his hand when he met his death she took down and polished up every day; but one gun she always kept loaded at the head of her bed in the inner room. She counted the stock every night and saw that the Kaffirs ploughed the lands, and she saw to the planting and watering of them herself.

Often as the years passed men of the countryside, and even from far off, heard of the young handsome widow who lived alone with her children and saw to her own stock and lands; and they came a-courting. But many of them were afraid to say anything when once they had come, and those who had spoken to her, when once she had answered them, never came again. About this time too the countryside began to fill in; and people came and settled as near as eight and ten miles away; and as people increased the game began to vanish, and with the game the lions, so that the one her husband killed was almost the last ever seen there.

But there was still game enough for food, and when her eldest son was twelve years old, and she gave him his father's smallest gun to go out hunting with, he returned home almost every day with meat enough for the household tied behind his saddle. And as time passed she came also to be known through the countryside as a "wise woman." People came to her to ask advice about their illnesses, or to ask her to dress old wounds that would not heal; and when they questioned her whether she thought the rains would be early, or the game plentiful that year, she was nearly always right. So they called her a "wise woman" because neither she nor they knew any word in that up-country speech of theirs for the thing called "genius." So all things went well till the eldest son was eighteen, and the dark beard was beginning to sprout on his face, and his mother began to think that soon there might be a daughter in the house; for on Saturday evenings, when his work was done, he put on his best clothes and rode off to the next farm eight miles away, where was a young daughter. His mother always saw that he had a freshly ironed shirt waiting for him on his bed, when he came home from the kraals on Saturday nights, and she made plans as to how they would build on two rooms for the new daughter. At this time he was training young horses to have them ready to sell when the traders came round: he was a fine rider and it was always his work. One afternoon he mounted a young horse before the door and it bucked and threw him. He had often fallen before, but this time his neck was broken. He lay dead with his head two feet from his mother's doorstep. They took up his tall, strong body and the next day the neighbours came from the next farm and they buried him beside his father, on the hillside, and another root was struck into the soil. Then the three who were left in the little farmhouse lived and worked on as before, for a year and more.

Then a small native war broke out and the young burghers of the district were called out to help. The second son was very young, but he was the best shot in the district, so he went away with the others. Three months after, the men came back, but among the few who did not return was her son. On a hot sunny afternoon, walking through a mealie field which they thought was deserted and where the dried yellow stalks stood thick, an assegai thrown from an unseen hand found him, and he fell there. His comrades took him and buried him under a large thorn tree, and scraped the earth smooth over him, that his grave might not be found by others. So he was not laid on the rise to the left of the house with his kindred, but his mother's heart went often to that thorn tree in the far north.

And now again there were only two in the little mud-house; as there had been years before when the young man and wife first settled there. She and her young lad were always together night and day, and did all that they did together, as though they were mother and daughter. He was a fair lad, tall and gentle as his father had been before him, not huge and dark as his two elder brothers; but he seemed to ripen towards manhood early. When he was only sixteen the thick white down was already gathering heavy on his upper lip; his mother watched him narrowly, and had many thoughts in her heart. One evening as they sat twisting wicks for the candles together, she said to him, "You will be eighteen on your next birthday, my son, that was your father's age when he married me." He said, "Yes," and they spoke no more then. But later in the evening when they sat before the door she said to him: "We are very lonely here. I often long to hear the feet of a little child about the house, and to see one with your father's blood in it play before the door as you and your brothers played. Have you ever thought that you are the last of your father's name and blood left here in the north; that if you died there would be none left?" He said he had thought of it. Then she told him she thought it would be well if he went away, to the part of the country where the people lived who had brought her up: several of the sons and daughters who had grown up with her had now grown-up children. He might go down and from among them seek out a young girl whom he liked and who liked him; and if he found her, bring her back as a wife. The lad thought very well of his mother's plan. And when three months were passed, and the ploughing season was over, he rode away one day, on the best black horse they had, his Kaffir boy riding behind him on another, and his mother stood at the gable watching them ride away. For three months she heard nothing of him, for trains were not in those days, and letters came rarely and by chance, and neither he nor she could read or write. One afternoon she stood at the gable end as she always stood when her work was done, looking out along the road that came over the rise, and she saw a large tent-wagon coming along it, and her son walking beside it. She walked to meet it. When she had greeted her son and climbed into the wagon she found there a girl of fifteen with pale flaxen hair and large blue eyes whom he had brought home as his wife. Her father had given her the wagon and oxen as her wedding portion. The older woman's heart wrapt itself about the girl as though she had been the daughter she had dreamed to bear of her own body, and had never borne.

The three lived joyfully at the little house as though they were one person. The young wife had been accustomed to live in a larger house, and down south, where they had things they had not here. She had been to school, and learned to read and write, and she could even talk a little English; but she longed for none of the things which she had had; the little brown house was home enough for her.

After a year a child came, but whether it were that the mother was too young, it only opened its eyes for an hour on the world and closed them again. The young mother wept bitterly, but her husband folded his arms about her, and the mother comforted both. "You are young, my children, but we shall yet hear the sound of children's voices in the house," she said; and after a little while the young mother was well again and things went on peacefully as before in the little home.

But in the land things were not going on peacefully. That was the time that the flag to escape from which the people had left their old homes in the Colony, and had again left Natal when it followed them there, and had chosen to face the spear of the savage, and the conflict with wild beasts, and death by hunger and thirst in the wilderness rather than live under, had by force and fraud unfurled itself over them again. For the moment a great sullen silence brooded over the land. The people, slow of thought, slow of speech, determined in action, and unforgetting, sat still and waited. It was like the silence that rests over the land before an up-country thunderstorm breaks.

Then words came: "They have not even given us the free government they promised"—then acts—the people rose. Even in that remote countryside the men began to mount their horses, and with their guns ride away to help. In the little mud-house the young wife wept much when he said that he too was going. But when his mother helped him pack his saddlebags she helped too; and on the day when the men from the next farm went, he rode away also with his gun by his side.

No direct news of the one they had sent away came to the waiting women at the farmhouse; then came fleet reports of the victories of Ingogo and Amajuba. Then came an afternoon after he had been gone two months. They had both been to the gable end to look out at the road, as they did continually amid their work, and they had just come in to drink their afternoon coffee when the Kaffir maid ran in to say she saw someone coming along the road who looked like her master. The women ran out. It was the white horse on which he had ridden away, but they almost doubted if it were he. He rode bending on his saddle, with his chin on his breast and his arm hanging at his side. At first they thought he had been wounded, but when they had helped him from his horse and brought him into the house they found it was only a deadly fever which was upon him. He had crept home to them by small stages. Hardly had he any spirit left to tell them of Ingogo, Laings Nek, and Amajuba. For fourteen days he grew worse and on the fifteenth day he died.

And the two women buried him where the rest of his kin lay on the hillside.

And so it came to pass that on that warm starlight night the two women were alone in the little mud-house with the stillness of the veld about them; even their Kaffir servants asleep in their huts beyond the kraal; and the very sheep lying silent in the starlight. They two were alone in the little house, but they knew that before morning they would not be alone; they were awaiting the coming of the dead man's child.

The young woman with her head on the table groaned. "If only my husband were here still," she wailed. The old woman rose and stood beside her, passing her hard, work-worn hand gently over her shoulder as if she were a little child. At last she induced her to go and lie down in the inner room. When she had grown quieter and seemed to have fallen into a light sleep the old woman came to the front room again. It was almost two o'clock and the fire had burned low under the large kettle. She scraped the coals together and went out of the front door to fetch more wood, and closed the door behind her. The night air struck cool and fresh upon her face after the close air of the house, the stars seemed to be growing lighter as the night advanced, they shot down their light as from a million polished steel points. She walked to the back of the house where, beyond the round hut that served as a storeroom, the woodpile lay. She bent down gathering sticks and chips till her apron was full; then slowly she raised herself and stood still. She looked upwards. It was a wonderful night. The white band of the Milky Way crossed the sky overhead, and from every side stars threw down their light, sharp as barbed spears, from the velvety blue-black of the sky. The woman raised her hand to her forehead as if pushing the hair farther off it, and stood motionless, looking up. After a long time she dropped her hand and began walking slowly towards the house. Yet once or twice on the way she paused and stood looking up. When she went into the house the

woman in the inner room was again moving and moaning.
She laid the sticks down before the fire and went into the
next room. She bent down over the bed where the younger
woman lay, and put her hand upon her. "My daughter," she
said slowly, "be comforted. A wonderful thing has happened to me. As I stood out in the starlight it was as though
a voice came down to me and spoke. The child which will
be born of you tonight will be a man-child and he will live
to do great things for his land and for his people."

Before morning there was the sound of a little wail in
the mud-house: and the child who was to do great things
for his land and for his people was born.

II

Six years passed; and all was as it had been at the little
house among the slopes. Only a new piece of land had been
ploughed up and added to the land before the house, so
that the ploughed land now almost reached to the ridge.

The young mother had grown stouter, and lost her pink
and white; she had become a working-woman, but she still
had the large knot of flaxen hair behind her head and the
large wondering eyes. She had many suitors in those six
years, but she sent them all away. She said the old woman
looked after the farm as well as any man might, and her son
would be grown up by and by. The grandmother's hair was
a little more streaked with grey, but it was as thick as ever,
and her shoulders as upright; only some of her front teeth
had fallen out, which made her lips close more softly.

The great change was that wherever the women went
there was the flaxen-haired child to walk beside them holding on to their skirts or clasping their hands.

The neighbours said they were ruining the child: they let
his hair grow long, like a girl's, because it curled; and they
never let him wear velschoens like other children but always shop boots; and his mother sat up at night to iron his
pinafores as if the next day were always a Sunday.

But the women cared nothing for what was said; to them

he was not as any other child. He asked them strange questions they could not answer, and he never troubled them by wishing to go and play with the little Kaffirs as other children trouble. When neighbours came over and brought their children with them he ran away and hid in the sloot to play by himself till they were gone. No, he was not like other children!

When the women went to lie down on hot days after dinner sometimes, he would say that he did not want to sleep; but he would not run about and make a noise like other children—he would go and sit outside in the shade of the house, on the front doorstep, quite still, with his little hands resting on his knees, and stare far away at the ploughed lands on the slope, or the shadows nearer; the women would open the bedroom window, and peep out to look at him as he sat there.

The child loved his mother and followed her about to the milk house, and to the kraals; but he loved his grandmother best.

She told him stories.

When she went to the lands to see how the Kaffirs were ploughing he would run at her side holding her dress; when they had gone a short way he would tug gently at it and say, "Grandmother, tell me things!"

And long before day broke, when it was yet quite dark, he would often creep from the bed where he slept with his mother into his grandmother's bed in the corner; he would put his arms round her neck and stroke her face till she woke, and then whisper softly, "Tell me stories!" and she would tell them to him in a low voice not to wake the mother, till the cock crowed and it was time to get up and light the candle and the fire.

But what he liked best of all were the hot, still summer nights, when the women put their chairs before the door because it was too warm to go to sleep; and he would sit on the stoof at his grandmother's feet and lean his head against her knees, and she would tell him on and on of the things he liked to hear; and he would watch the stars as they slowly set along the ridge, or the moonlight, casting bright-edged shadows from the gable as she talked. Often after the mother had got sleepy and gone in to bed the two sat there together.

The stories she told him were always true stories of the things she had seen or of things she had heard. Sometimes they were stories of her own childhood: of the day when she and his grandfather hid among the bushes, and saw the wagon burnt; sometimes they were of the long trek from Natal to the Transvaal; sometimes of the things which happened to her and his grandfather when first they came to that spot among the ridges, of how there was no house there nor lands, only two bare grassy slopes when they outspanned their wagon there the first night; she told of a lion she once found when she opened the door in the morning, sitting, with paws crossed, upon the threshold, and how the grandfather jumped out of bed and reopened the door two inches, and shot it through the opening; the skin was kept in the round storehouse still, very old and mangy.

Sometimes she told him of the two uncles who were dead, and of his own father, and of all they had been and done. But sometimes she told him of things much farther off: of the old Colony where she had been born, but which she could not remember, and of the things which happened there in the old days. She told him of how the British had taken the Cape over, and of how the English had hanged their men at the "Slachters Nek" for resisting the English government, and of how the friends and relations had been made to stand round to see them hanged whether they would or no, and of how the scaffold broke down as they were being hanged, and the people looking on cried aloud, "It is the finger of God! They are saved!" but how the British hanged them up again. She told him of the great trek in which her parents had taken part to escape from under the British flag; of the great battles with Moselikatse; and of the murder of Retief and his men by Dingaan, and of Dingaan's Day. She told him how the British government followed them into Natal, and of how they trekked north and east to escape from it again; and she told him of the later things, of the fight at Laings Nek, and Ingogo, and Amajuba, where his father had been. Always she told the same story in exactly the same words over and over again, till the child knew them all by heart, and would ask for this and then that.

The story he loved best, and asked for more often than all the others, made his grandmother wonder, because it did not seem to her the story a child would best like; it was not a story of lion-hunting, or wars, or adventures. Continually when she asked what she should tell him, he said, "About the mountains!"

It was the story of how the Boer women in Natal when the English Commissioner came to annex their country collected to meet him and pointing toward the Drakens Berg Mountains said, "We go across those mountains to freedom or to death!"

More than once, when she was telling him the story, she saw him stretch out his little arm and raise his hand, as though he were speaking.

One evening as he and his mother were coming home from the milking kraals, and it was getting dark, and he was very tired, having romped about shouting among the young calves and kids all the evening, he held her hand tightly.

"Mother," he said suddenly, "when I am grown up, I am going to Natal."

"Why, my child?" she asked him; "there are none of our family living there now."

He waited a little, then said, very slowly, "I am going to go and try to get our land back!"

His mother started; if there were one thing she was more firmly resolved on in her own mind than any other it was that he should never go to the wars. She began to talk quickly of the old white cow who had kicked the pail over as she was milked, and when she got to the house she did not even mention to the grandmother what had happened; it seemed better to forget.

One night in the rainy season when it was damp and chilly they sat round the large fireplace in the front room.

Outside the rain was pouring in torrents and you could hear the water rushing in the great dry sloot before the door. His grandmother, to amuse him, had sprung some dried mealies in the great black pot and sprinkled them with sugar, and now he sat on the stoof at her feet with a large lump of the sticky sweetmeat in his hand, watching the fire. His grandmother from above him was watching it also, and his mother in her elbow-chair on the other side of the fire had her eyes half closed and was nodding already with the warmth of the room and her long day's work. The child sat so quiet, the hand with the lump of sweetmeat resting on his knee, that his grandmother thought he had gone to sleep too. Suddenly he said without looking up, "Grandmother?"

"Yes."

He waited rather a long time, then said slowly, "Grandmother, did God make the English too?"

She also waited for a while; then she said, "Yes, my child; He made all things."

They were silent again, and there was no sound but of the rain falling and the fire cracking and the sloot rushing outside. Then he threw his head backwards on to his grandmother's knee and looking up into her face, said, "But, Grandmother, why did He make them?"

Then she too was silent for a long time. "My child," at last she said, "we cannot judge the ways of the Almighty. He does that which seems good in His own eyes."

The child sat up and looked back at the fire. Slowly he tapped his knee with the lump of sweetmeat once or twice; then he began to munch it; and soon the mother started wide awake and said it was time for all to go to bed.

The next morning his grandmother sat on the front doorstep cutting beans in an iron basin; he sat beside her on the step pretending to cut too, with a short, broken knife. Presently he left off and rested his hands on his knees, looking away at the hedge beyond, with his small forehead knit tight between the eyes.

"Grandmother," he said suddenly, in a small, almost

shrill voice, "do the English want *all* the lands of *all* the people?"

The handle of his grandmother's knife as she cut clinked against the iron side of the basin. "All they can get," she said.

After a while he made a little movement almost like a sigh, and took up his little knife again and went on cutting.

Some time after that, when a trader came by, his grandmother bought him a spelling-book and a slate and pencils, and his mother began to teach him to read and write. When she had taught him for a year he knew all she did. Sometimes when she was setting him a copy and left a letter out in a word, he would quietly take the pencil when she set it down and put the letter in, not with any idea of correcting her, but simply because it must be there.

Often at night when the child had gone to bed early, tired out with his long day's play, and the two women were left in the front room with the tallow candle burning on the table between them, then they talked of his future.

Ever since he had been born everything they had earned had been put away in the wagon chest under the grandmother's bed. When the traders with their wagons came round the women bought nothing except a few groceries and clothes for the child; even before they bought a yard of cotton print for a new apron they talked long and solemnly as to whether the old one might not be made to do by re-patching; and they mixed much more dry pumpkin and corn with their coffee than before he was born. It was to earn more money that the large new piece of land had been added to the lands before the house.

They were going to have him educated. First he was to be taught all they could at home, then to be sent away to a great school in the old Colony, and then he was to go over the sea to Europe and come back an advocate or doctor or a parson. The grandmother had made a long journey to the next town, to find out from the minister just how much it would cost to do it all.

In the evenings when they sat talking it over the mother

generally inclined to his becoming a parson. She never told the grandmother why, but the real reason was because parsons do not go to the war. The grandmother generally favoured his becoming an advocate, because he might become a judge. Sometimes they sat discussing these matters till the candle almost burnt out.

"Perhaps, one day," the mother would at last say, "he may yet become president!"

Then the grandmother would slowly refold her hands across her apron and say softly, "Who knows?—who knows?"

Often they would get the box out from under the bed (looking carefully across the corner to see he was fast asleep) and would count out all the money, though each knew to a farthing how much was there; then they would make it into little heaps, so much for this, so much for that, and then they would count on their fingers how many good seasons it would take to make the rest, and how old he would be.

When he was eight and had learnt all his mother could teach him, they sent him to school every day on an adjoining farm six miles off, where the people had a schoolmaster. Every day he rode over on the great white horse his father went to the wars with; his mother was afraid to let him ride alone at first, but his grandmother said he must learn to do everything alone. At four o'clock when he came back one or other of the women was always looking out to see the little figure on the tall horse coming over the ridge.

When he was eleven they gave him his father's smallest gun; and one day not long after he came back with his first small buck. His mother had the skin dressed and bound with red, and she laid it as a mat under the table, and even the horns she did not throw away, and saved them in the round house, because it was his first.

When he was fourteen the schoolmaster said he could teach him no more; that he ought to go to some larger school where they taught Latin and difficult things; they had not yet money enough and he was not quite old enough to go to the old Colony, so they sent him first to the High-veld, where his mother's relations lived and where there were good schools, where they taught the difficult things; he could live with his mother's relations and come back once a year for the holidays.

They were great times when he came.

His mother made him koekies and sasarties and nice things every day; and he used to sit on the stoof at her feet and let her play with his hair like when he was quite small. With his grandmother he talked. He tried to explain to her all he was learning, and he read the English newspapers to her (she could read in neither English nor Dutch), translating them. Most of all she liked his atlas. They would sometimes sit over it for half an hour in the evening tracing the different lands and talking of them. On the warm nights he used still to sit outside on the stoof at her feet with his head against her knee, and they used to discuss things that were happening in other lands and in South Africa; and sometimes they sat there quite still together.

It was now he who had the most stories to tell; he had seen Krugersdorp and Johannesburg, and Pretoria; he knew the world; he was at Krugersdorp when Dr. Jameson made his raid. Sometimes he sat for an hour, telling her of things, and she sat quietly listening.

When he was seventeen, nearly eighteen, there was money enough in the box to pay for his going to the Colony and then to Europe; and he came home to spend a few months with them before he went.

He was very handsome now; not tall, and very slight, but with fair hair that curled close to his head, and white hands like a town's man. All the girls in the countryside were in love with him. They all wished he would come and see them. But he seldom rode from home except to go to the next farm where he had been at school. There lived little Aletta, who was the daughter of the woman his uncle had loved before he went to the Kaffir war and got killed. She was only fifteen years old, but they had always been great friends. She netted him a purse of green silk. He said he would take it with him to Europe, and would show it her when he came back and was an advocate; and he gave her a book with her name written in it, which she was to show to him.

These were the days when the land was full of talk; it was said the English were landing troops in South Africa, and wanted to have war. Often the neighbours from the nearest farms would come to talk about it (there were more farms now, the country was filling in, and the nearest railway station was only a day's journey off), and they discussed matters. Some said they thought there would be war; others again laughed, and said it would be only Jameson and his white flag again. But the grandmother shook her head, and if they asked her why, she said, "It will not be the war of a week, nor a month; if it comes it will be the war of years," but she would say nothing more.

Yet sometimes when she and her grandson were walking along together in the lands she would talk.

Once she said: "It is as if a great heavy cloud hung just above my head, as though I wished to press it back with my hands and could not. It will be a great war—a great war. Perhaps the English government will take the land for a time, but they will not keep it. The gold they have fought for will divide them, till they slay one another over it."

Another day she said: "This land will be a great land one day with one people from the sea to the north—but we shall not live to see it."

He said to her: "But how can that be when we are all of different races?"

She said: "The land will make us one. Were not our fathers of more than one race?"

Another day, when she and he were sitting by the table after dinner, she pointed to a sheet of exercise paper, on which he had been working out a problem and which was covered with algebraical symbols, and said, "In fifteen years' time the government of England will not have one piece of land in all South Africa as large as that sheet of paper."

One night when the milking had been late and she and he were walking down together from the kraals in the starlight she said to him: "If this war comes let no man go to it lightly, thinking he will surely return home, nor let him go expecting victory on the next day. It will come at last, but not at first.

"Sometimes," she said, "I wake at night and it is as though the whole house were filled with smoke—and I have to get up and go outside to breathe. It is as though I saw my whole land blackened and desolate. But when I look up it is as though a voice cried out to me, 'Have no fear!'"

They were getting his things ready for him to go away after Christmas. His mother was making him shirts and his grandmother was having a kaross of jackals' skins made that he might take it with him to Europe where it was so cold. But his mother noticed that whenever the grandmother was in the room with him and he was not looking at her, her eyes were always curiously fixed on him as though they were questioning something. The hair was growing white and a little thin over her temples now, but her eyes were as bright as ever, and she could do a day's work with any man.

One day when the youth was at the kraals helping the Kaffir boys to mend a wall, and the mother was kneading bread in the front room, and the grandmother washing up the breakfast things, the son of the Field-Cornet came riding over from his father's farm, which was about twelve miles off. He stopped at the kraal and Jan and he stood talking for some time; then they walked down to the farmhouse, the Kaffir boy leading the horse behind them. Jan stopped at the round store, but the Field-Cornet's son went to the front door. The grandmother asked him in, and handed him some coffee, and the mother, her hands still in the dough, asked him how things were going at his father's farm, and if his mother's young turkeys had come out well, and she asked if he had met Jan at the kraals. He answered the questions slowly, and sipped his coffee. Then he put the cup down on the table, and said suddenly in the same measured voice, staring at the wall in front of him, that war had broken out, and his father had sent him round to call out all fighting burghers.

The mother took her hands out of the dough and stood upright beside the trough as though paralysed. Then she cried in a high, hard voice, unlike her own, "Yes, but Jan cannot go! He is hardly eighteen! He's got to go and be educated in other lands! You can't take the only son of a widow!"

"Aunt," said the young man slowly, "no one will make him go."

The grandmother stood resting the knuckles of both hands on the table, her eyes fixed on the young man. "He shall decide himself," she said.

The mother wiped her hands from the dough and rushed past them and out at the door; the grandmother followed slowly.

They found him in the shade at the back of the house, sitting on a stump; he was cleaning the belt of his new Mauser which lay across his knees.

"Jan," his mother cried, grasping his shoulder, "you are not going away? You can't go! You must stay. You can go by Delagoa Bay if there is fighting on the other side! There is plenty of money!"

He looked softly up into her face with his blue eyes. "We have all to be at the Field-Cornet's at nine o'clock tomorrow morning," he said. She wept aloud and argued.

His grandmother turned slowly without speaking, and went back into the house. When she had given the Field-Cornet's son another cup of coffee and shaken hands with him, she went into the bedroom and opened the box in which her grandson's clothes were kept, to see which things he should take with him. After a time the mother came back too. He had kissed her and talked to her until she too had at last said it was right he should go.

All the day they were busy. His mother baked him biscuits to take in his bag, and his grandmother made a belt of two strips of leather; she sewed them together herself and put a few sovereigns between the stitchings. She said some of his comrades might need the money if he did not.

The next morning early he was ready. There were two saddlebags tied to his saddle and before it was strapped the kaross his grandmother had made; she said it would be useful when he had to sleep on damp ground. When he had greeted them, he rode away towards the rise: and the women stood at the gable of the house to watch him.

When he had gone a little way he turned in his saddle, and they could see he was smiling; he took off his hat and waved it in the air; the early morning sunshine made his hair as yellow as the tassels that hang from the head of ripening mealies. His mother covered her face with the sides of her kappie and wept aloud; but the grandmother shaded her eyes with both her hands and stood watching him till the figure passed out of sight over the ridge; and when it was gone and the mother returned to the house crying, she still stood watching the line against the sky.

The two women were very quiet during the next days; they worked hard, and seldom spoke. After eight days there came a long letter from him (there was now a post once a week from the station to the Field-Cornet's). He said he was well and in very good spirits. He had been to Krugersdorp and Johannesburg, and Pretoria; all the family living there were well and sent greetings. He had joined a corps that was leaving for the front the next day. He sent also a long message to Aletta, asking them to tell her he was sorry to go away without saying goodbye; and he told his mother how good the biscuits and biltong were she had put into his saddlebag; and he sent her a piece of "vierkleur" ribbon in the letter, to wear on her breast.

The women talked a great deal for a day or two after this letter came. Eight days after there was a short note from him, written in pencil in the train on his way to the front. He said all was going well, and if he did not write soon they were not to be anxious; he would write as often as he could.

For some days the women discussed the note too.

Then came two weeks without a letter; the two women became very silent. Every day they sent the Kaffir boy over to the Field-Cornet's, even on the days when there was no post, to hear if there was any news.

Many reports were flying about the countryside. Some said that an English armoured train had been taken on the western border; that there had been fighting at Albertina, and in Natal. But nothing seemed quite certain.

Another week passed . . . Then the two women became very quiet.

The grandmother, when she saw her daughter-in-law left the food untouched on her plate, said there was no need to be anxious; men at the front could not always find paper and pencils to write with and might be far from any post office. Yet night after night she herself would rise from her bed saying she felt the house close, and go and walk up and down outside.

Then one day suddenly all their servants left them except one Kaffir and his wife, whom they had had for years, and the servants from the farms about went also, which was a sign there had been news of much fighting; for the Kaffirs hear things long before the white man knows them.

Three days after, as the women were clearing off the breakfast things, the youngest son of the Field-Cornet, who was only fifteen and had not gone to the war with the others, rode up. He hitched his horse to the post, and came towards the door. The mother stepped forward to meet him and shook hands in the doorway.

"I suppose you have come for the carrot seed I promised your mother? I was not able to send it, as our servants ran away," she said, as she shook his hand. "There isn't a letter from Jan, is there?" The lad said no, there was no letter from him, and shook hands with the grandmother. He stood by the table instead of sitting down.

The mother turned to the fireplace to get coals to put under the coffee to rewarm it; but the grandmother stood leaning forward with her eyes fixed on him from across the table. He felt uneasily in his breast pocket.

"Is there no news?" the mother said without looking round, as she bent over the fire.

"Yes, there is news, Aunt."

She rose quickly and turned towards him, putting down the brazier on the table. He took a letter out of his breast pocket. "Aunt, my father said I must bring this to you. It came inside one to him and they asked him to send one of us over with it."

The mother took the letter; she held it, examining the address.

"It looks to me like the writing of Sister Annie's Paul," she said. "Perhaps there is news of Jan in it"—she turned to them with a half-nervous smile—"they were always such friends."

"All is as God wills, Aunt," the young man said, looking down fixedly at the top of his riding whip.

But the grandmother leaned forward motionless, watching her daughter-in-law as she opened the letter.

She began to read to herself, her lips moving slowly as she deciphered it word by word.

Then a piercing cry rang through the roof of the little mud-farmhouse.

"He is dead! My boy is dead!"

She flung the letter on the table and ran out at the front door.

Far out across the quiet ploughed lands and over the veld to where the kraals lay the cry rang. The Kaffir woman who sat outside her hut beyond the kraals nursing her baby heard it and came down with her child across her hip to see what was the matter. At the side of the round house she stood motionless and openmouthed, watching the woman, who paced up and down behind the house with her apron thrown over her head and her hands folded above it, crying aloud.

In the front room the grandmother, who had not spoken since he came, took up the letter and put it in the lad's hands. "Read," she whispered.

And slowly the lad spelled it out.

"My Dear Aunt,

"I hope this letter finds you well. The Commandant has asked me to write it.

"We had a great fight four days ago, and Jan is dead. The Commandant says I must tell you how it happened. Aunt, there were five of us first in a position on that koppie, but two got killed, and then there were only three of us—Jan, and I, and Uncle Peter's Frikkie. Aunt, the khakies were coming on all round just like locusts, and the bullets were coming just like hail. It was bare on that side of the koppie where we were, but we had plenty of cartridges. We three took up a position where there were some small stones and we fought, Aunt; we had to. One bullet took off the top of my ear, and Jan got two bullets, one through the flesh in the left leg and one through his arm, but he could still fire his gun. Then we three meant to go to the top of the koppie, but a bullet took Jan right through his chest. We knew he couldn't go any farther. The khakies were right at the foot of the koppie just coming up. He told us to lay him down, Aunt. We said we would stay by him, but he said we must go. I put my jacket under his head and Frikkie put his over his feet. We threw his gun far away from him that they might see how it was with him. He said he hadn't much pain, Aunt. He was full of blood from his arm, but there wasn't much from his chest, only a little out of the corners of his mouth. He said we must make haste or the khakies would catch us; he said he wasn't afraid to be left there.

"Aunt, when we got to the top, it was all full of khakies like the sea on the other side, all among the koppies and on our koppie too. We were surrounded, Aunt; the last I saw of Frikkie he was sitting on a stone with blood running down his face, but he got under a rock and hid there; some of our men found him next morning and brought him to camp. Aunt, there was a khakie's horse standing just below where I was, with no one on it. I jumped on and rode. The bullets went this way and the bullets went that, but I rode! Aunt, the khakies were sometimes as near me as that tentpole, only the Grace of God saved me. It was dark in the night when I got back to where our people were, because I had to go round all the koppies to get away from the khakies.

"Aunt, the next day we went to look for him. We found him where we left him; but he was turned over on to his face; they had taken all his things, his belt and his watch, and the pugaree from his hat, even his boots. The little green silk purse he used to carry we found on the ground by him, but nothing it it. I will send it back to you whenever I get an opportunity.

"Aunt, when we turned him over on his back there were four bayonet stabs in his body. The doctor says it was only the first three while he was alive; the last one was through his heart and killed him at once.

"We gave him Christian burial, Aunt; we took him to the camp.

"The Commandant was there, and all of the family who are with the Commando were there, and they all said they hoped God would comfort you . . ."

The old woman leaned forward and grasped the boy's arm. "Read it over again," she said, "from where they found him." He turned back and reread slowly. She gazed at the page as though she were reading also. Then, suddenly, she slipped out at the front door.

At the back of the house she found her daughter-in-law still walking up and down, and the Kaffir woman with a red handkerchief bound round her head and the child sitting across her hip, sucking from her long, pendulous breast, looking on.

The old woman walked up to her daughter-in-law and grasped her firmly by the arm.

"He's dead! You know, my boy's dead!" she cried, drawing the apron down with her right hand and disclosing her swollen and bleared face. "Oh, his beautiful hair—Oh, his beautiful hair!"

The old woman held her arm tighter with both hands; the younger opened her half-closed eyes, and looked into the keen, clear eyes fixed on hers, and stood arrested.

The old woman drew her face closer to hers. "You . . .

do . . . not . . . know . . . what . . . has . . . happened!" she spoke slowly, her tongue striking her front gum, the jaw moving stiffly, as though partly paralysed. She loosed her left hand and held up the curved work-worn fingers before her daughter-in-law's face. "Was it not told me . . . the night he was born . . . here . . . at this spot . . . that he would do great things . . . great things . . . for his land and his people?" She bent forward till her lips almost touched the other's. "Three . . . bullet . . . wounds . . . and four . . . bayonet . . . stabs!" She raised her left hand high in the air. "Three . . . bullet . . . wounds . . . and four . . . bayonet . . . stabs! . . . Is it given to many to die so for their land and their people!"

The younger woman gazed into her eyes, her own growing larger and larger. She let the old woman lead her by the arm in silence into the house.

The Field-Cornet's son was gone, feeling there was nothing more to be done; and the Kaffir woman went back with her baby to her hut beyond the kraals. All day the house was very silent. The Kaffir woman wondered that no smoke rose from the farmhouse chimney, and that she was not called to churn, or wash the pots. At three o'clock she went down to the house. As she passed the grated window of the round outhouse she saw the buckets of milk still standing unsifted on the floor as they had been set down at breakfast time, and under the great soap-pot beside the woodpile the fire had died out. She went round to the front of the house and saw the door and window shutters still closed, as though her mistresses were still sleeping. So she rebuilt the fire under the soap-pot and went back to her hut.

It was four o'clock when the grandmother came out from the dark inner room where she and her daughter-in-law had been lying down; she opened the top of the front door, and lit the fire with twigs, and set the large black kettle over it. When it boiled she made coffee, and poured out two cups and set them on the table with a plate of biscuits, and then called her daughter-in-law from the inner room.

The two women sat down one on each side of the table, with their coffee cups before them, and the biscuits between them, but for a time they said nothing, but sat silent, looking out through the open door at the shadow of the house and the afternoon sunshine beyond it. At last the older woman motioned that the younger should drink her coffee. She took a little, and then folding her arms on the table rested her head on them, and sat motionless as if asleep.

The older woman broke up a biscuit into her own cup, and stirred it round and round; and then, without tasting, sat gazing out into the afternoon's sunshine till it grew cold beside her.

It was five, and the heat was quickly dying; the glorious golden colouring of the later afternoon was creeping over everything when she rose from her chair. She moved to the door and took from behind it two large white calico bags hanging there, and from nails on the wall she took down two large brown cotton kappies. She walked round the table and laid her hand gently on her daughter-in-law's arm. The younger woman raised her head slowly and looked up into her mother-in-law's face; and then, suddenly, she knew that her mother-in-law was an old, old woman. The little shrivelled face that looked down at her was hardly larger than a child's, the eyelids were half closed and the lips worked at the corners and the bones cut out through the skin in the temples.

"I am going out to sow—the ground will be getting too dry tomorrow; will you come with me?" she said gently.

The younger woman made a movement with her hand, as though she said "What is the use?" and redropped her hand on the table.

"It may go on for long, our burghers must have food," the old woman said gently.

The younger woman looked into her face; then she rose slowly and taking one of the brown kappies from her hand, put it on, and hung one of the bags over her left arm; the old woman did the same and together they passed out of the door. As the older woman stepped down the younger caught her and saved her from falling.

"Take my arm, Mother," she said.

But the old woman drew her shoulders up. "I only stumbled a little!" she said quickly. "That step has been always too high"; but before she reached the plank over the sloot the shoulders had dropped again, and the neck fallen forward.

The mould in the lands was black and soft; it lay in long ridges, as it had been ploughed up a week before, but the last night's rain had softened it and made it moist and ready for putting in the seed.

The bags which the women carried on their arms were full of the seed of pumpkins and mealies. They began to walk up the lands, keeping parallel with the low hedge of dried bushes that ran up along the side of the sloot almost up to the top of the ridge. At every few paces they stopped and bent down to press into the earth, now one and then the other kind of seed from their bags. Slowly they walked up and down till they reached the top of the land almost on the horizon line; and then they turned, and walked down, sowing as they went. When they had reached the bottom of the land before the farmhouse it was almost sunset, and their bags were nearly empty; but they turned to go up once more. The light of the setting sun cast long, gaunt shadows from their figures across the ploughed land, over the low hedge and the sloot, into the bare veld beyond; shadows that grew longer and longer as they passed slowly on pressing in the seeds ... The seeds! ... that were to lie in the dank, dark earth, and rot there, seemingly, to die, till their outer covering had split and fallen from them ... and then, when the rains had fallen, and the sun had shone, to come up above the earth again, and high in the clear air to lift their feathery plumes and hang out their pointed leaves and silken tassels! To cover the ground with a mantle of green and gold through which sunlight quivered, over which the insects hung by thousands, carrying yellow pollen on their legs and wings and making the air alive with their hum and stir, while grain and fruit ripened surely . . . for the next season's harvest!

When the sun had set, the two women with their empty bags turned and walked silently home in the dark to the farmhouse.

NINETEEN HUNDRED AND ONE

Near one of the camps in the Northern Transvaal are the graves of two women. The older one died first, on the twenty-third of the month, from hunger and want; the younger woman tended her with ceaseless care and devotion till the end. A week later when the British Superintendent came round to inspect the tents, she was found lying on her blanket on the mud-floor dead, with the rations of bread and meat she had got four days before untouched on a box beside her. Whether she died of disease, or from inability to eat the food, no one could say. Some who had seen her said she hardly seemed to care to live after the old woman died; they buried them side by side.

There is no stone and no name upon either grave to say who lies there . . . our unknown . . . our unnamed . . . our forgotten dead.

IN THE YEAR NINETEEN HUNDRED AND FOUR

If you look for the little farmhouse among the ridges you will not find it there today.

The English soldiers burnt it down. You can only see where the farmhouse once stood, because the stramonia and weeds grow high and very strong there; and where the ploughed lands were you can only tell because the veld never grows quite the same on land that has once been ploughed. Only a brown patch among the long grass on the ridge shows where the kraals and huts once were.

In a country house in the north of England the owner has upon his wall an old flintlock gun. He takes it down to show his friends. It is a small thing he picked up in the war in South Africa, he says. It must be at least eighty years old and is very valuable. He shows how curiously it is constructed; he says it must have been kept in such perfect repair by continual polishing for the steel shines as if it were silver. He does not tell that he took it from the wall of the little mud house before he burnt it down.

It was the grandfather's gun, which the women had kept polished on the wall.

In a London drawing room the descendant of a long line of titled forefathers entertains her guests. It is a fair room, and all that money can buy to make life soft and beautiful is there.

On the carpet stands a little dark wooden stoof. When one of her guests notices it, she says it is a small curiosity which her son brought home to her from South Africa when he was out in the war there; and how good it was of him to think of her when he was away in the back country. And when they ask what it is, she says it is a thing Boer women have as a footstool and to keep their feet warm; and she shows the hole at the side where they put the coals in, and the little holes at the top where the heat comes out.

And the other woman puts her foot out and rests it on the stoof just to try how it feels, and drawls "How f-u-n-n-y!"

It is grandmother's stoof, that the child used to sit on.

The wagon chest was found and broken open just before the thatch caught fire, by three private soldiers, and they divided the money between them; one spent his share in drink, another had his stolen from him, but the third sent his home to England to a girl in the East End of London. With part of it she bought a gold brooch and earrings, and the rest she saved to buy a silk wedding dress when he came home.

A syndicate of Jews in Johannesburg and London have bought the farm. They purchased it from the English government, because they think to find gold on it. They have purchased it and paid for it . . . but they do not possess it.

Only the men who lie in their quiet graves upon the hillside, who lived on it, and loved it, possess it; and the piles of stones above them, from among the long waving grasses, keep watch over the land.

CAN THEMBA

Daniel Canodoce Themba was born in 1924 near Pretoria, South Africa, and graduated with a first-class degree in English and a teacher's diploma from Fort Hare University College. He moved to Sophiatown, a vibrant center of black South African culture until it was razed by the white regime, and began writing short stories, one of which won the first fiction competition sponsored by *Drum* magazine. He then went to work for *Drum,* joining a group of hard-hitting and hard-drinking journalists who were said to live by a motto popularized in a 1949 film: "Live fast, die young, and have a good-looking corpse." He eventually lost his job at the magazine and moved to Swaziland, where he worked as a teacher. In 1966, all of his works were banned by the South African government on the grounds that he was a communist. He died in 1968, and not until the 1980s did his short stories finally become available with the publication of his two collections, *The Will to Die* (1972) and *The World of Can Themba* (1985). He was posthumously awarded the Order of Ikhamanga in Silver for "Excellent achievement in literature, contributing to the field of journalism and striving for a just and democratic society in South Africa."

The Suit
(1967)

Five-thirty in the morning, and the candlewick bedspread frowned as the man under it stirred. He did not like to wake his wife lying by his side—as yet—so he crawled up and out by careful peristalsis. But before he tiptoed out of his room with shoes and socks under his arm, he leaned over and peered at the sleeping serenity of his wife: to him a daily matutinal miracle.

He grinned and yawned simultaneously, offering his wordless Te Deum to whatever gods for the goodness of life; for the pure beauty of his wife; for the strength surging through his willing body; for the even, unperturbed rhythms of his passage through days and months and years — it must be — to heaven.

Then he slipped soundlessly into the kitchen. He flipped aside the curtain of the kitchen window, and saw outside a thin drizzle, the type that can soak one to the skin, and that could go on for days and days. He wondered, head aslant, why the rain in Sophiatown always came in the morning when workers had to creep out of their burrows; and then at how blistering heat waves came during the day when messengers had to run errands all over; and then at how the rain came back when workers knocked off and had to scurry home.

He smiled at the odd caprice of the heavens, and tossed his head at the naughty incongruity, as if, "Ai, but the gods!"

From behind the kitchen door, he removed an old rain cape, peeling off in places, and swung it over his head. He dashed for the lavatory, nearly slipping in a pool of muddy water, but he reached the door. Aw, blast, someone had made it before him. Well, that is the toll of staying in a yard where twenty . . . thirty other people have to share the same lean-to. He was dancing and burning in that climactic moment when trouser-fly will not come wide soon enough. He stepped round the lavatory and watched the streamlets of rainwater quickly wash away the jet of tension that spouted from him. That infinite after-relief. Then he dashed back to his kitchen. He grabbed the old baby bathtub hanging on a nail under the slight shelter of the gutterless roof-edge. He opened a large wooden box and quickly filled the bath-tub with coal. Then he inched his way back to the kitchen door and inside.

He was huh-huh-huhing one of those fugitive tunes that

cannot be hidden, but often just occur and linger naggingly in the head. The fire he was making soon licked up cheerfully, in mood with his contentment.

He had a trick for these morning chores. While the fire in the old stove warmed up, the water kettle humming on it, he gathered and laid ready the things he would need for the day: briefcase and the files that go with it; the book that he was reading currently; the letters of his lawyer boss which he usually posted before he reached the office; his wife's and his own dry-cleaning slips for the Sixty-Minutes; his lunch tin solicitously prepared the night before by his attentive wife; and, today, the battered rain cape. By the time the kettle on the stove sang (before it actually boiled), he poured water from it into a wash basin, refilled and replaced it on the stove. Then he washed himself carefully: across the eyes, under, in and out the armpits, down the torso and in between the legs. This ritual was thorough, though no white man a-complaining of the smell of wogs knows anything about it. Then he dressed himself fastidiously. By this time he was ready to prepare breakfast.

Breakfast! How he enjoyed taking in a tray of warm breakfast to his wife, cuddled in bed. To appear there in his supremest immaculacy, tray in hand when his wife comes out of ether to behold him. These things we blacks want to do for our own . . . not fawningly for the whites for whom we bloody-well got to do it. He felt, he denied, that he was one of those who believed in putting his wife in her place even if she was a good wife. Not he.

Matilda, too, appreciated her husband's kindness, and only put her foot down when he offered to wash up also.

"Off with you," she scolded him on his way.

At the bus stop he was a little sorry to see that jovial old Maphikela was in a queue for a bus ahead of him. He would miss Maphikela's raucous laughter and uninhibited, bawdy conversations in fortissimo. Maphikela hailed him nevertheless. He thought he noticed hesitation in the old man, and a slight clouding of his countenance, but the old man shouted back at him, saying that he would wait for him at the terminus in town.

Philemon considered this morning trip to town with garrulous old Maphikela as his daily bulletin. All the township news was generously reported by loud-mouthed heralds, and spiritedly discussed by the bus at large. Of course, "news" included views on bosses (scurrilous), the government (rude), Ghana and Russia (idolatrous), America and the West (sympathetically ridiculing), and boxing (bloodthirsty). But it was always stimulating and surprisingly comprehensive for so short a trip. And there was no law of libel.

Maphikela was standing under one of those token busstop shelters that never keep out rain nor wind nor sunheat. Philemon easily located him by his noisy ribbing of some office boys in their khaki-green uniforms. They walked together into town, but from Maphikela's suddenly subdued manner, Philemon gathered that there was something serious coming up. Maybe a loan.

Eventually, Maphikela came out with it.

"Son," he said sadly, "if I could've avoided this, believe you me I would, but my wife is nagging the spice out of my life for not talking to you about it."

It just did not become blustering old Maphikela to sound so grave and Philemon took compassion upon him.

"Go ahead, dad," he said generously. "You know you can talk to me about anything."

The old man gave a pathetic smile. "We-e-e-ll, it's not really any of our business . . . er . . . but my wife felt . . . you see. Damn it all! I wish these women would not snoop around so much." Then he rushed it. "Anyway, it seems there's a young man who's going to visit your wife every morning . . . ah . . . for these last bloomin' three months. And that wife of mine swears by her heathen gods you don't know a thing about it."

It was not quite like the explosion of a devastating bomb. It was more like the critical breakdown in an infinitely delicate piece of mechanism. From outside the machine just seemed to have gone dead. But deep in its innermost recesses, menacing electrical flashes were leaping from coil to coil, and hot, viscous molten metal was creeping upon the fuel tanks . . .

Philemon heard gears grinding and screaming in his head . . .

"Dad," he said hoarsely, "I . . . I have to go back home."

He turned round and did not hear old Maphikela's anxious, "Steady, son. Steady, son."

The bus ride home was a torture of numb dread and suffocating despair. Though the bus was now emptier Philemon suffered crushing claustrophobia. There were immense washerwomen whose immense bundles of soiled laundry seemed to baulk and menace him. From those bundles crept miasmata of sweaty intimacies that sent nauseous waves up and down from his viscera. Then the wild swaying of the bus as it negotiated Mayfair Circle hurtled him sickeningly from side to side. Some of the younger women shrieked delightedly to the driver, "*Fuduga!* . . . Stir the pot!" as he swung his steering wheel this way and that. Normally, the crazy tilting of the bus gave him a prickling exhilaration. But now . . .

He felt like getting out of there, screamingly, elbowing everything out of his way. He wished this insane trip were over, and then again, he recoiled at the thought of getting home. He made a tremendous resolve to gather in all the torn, tingling threads of his nerves contorting in the raw. By a merciless act of will, he kept them in subjugation as he stepped out of the bus back in the Victoria Road terminus, Sophiatown.

The calm he achieved was tense . . . but he could think now . . . he could take a decision . . .

With almost boyishly innocent urgency, he rushed through his kitchen into his bedroom. In the lightning flash that the eye can whip, he saw it all . . . the man beside his wife . . . the chestnut arm around her neck . . . the ruffled candlewick bedspread . . . the suit across the chair. But he affected not to see.

He opened the wardrobe door, and as he dug into it, he cheerfully spoke to his wife. "Fancy, Tilly, I forgot to take my pass. I had already reached town, and was going to walk up to the office. If it hadn't been for wonderful old Mr. Maphikela."

A swooshing noise of violent retreat and the clap of his bedroom window stopped him. He came from behind the wardrobe door and looked out from the open window. A man clad only in vest and underpants was running down the street. Slowly, he turned round and contemplated . . . the suit.

Philemon lifted it gingerly under his arm and looked at the stark horror in Matilda's eyes. She was now sitting up in bed. Her mouth twitched, but her throat raised no words.

"Ha," he said, "I see we have a visitor," indicating the blue suit. "We really must show some of our hospitality. But first, I must phone my boss that I can't come to work to-day . . . mmmm—er, my wife's not well. Be back in a moment, then we can make arrangements." He took the suit along.

When he returned he found Matilda weeping on the bed. He dropped the suit beside her, pulled up the chair, turned it round so that its back came in front of him, sat down, brought down his chin on to his folded arms before him, and waited for her.

After a while the convulsions of her shoulders ceased. She saw a smug man with an odd smile and meaningless inscrutability in his eyes. He spoke to her with very little noticeable emotion; if anything, with a flutter of humour.

"We have a visitor, Tilly." His mouth curved ever so slightly. "I'd like him to be treated with the greatest of con-sideration. He will eat every meal with us and share all we have. Since we have no spare room, he'd better sleep in here. But the point is, Tilly, that you will meticulously look after him. If he vanishes or anything else happens to him . . ." A shaft of evil shot from his eye . . . "Matilda, I'll kill you."

He rose from the chair and looked with incongruous supplication at her. He told her to put the fellow in the wardrobe for the time being. As she passed him to get the suit, he turned to go. She ducked frantically, and he stopped.

"You don't seem to understand me, Matilda. There's to be no violence in this house if you and I can help it. So, just look after that suit." He went out.

He went out to the Sophiatown Post Office, which is placed on the exact line between Sophiatown and the white man's surly Westdene. He posted his boss's letters, and walked to the beerhall at the tail end of Western Native Township. He had never been inside it before, but somehow the thunderous din laved his bruised spirit. He stayed there all day.

He returned home for supper . . . and surprise. His dingy little home had been transformed, and the air of stern masculinity it had hitherto contained had been wiped away, to be replaced by anxious feminine touches here and there. There were even gay, colourful curtains swirling in the kitchen window. The old-fashioned coal stove gleamed in its blackness. A clean, chequered oilcloth on the table. Supper ready.

Then she appeared in the doorway of the bedroom. Heavens! here was the woman he had married; the young, fresh, cocoa-coloured maid who had sent rushes of emotion shuddering through him. And the dress she wore brought out all the girlishness of her, hidden so long beneath German print. But no hint of coquettishness, although she stood in the doorway and slid her arm up the jamb, and shyly slanted her head to the other shoulder. She smiled weakly.

"What makes a woman like this experiment with adultery?" he wondered.

Philemon closed his eyes and gripped the seat of his chair on both sides as some overwhelming, undisciplined force sought to catapult him towards her. For a moment

some essence glowed fiercely within him, then sank back
into itself and died . . .

He sighed and smiled sadly back at her. "I'm hungry,
Tilly."

The spell snapped, and she was galvanised into action.
She prepared his supper with dexterous hands that trembled a little only when they hesitated in midair. She took
her seat opposite him, regarded him curiously, clasped her
hands waiting for his prayer, but in her heart she murmured
some other, much more urgent prayer of her own.

"Matilda!" he barked. "Our visitor!" The sheer savagery
with which he cracked at her jerked her up, but only when
she saw the brute cruelty in his face did she run out of the
room, toppling the chair behind her.

She returned with the suit on a hanger, and stood there
quivering like a feather. She looked at him with helpless
dismay. The demoniacal rage in his face was evaporating,
but his heavy breathing still rocked his thorax above the
table, to and fro.

"Put a chair, there." He indicated with a languid gesture
of his arm. She moved like a ghost as she drew a chair to the
table.

"Now seat our friend at the table . . . no, no, not like that.
Put him in front of the chair, and place him on the seat so
that he becomes indeed the third person."

Philemon went on relentlessly: "Dish up for him. Generously. I imagine he hasn't had a morsel all day, the poor
devil."

Now, as consciousness and thought seeped back into
her, her movements revolved so that always she faced this
man who had changed so spectacularly. She started when
he rose to open the window and let in some air.

She served the suit. The act was so ridiculous that she
carried it out with a bitter sense of humiliation. He came
back to sit down and plunge into his meal. No grace was
said for the first time in this house. With his mouth full, he
indicated by a toss of his head that she should sit down in
her place. She did so. Glancing at her plate, the thought oc-

curred to her that someone, after a long famine, was served a sumptuous supper, but as the food reached her mouth it turned to sawdust. Where had she heard it?

Matilda could not eat. She suddenly broke into tears.

Philemon took no notice of her weeping. After supper, he casually gathered the dishes and started washing up. He flung a dry cloth at her without saying a word. She rose and went to stand by his side drying up. But for their wordlessness, they seemed a very devoted couple.

After washing up, he took the suit and turned to her. "That's how I want it every meal, every day." Then he walked into the bedroom.

So it was. After that first breakdown, Matilda began to feel that her punishment was not too severe, considering the heinousness of the crime. She tried to put a joke into it, but by slow, unconscious degrees, the strain nibbled at her. Philemon did not harass her much more, so long as the ritual with the confounded suit was conscientiously followed.

Only once, he got one of his malevolent brainwaves. He got it into his head that "our visitor" needed an outing. Accordingly the suit was taken to the dry cleaners during the week, and, come Sunday, they had to take it out for a walk. Both Philemon and Matilda dressed for the occasion. Matilda had to carry the suit on its hanger over her back and the three of them strolled leisurely along Ray Street. They passed the church crowd in front of the famous Anglican Mission of Christ the King. Though the worshippers saw nothing unusual in them, Matilda felt, searing through her, red-hot needles of embarrassment, and every needle-point was a public eye piercing into her degradation.

But Philemon walked casually on. He led her down Ray Street and turned into Main Road. He stopped often to look into shop windows or to greet a friend passing by. They went up Toby Street, turned into Edward Road, and back home. To Philemon the outing was free of incident, but to Matilda it was one long, excruciating incident.

At home, he grabbed a book on Abnormal Psychology,

flung himself into a chair and calmly said to her, "Give the old chap a rest, will you, Tilly?"

In the bedroom, Matilda said to herself that things could not go on like this. She thought of how she could bring the matter to a head with Philemon; have it out with him once and for all. But the memory of his face, that first day she had forgotten to entertain the suit, stayed her. She thought of running away, but where to? Home? What could she tell her old-fashioned mother had happened between Philemon and her? All right, run away clean then. She thought of many young married girls who were divorcees now, who had won their freedom.

What had happened to Staff Nurse Kakile? The woman drank heavily now, and when she got drunk, the boys of Sophiatown passed her around and called her the Cesspot.

Matilda shuddered.

An idea struck her. There were still decent, married women around Sophiatown. She remembered how after the private schools had been forced to close with the advent of Bantu Education, Father Harringay of the Anglican Mission had organised Cultural Clubs. One, she seemed to remember, was for married women. If only she could lose herself in some cultural activity, find absolution for her conscience in some doing good; that would blur her blasted home life, would restore her self-respect. After all, Philemon had not broadcast her disgrace abroad . . . nobody knew; not one of Sophiatown's slander-mongers suspected how vulnerable she was. She must go and see Mrs. Montjane about joining a Cultural Club. She must ask Philemon now if she might . . . she must ask him nicely.

She got up and walked into the other room where Philemon was reading quietly. She dreaded disturbing him, did not know how to begin talking to him . . . they had talked so little for so long. She went and stood in front of him, looking silently upon his deep concentration. Presently, he looked up with a frown on his face.

Then she dared, "Phil, I'd like to join one of those Cultural Clubs for married women. Would you mind?"

He wrinkled his nose and rubbed it between thumb and index finger as he considered the request. But he had caught the note of anxiety in her voice and thought he knew what it meant.

"Mmmm," he said, nodding. "I think that's a good idea. You can't be moping around all day. Yes, you may, Tilly." Then he returned to his book.

The Cultural Club idea was wonderful. She found women like herself, with time (if not with tragedy) on their hands, engaged in wholesome, refreshing activities. The atmosphere was cheerful and cathartic. They learned things and they did things. They organised fêtes, bazaars, youth activities, sport, music, self-help and community projects. She got involved in committees, meetings, debates, conferences. It was for her a whole new venture into humancraft, and her personality blossomed. Philemon gave her all the rein she wanted.

Now, abiding by that silly ritual at home seemed a little thing . . . a very little thing . . .

Then one day she decided to organise a little party for her friends and their husbands. Philemon was very decent about it. He said it was all right. He even gave her extra money for it. Of course, she knew nothing of the strain he himself suffered from his mode of castigation.

There was a week of hectic preparation. Philemon stepped out of its cluttering way as best he could. So many things seemed to be taking place simultaneously. New dresses were made. Cakes were baked; three different orders of meat prepared; beef for the uninvited chancers; mutton for the normal guests; turkey and chicken for the inner pith of the club's core. To Philemon, it looked as if Matilda planned to feed the multitude on the Mount with no aid of miracles.

On the Sunday of the party, Philemon saw Matilda's guests. He was surprised by the handsome grace with which she received them. There was a long table with enticing foods and flowers and serviettes. Matilda placed all her guests round the table, and the party was ready to begin in the mock-formal township fashion. Outside a steady rumble of conversation went on where the human odds and ends of every Sophiatown party had their "share."

Matilda caught the curious look on Philemon's face. He tried to disguise his edict when he said, "Er . . . the guest of honour."

But Matilda took a chance. She begged, "Just this once, Phil."

He became livid. "Matilda!" he shouted, "Get our visitor!" Then with incisive sarcasm, "Or are you ashamed of him?"

She went ash-grey; but there was nothing for it but to fetch her albatross. She came back and squeezed a chair into some corner, and placed the suit on it. Then she slowly placed a plate of food before it. For a while the guests were dumbfounded. Then curiosity flooded in. They talked at the same time. "What's the idea, Philemon?" . . . "Why must she serve a suit?" . . . "What's happening?" Some just giggled in a silly way. Philemon carelessly swung his head towards Matilda. "You better ask my wife. She knows the fellow best."

All interest beamed upon poor Matilda. For a moment she could not speak, all enveloped in misery. Then she said, unconvincingly, "It's just a game that my husband and I play at mealtime." They roared with laughter. Philemon let her get away with it.

The party went on, and every time Philemon's glare sent Matilda scurrying to serve the suit each course; the guests were no-end amused by the persistent mock-seriousness with which this husband and wife played out their little game. Only, to Matilda, it was no joke; it was a hot poker down her throat. After the party, Philemon went off with one of the guests who had promised to show him a joint "that sells genuine stuff, boy, genuine stuff."

Reeling drunk, late that sabbath, he crashed through his kitchen door, onwards to his bedroom. Then he saw her.

They have a way of saying in the argot of Sophiatown, "Cook out of the head!" signifying that someone was impacted with such violent shock that whatever whiffs of alcohol still wandered through his head were instantaneously evaporated and the man stood sober before stark reality.

There she lay, curled, as if just before she died she begged for a little love, implored some implacable lover to cuddle her a little . . . just this once . . . just this once more.

In screwish anguish, Philemon cried, "Tilly!"

Ngugi wa Thiong'o

Thiong'o was born James Thiong'o in Limuru, Kenya, in 1938; he changed his name in 1977 because of its associations with Christianity and colonial oppression. He was educated at Makerere University and the University of Leeds, returning to Kenya to teach at the University of Nairobi, where he convinced the administration to transform its Department of English into the Department of African Languages and Literature. Thiong'o was both critical of British rule in Kenya and disappointed in the new black ruling class after Kenya gained its independence, and his fiction has frequently depicted ordinary Kenyans juxtaposed against corrupt politicians and greedy entrepreneurs. His first novel, *Weep Not, Child* (1964), described how the Mau Mau rebellion against the British administration in the 1950s affected the lives of a young boy and his family. He is also the author of plays, short stories, and copious nonfiction, most notably *Decolonising the Mind: The Politics of Language in African Literature* (1986).

Minutes of Glory
(1975)

Her name was Wanjiru. But she liked better her Christian one, Beatrice. It sounded more pure and more beautiful. Not that she was ugly; but she could not be called beautiful either. Her body, dark and full fleshed, had the form, yes, but it was as if it waited to be filled by the spirit. She worked in beer halls where sons of women came to drown their inner lives in beer cans and froth. Nobody seemed to notice her. Except, perhaps, when a proprietor or an impatient customer called out her name, Beatrice; then other customers would raise their heads briefly, a few seconds, as if to behold the bearer of such a beautiful name, but not finding anybody there, they would resume their drinking, their ribald jokes, their laughter and play with the other serving girls. She was like a wounded bird in flight: a forced landing now and then but nevertheless wobbling from place to place so that she would variously be found in Alaska, Paradise, The Modern, Thome and other beer halls all over Limuru. Sometimes it was because an irate proprietor found she was not attracting enough customers; he would sack her without notice and without a salary. She would wobble to the next bar. But sometimes she was simply tired of nesting in one place, a daily witness of familiar scenes; girls even more decidedly ugly than she were fought over by numerous claimants at closing time. What do they have that I don't have? she would ask herself, depressed. She longed for a bar-kingdom where she would be at least one of the rulers, where petitioners would bring their gifts of beer, frustrated smiles and often curses that hid more lust and love than hate.

She left Limuru town proper and tried the mushrooming townlets around. She worked at Ngarariga, Kamiritho, Rironi and even Tiekunu and everywhere the story was the same. Oh yes, occasionally she would get a client; but none cared for her as she would have liked, none really wanted her enough to fight over her. She was always a hard-up customer's last resort. No make-believe even, not for her that sweet pretence that men indulged in after their fifth bottle of Tusker. The following night or during a payday, the same client would pretend not to know her; he would be trying his money-power over girls who already had more than a fair share of admirers.

She resented this. She saw in every girl a rival and adopted a sullen attitude. Nyagūthiĩ especially was the thorn that always pricked her wounded flesh. Nyagūthiĩ, arrogant and aloof, but men always in her courtyard; Nyagūthiĩ, fighting with men, and to her they would bring propitiating gifts which she accepted as of right. Nyagūthiī could look bored, impatient or downright contemptuous and still men would cling to her as if they enjoyed being whipped with biting words, curled lips and the indifferent eyes of a free woman. Nyagūthiī was also a bird in flight, never really able to settle in one place, but in her case it was because she hungered for change and excitement: new faces and new territories for her conquest. Beatrice resented her very shadow. She saw in her the girl she would have liked to be, a girl who was both totally immersed in and yet completely above the underworld of bar violence and sex. Wherever Beatrice went the long shadow of Nyagūthiī would sooner or later follow her.

She fled Limuru for Ilmorog in Chiri District. Ilmorog had once been a ghost village, but had been resurrected to life by that legendary woman, Nyang'endo, to whom every pop group had paid their tribute. It was of her that the young dancing Muthuu and Muchun g' wa sang:

> *When I left Nairobi for Ilmorog*
> *Never did I know*
> *I would bear this wonder-child mine*
> *Nyang'endo.*

As a result, Ilmorog was always seen as a town of hope where the weary and the downtrodden would find their rest and fresh water. But again Nyagūthiī followed her.

She found that Ilmorog, despite the legend, despite the songs and dances, was not different from Limuru. She tried various tricks. Clothes? But even here she never earned enough to buy herself glittering robes. What was seventy-five shillings a month without house allowance, posho, without salaried boyfriends? By that time Ambi had reached Ilmorog and Beatrice thought that this would be the answer. Had she not, in Limuru, seen girls blacker than herself transformed overnight from ugly sins into white stars by a touch of skin-lightening creams? And men would ogle them, would even talk with exaggerated pride of their newborn girlfriends. Men were strange creatures, Beatrice thought in moments of searching analysis. They talked heatedly against Ambi, Butone, Firesnow, Moonsnow, wigs, straightened hair, but they always went for a girl with an Ambi-lightened skin and head covered with a wig made in imitation of European or Indian hair. Beatrice never tried to find the root cause of this black self-hatred; she simply accepted the contradiction and applied herself to Ambi with a vengeance. She had to rub out her black shame. But even Ambi she could not afford in abundance; she could only apply it to her face and to her arms so that her legs and her neck retained their blackness. Besides there were parts of her face she could not readily reach—behind the ears and above the eyelashes, for instance—and these were a constant source of shame and irritation to her Ambi-self.

She would always remember this Ambi period as one of her deepest humiliation before her later minutes of glory. She worked in Ilmorog Starlight Bar and Lodging. Nyagūthiī, with her bangled hands, her huge earrings, served behind the counter. The owner was a good Christian soul who regularly went to church and paid all his dues to Harambee projects. Potbelly. Grey hairs. Soft-spoken. A respectable family man, well-known in Ilmorog. Hardworking even, for he would not leave the bar until the closing hours, or more precisely, until Nyagūthiī left. He had no eyes for any other girl; he hung around her, and surreptitiously brought her gifts of clothes without receiving gratitude in kind. Only the promise. Only the hope for tomorrow. Other girls he gave eighty shillings a month. Nyagūthiī had a room to herself. Nyagūthiī woke up whenever she liked to take the stock. But Beatrice and the other girls had to wake up at five or so, make tea for the lodgers, clean up the bar and wash dishes and glasses. Then they would hang around the bar in shifts until two o'clock when they would go for a small break. At five o'clock they had to be in again, ready for customers whom they would now serve with frothy beers and smiles until twelve o'clock or for as long as there were customers thirsty for more Tuskers and Pilsners. What often galled Beatrice, although in her case it did not matter one way or another, was the owner's insistence that the girls should sleep in Starlight. They would otherwise be late for work, he said. But what he really wanted was for the girls to use their bodies to attract more lodgers in Starlight. Most of the girls, led by Nyagūthiī, defied the rule and bribed the watchman to let them out and in. They wanted to meet their regular or one-night boyfriends in places where they would be free and where they would be treated as not just barmaids. Beatrice always slept in. Her occasional one-night patrons wanted to spend the minimum. Came a night when the owner, refused by Nyagūthiī, approached her. He started by finding fault with her work; he called her names, then as suddenly he started praising her, although in a grudging, almost contemptuous manner. He grabbed her, struggled with her, potbelly, grey hairs and everything. Beatrice felt an unusual revulsion for the man. She could not, she would not bring herself to accept that which had so recently been cast aside by Nyagūthiī. My God, she wept inside, what does Nyagūthiī have that I don't have? The man now humiliated himself before her. He implored. He promised her gifts. But she would not yield. That night she too defied the rule. She jumped through a window; she sought a bed in another bar and only came back at six. The proprietor called her in front of all the others and dismissed her. But Beatrice was rather surprised at herself.

She stayed a month without a job. She lived from room to room at the capricious mercy of the other girls. She did not have the heart to leave Ilmorog and start all over again in a new town. The wound hurt. She was tired of wandering. She stopped using Ambi. No money. She looked at herself in the mirror. She had so aged, hardly a year after she had fallen from grace. Why then was she scrupulous, she would ask herself. But somehow she had a horror of soliciting lovers or directly bartering her body for hard cash. What she wanted was decent work and a man or several men who cared for her. Perhaps she took that need for a man, for a home and for a child with her to bed. Perhaps it was this genuine need that scared off men who wanted other things from barmaids. She wept late at nights and remembered home. At such moments, her mother's village in Nyeri seemed the sweetest place on God's earth. She would invest the life of her peasant mother and father with romantic illusions of immeasurable peace and harmony. She longed to go back home to see them. But how could she go back with empty hands? In any case the place was now a distant landscape in the memory. Her life was here in the bar among this crowd of lost strangers. Fallen from grace, fallen from grace. She was part of a generation which would never again be one with the soil, the crops, the wind and the moon. Not for them that whispering in dark hedges, not for her that dance and lovemaking under the glare of the moon, with the hills of TumuTumu rising to touch the sky. She remembered that girl from her home village who, despite a life of apparent glamour being the kept mistress of one rich man after another in Limuru, had gassed herself to death. This generation was not awed by the mystery of death, just as it was callous to the mystery of life; for how many unmarried mothers had thrown their babies into latrines rather than lose that glamour? The girl's death became the subject of jokes. She had gone metric—without pains, they said. Thereafter, for a week, Beatrice thought of going metric. But she could not bring herself to do it.

She wanted love; she wanted life.

A new bar was opened in Ilmorog. Treetop Bar, Lodging and Restaurant. Why Treetop, Beatrice could not understand unless because it was a storeyed building: tea shop on the ground floor and beer shop in a room at the top. The rest were rooms for five-minute or one-night lodgers. The owner was a retired civil servant but one who still played at politics. He was enormously wealthy with business sites and enterprises in every major town in Kenya. Big shots from all over the country came to his bar. Big men in Mercedes. Big men in their Bentleys. Big men in their Jaguars and Daimlers. Big men with uniformed chauffeurs drowsing with boredom in cars waiting outside. There were others not so big who came to pay respects to the great. They talked politics mostly. And about their work. Gossip was rife. Didn't you know? Indeed so and so has been promoted. Really? And so and so has been sacked. Embezzlement of public funds. So foolish you know. Not clever about it at all. They argued, they quarrelled, sometimes they fought it out with fists, especially during the elections campaign. The only point on which they were all agreed was that the Luo community was the root cause of all the trouble in Kenya; that intellectuals and university students were living in an ivory tower of privilege and arrogance; that Kiambu had more than a lion's share of developments; that men from Nyeri and Muranga had acquired all the big business in Nairobi and were even encroaching on Chiri District; that African workers, especially those on the farms, were lazy and jealous of "us" who had sweated ourselves to sudden prosperity. Otherwise each would hymn his own praises or return compliments. Occasionally in moments of drunken ebullience and self-praise, one would order two rounds of beer for each man present in the bar. Even the poor from Ilmorog would come to Treetop to dine at the gates of the nouveaux riches.

Here Beatrice got a job as a sweeper and bedmaker. Here for a few weeks she felt closer to greatness. Now she made beds for men she had previously known as names. She watched how even the poor tried to drink and act big in front of the big. But soon fate caught up with her. Girls flocked to Treetop from other bars. Girls she had known at Limuru, girls she had known at Ilmorog. And most had attached themselves to one or several big men, often playing a hide-and-not-to-be-found game with their numerous lovers. And Nyagũthiĩ was there behind the counter, with the eyes of the rich and the poor fixed on her. And she, with her big eyes, bangled hands and earrings maintained the same air of bored indifference. Beatrice as a sweeper and bed-maker became even more invisible. Girls who had fallen into good fortune looked down upon her.

She fought life with dreams. In between putting clean sheets on beds that had just witnessed a five-minute strug-gle that ended in a half-strangled cry and a pool, she would stand by the window and watch the cars and the chauffeurs, so that soon she knew all the owners by the number plates of their cars and the uniforms of their chauffeurs. She dreamt of lovers who would come for her in sleek Mer-cedes sports cars made for two. She saw herself linking hands with such a lover, walking in the streets of Nairobi and Mombasa, tapping the ground with high heels, quick, quick short steps. And suddenly she would stop in front of a display glass window, exclaiming at the same time: Oh darling, won't you buy me those . . . ? Those what, he would ask, affecting anger. Those stockings, darling. It was as an owner of several stockings, ladderless and holeless, that she thought of her well-being. Never again would she mend torn things. Never, never, never. Do you understand? Never. She was next the proud owner of different coloured wigs, blond wigs, brunette wigs, redhead wigs, Afro wigs, wigs, wigs, all the wigs in the world. Only then would the whole earth sing hallelujah to the one Beatrice. At such moments, she would feel exalted, lifted out of her murky self, no longer a floor sweeper and bedmaker for a five-minute instant love, but Beatrice, descendant of Wangu Makeri who made men tremble with desire at her naked body bathed in moonlight, daughter of Nyang'endo, the founder of modern Ilmorog, of whom they often sang that she had worked several lovers into impotence.

Then she noticed him and he was the opposite of the lover of her dreams. He came one Saturday afternoon driving a big five-ton lorry. He carefully parked it beside the Benzes, the Jaguars and the Daimlers, not as a lorry, but as one of those sleek cream-bodied frames, so proud of it he seemed to be. He dressed in a baggy grey suit over which he wore a heavy khaki military overcoat. He removed the overcoat, folded it with care and put it on the front seat. He locked all the doors, dusted himself a little, then walked round the lorry as if inspecting it for damage. A few steps before he entered Treetop, he turned round for a final glance at his lorry dwarfing the other things. At Treetop he sat in a corner and, with a rather loud defiant voice, ordered a Kenya one. He drank it with relish, looking around at the same time for a face he might recognize. He indeed did recognize one of the big ones and he immediately ordered for him a quarter bottle of Vat 69. This was accepted with a bare nod of the head and a patronizing smile; but when he tried to follow his generosity with a conversation, he was firmly ignored. He froze, sank into his Muratina. But only for a time. He tried again: he was met with frowning faces. More pathetic were his attempts to join in jokes; he would laugh rather too loudly, which would make the big ones stop, leaving him in the air alone. Later in the evening he stood up, counted several crisp hundred-shilling notes and handed them to Nyagūthiī behind the counter ostensibly for safekeeping. People whispered; murmured; a few laughed, rather derisively, though they were rather impressed. But this act did not win him immediate recognition. He staggered towards room number 7 which he had hired. Beatrice brought him the keys. He glanced at her, briefly, then lost all interest.

Thereafter he came every Saturday, at five when most of the big shots were already seated. He repeated the same ritual, except the money act, and always met with defeat. He nearly always sat in the same corner and always rented room 7. Beatrice grew to anticipate his visits and, without being conscious of it, kept the room ready for him. Often after he had been badly humiliated by the big company, he would detain Beatrice and talk to her, or rather he talked to himself in her presence. For him, it had been a life of struggles. He had never been to school although getting an education had been his ambition. He never had a chance. His father was a squatter in the European settled area in the Rift Valley. That meant a lot in those colonial days. It meant among other things a man and his children were doomed to a future of sweat and toil for the white devils and their children. He had joined the freedom struggle and like the others had been sent to detention. He came from detention the same as his mother had brought him to this world. Nothing. With independence he found he did not possess the kind of education which would have placed him in one of the vacancies at the top. He started as a charcoal burner, then a butcher, gradually working his own way to become a big transporter of vegetables and potatoes from the Rift Valley and Chiri districts to Nairobi. He was proud of his achievement. But he resented that others, who had climbed to their present wealth through loans and a subsidized education, would not recognize his like. He would rumble on like this, dwelling on education he would never have, and talking of better chances for his children. Then he would carefully count the money, put it under the pillow and then dismiss Beatrice. Occasionally he would buy her a beer but he was clearly suspicious of women whom he saw as money-eaters of men. He had not yet married.

One night he slept with her. In the morning he scratched for a twenty-shilling note and gave it to her. She accepted the money with an odd feeling of guilt. He did this for several weeks. She did not mind the money. It was useful. But he paid for her body as he would pay for a bag of potatoes or a sack of cabbages. With the one pound, he had paid for her services as a listener, a vessel of his complaints against those above, and as a one-night receptacle of his man's burden. She was becoming bored with his ego, with his stories that never varied in content, but somehow, in him, deep inside, she felt that something had been there, a fire, a seed, a flower which was being smothered. In him she saw a fellow victim and looked forward to his visits. She too longed to talk to someone. She too longed to confide in a human being who would understand.

And she did it one Saturday night, suddenly interrupting the story of his difficult climb to the top. She did not know why she did it. Maybe it was the rain outside. It was softly drumming the corrugated iron sheets, bringing with the drumming a warm and drowsy indifference. He would listen. He had to listen. She came from Karatina in Nyeri. Her two brothers had been gunned down by the British soldiers. Another one had died in detention. She was, so to speak, an only child. Her parents were poor. But they worked hard on their bare strip of land and managed to pay her fees in primary school. For the first six years she had worked hard. In the seventh year, she must have relaxed a little. She did not pass with a good grade. Of course she knew many with similar grades who had been called to good government secondary schools. She knew a few others with lesser grades who had gone to very top schools on the strength of their connections. But she was not called to any high school with reasonable fees. Her parents could not afford fees in a Harambee school. And she would not hear of repeating Standard Seven. She stayed at home with her parents. Occasionally she would help them in the shamba and with house chores. But imagine: for the past six years she had led a life with a different rhythm from that of her parents. Life in the village was dull. She would often go to Karatina and to Nyeri in search of work. In every office they would ask her the same questions: what work do you want? What do you know? Can you type? Can you take shorthand? She was desperate. It was in Nyeri, drinking Fanta in a shop, tears in her eyes, that she met a young man in a dark suit and sunglasses. He saw her plight and talked to her. He came from Nairobi. Looking for work? That's easy; in a big city there would be no difficulty with jobs. He would certainly help. Transport? He had a car—a cream-white Peugeot. Heaven. It was a beautiful ride, with the promise of dawn. Nairobi. He drove her to Terrace Bar. They drank beer and talked about Nairobi. Through the window she could see the neon-lit city and knew that here was hope. That night she gave herself to him, with the promise of dawn making her feel light and gay. She had a very deep sleep. When she woke in the morning, the man in the cream-white Peugeot was not there. She never saw him again. That's how she had started the life of a barmaid. And for one and a half years now she had not been once to see her parents. Beatrice started weeping. Huge sobs of self-pity. Her humiliation and constant flight were fresh in her mind. She had never been able to take to bar culture, she always thought that something better would come her way. But she was trapped, it was the only life she now knew, although she had never really learnt all its laws and norms. Again she heaved out and in, tears tossing out with every sob. Then suddenly she froze. Her sobbing was arrested in the air. The man had long covered himself. His snores were huge and unmistakable.

She felt a strange hollowness. Then a bile of bitterness spilt inside her. She wanted to cry at her new failure. She had met several men who had treated her cruelly, who had laughed at her scruples, at what they thought was an ill-disguised attempt at innocence. She had accepted. But not this, Lord, not this. Was this man not a fellow victim? Had he not, Saturday after Saturday, unburdened himself to her? He had paid for her human services; he had paid away his responsibility with his bottles of Tusker and hard cash in the morning. Her innermost turmoil had been his lullaby. And suddenly something in her snapped. All the anger of a year and a half, all the bitterness against her humiliation were now directed at this man.

What she did later had the mechanical precision of an experienced hand.

She touched his eyes. He was sound asleep. She raised his head. She let it fall. Her tearless eyes were now cold and set. She removed the pillow from under him. She rummaged through it. She took out his money. She counted five crisp pink notes. She put the money inside her brassiere.

She went out of room number 7. Outside it was still raining. She did not want to go to her usual place. She could not now stand the tiny cupboard room or the superior chatter of her roommate. She walked through mud and rain. She found herself walking towards Nyagũthiĩ's room. She knocked at

the door. At first she had no response. Then she heard
Nyagūthiī's sleepy voice above the drumming rain.

"Who is that?"

"It is me. Please open."

"Who?"

"Beatrice."

"At this hour of the night?"

"Please."

Lights were put on. Bolts unfastened. The door opened.
Beatrice stepped inside. She and Nyagūthiī stood there face
to face. Nyagūthiī was in a see-through nightdress: on her
shoulders she had a green pullover.

"Beatrice, is there anything wrong?" she at last asked, a
note of concern in her voice.

"Can I rest here for a while? I am tired. And I want to
talk to you." Beatrice's voice carried assurance and power.

"But what has happened?"

"I only want to ask you a question, Nyagūthiī."

They were still standing. Then, without a word, they both
sat on the bed.

"Why did you leave home, Nyagūthiī?" Beatrice asked.
Another silent moment. Nyagūthiī seemed to be thinking
about the question. Beatrice waited. Nyagūthiī's voice
when at last it came was slightly tremulous, unsteady.

"It is a long story, Beatrice. My father and mother were
fairly wealthy. They were also good Christians. We lived under regulations. You must never walk with the heathen.
You must not attend their pagan customs—dances and cir-
cumcision rites, for instance. There were rules about what,
how and when to eat. You must even walk like a Christian
lady. You must never be seen with boys. Rules, rules all the
way. One day instead of returning home from school, I and
another girl from a similar home ran away to Eastleigh. I
have never been home once this last four years. That's all."

Another silence. Then they looked at one another in
mutual recognition.

"One more question, Nyagūthiī. You need not answer

it. But I have always thought that you hated me, you despised me."

"No, no, Beatrice, I have never hated you. I have never hated anybody. It is just that nothing interests me. Even men do not move me now. Yet I want, I need instant excitement. I need the attention of those false flattering eyes to make me feel myself, myself. But you, you seemed above all this—somehow you had something inside you that I did not have."

Beatrice tried to hold her tears with difficulty.

Early the next day, she boarded a bus bound for Nairobi. She walked down Bazaar Street looking at the shops. Then down Government Road, right into Kenyatta Avenue and Kimathi Street. She went into a shop near Hussein Suleman's street and bought several stockings. She put on a pair. She next bought herself a new dress. Again she changed into it. In a Bata Shoeshop she bought high-heeled shoes, put them on and discarded her old flat ones. On to an Akamba kiosk, and she fitted herself with earrings. She went to a mirror and looked at her new self. Suddenly she felt enormous hunger as if she had been hungry all her life. She hesitated in front of Moti Mahal. Then she walked on, eventually entering Fransae. There was a glint in her eyes that made men's eyes turn to her. This thrilled her. She chose a table in a corner and ordered Indian curry. A man left his table and joined her. She looked at him. Her eyes were merry. He was dressed in a dark suit and his eyes spoke of lust. He bought her a drink. He tried to engage her in conversation. But she ate in silence. He put his hand under the table and felt her knees. She let him do it. The hand went up and up her thigh. Then suddenly she left her unfinished food and her untouched drink and walked out. She felt good. He followed her. She knew this without once turning her eyes. He walked beside her for a few yards. She smiled at herself but did not look at him. He lost his confidence. She left him standing sheepishly looking at a glass window outside Gino's. In the bus back to Ilmorog, men gave her seats. She accepted this as of right. At Treetop Bar she went straight to the counter. The usual crowd of big men was there. Their conversations stopped for a few seconds at her entry. Their lascivious eyes were turned to her. The girls stared at her. Even Nyagūthiī could not maintain her bored indifference. Beatrice bought them drinks. The manager came to her, rather unsure. He tried a conversation. Why had she left work? Where had she been? Would she like to work in the bar, helping Nyagūthiī behind the counter? Now and then? A barmaid brought her a note. A certain big shot wanted to know if she would join their table. More notes came from different big quarters with the one question: would she be free tonight? A trip to Nairobi even. She did not leave her place at the counter. But she accepted their drinks as of right. She felt a new power, confidence even.

She took out a shilling, put it in the slot and the jukebox boomed with the voice of Robinson Mwangi singing Hūnyū wa Mashambani. He sang of those despised girls who worked on farms and contrasted them with urban girls. Then she played a Kamaru and a D. K. Men wanted to dance with her. She ignored them, but enjoyed their flutter around her. She twisted her hips to the sound of yet another D. K. Her body was free. She was free. She sucked in the excitement and tension in the air.

Then suddenly at around six the man with the five-ton lorry stormed into the bar. This time he had on his military overcoat. Behind him was a policeman. He looked around. Everybody's eyes were raised to him. But Beatrice went on swaying her hips. At first he could not recognize Beatrice in the girl celebrating her few minutes of glory by the jukebox. Then he shouted in triumph: "That is the girl! Thief! Thief!"

People melted back to their seats. The policeman went and handcuffed her. She did not resist. Only at the door she turned her head and spat. Then she went out followed by the policeman.

In the bar the stunned silence broke into hilarious laughter when someone made a joke about sweetened robbery without violence. They discussed her. Some said she should have been beaten. Others talked contemptuously about "these bar girls." Yet others talked with a concern noticeable in unbelieving shakes of their heads about the rising rate of crime. Shouldn't the Hanging Bill be extended to all thefts of property? And without anybody being aware of it the man with the five-ton lorry had become a hero. They now surrounded him with questions and demanded the whole story. Some even bought him drinks. More remarkable, they listened, their attentive silence punctuated by appreciative laughter. The averted threat to property had temporarily knitted them into one family. And the man, accepted for the first time, told the story with relish.

But behind the counter Nyagūthiī wept.

ZOË WICOMB

Zoë Wicomb was born in 1948 in Namaqualand, South Africa, and was educated at the University of the Western Cape. Upon graduation in 1970, she traveled to England and continued her studies at Reading University. She lived in Glasglow and Nottingham and returned to South Africa in 1990 to teach at the University of the Western Cape. She came to the attention of the reading public with her first collection of short stories, *You Can't Get Lost in Cape Town* (1987), which addresses the issue of apartheid. Among her other acclaimed works are *David's Story* (2000), *Playing in the Light* (2006), and *The One That Got Away* (2008). Wicomb teaches creative writing and postcolonial literature at the University of Strathclyde in Glasglow.

N2

(2008)

They argued all the way from Stellenbosch.

Something odd, as they sat around the table toasting Jaap's prize-winning pinot noir—later she thought of a spiked drink—slipped into what she had described to her girlfriends as a nice 'n' easy relationship. A lovely evening it was too, with the mountain just taking colour, and in her hand the crystal flute with those divine little beads jostling at the brim.

Now for this barbarian, she had smiled into Jaap's sunburnt face, you must fill it right up, almost to the brim, yes, just so, so I can watch the suicide leap of the bubbles. No half-glass for me.

As a child Mary loved weddings. Then grown-ups sipped from wide-brimmed coupes at darling little ponds of champagne. She supposed it hadn't been real but what did she care about such snobbish distinctions, méthode champenoise sounded grand enough for her; it was the effervescence that counted. She watched the sparkles rising from the bottom in a stream of light and bubble at the brim. Oh, there was nothing like it, bubbles that hurled themselves at her, that couldn't wait to be taken. That's what's best, the moment before, when for seconds you are queen of a world of pleasure that awaits. Mary saw herself fixed in a photograph, with glass held to lips moist with expectation, chin — still young and firm — regally lifted, but there you are, who can resist greed, even when you know that that moment is best, that the actual thing falls just short of its promise. Like sex, she supposed, and surprised herself by casting a resentful look across the table at Harold.

Harold, only half-focused on the still-life of crystal, liquor and lips, was asking about vines cultivated on higher slopes, about the heavy sandstone loams, and so caught that ugly look with puzzlement. Was she bored? Uncomfortable about something or other? Not that her demand for a full-to-the-brim flute was not charming. He had half-smiled, solicitously. No wonder she felt cross, not knowing what to make of such a hybrid look.

Yes, sex. She would have liked to have said it out loud. That's what people like Harold with all their talk of politics don't think of, that there are now all kinds of freedoms. Just think, that a man who had sat in prison for decades, no champagne, no sex, was the one to push the country into the twentieth century, into the civilised world; she had been to Amsterdam where they made no bones about these things. Now everyone here at home could talk about it, see it on television, read about it in magazines, even in poems. No need any longer for men to make sinful trips to the Wild Coast or Sun City, it was all there to be had at home. And what's more, for women as well. Sex between all kinds, although she would have drawn the line there, perhaps taken

one step at a time, no good being too advanced, even stepping ahead of England, but that's freedom for you, just as
De Klerk said, freedom is unstoppable.

All of which prolonged the moment of anticipation, for
the glass was still held to her mouth while she pondered
liberation, until Harold, now attentive, watched the compo-
sition come to life: the glass pressed against cherry-red lips
parted, the liquor spurting. Behind her, the sun was dipping
fast, drunkenly, in the usual gold and reds, and then the
light, how the light ricocheted from the crystal as she tilted
it to her lips. The *something* flare of lightning . . . beaded
bubbles *something* at the brim . . . Mary thought of lines
that were once, perhaps, recited at school; she couldn't
quite remember.

It was getting late. From below in Idas Valley the smell
of location woodsmoke rose, and the skelbek of a drunk
woman could be heard above the distant beat of kwela music. It was time they went home.

Drink up, said Harold, still smiling. Only one glass for
him; he was driving. Jaap pushed a bottle across the table.
To lay down.

Ag, no man, what's the use of a prizewinner if you can't
pass it round?

And again, Drrringcupp. Crass like the skelbek that
drifted onto the terrace, his voice cut through the first sift-
ing of frangipani as the light drained quickly, helter-
skeltering after an already-sunken sun.

She turned to Jaap. What a beauty you have here — has
she said that before? — top marks from me.

Oh, I can't take all the credit. I've got some first-class
men working for me. My manager, he can tell just the right
moment to irrigate, that's crucial you see, and I've even got
a chap here from Idas Valley who knows everything there
is to know about hanepoot.

He smiled, shyly for such a big man who stretched comfortably, brown arms flung out as if blessing the table. But
the table too had had it. Others had left their traces on
crumpled napkins; the cloth was stained with wine; and be-

side the posy of wild flowers an oyster canapé lay capsized, its crushed stern flung to the edge, to the printed border of guinea-fowl craning their speckled necks onto the table. Mary folded her napkin, placed it over the scrap of pastry. Post-prandial sadness flitted across her face.

Time we went, Harold announced in a first-time voice.

Ah, she thought, a spike of jealousy. That's what it was, jealous of Jaap who travelled to Europe once, twice a year with his estate wines. And oh yes, what if she were not ready to go, what if she did not think it time? But coming as it did, belatedly, the thought slunk off. So she looked deep into the empty glass, spun the stem, set it down, and pinged with her perfect nail against the crystal. Which made the men rise. Their chairs scraped against the stone paving of the terrace.

Ja-nee, said Jaap, that motorway is no joke in the dark. I see those squatter people have started throwing stones from the bridge again, something in this morning's Cape Times about the N2. Kapaah! he beat together his large hands. Also onto a Merc it was, but on the other side, coming from Cape Town. Luckily it hit the back.

Mary thought of the three wild men. On the N2 that morning, as they drove to Stellenbosch, the black men leapt naked, except for skimpy loincloths, out of the bush, ran across the dual carriageway jumping the barriers, and disappeared into the bush on the other side. Their faces were covered in grey clay. They may have carried shields and spears.

Ag what can one do, she shrugged, there's nothing to do other than brave it out. That's now the new life for us hey, just braving it out on that chicken-run.

Jaap's kapaah! hands fell, See-you-soon, on her shoulders. Then she felt quite sober.

Princess's boy, the eldest, it was not that he did anything in particular, he just was funny, different from other children. Mrs. Matsepe could not put her finger on it. Êh, that Themba was deep-deep, which may have made for a charm-

ing little boy, always with his head tilted asking funny questions like an old man, but now that he was no longer little,
there was a strange brooding air about him that surely
would bring trouble. And what can you do?—you can pray
and pray to God to keep the children safe, but that's life,
nothing but trouble, nothing to do, just the business of
braving it out.

Funny how children grow overnight, and for that matter
a boy who doesn't eat much. Even over the big days, Christmas and New Year, just like that turning fussily away from
all the special food, and still shooting tall and broad into his
eighteenth year, a good-looking boy with Princess's firm
chin and deep black skin, so that she wrote to her sister to
say how fine he looked, never mind the strangeness that
had already started to set in, she supposed, when his voice
finally broke.

Princess wrote to say that yes, Themba had written,
Themba now wanted to go back to school, start where he
left off in Standard Six, Themba wanted to be a photogra-
pher. And in the envelope was twenty rand. Twenty rand,
êh, the girl must be mad sending big notes in the post with
all these skelm postmen who sit in the dunes with the mail-
bags and a tube of glue, going through people's letters before delivering them, late in the day, when the sun is already
sitting in the middle of the sky. But miracle of miracles, the
money slipped past the hands of those skelms, which is
something to be thankful for, and another thing, at least
Themba didn't want to be a postman.

But still, Mrs. Matsepe was hurt. The boy was her own
since so-so high, since before she herself had children. Why
had he not spoken to her? If only she had thought of it first,
that he should go back to school, that they could manage
again now that things were getting better. But Jim said, and
Jim too was no less than his father, Jim said it was only
right, it was only respectful that he should write to Princess
first, that he appreciated having two mamas, that he should
test out his ideas on paper before blurting out things that
might come out wrongly. That was when she stopped listen-

ing. Having given her this bullshit wisdom he would in any case expect her to speak to Themba. Which was just as well. Only last week, when she complained about the boy's strangeness, Jim of all people came up with such a kaffir-idea that she just had to shake her head.

About this Themba business, he said, I thi-ink . . . and then stared deeply into his mug as if she had nothing better to do than stand around waiting. As if she were not about to take her life in her hands as she did every morning be-fore sunrise, squash herself into a show-off taxi that would hurl itself recklessly all over the N2, as if driving people under cover of pounding music into a death of steel and fire were better than delivering them to their places of work. Not for Mrs. Matsepe—she adjusted her beret—that was her name, that's who she was, since the day she decided to hell with laws and in-laws and came to the city after Jim, her lawfully-wedded husband. No, after all those troubles—and now also Jim with a head full of foolish ideas—she would survive any taxi-ride to get to her Green-oaks Nursing Home, where she was in charge of all the cleaning girls. No, for her it was nice to get out to Rosebank every day, nice to be spread out amongst trees and purple flowering bushes, away from the noise of the motorway, from the filth of Crossroads. She would not give up hope that they'd get away; it was just a matter of time.

Jim cleared his throat to continue, but then the blue work van hooted, and without grabbing his lunch-pack he rushed off. So now he'd have to spend money on slap-chips. It was she, Mrs. Matsepe, who got up early, got everyone ready for the day, packed his bread with peanut butter and a nice sprig of parsley she took from the Greenoaks gar-den. She admired the way cook put a curly bit of green on the dinner plates, made everything so nice and appetising, but that man of hers was too stupid. It was not till night-time, in the creaking bed, whispering so as not to wake the children, and worried about Themba who was not yet home, it was not till then, and with an elbow nudge from her, that he returned to his thought.

Themba must go to the bush, to initiation, it's the right way to turn him into a man, help him over this difficult business of growing up. He must go into the bush.

She could tell from his voice that his heart wasn't in it, but still, she really didn't expect such a backward idea from a Christian man. What could have got into Jim?

The bush, she exploded, call that strip along the N2 a bush? Just a rubbish scrap of trees left there to keep our place out of sight.

Yes, but it's still our bush, that's what we've made of it; we must make do, it's all we have for the young ones to go to, to become men. Even the students have started going to the bush . . .

As if that meant anything, Mrs. Matsepe snorted. Those students were toyi-toying fools, always going on strike, loafing about at weekends, doing those terrible things to girls in the hostels and then talking rubbish about roots and traditional culture. She supposed that that was what Themba wanted to be, a student.

I'm saying to you now and I won't say it again, Jim. No people of mine are going to have anything to do with such backward things. A pretend-bush in Town, that's the very last I want to hear of it.

But now, with Themba back at school, now a young man, who carried on scowling and shrugging his shoulders and going about with others who looked as if they carried guns, she did not know what to think. What if she were wrong? If it were the only way to pull him right, should she not think again about initiation? If the boy himself were to ask, would she not say, yes anything?

But Themba said nothing. Themba did not speak; he sat with his head buried in books.

For a few seconds before he braked sharply, the car hobbled as if the road had grown potholed. Mary raised her eyebrows and turned away disdainfully. The last straw, said her look.

So now I'm responsible for the behaviour of the car, he said.

I said nothing at all. I don't care who's responsible, but I would like to get back to civilisation. This is no place to get stuck in the dark.

We're not stuck, he hissed. Then, resolving to be patient, it was after all no joke for a woman to find herself in the middle of nowhere: It won't take a minute, just a puncture, just a matter of changing the wheel. I got the spare checked just the other day.

He opened his door a fraction, and in the light leant over her to scrabble in the cubbyhole for a torch. Mary shrank into the corner, her head turned to look into the moonless night.

Themba heard the screech of the car coming to a halt just yards away. He had made himself a hideout in the Port Jackson bushes, had cleared the space of rubbish blown from the houses, and had dug out with his hands something of a dip in which to settle himself comfortably. Here he often sat in the dark, with the smell of earth not quite smothered by petrol fumes, the sound of the traffic a steady whoosh and hum, and through the screen of reeds and bushes his eyes followed the flashes of light and the sleek shapes of cars sailing by in the black night. Behind him, Crossroads was drowned in darkness.

Themba sat up, squatting to see the yellow light spill onto the shoulder of the road, the light on the woman's cropped yellow head. He watched the man wrenching at the handbrake, swinging his long legs out onto the tarmac and, in another pool of propped torchlight, opening the boot and lifting out a jack. Themba could see that he hasn't done this before, not on the chassis of this car. The man groped for a place to fit the jack, looked about ruefully for a second, then slid on his back under the belly of the car, a silver beauty of a Mercedes Benz . . . yes he'd found it, the jackpoint. Now he reached for the wheel brace to loosen off the nuts.

In the intimate interior of the car the woman's yellow head was bent over a handbag in which she pushed things about, groping for something at the bottom. Another flash of light within that lit space, then a glowing circle of red as she drew deeply from a cigarette. She stared straight ahead. A car rushed past. For a second, her face shone white and still.

Fuck. Fuck. The voice cracked into the night so that Themba started, losing his balance. The man threw down the brace in a rage, then picking it up again, pushed with all his might, with clenched teeth, at the nut that would not budge. The woman's head was turned, towards the bush; she had heard a branch give as Themba toppled on tensed ankles. Oblivious to the angry grunting of the man, her hand groped in the bag, while her eyes flitted in search of the invisible branch.

Themba squirmed with guilt. For spying on them, for not helping the man. But it was not his fault that they had landed right there at his private place, displaying themselves in their own light, acting out their business in slow motion it seemed, before his eyes, and hearing Mrs. Matsepe's voice to keep away from white people, to keep out of trouble, he hesitated.

Then he stood up, parted the branches noisily and walked straight out onto the road. The man's back was turned. The mlungu woman was out of the car in a flash, like a movie star, kicking open the door; her gun was clasped in both hands trained on him. He held up his hands, stuttered, Hô-hôkaai lady, I'm just coming to help, get the wheel loose so we can put on the new one lady. Stupidly betraying himself as spy.

In slow motion the hands were lowered, a slow smile twitched on her face as she looked him in the eye, the moody boys' eyes, ag he was only a kid, and her lips settled, smiling, Yes, sorry, you know what it's like on the N2 . . .

The man was taking the gun out of her hand, pushing it casually into his own back pocket, smiling energetically at Themba. Ag man, she's just a bundle of nerves, and pointing to the wheel, it's these bladdy nuts, you can have a go if you like but I've been trying all this time you know.

We must put something by the front wheel, the boy said.

Themba picked up the torch to search the ground and pointed the light at a suitable stone. A moment's hesitation before the man bent down to pick it up himself. With the front wheel wedged, he tried again and shook his head. He watched the boy straining against the brace. Just his luck that the boy should be the one to shift the nuts.

I think, said Themba, as if he hadn't managed it, they'll perhaps come loose under the jack. Together they pushed aside the clutter in the boot, the toolbag, an old rug and what looked like a brand-new Nikon camera, shifted these to lift out the spare, and in a jiffy the car was jacked up, the old wheel off, the new one fixed.

Themba was wiping his hands on his trousers as they got into the car. The windows rolled down simultaneously. Together they spoke their scrambled words of thanks, then her voice above his, laughing It's so good of you I don't know what . . . and the man's, Yes, that was a devil of a wheel, thank you man, and one day I'll be the one to roll a stone out of your path hey.

Again the noise as their voices merged, and the key turned and the Merc started up, and it was as if from a distance, joining the gibberish of thanks, that he heard a thin sound coming from an unknown place inside and distinctly the words, Please sir, madam, have you please got some rand? Then the scramble in pockets, in the handbag, and two sets of white hands dropped the notes—Yes of course, ag shame man, sorry we just weren't thinking—into the bowl of his very own prosthetic hands.

His hands were on fire. Themba stuffed a burning note into each of his pockets, felt the fire running down his legs and back up through his body, so that he sprinted home with the repetition of his own voice in tinny echo, Please sir madam have you please got some rand some rand some rand . . .

Mrs. Matsepe dropped her dishcloth right there on the floor and followed the boy, a streak of fire she could have sworn, into the room where the youngest was already asleep. Themba whipped the money out of his pockets, two twenty-rand notes, and threw them on the bed.

It's for you, he whispered, from the people on the road.
I helped them change a wheel.

And they gave you money?

Themba dropped his eyes. Some rands, some rands,
some rands, echoed in his head. He said slowly, watching his
hands curve once again into a cup: I asked for the money.
From mlungu in a Merc. I begged.

With her eyes fixed on the boy, on the face twitching
with shame, Mrs. Matsepe took the notes, folded them together, then tore them, carefully, into halves, into quarters,
into eighths, and again, into tiny scraps of paper that she
held aloft, clenched in fists, before showering them onto
the bed.

READ THE TOP 20
SIGNET CLASSICS

Animal Farm by George Orwell

1984 by George Orwell

The Inferno by Dante

Frankenstein by Mary Shelley

Beowulf (Burton Raffel, translator)

The Odyssey by Homer

The Federalist Papers by Alexander Hamilton

The Hound of the Baskervilles
   by Sir Arthur Conan Doyle

Narrative of the Life of Frederick Douglass
   by Frederick Douglass

Dr. Jekyll and Mr. Hyde by Robert Louis Stevenson

Hamlet by William Shakespeare

The Scarlet Letter by Nathaniel Hawthorne

Les Misérables by Victor Hugo

Heart of Darkness and The Secret Sharer
   by Joseph Conrad

Wuthering Heights by Emily Brontë

A Midsummer Night's Dream by William Shakespeare

Nectar in a Sieve by Kamala Markandaya

Ethan Frome by Edith Wharton

Adventures of Huckleberry Finn by mark twain

A Tale of Two Cities by Charles Dickens

SIGNETCLASSICS.COM
FACEBOOK.COM/SIGNETCLASSIC